HEIR OF THE LINE

Eric James Stone

Robot Sorcerer Press

Copyright © 2022 Eric James Stone

All rights reserved.

Originally serialized on Kindle Vella.

The characters and events portrayed in this book are fictitious. Any similarity to real persons, living or dead, is coincidental and not intended by the author.

No part of this book may be reproduced, or stored in a retrieval system, or transmitted in any form or by any means, electronic, mechanical, photocopying, recording, or otherwise, without express written permission of the publisher.

ISBN-13: 978-1-7353717-4-0

Cover art by: Chrissy Ellsworth

Printed in the United States of America

To Honor and Link, the heirs of my line

Prologue

Balunor

"It's time to go," Elesi said, her voice calm.

High Protector Balunor cast aside the paperwork about guard shifts and sprang from his chair. "Time? Now? The baby?"

Elesi laughed, then grimaced slightly as she tried to sit up in their bed. "Yes, the baby."

"Here, let me help." Balunor reached down and scooped her up in his arms.

"Put me down, you silly man. I can still walk."

"I can carry you." The birthing room in the Inner Keep of Aud Sapeer was only two corridors and a flight of stairs away.

"Yes, you're a fine, strong man, my love, and I've no doubt you could carry me all the way to Bargas and back. But your armor does make lying in your arms a mite uncomfortable."

He gently lowered her to her feet. "Sorry, forgot I was wearing it." Forged by a good ferromancer, his armor was far lighter and thinner than ordinary steel. He wore it so often it felt like a second skin.

Jesana was already at the birthing room getting things ready when they arrived. Royal Omnimancer Selima had predicted their boy would be born today. After he helped Elesi onto the bed, Jesana shooed him from the room. "Out with you. This is no place for a man."

Placing a kiss on his wife's cheek, he said, "I love you, Elesi."

She smiled. "I believe that's what got me into this situation." She pointed her chin at the door. "Now, go on. Next time you see me I'll have our son in my arms."

◆ ◆ ◆

When the door to the birthing room opened, Jesana came out, her face lined with worry.

"What's wrong?" asked Balunor.

"She's breech," said Jesana, "and as I was trying to move the baby around, I found the cord has twisted around his neck several times."

"Is he alive?"

To Balunor's relief, Jesana nodded. "Selima can see inside the womb, which will make it easier to untangle him. Go get her."

Selima would be in the queen's chambers. He began to run, his armored boots ringing out on the stone floor with every step.

Elesi was not the only pregnant woman in the Inner Keep. Queen Anutia's child was not due for another forty days, but her pregnancy had been difficult. She had been confined to her bed since the beginning of summer, with Royal Omnimancer Selima almost constantly at her side to ensure the health of both mother and child. Elesi had mentioned frequently how fortunate she felt that her pregnancy was easier than the queen's. Now Elesi was having problems, too. Balunor felt a stinging in his eyes and he blinked back tears. Elesi would be all right. She had to be.

As he approached the queen's chambers he steadied his breathing. It would not do for one of the sixteen High Protectors to appear as a panicked child. Reaching forward, he pressed his palm against the shimmering air that marked the edge of the multilayered wards around the queen's chambers. As he said the first of the secret keywords to open a portal in the wards, they flickered in acknowledgement. When he finished the keywords, there was a small pop as the shimmering stopped in front of him.

One of the queen's chambermaids answered his knock.

"I need Selima," he said.

Moments later, Selima came to the door.

"What is it, Balunor?"

"It's Elesi. There's something wrong—"

The sudden clanging of one of the Outer Keep's alarm bells was quickly joined by several others, and Balunor instinctively drew his sword. As it cleared the scabbard the enchanted blade turned an angry yellow instead of its normal blue glow: the High Protectors' swords could sense when the Heir of the Line was in danger.

Forcing all thought of Elesi to the back of his mind, Balunor began running toward the passageway connecting the Inner Keep with the Outer.

"Wait," said Selima. "Stay and guard the queen." There was a puff of air as she reestablished the wards around the queen's chambers.

Balunor stopped. "My place is with—"

"Stay!" Selima passed him and sprinted toward the Outer Keep.

He knew what she was thinking—if King Ordil, the current Heir of the Line of Orcan, were killed, then protecting his unborn child would become the most important job in the world.

The prophecy that led to the creation of the Protectors of the Line five hundred years earlier was clear: *Only one shall have power to kill the High Priestess of the Dark God, and that one shall be the Heir of the Line of Orcan. The Heir must live to confront the Dark Priestess, else all will be lost.*

Balunor whispered to himself the Protector's Oath. "I swear upon my life that I will protect the line of Orcan att'Fenisak of Aud Sapeer from this day until I let my last breath out." He might not be protecting the current Heir, but he could still protect the line.

Balunor walked back to the faint shimmer of the wards.

According to Selima, nothing could penetrate the wards without a vast amount of time and magical power. So all he needed to do was make sure nobody tried to bring them down.

He wished he could return to Elesi's side, but he could not until the danger to the Heir had passed. He said a silent prayer to each of the three Gods of Light. It was all he could do.

◆ ◆ ◆

Balunor readied his sword when he heard footsteps in the hall, then relaxed when he recognized Veratur, another of the sixteen High Protectors who led the Protectors of the Line.

"Do you know what's happening?" asked Balunor.

Veratur shook his head. "All I know is that the Outer Keep sounded the alarm. I came here to check on the queen. Have you alerted Selima?"

"Didn't you pass her in the hallway?" asked Balunor.

"No. But you're sure she's gone to help the king?"

Balunor stared at his friend. The tone of the question seemed strange. Veratur stood before him, hand on his sword hilt. The sword was still in its sheath. Any Protector should instinctively have drawn his sword when the alarm sounded, and would probably not sheath it again until he could see the danger to the king was over.

"Draw your sword, Veratur," said Balunor. Since the sword's enchantment only worked when it was wielded on behalf of the Heir of the Line, if Veratur's sword did not glow when removed from its sheath, it would prove treachery. Balunor raised his sword, still glowing yellow, and pointed it at Veratur's heart.

"Balunor, what are you doing?" Veratur stepped back.

"If I'm wrong, forgive me. Draw it."

Veratur slowly withdrew the sword from the sheath. When the tip came out, the blade's glow did not appear. "That's strange. I don't know—"

"Quiet," said Balunor. He found it hard to believe that a High

Protector would betray his oath, but the evidence was clear. "Drop it."

Veratur let the sword clatter on the floor.

Balunor kicked it away. His eyes were only off Veratur for a moment, but as he looked back, he saw that the traitor was removing something from a pocket in his tunic.

"What are you…" began Balunor.

Veratur jumped back. He threw a handful of small objects at Balunor. They looked like dragon's teeth, but they bounced harmlessly off his armor. Balunor started after Veratur.

"Attack him," ordered Veratur.

"I won't fall for—" Hearing a noise behind him, Balunor whirled about just in time to chop off the paw of one of the six Soulless who had appeared in the hallway.

The Soulless were unnatural hybrids—men and animals fused together through biomancy. Now four bear-like ursiks and two scorpion-like scorpiks were in the Inner Keep, separated only by Selima's wards from the queen. The dragon's teeth must have been enchanted to summon the creatures. That meant Veratur was in league with the Dark Priestess.

Balunor was outnumbered, but he had an advantage that swung the odds in his favor. The enchantment on a High Protector's sword made the edges capable of cutting through normal materials as if they were not even there.

In a blur of glowing yellow, Balunor backhanded his blade through the torso of the ursik he had just de-pawed. As it collapsed to the floor the next came after him, but a single stroke sent it to join the first.

Now Balunor was on the attack, and he charged forward, letting the blade sweep through the other two ursiks in a single motion.

One of the scorpiks raised a claw to deflect the unstoppable blade.

And the sword's yellow glow disappeared.

Balunor stumbled as his blade met the unexpected resistance of the scorpik's exoskeleton. The scorpik's stinger, filled with a deadly paralyzing poison, flipped over its head. Balunor barely recovered in time to parry it. But that left him open for an attack by a claw, which broke through the seam between the bottom of his breastplate and the faulds protecting his lower abdomen. His flesh tore as he leapt away. Warm blood began to soak the clothing under his armor.

Suddenly on the defensive, Balunor backed off from the scorpiks. He knew he was still loyal, so there could be only one explanation as to why his sword's enchantment had failed: King Ordil was dead. Until his child was born, there was no Heir of the Line to protect, and enchantments could be very literal sometimes. The rest of the Protectors would be on their way here—all he needed to do was hold off the scorpiks until help arrived.

Then he heard Veratur speak the first of the keywords to open a portal in the wards around the queen's chambers.

Turning his back on the scorpiks, Balunor lunged toward the traitor. But a chitinous claw grabbed his right shoulder and squeezed. Balunor couldn't help crying out in pain as the ferromancy-enhanced steel of his armor crumpled under the force of the scorpik's grip.

He dropped his sword, but he managed to rip free, leaving his spaulder behind in the scorpik's grasp.

The wards flashed, and Balunor knew Veratur was only moments from opening a portal.

He charged forward and tackled Veratur, but he was a moment too late—an imploding pop of air signaled the portal was open.

Veratur managed to get to his feet first, and retreated behind the scorpiks. "Go in and kill the pregnant woman."

After picking up Balunor's sword, Veratur darted down the corridor and disappeared.

The two scorpiks skittered toward the opening in the wards.

Looking around desperately for a weapon, Balunor spotted Veratur's sword lying on the floor where he had kicked it. He scooped it up and dove through the opening under the hind legs and tail of the first scorpik.

He jabbed the sword upwards, but without its enchantment, it failed to penetrate the scorpik's carapace.

Balunor said the first keyword for restoring the wards. A slight shimmer appeared in the air and the scorpik hissed and jumped forward as its tail was jolted by the ward. The second scorpik, trapped outside, began to batter against the ward with its claws, its eight legs churning against the stone floor.

One ward was too weak to stand for long, but it meant he only had a single enemy to deal with for the moment. Balunor leapt to his feet and charged after it into the queen's bedchamber. He shouted the rest of the keywords as he ran, hoping that would work to restore all the wards.

Queen Anutia weakly tried to sit up on her bed, shielded by her chambermaid Irini, who was brandishing a small dagger.

Balunor had underestimated the scorpik's speed. Even without a stinger, the scorpik was still capable of killing both women before Balunor could catch it.

Irini must have realized that, and she jumped off the bed and ran toward the Soulless with her dagger stretched out before her. It swung a massive pincer to bat her out of the way, but she ducked under the swing and stabbed at it. The dagger deflected harmlessly off its carapace. She then grabbed onto its left front leg, wrapped herself around it and tried to pierce a leg joint with her dagger. The scorpik reached its right pincer over, snapped her neck, and peeled her body off its leg.

The queen shrank back on her bed.

But Irini had delayed the scorpik enough for Balunor to catch up. One well-aimed swing was sufficient to sever a rear leg at its joint. The Soulless turned toward him and tried to grab him, but Balunor's blade was already in motion, and he caught the segmented neck in the right spot. Its head landed on the floor two feet from the queen's bed.

"Thank the Gods you were here." The queen's voice was filled with relief.

"No time, Your Majesty," he said over his shoulder as he

raced back to the wards. If he could only complete the keywords in time and restore the full wards, the queen—and her unborn child—would be secure.

But he was too late. The final scorpik charged through the doorway into the room.

Balunor positioned himself between the Soulless and the queen.

Its tail whipped toward him and he swung up to cut off its stinger. He realized too late that the tail attack was a feint and his sword was too high to get back in position to parry the pincer that grabbed the wrist of his left arm and twisted.

With a sharp crack, the bones in his forearm broke. The scorpik kept twisting, and the jagged edges of bone cut through his flesh.

Balunor screamed, and his vision blurred. He brought his sword down on the pincer and it let go, but the other pincer locked onto his right leg and pulled it out from under him. He went down awkwardly, and without his left arm to help, he almost dropped his sword in trying to roll to his feet. The Soulless had started toward the queen and he charged after it. He leapt on its back as it reached the bed and the two of them crashed to the floor.

He felt a crushing blow to his left ankle as the scorpik's weight came down on it hard, but Balunor managed to get to his feet between it and the bed. The scorpik raised itself off the floor and began to approach. Balunor lifted his sword into a defensive position. The Soulless charged forward and impaled itself on his sword, its momentum pushing Balunor back onto the bed.

And its tail flipped up and over Balunor's head until its stinger struck the queen's foot.

"No," she gasped.

The Soulless collapsed on top of Balunor, dead. But it was too late. He had failed to protect the queen. He had failed the protect the king. He had failed utterly.

"Balunor!" The queen's voice was weak. "Cut him out."

"What?" He struggled to push the dead scorpik off himself.

"Quickly. Cut open my womb."

He turned to face her. Tears were running down her cheeks.

"But I don't know—"

"You know how to follow orders. The Heir must..." Her jaw went slack as the poison reached her head but he could still see the pleading in her eyes.

Hoping that the poison would take longer to pass along the umbilical cord into the baby, he took his sword and carefully cut a slit from the top of queen's belly to the bottom. Blood and water gushed out. Propping the cut open with his otherwise useless left hand, he cut the wall of the womb, then dropped his sword and reached inside and found the baby. He seemed very small.

Balunor pulled him out and laid him on the bed, then reached for his sword to cut the cord. As he brought the blade up, he saw it again glowed with blue flame. He sliced through the cord. Blood oozed from it, so after a bit of fumbling with one hand he managed to tie it in a simple knot.

When the glow of his sword turned from blue to yellow, he grabbed it and spun around to face whatever new danger had appeared, but there was no one there. He turned back to the baby, and realized the child wasn't breathing. He tried to remember what he'd heard about birthing babies. There was something about holding the baby upside down and slapping him, but he wasn't sure how to do that with one hand. He held him upside down anyway, and watched as liquid drained out of his tiny mouth and nose.

"I'm sorry, Your Majesty," said Balunor as he willed the baby to live. The baby had to live. "I'm well-trained in the art of combat, but no one ever thought to train me as a midwife."

The baby gave a tiny cough that expelled some more liquid, and then took his first breath. Balunor's sword returned to its blue glow, and he let out a sigh.

"Very good, Your Majesty. Just keep doing that, please."

He laid the baby on the bed, then limped back outside the

queen's chambers and hastily recited the keywords to restore the wards.

The air did not shimmer.

He tried again, more slowly. Nothing happened. The Soulless breaking through after his previous interrupted attempt must have dispelled the wards completely.

As he returned to the bed, he almost collapsed from dizziness. The blood loss from the wounds on his stomach, arm, and shoulder were taking their toll. He needed to get the king to someone else, someone who could properly care for a baby. Jesana would know what to do.

He couldn't carry sword and baby in the same hand, so he cut a wide swath of bedsheet and made a makeshift sling for his arm. He cradled the tiny king in his broken arm inside the sling. The baby's eyes were closed, somehow sleeping peacefully despite his violent birth.

"Shall we get you to the birthing room, Your Majesty? That's where you should have been born. Perhaps you can meet my son. Today's his birth day, too." He grabbed his sword and limped as quickly as he could back toward the birthing room.

◆ ◆ ◆

The birthing room was only twenty paces farther down the corridor when Balunor's knees refused to carry him any farther. As he fell, he twisted his body to keep his left arm—and its precious cargo—from being crushed.

He was about to call out to Jesana for help when he heard an unfamiliar male voice say, "What was that?"

Two men came around a corner at the far end of the hallway. Their midnight-black armor seemed to reflect no light and revealed their identity as Knights of the Dark God.

One of the knights snickered. "Another wounded Protector, running for his life."

"Maybe this one will talk," said the second.

Balunor lifted his sword, which glowed an enraged yellow.

But he could not hold it up for more than a moment, and it sank back to the floor.

He tried to yell for help, but could not manage more than a hoarse whisper.

When the knights got close enough, they would spot the Heir hidden in his sling, and they would kill the baby. There was nothing he could do to stop them.

The knights were only two paces away when a sound from the birthing room made them stop.

A baby had started crying.

"The new Heir!" said one of the knights, and they both turned ran back to the birthing room door. When it refused to open, they began to break it down.

The crying baby had to be his son. Elesi had given birth, and the knights would kill his child unless he could stop them. Balunor tried once more to rise, but his muscles refused to lift him.

The only way to save his son would be to surrender the Heir.

Balunor had known he might have to sacrifice his own life to protect the Heir, but he had never contemplated sacrificing his son's life. Yet every moment the knights took in killing his son was another chance for the Protectors of the Line to arrive and rescue the Heir.

"Forgive me, my son," he whispered.

And that's when four Protectors of the Line came charging around the corner. The Knights of the Dark God abandoned their attempt to break down the door and turned to face the threat. One of the Protectors carried a High Protector's sword, and as Balunor's vision dimmed, the last thing he saw was the bright yellow blade slicing off a black-helmeted head.

◆ ◆ ◆

Consciousness returned slowly. He looked up at the stone ceiling and groaned.

Selima rushed to Balunor's side and clapped her hand to his

forehead. In a moment, all his pain seemed distant, as if it weren't really his.

"I'm sorry we couldn't get here any sooner," she said.

"The Heir?"

"He's safe." Selima winced. "But your wounds are too severe. I can't heal you."

He had suspected as much. But he had to let her know what happened. "Veratur..."

"I have not seen him," said Selima. "I don't know if he lives."

"He's a traitor. He summoned..."

Her eyes widened. "He will pay dearly for that."

Balunor looked around and realized he was in the birthing room. Elesi was on a bed next to him. Her eyes were closed. "Elesi?"

"She's gone before you to the World of the Dead." Selima shook her head. "The breech birth. If I could have..."

"My son cried," Balunor said. "Distracted them."

"Your son lives," said Selima. "He's weak, but he'll live."

Balunor coughed. He tasted blood. "See him?"

Jesana brought his son over, wrapped in swaddling.

It was getting dark, despite the torches that lined the walls, and it was hard to breathe. But he managed to say, "Geradin." He and Elesi had chosen to name the boy after her father. "Call him Geradin."

He could see tears in Selima's eyes. He tried to tell her it wasn't her fault, but his voice would not cooperate.

"The Heir is safe, thanks to you," Selima said. "You have fulfilled your oath. Go now and join Elesi. And fear not for your son, I will raise him to honor your name and care for him as if he were my own."

Balunor nodded and closed his eyes. As he let out his last breath, he could hear Elesi's voice say, "It's time to go."

Chapter One

Geradin

"You are not really Balunor's son."

As Geradin reflexively wove a defensive pattern with his sword he mentally pushed aside Ytanor's words. *There are no distractions. There is nothing but the fight.*

"Your slut mother…" Ytanor's breathing was labored.

Parry. Feint. Wait for the opening.

"…was Veratur's private whore."

Wait.

"With a harlot for a mother and a traitor for—"

There. Ytanor's slash was slightly too strong, and instead of parrying Geradin suddenly moved back and allowed it to swing through empty air. With Ytanor slightly off-balance, Geradin lunged, swinging his sword up toward Ytanor's exposed throat. He stopped it less than a thumbwidth from contact.

Ytanor's face was flushed, and drops of sweat had left streaks in the dust below his graying sideburns. His breath came in large gulps, but other than that he remained as motionless as Geradin. The light brown cloud of dust kicked up during their combat began to return to the dirt of the training yard.

"Well done, Geradin." Ytanor stepped back from the sword at his throat and bowed. "I did not even realize I had given you that opening. And you refused to allow yourself to be distracted."

Geradin did not return the bow. "There are no distractions. There is only the fight. You taught me that." He straightened from the lunge position but kept his sword extended, still pointing at Ytanor's throat. The fight was over. Now he could allow himself to consider Ytanor's words. Thinking about his mother brought a sting to his eyes, but he forced his face to remain the calm mask that he always wore while fighting.

Ytanor glanced at Geradin's sword and cocked his head. "You have something you wish to say?"

"I will thank you not to insult the memory of my mother again, Swordmaster Ytanor." The stilted excesses of court speech came naturally to Geradin. Growing up in the Keep he could not avoid it, and now he used its formality to mask the emotion from his voice and technically show the respect a student owed a teacher. Such a ploy would not fool Ytanor, but it was all he could do to save his mother's honor. He might have killed her with his birth, but he was not going to leave her undefended now.

"If I am so inclined, I will insult your mother, or your father—even Gods of Light themselves—in order to further your training. Tell me, Pupil Geradin," he said, emphasizing the formal words, "why would I do such a thing?" He stared intently into Geradin's eyes.

Geradin held his sword up a moment longer, then let it drop to his side. "Because there is nothing but the fight. If I am to be a Protector, I need the best training possible. And of course, an enemy would not hesitate to use any means to distract me." A stupid error, he thought. I already knew all of that, but I let my feelings blind me. "I'm sorry; I need to work on controlling my emotions."

Ytanor chuckled. "You did well enough at controlling them during the fight. You had no reaction at all while I was slandering your mother. And after the fight…Well, I think a little excessive formality can be excused. If only my other students controlled their emotions as well during a fight as you did after."

Geradin nodded, then brought the tip of his sword up beside his head and dipped it slightly in salute.

Ytanor returned his salute. "I think that will be all for today. Since tomorrow is Midsummer Day, we will skip tomorrow's training session."

"Thank you, Swordmaster."

As he watched Ytanor walk away, he wondered what to do about his training. He liked his teacher, and there was no better instructor in Aud Sapeer, but it was now eight days since Ytanor had even landed a touch on him during their bouts. He wondered how he was supposed to improve his skill when he was a better swordsman than his teacher.

He looked down at his sword. It was only a practice sword, with a blunt end and no edge. Getting hit by it still hurt, but it was unlikely to cause any real damage. Some of the other students never wore their practice swords except during training, but his practice sword was constantly at his side, just as his real sword would be when he became a Protector. That time might still be a few years off, but he would be ready.

He glanced at the clock. Time enough to see how Mek was doing before going into the city. The daily meeting with the Regency Council probably wasn't finished yet, so he made his way toward the Council Room in the Inner Keep.

Two Protectors of the Line stood guard outside the door, so he knew Mek was still inside. He greeted them by name and asked, "How are things going in there?"

"Same as usual, I'm afraid. You want to go in or just wait for him out here?"

Geradin sighed. "I'll go on in. Light, I hate politics." Selima didn't like it when he swore, but if the Gods of Light took offense, it had been two thousand years since they'd done anything about it.

"It's the types that like politics you have to watch for."

"I'll remember that." He slipped through the door and they

closed it behind him.

"...the lifeblood of our kingdom. But if the merchants do not feel safe on our roads, they will find other routes. They ask why they should pay our highway taxes if they are not protected from common bandits. And I can't say I blame them. Something must—" Lady Uwixa paused as Kindul, Lord Regent, raised his palm.

"I see our young king's friend has joined us. Perhaps he has an urgent message for us. What news, young Lord Geradin?" The Lord Regent smiled.

Geradin was about to reply that he had no news, but Mek spoke first. "Perhaps Lord Geradin's news is of such troubling nature that he dare not speak it in your presence, my ancient and revered Lord Regent, for fear that your heart could not bear it."

"There is nothing wrong with my heart, Your Majesty."

"Indeed? I am most glad to hear that a man of your age still has a sound heart. But it is best not to take any chances. If the members of the council would be so good as to wait outside while Lord Geradin gives me his report?"

Selima, Lady Uwixa, and two others arose at once saying, "Yes, Your Majesty."

Two arose more slowly, and three looked at the Lord Regent until he nodded before they rose to their feet. All ten members of the council made their way toward the door.

"Oh, my Lord Regent," said Mek.

"Yes, Your Majesty?"

"Perhaps while you wait you could be thinking about a solution to Lady Uwixa's merchant problems that is more effective than a mere change of subject?"

"Of course, Your Majesty." The Lord Regent bowed ever so slightly, then exited and the door was closed behind him. The two of them were left alone, not counting the ever-present Protectors behind Mek's chair.

"I don't have any news."

"I know. And all of them know it, too. But it gave me a good excuse to try to take Kindul down a peg." He sighed. "Four years and one day left before I turn twenty and can rule in my own right. If only..."

Geradin waited, then finally said, "If only what?"

"Ger, why didn't you take the Tests of Majority on our birthday last year?"

Geradin's eyes wandered the room, looking anywhere but Mek. "I...Well, I didn't think I was ready. I'm still not." He didn't want to embarrass his best friend.

"Not ready yet? Hah. Perhaps I should have the Lord Regent teach you some lessons in the art of lying. You could probably have passed the day we turned thirteen, if they'd let you try."

By law, citizens of Aud Sapeer aged fifteen through nineteen could become adults by passing the Tests of Majority on their birthday. At the age of twenty, they became adults automatically.

"Why should I take on adult responsibilities before I want to?" said Geradin. *And before my best friend can?*

"Oh, I don't know. Perhaps because you could swear your oath and become a Protector, which is all you've dreamed about for as long as I can remember."

Geradin said nothing. Of course Mek knew why he hadn't taken the Tests. How had he ever thought that his friend wouldn't figure it out?

"Ger, I know I could never pass the Tests." Mek's eyes fell for a moment to his useless legs. "But that doesn't mean you have to wait until you're twenty to get your majority."

"But if I take the Tests it will remind the Council that you can't."

"I don't need you to protect my feelings."

"But they'd use it against you. Kindul would call attention to it in his plan to make the Regency permanent."

Mek shook his head. "I know you're just trying to protect me, but it doesn't make much difference. Kindul could even use the fact that you don't take the Tests against me, claiming I am holding you back out of vanity."

"I...I didn't think of that." He should have anticipated that. He should have looked at all the possibilities. Another lesson he already knew, but had failed to use properly.

"It doesn't really matter. What does matter is that I need someone I can trust to do things for me. And there's no one I trust more than you. I need you to have your majority. So you take the Tests tomorrow, agreed?"

"Agreed."

"Well, I think we've let the Council stew long enough. Ask them to come back in, and then stand behind Kindul's chair until I ask you to leave."

Geradin grinned. "That will make him a bit jumpy. He knows I don't like him."

"You only have a practice sword. You can't cut off his head with that."

"Oh, I could do it. It would be a slow, painful process, and it might get rather messy, but if Your Majesty commands..."

Mek snickered. "My Majesty will give the matter serious consideration."

Geradin opened the door, and said, "My lords and ladies, His Majesty is ready for you now."

They filed back into the room and took their seats. Geradin conspicuously positioned himself three feet behind the Lord Regent's chair and stood with his hand on the hilt of his sword.

The Lord Regent stared at Geradin for a moment, then turned to Mek and began, "Your Majesty—"

"A moment, my Lord Regent," said Mek. "Lord Geradin and I were discussing a matter of grave importance, and a legal question came up. Since you are well versed in the law, I thought you might settle the question." His face wore a puzzled frown.

"Of course, Your Majesty."

"Is the punishment for high treason death by beheading or death by hanging?"

"High treason? You have discovered a traitor?"

"Do you not know the answer, my Lord Regent, or is

there some other reason why you do not wish to discuss the subject?"

"I beg your pardon, Your Majesty. It was only out of concern about a possible traitor that I—"

"Your loyalty to me is most touching, my Lord Regent. Now if you be so good as to actually answer the question that I have asked, my joy in your service will be full."

"The penalty is death by hanging, Your Majesty."

"Ah, I was wrong. I thought it was death by beheading. Never mind, Lord Geradin, you may leave now."

"As Your Majesty commands." He bowed low and made his way out the door. Once he was safely out in the corridor with the door shut behind him, he chuckled. Mek would have to describe the Lord Regent's face later. He and Mek had pulled plenty of pranks when they were younger, but with his training and Mek's responsibilities it was something they rarely did any more. But it was good to see Mek hadn't lost his touch.

He went to his room to get the money he had been saving out of the allowance Selima gave him four times each season. Suddenly he realized that would change after he took the Tests of Majority. He would have to earn his own money. It was not as if he would have to look for a job, for he knew the Protectors of the Line would accept him without question, but the idea was still strange to him. Yesterday he'd thought his majority was four years in the future, but now it was less than a day away.

The moneybox on his desk held seven gold dinars and some silver—enough to buy a birthday gift for Mek and make a deathday offering for his mother. He put the money into a purse and tied it firmly to his belt next to his sword.

Chapter Two

Aumekor

Aumekor wished he could follow Geradin out the door of the Council Room so they could have a good laugh. It had been too long since they'd pulled a prank together. Instead, he kept his brow wrinkled and his lips pursed. Grave concern tempered by honest curiosity was the signal he wanted to send.

He looked at Kindul, Lord Regent, who was bringing his wide eyes back into a mask of utter calm. By now he would have realized that it was merely an attempt to rattle him, and while he might be furious he was experienced enough to know that he could not object to the joke without making himself look like a fool in the eyes of the members of the Regency Council. His best course would be to continue the meeting as if it had never been interrupted.

Which meant that Aumekor's best course was to interrupt the planned flow of the meeting, but it could not be another attack on Kindul: That would be seen as frivolous. It needed to be something serious. Unfortunately, the Lord Regent had the advantage of directly controlling the bureaucracy of Aud Sapeer's government, which meant he filtered most of the information about the kingdom before it reached Aumekor. Some of the gaps could be filled by Selima, who had her own sources of information, magical and otherwise. Although Aumekor had never been outside the walls of the Keep,

Geradin was his eyes and ears in the city, and Geradin's ability to get along with commoners gave him a perspective that the lords and ladies of the Regency Council did not share. And the Protectors of the Line were by law under the direct control of the Heir of the Line, not the Lord Regent's, and that gave him an additional independent source of information.

None of those sources had given him anything new to use against Kindul, but Lady Uwixa's complaint about bandit attacks on the roads sounded serious enough. Not only might it be a problem of some urgency, but it also had the potential to embarrass the Lord Regent, who, after all, controlled the police.

"My Lord Regent, if you would care to resume our council?" He was betting that Kindul would try to skip past the issue of bandits, and that would give him the opening to show dominance by forcing the issue.

"Of course, Your Majesty. I am sorry to report that Prince Jupuruk att'Kosarim of Cirkepam was thrown from his horse and killed a few days ago. May his soul rise in the Light to eternal happiness in Velia."

After a moment of stunned silence, all the members of the council rose and recited, "May his soul rise in the Light."

Although it was his kingly prerogative to remain seated, Aumekor would have given up his throne in exchange for the strength to rise to his feet for the ritual with the others. But he spoke the traditional words by rote as his mind tried to think through the implications. Of course, he had to abandon his plan to pressure Kindul regarding the bandits—this news would have far-reaching consequences.

Prince Jupuruk was—had been—the only surviving child of Queen Onara, and she was long past childbearing age. Unfortunately, while she had borne four children, three of them had been of a sickly disposition. Not that he himself had much room for boasting on that account, but while his legs and left arm were completely useless and his right arm almost so, he was otherwise healthy. Despite the best care possible, the first three of Queen Onara's children had died before their tenth birthdays. Blaming her husband, she had divorced him and married again. Much to everyone's surprise, the change of husbands appeared to have worked, as Prince Jupuruk had been by all accounts healthy as a dragon. More than that, he had been loved by the people of Cirkepam, and because his mother's health was starting to fade there had been rumors that she was about to abdicate her throne in his favor.

The plotting Geradin despised here in Aud Sapeer, with only a regency at stake, was petty compared to what the nobles in Cirkepam would do to position themselves to take the throne for themselves and their heirs. Queen Onara was not dead yet, so there would probably not be any open fighting, but such instability in a kingdom bordering Aud Sapeer was potentially dangerous.

"My Lord Regent," said Mek. "This is grievous news indeed. How is Her Majesty dealing with the tragedy?"

"My sources tell me that her health has suffered a terrible blow, Your Majesty. While it is possible she may recover and yet lead Cirkepam for many years, we must anticipate the possibility that she may die at any time."

Lady Uwixa asked, "Please correct me if I mistake myself, My Lord Regent, but am I correct in thinking Her Majesty does not have any siblings to whom the crown could pass?"

"That is correct, Lady Uwixa."

"Then she is the last of her line. What is the likelihood of civil war when Her Majesty passes on? Is there one of the nobles powerful enough to claim the throne without bloodshed?"

"Unfortunately, it appears that there could be as many as four powerful nobles who might try to claim the throne, and with enough bad blood between them that it is unlikely that any of them would gain the support of any of the other three. And of course, in a situation like this, some of the lesser nobles might unite behind yet another candidate. If there is a civil war, it could last for several years."

Aumekor kept his face calm, but he was surprised the situation was that bad. Queen Onara must have been playing a balance of power game to prevent any one noble from getting too much power. "Could you tell me, My Lord Regent, out of the potential successors, are there some who are less disposed to be friendly toward our kingdom than their rivals?"

Kindul raised his eyebrows as if shocked. "Your Majesty, it would be…most improper for Aud Sapeer to involve itself in a purely internal matter of one of the other Free Kingdoms."

Mirroring the Lord Regent's look, Aumekor said, "Most improper indeed, My Lord Regent. I am surprised the idea even occurred to you, and I hope you will not mention such a thing again. I merely thought we might want to make an effort to improve relations with anyone who might become monarch of a kingdom along our borders."

"Perhaps it is improper for Aud Sapeer to interfere in the internal affairs of another Free Kingdom, Your Majesty," said Selima, "but a prolonged civil war would weaken the Free Kingdoms as a whole and perhaps invite an attack by the Armies of the Dark God. Thus, it is not a purely internal affair, but it concerns all of the Free Kingdoms."

"Of course it concerns us, Omnimancer Selima," said Lord Wintog, one of Kindul's allies on the council. "But for us to become involved in another kingdom's civil war would have repercussions. Severe repercussions on the very alliance of the Free Kingdoms."

Selima shook her head. "I am not talking about getting involved in a civil war, Lord Wintog. I am talking about avoiding one."

Over the years Aumekor had learned that if Selima had an idea, it was almost always a good one. "Omnimancer Selima, since avoiding a tragic civil war must be the desire of everyone at this table, please explain what you would propose to do."

"Thank you, Your Majesty. There is historical precedent for an outside power choosing a successor when a monarch dies with no heir. There were several cases in the Age of Light when the Gods themselves chose a new monarch through some sign, as in the legend of the sword in the anvil. But since the departure of the Gods of Light—may they return when we are worthy—there have been at least three instances where a monarch was chosen by a Conclave of Monarchs. The most recent time was about three hundred and fifty years ago, when the monarchs of the Free Kingdoms chose Gelsina beh'Yttana as Queen of Crez Pecui."

"But how would you get the nobles to agree to have the question decided by a Conclave of Monarchs?" asked Lord Wintog, his tone clearly conveying that he thought such a thing impossible. "If they believe they can gain the crown by force of arms, they will ignore the Conclave. Or are you proposing that the other monarchs support their choice by force of arms?"

"What I am proposing is that we encourage Her Majesty Queen Onara to call a Conclave of Monarchs to choose her successor. In fact, it is possible that she is already considering such a course of action, as I very much doubt that all her advisors are ignorant of history, Lord Wintog."

Aumekor refrained from smiling at Lord Wintog, who was doing his best to control his anger at being insulted. Suddenly, the Protector standing behind his left shoulder leaned forward and whispered, "A word, Your Majesty?"

Raising his palm to signal a pause in the meeting, Aumekor said, "My Lords and Ladies, if we might pause this discussion for a moment?"

"As Your Majesty commands," said Kindul.

Turning to the Protector, Aumekor said quietly, "What is it, Potonil?"

"Forgive the interruption, Your Majesty, but if such a Conclave would require you to leave the Keep, I know the High Protectors would be strongly opposed."

Aumekor nodded slowly. Though there were times he resented being almost a prisoner in his own castle, he knew the Protectors were only trying to keep him safe. Not only that, but it was only his isolation in the Keep that made it possible to hide from the world the fact that he was crippled. During his annual appearances at the Midsummer Festival Selima would magically support him so that he appeared to walk, and all his other public appearances were in the throne room of the Inner Keep, where he could remain seated as visitors were brought before him.

Only those who lived or worked in the Inner Keep, plus the members of the Regency Council, were aware that he could not even stand on his own, and all of them were sworn to keep the matter secret. Remarkably, as far as he knew the secret had not leaked out. Although it was perhaps not quite so remarkable at that, considering the fact that the oaths were taken under a bond of magic.

To leave the Keep in order to attend the Conclave of Monarchs would not only make it harder for the Protectors of the Line to do their duty, but it would place him in situations where he would be expected to stand and walk. While Selima could handle that on rare occasions, it would require too much magical energy for her to do it several times a day for as long as the Conclave lasted.

Turning to Selima and fixing her with his eyes, he said, "Omnimancer Selima, where would tradition and history indicate that such a Conclave should be held?"

Her eyes flickered to the Protector who had just spoken with him, and she nodded almost imperceptibly. "There does not appear to be any required meeting place, Your Majesty."

"My Lord Regent, My Lords and Ladies," he said, eyeing them each in turn, "then I propose that we immediately send an embassy to Her Majesty Queen Onara proposing that she call a Conclave of Monarchs to choose her successor, and that we offer the hospitality of the Keep of Aud Sapeer to host the Conclave."

Kindul nodded, obviously understanding why the Conclave must be held in Aud Sapeer. "As you command, Your Majesty. I shall see to the arrangements personally. To that end, unless there is any objection I propose that we adjourn this meeting and postpone all other business until the day after tomorrow."

Now was not the time to deal with the bandit situation, so Aumekor did not object. Neither did anyone else. The council members rose from their seats, and each bowed to him as they exited the room. Only Selima remained behind.

She sighed and shook her head. "Poor Onara. She must be taking it very hard. I'll be surprised if she lasts till next Midsummer."

"We should be able to arrange for the Conclave by late autumn. Perhaps sooner."

"Yes, sooner would be better." She eyed him speculatively. "Of course, the selection of a new monarch for Cirkepam is not the only business that might be conducted at a Conclave of Monarchs."

Aumekor frowned thoughtfully. "Yes, such a meeting would allow for discussions on improving the fortifications for the Barrier Guard, perhaps even drawing up contingency plans for additional manpower in case the Dark Priestess decides to attack."

"Oh, I had in mind something much more important than that."

He paused before responding. "What would that be?"

Selima laughed dryly. "Why, arranging your marriage, of course."

Chapter Three

Geradin

As Geradin went through the gates out into the bustle of Keep Street, he tried to think of a good gift for Mek. It needed to be something no one else would give him. Not lavish or expensive, but unusual. He decided to buy his deathday offering for his mother first, and then he would grab something to eat as he shopped for Mek's birthday gift.

Yellow and blue ribbons for the Midsummer Festival crisscrossed Temple Street above his head. He ducked into one of the small shops near the Temple of Light, and browsed for a while, finally selecting a delicate offering box, light blue with a golden sun painted on top. He handed one gold dinar to the shopkeeper.

"May I assist you in writing the offering, Lord Geradin?" The shopkeeper picked up a pen and a sheet of offering paper.

"No, thank you." He took the pen and paper and moved to a writing-desk near the back of the shop.

Gods of Light, I thank you for my mother, though I never knew her. I ask that she rest easy in the World of the Dead and that she know of my love for her.

The shopkeeper could have written him something longer and fancier, perhaps even rhyming, but ever since Selima had taught him to write he had written his own offerings. He rolled the offering paper up and slipped it inside the box. He blinked several times to clear his eyes before he turned back to face the shopkeeper, who took the box, wrapped it in brown paper, bound it up with twine and returned it to him.

After tying the package to his belt, he left the shop and headed south toward Trader's Square. He had decided the best place to look for Mek's gift was among the foreign merchants. They always seemed to have unusual things: artifacts of far-off places or long-past times, if you could believe their claims. Of course, the local merchants were no better, but if the foreigners told him lies, at least they were lies he had not heard before.

He bought a grilled sausage on a skewer and a small loaf of bread from a vendor on the street. As he threaded himself through the crowded streets, he alternated between bites of sausage and small chunks of bread.

The Midsummer Festival always attracted a large number of visitors from outlying areas of the kingdom, so Geradin practiced his observation skills, trying to train himself to instantly spot people who were out of place. With some it was easy, for their simple homespun clothing marked them as farmers who did not live near the city. Others presented more of a challenge, and he had to notice small details such as the way they looked about them or the speed at which they walked. Aud Sapeer residents tended to look straight ahead and walk more quickly.

Soon Geradin arrived in Traders' Square. Ignoring the shouted pitches for his attention, he passed the permanent stalls of the locals to reach the makeshift stalls and wagons of the foreigners.

After spending about a quarter of the afternoon working his way methodically through the market, Geradin reached the back corner of the square. He had heard quite enough about fortuitous discoveries of ancient magical artifacts from the Age of Light and rare objects discovered hidden beneath the Burn, the scarred expanse that remained from when the Dark God burned half the world.

Suddenly, his eye caught something small moving on the

ground. He turned to see what it was, then blinked as a knight two palmwidths tall in a full suit of armor marched toward him waving a tiny sword.

"Don't worry, milord, it's only a toy," said a man to his left.

Geradin glanced at the vendor. He was missing his left arm. On his right hand he wore a chainmail glove and he was walking two of his fingers across the small, empty table in front of him. He stopped and the miniature knight halted.

"You see, milord? The glove controls its legs." He wiggled his fingers, and the knight mimicked the motion. "Would you like to try it?" When he removed the glove, the knight collapsed on the cobblestones.

"Yes." Geradin took the glove and put it on. The figure sprang to its feet, and with a little practice he had it marching along.

It was remarkable—so remarkable that he began to suspect it might be a trick.

When he was thirteen, a traveling merchant had sold him "an ancient charm from the Age of Light" that would increase the strength of its possessor. At the merchant's urging, he had tested it on the spot by lifting a large rock. He had rushed back to the Keep, eager to give the charm to Mek. But on examining the charm with her power, Selima had found that it had no magical properties. The merchant had evidently used some magic to make the rock seem lighter in order to fool him. Was it possible that the merchant was doing something similar, controlling the little knight directly rather than through the glove?

Geradin hid the glove behind his back, and it still followed his movements. After trying some sudden starts and stops that were mimicked instantly by the little suit of armor, Geradin was convinced.

"I've never seen anything like it," said Geradin. "Where does it come from?"

"My son here made the armor," the merchant said, indicating the young man unloading boxes from a wagon behind him, "and my daughter enchanted it. She's got a talent for ferromancy." The pride in his voice was unmistakable.

"Your daughter is very talented." Geradin was sure that none of the commercial mancers in Aud Sapeer had made anything like this. Selima probably could, but as far as he knew she hadn't.

"You are a mancer yourself, milord?"

"No, but I have studied the subject. I know my teacher would love to meet your daughter. Did she come with you to Aud Sapeer?"

"Yes, milord. She went looking for an inn for us to sleep tonight while my son and I set up here."

Geradin looked around. The merchants in the back corner of Traders' Square did not get much traffic. He wouldn't have come here himself if he hadn't been so systematic in his search for a gift. "This is hardly a prime spot to set up your wares."

"I know, milord. We had hoped to rent a better position, but we ended up having to pay...tolls along the way." There was anger beneath his words.

"Tolls. I see." Geradin knew immediately what had happened. The highway taxes were not high enough to cause much problem, and their cost would hardly be a surprise. But the bandits that seemed to be increasingly common in the countryside rarely stole a merchant's goods—or even his money. Instead, they offered a merchant "protection" along the road. A merchant who refused would most likely encounter trouble on his journey, and so most of them paid. As this man obviously had. "Where did you come from?"

"Glicken, milord. It's a small village about three days south."

"You aren't a traveling merchant by trade, are you?"

"No, milord. I was a blacksmith by trade until I lost my arm serving my turn in the Barrier Guard. My son Pagil here, he was only twelve when that happened, but he took over the work. It was hard at first, but he turned into a fine smith."

"The workmanship on this armor is impressive. How much are you selling this knight for?" Geradin asked, hoping the price would be low enough but certain it wouldn't be.

"Twenty gold dinars, milord."

Geradin sighed. Mek would have loved it. "You wouldn't happen to have any other remarkable items that you would sell for six gold?"

"Sorry, sir. We only have the knights."

"You mean this isn't the only one?"

"No, sir. We have thirty of them."

Apparently his lack of money had demoted him from a lord in the eyes of the vendor. Normally, he wouldn't have minded. He didn't particularly want to be a lord, and he had done nothing to deserve such an honor. But he wanted to give Mek one of those knights, and now he wished he had the kind of wealth usually associated with his noble status.

Then again, wealth wasn't the only thing associated with noble status.

"I was really hoping to buy one as a birthday gift for a friend," Geradin said. "I don't have much money because I have not yet achieved my majority, but I can promise you that if you sell me one for six gold, you will be able to sell the rest of them within two days for fifty gold apiece. And after I have achieved my majority and earned some money, I will pay you fifty for this one."

That earned him a skeptical look. "A fine promise, indeed, sir. And how would that promise come to pass?"

Geradin grinned. "Tomorrow I will present one of your knights to His Majesty, King Aumekor, during his birthday celebration. Believe me, after that, many of the richest people in Aud Sapeer will be here demanding to purchase one for themselves."

The vendor had a pensive look in his eyes. "They probably would, at that. But how can I be sure that you will actually give this to the king?" As an afterthought, he added, "No offense, milord."

"None taken." After a moment's thought, Geradin said, "I could give you my word of honor, but since you don't know whether I am honorable, that is not much help. Come with me to some of the local vendors and ask them who I am and whether they would trust my word."

"I suppose that would work, milord." He turned to his son. "Pag, stop unloading. We may be closing up shop until tomorrow afternoon. Keep an eye on things while I go with this young man for a bit."

"Yes, Pa."

The two of them walked through the foreign traders until they reached the permanent stalls.

"You can start asking around here. I'm sure some of them recognize me. Or we could go into the city further if you want."

The vendor approached a rug merchant. "Excuse me, sir, but is that young man over there generally considered trustworthy?" he said, waving his hand in Geradin's direction.

The merchant laughed. "You must be new in town. Even if he were only half as trustworthy as his father you could still trust him with your life. If Lord Geradin att'Balunor wants credit, give it to him." He laughed again. "Would you care for a fine rug, Lord Geradin? I'll make you a good price."

"No, but I thank you for your assistance."

The vendor turned back to Geradin. His eyes stared at Geradin's feet. "I beg your pardon, milord, for doubting you, milord." His head bobbed on each "milord."

"Never mind that." He felt a bit guilty for taking advantage of his title. "Now that you know my name, why don't you tell me yours and we can walk back to your table like old friends?"

"My name is Egen att'Olun, milord."

"Well, Egen, do we have a deal?"

"Yes, milord."

"Good. His Majesty will love it."

As they approached Egen's table again, a young woman popped up from sitting on a box.

"Papa, where have you been? Pag's stopped unloading and when I asked him why he said to ask you. We need to sell something today. I've been to several inns and we haven't—" She stopped suddenly as she looked at Geradin.

"Lord Geradin, allow me to present my daughter Allonna."

She wasn't pretty enough to turn many heads at a noble's ball, he judged, especially in that homespun dress. But he could almost see her vibrate with energy. He bowed before her. "It is a pleasure to meet you. I stand in awe of your talents."

She blushed and gave a flustered bow. "I am honored, milord."

He turned to Egen. "I must return to the Keep shortly. If you could put the knight into a box for me, I would appreciate it."

"Of course, milord." He scooped up the tiny suit of armor and the controlling glove and placed them in a rough wooden box. "Here you are, milord."

Geradin opened his purse and removed the six gold dinars.

"No need, milord. Your credit is good with me."

Geradin saw Allonna open her mouth to say something, but he spoke first. "Thank you for your trust, but I insist that you take this as token of my good faith."

"You are most kind, milord."

After bidding them all a good day, Geradin returned to the Keep, but stopped short of the gate. He called out to the Protectors on guard, "I have a magical item that needs to be approved."

"We'll have someone meet you in the gatehouse."

He went into the gatehouse built alongside the wall of the Outer Keep and sat down to wait. He was certain that the little knight was not part of a plot to kill the Heir, but any unapproved magical item brought into the Keep would set off alarms. He knew better than most the reason for such precautions; he just wished they had been in place sixteen years earlier.

◆ ◆ ◆

The door to the gatehouse opened, and Selima walked in. "So, Geradin, another artifact from the Age of Light?" There was a trace of amusement in her voice.

Geradin winced at the reference to his gullibility. "I hope I am not as easy to fool as I was then." He opened the box, took out the limp suit of armor and laid it on the table. Taking out the glove, he put it on, and the little knight sprang to its feet. Selima gasped as he walked the knight to and fro on the table.

"Where did you get this?" she asked. "Is it from the Age of Light? It seems to be in perfect condition."

"I bought it from a vendor in Trader's Square. He says his son forged the armor and his daughter enchanted it."

"Amazing. Something like this would take a great deal of power and skill. I only hope the girl did not flare herself out creating this."

"I doubt she did." He paused, holding back a grin. "It would have made the other twenty-nine very hard to make."

"Twenty-nine more? It cannot be. And yet...You are certain there are more?"

"Well, I didn't actually see them. But there's no way Egen would have sold this one to me at that price if there weren't more. Although, his daughter didn't seem too pleased about it..."

"She is here?" Selima shut her eyes a moment. "You must take me to her."

As they walked briskly toward Traders' Square, Geradin said, "I thought you'd want to meet her, but why is it so urgent?"

"I can tell how much power it took to enchant that knight, and it is well within my capacity." Selima took a deep breath. "But it would take me at least a season to gather that much power."

Growing up as Selima's ward, Geradin had learned a lot about the workings of magic, even though he had no talent for it himself. Magical power permeated the universe, but it was directly available only to those who had the talent to draw it into themselves—and that talent was not given equally to all. Geradin worked out the implications. If it took Allonna one season per knight she enchanted, it would have taken her seven-and-a-half years to enchant thirty. Obviously it couldn't take her that long. "So she must gather power very quickly."

"Precisely. And that's what concerns me."

"Because she may be more powerful than you?"

"Because anyone in the kingdom capable of gathering and wielding that much power should have been detected long ago. There are two possibilities, and both have troublesome implications."

"I've met her, Selima. I don't think she's a servant of the Dark Priestess, if that's what you're thinking."

"Even if she is but an innocent girl who was somehow overlooked by the Testers, without proper training she is a danger to herself and others. With so much power available, who knows how much damage she could cause if she were to flare herself out?"

Over the years Geradin had met a few mancers who had tried to use too much power at once and had flared themselves out, unable to stop wielding their power until they had consumed all the power they had gathered. Afterwards, they were never able to use mancy again. They had come to Selima for help. He'd asked her what would become of them, and she'd told him that they would most likely die within a few seasons. Using magic tended to prolong the lives of mancers for hundreds of years beyond the normal span—and the more power they used, the longer they tended to live. But mancers who flared themselves out seemed to grow old quickly. That was, perhaps, a mercy for them, as they seemed to be in constant pain. There was no way to restore their ability to use magic; the most Selima could do for them was to use her healing abilities to dull their pain.

Remembering how Allonna seemed so full of energy, Geradin hoped she would never flare herself out.

❖ ❖ ❖

When they arrived at the back corner of Traders' Square, Egen and Allonna were gone, but Pag was still there securing their trade goods in the wagon. At Selima's questioning he told them that his father and sister had gone to an inn called the Traveler's Rest.

As Geradin and Selima walked to the inn, she said, "If I take this young woman as my apprentice, we'll bring her family to stay at the Keep tonight. If I tell you you're needed at the Keep, I want you to go tell Jialla to prepare a room in the Outer Keep for Allonna and another for Egen and his son."

Keeping his face serious, Geradin nodded. "Are you certain you don't want to signal me by twice cawing like a crow while winking your left eye?"

Selima shook her head, smiling. "And Swordmaster Ytanor keeps telling me you're such a serious boy."

Chapter Four

Allonna

Allonna finished counting the coins and carefully gathered them off the worn blanket and put them back in her purse. She shouldn't have left Papa and Pag alone for so long while looking for an inn. Well, Pag would have waited for her to get back, but Papa...Papa thought of himself as a good negotiator. He'd been making deals since before she was born, he'd remind her. It had been hard for him to turn that duty over to her two years ago. He'd been sick abed for nine days and during that time she'd managed to get their firewood supplier to cut his prices while convincing Lord Hilsakut's head stableman to pay more for horseshoes. Since then, he'd usually let her do the negotiating.

But no, Papa couldn't wait for her to get back. He just had to make a deal with that young lord. For some reason, Papa always trusted nobles and gave them credit, even when some of them still owed him for work done ten years past. And this lord was young—didn't even have his majority yet, Papa said, as if that excused anything—and while he might be tall and proud-looking and wearing a fancy tunic, he obviously didn't have much money. Wouldn't come into his inheritance for years, no doubt. He'd told Papa he had connections to the King, but what lord didn't claim that?

No, they had been cheated. Of course they had. First those bandits on the road, claiming they were taking a toll, and now this lordling with his fancy talk and promises, thinking to take advantage because they weren't city folk. Well, she would show them. They would think her a simple county girl, but she would teach them a thing or two about negotiating. She smiled to herself. Of course, they wouldn't realize they'd been taught until after the deal was done...

Her thoughts were interrupted as Papa burst into the room and quickly shut the door behind him. She turned to face him.

"Papa, I hope you haven't spent too much on drinking. We only have enough money left to stay here another ten days. You should not have charged that lord so little. If he tells others the price he paid, no one will pay us enough to make our trip here worth the effort. And his suggestion about buying boxes cost us—" She stopped when he raised his palm to quiet her.

"Quick, make yourself presentable while I straighten up this mess," he said, waving his hand at the clothes she had laid out on one of the two beds to try to get some of the wrinkles out.

She looked down at her blouse and skirt, and automatically began brushing off some of the dust from the road. The inn actually had baths, but she hadn't had a chance to go there and get cleaned up from their journey yet. "What's wrong with how I look? And who's coming? Not that young lord again, hoping to cheat us some more?"

Papa sighed. "He didn't cheat us, Lonna. I've explained it already. And he is here, but he's not the one who came to see you."

"To see me?" Allonna was puzzled. Who would even know she was here?

"It's Royal Omnimancer Selima. She's the one who wants to see you. Lord Geradin showed her the knight, and she wants to see you."

She stopped brushing at her skirt, then started brushing even harder. Papa had finished putting the clothes back in their trunk, and he looked her over.

"That'll have to do; can't keep them waiting in the hall any longer. Just try to keep a civil tongue and do whatever the

Omnimancer asks."

Allonna nodded. Suddenly her palms felt wet with perspiration and she tried to dry them on her skirt as Papa opened the door. In came an elegantly dressed woman followed by the young lord.

Papa bowed his head. "Omnimancer Selima beh'Tenika, I beg leave to present to you my daughter, Allonna beh'Wefanna."

For as long as she could remember, Allonna had heard stories about Royal Omnimancer Selima. How she had advised generations of kings and queens. How she could instantly heal a man on the brink of death. How she could utter a word and a strong man would be dead before his heart could beat even once more. So the short, slight-figured woman who stood before her did not fit Allonna's image of what an all-powerful omnimancer should look like. Yet the confident way she carried herself and the reserved power Allonna could sense in a way she didn't really understand allowed no doubt.

"Milady, I am most honored to meet you." Remembering her manners, she bowed.

Omnimancer Selima smiled at her. "And I am honored to meet you, Allonna. It is rare indeed to find someone of your magical abilities."

Heat rose in her cheeks. "My abilities are humble, milady, compared to an omnimancer such as you." Why was Omnimancer Selima here?

"Why don't you let me be the judge of that? From what I have seen, you may have great potential. Is it true that you have enchanted thirty little knights like the one your father sold to Lord Geradin?"

"Yes, milady."

"How did you learn to do that? Have you had any training in mancy?"

"No, milady. I just...did it. My mother had a talent for healing, and I got that from her, but I never did anything with metal before."

"And how long did it take you to gather the power to

enchant one?"

Allonna frowned. She wasn't sure what Omnimancer Selima meant. She thought magical power was just there to be used when needed. "Gather the power, milady? I don't understand."

"You have a reservoir of magical power within you that you have drawn from the world around you. Enchanting one of those knights would have used a lot of power, so it would take some time for you to fill the reservoir again by gathering power."

"I'm sorry, milady. I don't know how to gather power." Her cheeks flushed slightly. She felt so ignorant. Her mother had taught her what little she knew, but since her mother had died when she was ten years old, she really hadn't had a chance to learn much. If only she had known how to gather power, perhaps she could have gathered enough to heal her mother. Her eyes stung a moment at the thought.

"Don't be sorry, Allonna." Omnimancer Selima's voice was cheerful. "You probably just do not realize that you are doing it. What gave you the idea to enchant the suits of armor?"

"Well, milady, my brother had forged them as a trial of a new method of smithing, and I was admiring one of them, and I thought it would be fun if it could march around like there was a little knight inside it, and I touched it and…I guess I just wanted it to move, and it did. It started marching. Scared me half to death, it did, milady, especially when it wouldn't stop marching until I made it stop."

"I see. So when you first enchanted one, it was just marching, and not under the control of a gauntlet?"

"Yes, milady. The gauntlet was Pag's idea."

"So you then enchanted a knight and the gauntlet to go with it."

"Yes, milady."

"And after you did that, how long was it before you could enchant another?"

"After I did the first one and it worked, we showed Papa. He realized we could sell them, so we went back to the smithy and I enchanted the rest."

Selima did not say anything. After the rapid pace of the questions, the sudden silence made Allonna nervous. Had she just admitted something she shouldn't have done? Perhaps they weren't supposed to sell magical items without permission. Allonna finally raised her eyes from the floor and was surprised to see the omnimancer staring at her with raised eyebrows.

Then Omnimancer Selima spoke softly. "You enchanted the rest of them that same day?"

Relieved that she did not appear to be in any trouble, she replied, "Yes, milady. Well, the first time I did it I made a proper mess of things because I enchanted them all at once, and all the gauntlets made all the knights move, so I had to do each one again on their own."

Selima stood very still for what seemed to be a very long time. Finally she shook her head slowly and said, "Allonna, would you be willing to do a simple spell for me here?"

"If you wish, milady. Although I really don't know how to do much." Allonna was very puzzled by Omnimancer Selima's reaction. Why did someone so powerful want her to cast a spell?

"It will be very simple. I trust you know how to undo someone else's spell?"

"Yes, milady. My mother taught me that much."

Omnimancer Selima made a bowl shape with her hands and spoke a few words that Allonna couldn't understand. Then she pulled her hands away leaving a glowing ball made of blue light floating before her. A simple light spell; Allonna had learned to do that when she was about five years old.

"Undo this spell, please," said Omnimancer Selima.

Undoing spells was so simple she wondered why Omnimancer Selima was asking her to demonstrate it. "Yes, milady." Pointing her finger at the glowing ball, she focused a quick flash of magical power toward it as she said, "Be undone."

On reaching the center of the light, she could feel her burst of power break apart, as if it had shattered on a rock. Her eyes went wide. The light still shone unwavering, as if she had done nothing. But it should have worked. Undoing spells always worked. Well, sometimes other people had trouble undoing her spells, but she'd never had trouble—Suddenly she realized that she'd been very casual in undoing the spell, as if it were one of her neighbors who had cast it, and not the most powerful omnimancer in the Free Kingdoms. Determination surged within her; she would pass this test.

"I'm sorry, milady. That's never happened before. Let me try again." She breathed deeply and sent a burst of power that, though brief, was about as large as she had ever done before. "Be undone!"

The moment her power touched the center of the light, it disappeared completely except for a faint red afterglow. Allonna almost sighed with relief. If that hadn't worked, she would have had to use more power, and she wasn't sure how much she could use without flaring herself out.

Omnimancer Selima turned to Lord Geradin and said, "Lord Geradin, I believe you are needed at the Keep."

Allonna was somewhat startled at this sudden change in the conversation. The young lord had not spoken the whole time, and she had mostly forgotten he was even there. The fact that he was here with Omnimancer Selima made her revise the opinion she had formed that he was not the influential person he had claimed to be when negotiating with Papa. And then suddenly her mouth formed a silent "Oh" as her mind for the first time connected this Lord Geradin with Geradin, the infant son of Aud Sapeer's greatest hero—the baby who had saved the Heir by crying at the right time. She'd heard storytellers recite "Balunor's Stand" in the village square in back in Glicken since she was a small child. She had known that Balunor's son and the king were raised together by Royal Omnimancer Selima. Yet it had not occurred to her when her father had introduced

Lord Geradin to her, and in their later discussions about the deal he had made she had not made the connection. She just had never expected to actually meet anyone from a teller's tale.

"I shall go at once, milady," said Lord Geradin. Bowing to Papa and then her, he said, "Egen, I hope to see you again soon, and you as well, Miss Allonna."

"Go in the Light, milord," she said automatically in unison with Papa, although her mind was still reeling from her new understanding of who he was. They both bowed to the young lord, who turned quickly and exited the room.

They both looked to Omnimancer Selima expectantly. She in turn was looking at Allonna appraisingly.

"How old are you, Allonna?"

"I'm nineteen, milady."

"When you were younger, were you ever tested to determine the strength of your talent?"

"Yes, milady. Once when I was nine, I think, and again when I was fifteen, a Tester came to Glicken—that's our village—and he tested all the children and youth."

The omnimancer frowned at her, and she felt her heart thud within her. Had she said something wrong?

The frown vanished from Omnimancer Selima's face. "Don't worry, Allonna. I am not angry with you. It's just that I am very puzzled that the Tester did not realize the extent of your talent. Someone like you should have been trained by an omnimancer from when you were a girl."

"You mean because I can enchant metal? I didn't know myself, milady, until last season. I thought I could only do healing."

"It's not that, exactly. Forgive me, but I must ask this: your mother is no longer living, is she?"

"No, milady. She died when I was ten years old."

"So she did not teach you much about the theory of magic. She only taught you to use your talent in a practical manner."

Allonna thought a moment. "Yes, milady, I guess that's true."

"Did she teach you about the need to restrain your power?"

"She warned me I should never use too much power or I might flare myself out. Always use as little power as possible, she told me."

Nodding her head, Omnimancer Selima said, "And when the Tester came and started drawing power out of you to see how much you could use..."

Allonna realized where the omnimancer was headed. "...I was afraid of flaring myself out, so I only let him take a small amount. Yes, milady. I didn't realize what I was doing at the time, but you've seen the truth of it."

The omnimancer shook her head. "It takes a great deal of talent to fool a Tester—the very kind of talent the Testers are supposed to be looking for. The man was obviously incompetent." She sighed. "But what's done is done. The question is, what are you going to do now?"

"What am I going to do?" What was she supposed to do? What did Omnimancer Selima want her to do?

"Yes. Do you have your majority?"

"No, milady."

Turning to Papa, Omnimancer Selima said, "Master Egen, since your daughter is under your care, I would like to beg your permission to take Allonna as my apprentice, if she is willing."

Her breath caught in her throat. Apprentice? To Omnimancer Selima? Pride at being asked mingled with fear: fear that she wouldn't be able to live up to the omnimancer's expectations, fear of change. To leave her family, to leave her friends, to leave her village, to live in this giant city, to live among strangers and perhaps to die among them: these were not things she had dreamed of.

Papa scratched his head and said, "If she be willing, milady, I doubt I could do anything to stop her, so I'd best give my permission."

"Allonna, I would like you to become my apprentice. You do not need to decide right now, because this is a decision that will change the course of your life."

She paused. "Let me tell you what Omnimancer Jiltunok said to me when he asked me to become his apprentice. He said, 'I will not lie to you. If you choose this path, it will not be easy. You will study hard and you will work hard. But in the end, it will be worth it. You will learn things you've never dreamed existed, and you will be a powerful force for Light in our world.' Allonna, I say the same to you. I cannot lie to you: a hard future is rushing toward us, and I need your help to shape it for good. It may be dangerous, it may be full of sorrow, but the cause of Light is worth the cost. So I ask you to please consider my offer."

A chill ran down the back of Allonna's neck. The future must be hard indeed if Omnimancer Selima was asking her for help. Part of her, the part that thrilled with excitement to hear a teller's tales in the village square, wanted to say yes right now, wanted to join with Omnimancer Selima in her fight against the Dark. But the chill she'd felt stopped her.

"I..." She steadied her voice. "I will consider it, milady."

Flashing a smile at her, Omnimancer Selima said, "That's all I ask. I do not mean to frighten you, but it would not be fair to you if you thought an apprenticeship was going to be easy. Now, Master Egen, go downstairs and tell the innkeep that you will not be requiring this room after all and to have him summon a cart for your things."

"We have a cart, milady, with my son. But why must we leave this room?"

"Because you're coming to stay at the Keep. I want Allonna to get a good idea of where she would be living if she becomes my apprentice, and it would hardly do to have her staying at the castle while you and your son stay at an inn all the way across the city."

"That's very kind of you, milady, but it's not necessary—"

"Master Egen," she said, smiling, "my mind is quite made up. Do you see any point in arguing with me?"

"Ah, no, milady." He grinned sheepishly. "I'll just go down and have a word with the innkeep."

The rest of the day was a blur to Allonna. Arriving with Papa and Pag at the huge stone Keep that merged into the side of a mountain, being shown to a bedroom all her own that seemed as big as their house back in Glicken, having a bath in steaming hot water—it all seemed too much to take in. After a Midsummer's Eve feast which had more food than she'd ever seen in one place outside a market, she'd ended up watching fireworks out the window of her room until she was so tired that not even the continuing celebration could keep her from falling asleep in the softest bed she had ever known.

Chapter Five

Geradin

The Midsummer's Eve festivities had kept him up past midnight, but Geradin arose and got dressed before dawn on Midsummer Day. He wanted to make his mother's deathday offering before the Temple of Light got too crowded. With the offering box secured to his belt, he bade good day to the ever-watchful Protectors at the front gate of the Keep and made his way to the Temple of Light.

There were few people on the streets at this time of day—some tradesmen moving supplies for the day's celebrations, a handful of revelers making their way to bed—so Geradin was able to reach the temple grounds before sunrise. The cloudless sky allowed a clear view of the Nightglow, and Geradin spotted the shape of the Dragon's Egg almost directly overhead, which was said to be an omen for a good beginning.

Of course, Selima put no stock in such superstition. She said the Nightglow was merely the sun reflecting off clouds of dust at the edges of the universe, and its shapes held no meaning for good nor bad.

Set on a hill overlooking the city, the Temple of Light in Aud Sapeer looked as if it had been sculpted from blue flames. For all Geradin knew, it had been, for it was a creation of the Gods of Light. The temple's walls shimmered in the darkness, and its three spires, taller than anything ever built by men, seemed to rise up to join with the Nightglow stretching across the sky.

As he followed the path that curved around the hill up to the entrance on the east side of the temple, he spotted the bright pinpoint of Velia, the World of the Dead, glowing in the slowly reddening dawn sky. Even though he knew that when making an offering for the dead it did not matter whether Velia was visible in the sky or not, seeing it made him feel sure that his offering would reach his mother..

There was no line at the offertorium, and he took his place before the altar.

"Who comes before the altar of Attol?" asked the priest as he took the box from Geradin's outstretched hands.

"It is I, Geradin att'Balunor."

"Who comes before the altar of Beska?"

"It is I, Geradin beh'Elesi."

"Who comes before the altar of Clanni?"

"It is I, Geradin, a Follower of the Light."

"For whom is this offering made to the Gods of Light?"

"For my mother who is dead, Elesi beh'Ehanna."

The priest placed the box in the crucible on the altar, then marked a pattern in the air above it with his finger. The box burst into flame and began to burn rapidly. When the offering paper inside started to burn, the smoke from the crucible turned white. The smoke rose toward the triangular opening in the ceiling of the offertorium and joined the sky.

"Let the spirit of this offering rise to the World of the Dead and give comfort to the dead." The priest bowed.

Geradin returned the bow, then exited the offertorium.

"A moment, Lord Geradin?" said a male voice in the darkness outside.

Geradin turned to face the speaker, then bowed when he saw who it was. "High Priest Kogyrinem. I am honored to speak with you."

"You were making a deathday offering for your parents?"

"For my mother, Your Grace."

"Ah." Kogyrinem smiled, but his eyes were sad. "That is what I thought. I do not wish to give offense, but it has come to my attention that in recent years you have not made an offering for your father."

"Your Grace is correct."

High Priest Kogyrinem said nothing but continued looking at him. The silence grew heavy, and finally Geradin felt compelled to explain.

"My father always receives much honor and remembrance on his deathday, Your Grace. There is no need for me to make an offering for him." He hoped this explanation would be sufficient to ward off further questions.

Again Kogyrinem did not speak. Finally, Geradin said, "If there is nothing further, Your Grace, I must prepare to take my Tests of Majority."

Kogyrinem nodded slowly. "Go with the Light, Lord Geradin."

"I follow the Light, Your Grace," he said, bowing before Kogyrinem before turning and leaving the temple.

He wasn't hungry, so going back to the Keep for breakfast would serve no purpose. It would be a while yet before the Tests of Majority would begin, but he decided to wait at the Arena of Judgment until then. He did not hurry as he walked the wakening streets of the city to the place where he would officially become an adult in the eyes of gods and men.

Mek was right, of course. He would have no difficulty passing the Tests themselves. But growing up he had imagined that Mek would be there beside him, that they would both achieve their majority and enter the world of adults together. When he had realized that Mek's useless legs and weak arms would prevent him from passing the Test of Body, he'd still clung to the hope that somehow, Selima would find a cure for Mek's condition so they could go through this together. But now he would best serve Mek as an adult, and so he must put away his childish dreams.

The outer wall of the arena loomed over him, and he walked up to the Gate of the Champions. In the distant past, the primary purpose of the Arena of Judgment had been to conduct trials by combat. Now it was used for tournaments on special occasions—the traditional Midsummer Tournament would be held here that afternoon—but an element of its former purpose remained in the Tests of Majority, passing judgment on the worthiness of children to become adults.

On any other occasion, Geradin would be entering through the Gate of the Champions, for he had won the youth division of every tournament for the past three years. Today, though, he would enter through the Gate of the Petitioners, as would all the others who wished to take the Tests of Majority. Gods willing, he would leave through the Gate of the Citizens.

There was already someone at the Gate of the Petitioners. He stood taller than Geradin by a head and beneath a rough homespun tunic his shoulders were wide as two men standing together. The wooden practice sword seemed almost a twig in his hand as he moved it through various practice swings.

Geradin had never faced anyone so large and strong in the tournaments. Instinctively he began searching for weaknesses. This was not someone who had been trained in using the sword; while powerful, the practice swings were slow and hesitant. Geradin now recognized him as a laborer for one of the builders in town, who was often in the streets easily carrying on each shoulder a wooden beam which would have been a heavy load for an ordinary man.

When he saw the other pause in his practice, Geradin spoke up. "Good day to you, sir."

With a start, he turned toward Geradin. "Good day to you, Lord Geradin," he said, bowing his head.

It still caught Geradin off guard sometimes when people he didn't know knew him. "And what is your name?"

"Holoran, milord."

"Well, Holoran, it looks like we are the most anxious to leave our childhood behind. I did not expect anyone to be here so early."

"If it please you, milord, I can return later."

"No, no. You have as much right to be here as I. Please, feel free to continue with your practice."

Holoran looked down at the sword in his hand, then sheathed it with a sigh. "I don't reckon it makes no difference anyway, milord. I've no skill with the blade. I just... I'm sorry, milord."

"Sorry for what?"

"I needn't burden you with my problems, milord."

"Don't think of me as a lord. Like you, I am just another youth born on Midsummer Day. Call me Geradin."

"As you wish, mi—Geradin."

"So tell me, Holoran, you have not had much training in the sword?"

"No, m—, not really. Some of my fellow workers have tried to teach me, especially after..."

"After what?"

"After I failed the first time."

Geradin grimaced in sympathy. Young nobles could fail the Tests of Majority, and it was passed off as the carelessness of the young. He should have studied more, they would say. Among the lower classes, though, it was considered a disgrace to take the Tests of Majority and fail. Trying to get ahead before his time, they would say. Most people just waited until they turned twenty and received their majority automatically, unless they had some pressing reason.

"And so you're here to try a second time."

Holoran ducked his head down. "Third, milord," he said, his voice quiet, as if trying to hide.

Geradin realized he'd stepped in the mire. "Well, this is my first time. Perhaps you could give me some pointers, things to watch for. And perhaps I could give you a few tips about the sword."

"Would you, milord? I seen you in the tourneys. I never seen anyone who could fight like you."

Geradin coughed to hide his embarrassment. "That's enough with the milords, please." Drawing his practice sword, he said, "Now, show me how you would attack me."

Holoran drew his sword, and then lumbered forward while swinging his sword in a wide arc. Geradin stepped lightly aside and the sword missed him completely as Holoran passed him by.

"You see my problem, m—Geradin? How am I supposed to get three touches on my opponent when he won't stand still so as I can hit him?"

In the Test of Body by Combat, the youth would face off against a soldier, and was required to get three touches before the soldier could get five. The soldiers involved were average swordsmen at best, nowhere near the caliber of Swordmaster Ytanor, and so Geradin was sure that he could get his three touches without even being touched himself. But Holoran...

"Well, here's the first bit of strategy I have for you. Stand your ground. Make him come to you. Once you get moving, it's hard for you to change direction, which lets your opponent slip around you. Stand in one place, and you can turn to face him in any direction."

Biting his lip, Holoran nodded.

"Now, let me see how fast you can thrust with your sword."

The sword tip came up and moved forward as if it were moving under water.

"Again. Faster."

No difference. Even a below-average soldier would be able to avoid those blows. Holoran had strength to spare, but no speed.

"It's no use, m—Geradin. I know I am too slow. But I have to try, anyway." He sheathed his sword.

Geradin nodded reluctantly. "Why is it so important to you to pass the Tests? Why not just wait until you're twenty?"

Holoran ducked his head. "Well, ah, there's this girl..."

Suppressing a grin, Geradin said, "The things we men do for women."

"She got her majority three years ago, so she can marry, but as I have not my majority, her father can still forbid the match. And I don't want to wait two more years."

Geradin frowned. "She has her majority, and her father still stands in her way?"

"He thinks me unworthy of her. He hopes that as time passes, she will give up on me, and marry into a merchant family. I'm just a common laborer."

At that last word, Geradin's head snapped up. "But that's the answer! Why are you taking the Test of Body by Combat? Why not take the Test of Body by Labor?"

"I am no coward, milord." His voice was stiff.

"But I'm sure you could pass it, and then you'd have your majority." The assignments given out for the Test of Body by Labor consisted of a half-day of grueling work in the service of the city. Anyone fit of body could do it.

Holoran shook his head. "Only cowards and women take the Test of Body by Labor. I'll not be thought a coward."

"But—"

"It's all very good for you, Geradin. As a lord, none dare speak ill of you."

How little he knew of court politics, thought Geradin.

"But for me to live my life, having all around me call me a coward? I could not bear it. I would rather fail honorably than succeed at such a cost."

Slowly, Geradin nodded. "I see what you mean. It takes great courage, Holoran, to go into a battle knowing you will lose, yet trying your hardest all the same. Come, I will try to teach you a few tricks, and who knows but what you'll get lucky?"

Chapter Six

Aumekor

Aumekor lay on his back on his overly large bed. It was ridiculous to have so much space for himself when a cot would suffice. It was not as if he were going to roll around in it. In the sixteen years since he'd been born—if such a commonplace term could be used to describe being cut from your mother's womb with a sword—he had never so much as turned himself onto his side without aid. Sixteen years old, and weak as a babe in arms. Weaker, even.

The light of the torches that ringed his room flickered over the bed. He turned his head to see the ever-vigilant protectors standing watch over him. Sixteen years of sleeping in a well-lit room so no one could sneak up on him in the darkness. But the light was not the gentle luster of the Nightglow coming through a window — something he had only read about. There were no windows in the Inner Keep.

And today, for only the sixth time in sixteen years, he would go outside the Inner Keep. Only as far as the Outer Keep, to be sure, but he would be beneath the sun and sky, with nothing between them and him. Unless you counted the magical protective shielding that Selima and the other mancers would be weaving around him. But Midsummer Day was his one chance to get outside, and he would take it.

He'd been almost eleven years old when he first read the Charter of Aud Sapeer. His history tutor had shown it to him as part of a lesson on how the government of Aud Sapeer was formed nearly two thousand years ago. The Charter had been amended hundreds of times, and was a fascinating lesson in itself regarding the constant fluctuations of the distribution of power between the monarch, the nobility, and the commoners. But what had struck him instantly the first time he read it was a clause, never amended, which stated, "The Monarch shall deliver, each Midsummer Day, a Speech before the Public detailing the State of the Kingdom, and showing Himself to the People to be their just and rightful Ruler."

Until he read those words, he had been a very compliant child, always accepting the explanations of adults as to why it was not safe for him to go outside. After all, what could he do with his weak body against the powerful adults surrounding him?

But those words had become his weapon, and with them he had beaten down every objection from the Regency Council, from the High Protectors, even from Selima herself. He had a duty, he told them, and he was going to perform that duty, and if they obstructed him in the performance of his duty under the Charter that was the very foundation of the Kingdom of Aud Sapeer, then they were traitors all and he would be under no obligation to follow their counsel in any matter whatsoever.

Eventually they had found it easier to let him give a speech from a terrace of the Outer Keep, surrounded by Protectors and warded about by magic, before an audience of a few dozen carefully-screened people, than to put up with his refusal to cooperate with anything they wanted him to do.

He laughed as he remembered that first speech. The Regency Council had wanted to write it for him, but he'd insisted on painfully scratching it out himself, with Ger on hand to dip the pen in the inkwell for him. It had consisted of no more than twenty sentences: a child's imagining of a great speech, bejeweled with phrases about the greatness of Aud Sapeer and crowned by an improbable but sincere promise to be the best king ever. But he'd memorized his speech so he could spend that short while looking up into the sky or over the wall of the Outer Keep to the city beyond, and feeling the freshness of wind on his face. When he finished speaking he'd had a moment to revel in the probably insincere and certainly excessive cheering by the handpicked listeners, and then he'd been bundled back inside.

Now that he was older, he more fully understood the threat the High Priestess of the Dark God posed, not just to him but to everyone who lived in the sixteen Free Kingdoms. So he went along with the extensive efforts to protect him. But he adamantly insisted on giving the Midsummer Day speech. He had to. Not because it was his duty under the Charter; that duty was subordinate to the need to preserve the Line of Orcan. Not because he wanted his one yearly chance to see the sun and sky, although he did treasure that aspect. No, he had to do it because that was the first thing in which he had ever exercised his power as king. To back off from it would be seen as a sign of weakness.

And he must not appear weak. Kindul made sure of that. By constantly seeking any weakness to exploit, Kindul had forced him to become strong. Aumekor snorted softly. Perhaps he should thank Kindul for that.

The irony was that Kindul, who had been Lord Chancellor to his father, should have been his greatest supporter, not his greatest enemy. Well, his greatest enemy after the Dark Priestess. The Lords Chancellor of Aud Sapeer had traditionally done their best to strengthen the monarch they served—if the time came for the prophecy to be fulfilled, the more power the Heir of the Line could command, the more likely he would win that crucial battle.

From what Selima and others had told him, he knew that Kindul had been following in that grand tradition. Sixteen years ago, Lord Chancellor Kindul had rightfully stood at King Ordil's right hand as the king delivered his Midsummer address. Lord Chancellor Kindul had taken a sword blade through the shoulder trying to shield his monarch and friend from a Knight of the Dark God. And Lord Chancellor Kindul had arisen from the carnage that day to find his king and queen dead, leaving only a sickly infant as the Heir of the Line. He was the natural choice of the Assembly of Lords to become Lord Regent, and his wisdom and skill had kept Aud Sapeer mostly prosperous and peaceful for sixteen years; whether by negotiating trade agreements or by playing off one neighboring monarch against another.

Aumekor sighed. His father, King Ordil, had been a strong man, a mighty warrior—even at the last, unarmed and unarmored, he had killed two Knights of the Dark God before he was swarmed under and killed. If Aumekor had been born healthy like Geradin, things might have been different. Kindul might have been different: he might have been surrogate father to him as Selima had been surrogate mother.

But Kindul did not see in him the son of his friend King Ordil. No, he saw a pitiful weakling—a usurper, even—sitting on the throne of the man he had given his life to and almost given his life for. The King of Aud Sapeer must be strong. The Heir of the Line must be strong. The man Kindul served must be strong, and thus he could not forgive Aumekor his weakness. The Lord Regent would give Aumekor the exquisite courtesies due to him by right of birth, but though unquestionably loyal to the throne of Aud Sapeer, he would not be friend to him who sat upon it.

This was all speculation, Aumekor reminded himself. As far as he knew, Kindul had never expressed these thoughts to anyone. Aumekor knew his ability to analyze the words and deeds of others and gain insight into their motives was useful in predicting what his opponents might do and allowing him to take preventive measures, but he also knew it was not perfect. So while he might feel he understood Kindul, he had to be careful not to become overconfident in his own analysis.

The door to his bedchamber opened, and Aumekor turned his head to see Nikufed, his valet, carrying a tray with several pastries cut into bite-sized pieces, a dish of cream, and a pot of tea.

"Good morning, Your Majesty. Are you ready for breakfast?"

"Yes, thank you, Kuf."

Nikufed helped him into a sitting position, then snapped the legs of the silver tray into position and placed it over his lap. Aumekor dipped one of the pieces of pastry in the cream, then lifted it to his mouth and savored the mixture of sweet and tart flavors in the berry filling.

"The cooks have outdone themselves again. Have you had one of these?"

"Yes. I had to make sure they weren't trying to poison you. I had three, to make thrice sure."

Chuckling, Aumekor took another piece. Since the food was tested magically for poison, no one actually had to risk his life as a food taster. Kuf's constant jokes about security helped make it all less oppressive somehow. Most of the people he knew were very serious about keeping him safe, and while he knew they were right about how important it was, he wished they could be more light-hearted about it. But many of them had memories of sixteen years ago to sober their thoughts about security, and that attitude infected the younger inhabitants of the Inner Keep. Even Ger, who would joke with him about just about anything, tended to grow grave when it came to anything related to protecting the Heir of the Line.

"Have you decided what you will wear for your speech today?"

As if he had a choice. Aumekor smiled and played along. "I was thinking...perhaps some colorful silk pantaloons and a vest?"

"Oh no, Your Majesty." Kuf shook his head in mock disapproval. "Silk pantaloons are no longer the style. I had no idea you were so out of touch with the current fashions. Comes from locking yourself away in this castle, I'd guess. No, Your Majesty. I will tell you what the fashionable monarch is wearing for speeches these days."

"And what is that?"

"Why, nothing less than steel, Your Majesty. Encasing yourself from toe to crown in fabulous, shiny steel is thought the pinnacle of good taste."

"I seem to recall that steel was considered fashionable last Midsummer Day as well. I thought fashion was changeable as the wind."

"Good steel never goes out of style. That's what I always say."

"No, I guess it doesn't. I'll go with the steel, then, Kuf."

"A wise choice indeed, Your Majesty. You're fortunate to have someone like me to advise you in such matters."

There was a knock at the door, and one of the Protectors looked out to see who it was, then announced that Selima wanted to see him. He nodded, and she was ushered in.

"Good Midsummer, Selima."

"Good Midsummer, Aumekor. And happy birthday."

"Thank you." He smiled at her a moment, then grew more serious. "Did…Have you had a chance…"

Selima nodded. "I made offerings for your parents early this morning."

"I appreciate you doing that for me."

Selima sat on the edge of his bed. "Your parents were wonderful people. I wish you'd had a chance to know them. They were both so happy that you were going to be born." She shook her head. "And now here you are, sixteen years old. I'm sure your parents are very proud of the man you've become."

She sighed. "I know I haven't been a good replacement as a mother, for you or for Geradin—" She raised her palm to silence his objection. "—but I'm proud of you both. No one could ask for two finer…Well, I'm just proud of you both."

Aumekor wasn't used to having Selima express her emotions and he wasn't sure what to say, so he finally settled on a simple thank you. To know that he was living up to her expectations despite his weakness made him feel a warmth in his chest. Yet he still felt embarrassed that she was telling him this. He decided to change the subject.

"Geradin told me last night you may have found an apprentice?"

"Yes, if she accepts, which I think she will. Allonna is her name. She lacks all but the most basic training, but she's very powerful. Far more powerful than I am, in fact."

Aumekor started in surprise, then involuntarily looked down at his legs.

Selima caught the movement of his eyes, and shook her head sadly. "No, Aumekor. I'm sorry. With your paralysis, it's not a matter of more power being able to help; it's a lack of knowledge. The gods themselves, perhaps some mancers from long ago could have cured you. But so much was lost when the Gods of Light disappeared, and even more when the Dark God burned the world."

"I know, Selima. I know. It's not your fault."

Selima turned away from him. "I should never have left your mother. As it was, I was too late to save your father. And if it hadn't been for Balunor, you would have been killed along with your mother. If I'd only stayed..."

"You did what you thought was right. I don't blame you—nobody does. And you've been doing a marvelous job of protecting me ever since. I probably haven't thanked you enough for that."

Selima straightened her back and turned to face him again, a half-smile on her lips. "No, you haven't. In fact, you've complained about it far too much. But it's your birthday, so I forgive you."

He was glad to see her coming back into her usual spirits. "If you're in a forgiving mood, let me see if there's anything else I need to confess..."

Kuf coughed discreetly.

"Oh, it looks like it's time for Kuf to take me to the baths. Have to be spruced up so the people will know I'm their rightful king, after all." He paused, then added, "Thank you again for making the offerings for my parents, Selima."

"It was an honor. I guess I'll see you this afternoon to prepare for your speech?"

"Yes."

Selima nodded, then left the bedchamber.

Aumekor turned to Kuf. "Well, my good Nikufed, the time has come for me to face mine ancient enemy, the bath. It hasn't managed to drown me yet, and with luck, I shall once again emerge victorious. And clean."

"Never fear, my liege," said Kuf, as he lifted Aumekor into his rolling chair. "I will be at your side, and should you fall, I swear to avenge you an hundred-fold and more, till there be no baths left in all the kingdom. I shall personally drain each one."

Chapter Seven

Geradin

Only the Test of Body remained. Geradin and the other seven candidates followed the Proctor into the field of the arena.

Geradin had been most worried about the Test of Spirit. He'd known he could read and do arithmetic well enough to pass the Test of Mind without difficulty, and of course there would be no problem with the Test of Body. But the Test of Spirit required him to remember his theology, a subject which did not interest him much, and he'd heard that the priests who asked the questions had little tolerance for mistakes.

He had almost sighed in relief when the first question had asked him to explain why demigods were both greater than and less than men, and give an example.

"The demigods are greater than men because the Gods granted them power second only to the Gods themselves," he had answered. "The demigods are less than men because the Gods did not grant them free will, but bound them to their tasks. Kairith, for example, is the demigod of death. He is bound to take the souls of those who die to the world of the dead." The priest had nodded approvingly, and Geradin had felt more at ease. He'd been stumped by his final question, which was something about some prophecy that had already been fulfilled. When studying prophecy, he'd always focused on what was going to happen, not what had already happened.

Fortunately he had done well enough before that question to pass.

Holoran had done better than he on the Test of Spirit, answering each question without hesitation. But now, as they came into the sunlight of the arena, Geradin could see those huge shoulders slumping. Despite what Geradin had taught him, unless a particularly incompetent soldier was chosen to be his opponent, Holoran would fail a third time.

The people in the stands were sparse. Some were merely there to get well-positioned for the tournament that afternoon, but most of them were relatives or friends of those taking the Tests. Geradin had no relatives, and he knew that Selima's duties would prevent her from coming. And of course, Mek never left the protection of the Keep.

"She's here," said Holoran, looking into the stands. "I'd thought she might not come to see me fail again."

"Where is she?" Geradin asked, trying to follow Holoran's gaze.

"The one there in the green dress, waving with both arms."

The movement drew his eye and Geradin spotted the busty brunette instantly. "Ah, Holoran, I can see why you're so anxious to get your majority." Giving him a clap on the shoulder, he said, "With an incentive like that, I'm sure you'll manage your three touches."

"I've had that incentive the last two times. It's not enough. A miracle is what I need."

Holoran was already defeated before a blade was lifted against him, Geradin could see. And even if Geradin could find some way to boost Holoran's morale, what good would it really do? What good is hope when you cannot win the battle?

The eight of them stood in the middle of the arena. The three women were not wearing practice swords, so it was obvious that none of them was planning to choose the Test of Body by Combat. They would be led off to work for a half-day before being brought back to swear their oaths. The combat here in the arena would last only a short while, after which the victors would swear their oaths, and the vanquished would leave in disgrace.

The Proctor's voice called all eyes to him. "To be fully worthy of your majority, you must prove that you are fit enough to contribute to the good of all. You may prove that you are willing to defend our kingdom and the Light by choosing the Test of Body by Combat. Or you may prove that you are willing to labor with your strength to build up our kingdom and the Light by choosing the Test of Body by Labor." He walked slowly in front of them, looking each of them in the eyes. "The time has come to make your choice."

If you cannot win the battle, you are fighting the wrong battle. Geradin did not remember in which book of tactics he'd read that maxim, but he knew Holoran was going to make the wrong choice again. For fear of being considered a coward, he would fight the wrong battle. But perhaps there was a way to change the situation.

"My Lord Proctor, might I be permitted to speak before we make our choices?"

The Lord Proctor frowned. Geradin's request did not fit the ceremonial pattern.

Geradin knew he had put the Lord Proctor in an awkward position. The man who served as Lord Proctor was not truly a lord: on any particular day, whoever conducted the Tests of Majority was the Lord Proctor. The lordship was bestowed on the position, not the man. This allowed someone who was not normally a lord to give orders to the nobles taking the Tests of Majority without violating propriety. Thus, while the Lord Proctor today certainly had the authority to refuse Geradin's request, the man himself had to be considering whether it made sense to possibly offend an actual lord who was known to be the king's best friend.

Finally the Lord Proctor nodded. "You may speak, Lord Geradin."

"I give you thanks, My Lord Proctor." He would apologize to the man later for having put him in such a dilemma. He raised his voice to the people in the stands. "I have been told that only cowards and women choose the Test of Body by Labor. I want to declare to you today that I am not a woman, although I hope you will take my word for it rather than have me prove it by undressing before you."

There was a smattering of laughter.

"I also declare before you that I am not a coward. On that, you need not take my word, as I believe I have proved my bravery and skill before you in this very arena on other occasions. And I believe nothing would give me more pleasure than to demonstrate to you my skill with the sword this morning by rapidly dispatching my opponent in combat."

Someone in the crowd began chanting "Ger-a-din! Ger-a-din!" A few others joined in, but Geradin raided his palm to silence them.

"By choosing the Test of Body by Combat, I could leave through the Gate of Citizens with my majority in moments. Meanwhile, the 'cowards' and women who choose the Test of Body by Labor will spend half a day working to improve our city to the benefit of all. But what does our city gain from my bravery if I get three touches with the sword? Nothing. Yet if I am a coward and give my labor, our city is the better for it. The easy path is before me. If I am afraid of a little hard work, I can choose the path of combat. But I will not take the easy path. I will not shrink from getting my hands dirty, from straining my muscles to the utmost to improve our city.

"I will choose the Test of Body by Labor. If this be cowardice, then call me coward to my face. But remember when you do, I will have my majority, and the sword I will wield in defense of my honor will be made of fine steel, not wood." He pulled his practice sword from its sheath and threw it to the ground, then turned to the others standing with him.

"I know that most of you have planned to take the Test of Body by Combat. And some of you may have commitments that would prevent you from spending the next half-day laboring. If you choose combat, I cannot fault you for it. But if you do not fear to labor, I ask you to join with me in making our fair city even fairer. For it is not cowards and women who choose the Test of Body by Labor. It is brave men and women who love our city. And I would be numbered among them."

He looked to the Lord Proctor. "That is all I wished to say, My Lord Proctor."

Out in the crowd someone began to clap, and others quickly joined in. The chant of "Ger-a-din! Ger-a-din!" began again and grew in volume. Large crowds had chanted his name before, much louder, but he'd never felt so good about it as he did now.

The Lord Proctor raised his hand until the crowd went quiet. "It appears that Geradin att'Balunor has made his choice. For the rest of you, the time has come to make your choice." He turned to the young man closest to him. "Jilmor att'Besok, what is your choice?"

Jilmor's right hand fumbled on the hilt of his practice sword. He glanced at Geradin, then said, "I...I choose the Test of Body by Labor."

A cheer went up from the crowd, and the Lord Proctor had to still them again. He stepped to the next in line, one of the women. "Lemili beh'Nara, what is your choice?"

"I choose the Test of Body by Labor."

"Soraden att'Waverilon, what is your choice?"

"I choose the Test of Body by Labor."

"Holoran att'Kemol, what is your choice?"

Geradin was surprised to see Holoran frown at him. The silence stretched. Holoran turned and looked at the woman he loved. She was standing, very still. Finally, Holoran shook his head and said, "I choose the Test of Body by Labor." His voice was disgusted.

As the rest of them were asked to choose, Geradin tried to figure out why Holoran was unhappy with the situation. Finally he concluded that Holoran must have been putting on a show of reluctance in order to further protect himself from being called a coward.

The Lord Proctor quieted the final cheers after all of them

had chosen. He turned to the soldiers waiting nearby, and said, "None having chosen the Test of Body by Combat, your services will not be needed. Go with the Light."

"We follow the Light," they answered in unison, then turned and marched away.

"Taskmaster Ulinor, here are eight who have chosen the Test of Body by Labor. I charge you to take them and put them in the service of our city. Let them labor with their might; let them not slacken nor complain lest they prove themselves unworthy."

"My Lord Proctor, it shall be as you command. I shall return my charges to your hands when they are finished with their labors."

The Lord Proctor turned back toward them and said, "Go with the light."

"We follow the Light," Geradin said along with the others, and then they followed the Taskmaster out of the field of the arena to the Gate of the Servants. Outside the gate, he assigned the three women to go with someone who was waiting there, then turned to the men.

"I was not expecting to assign any men to labor, and I've never had more than one, let alone five. But don't you worry, I've got just the task for you." He chuckled. "You'll labor enough to earn your majority. Follow me." He chuckled again.

He took them into a storehouse. "Each of you grab a pickaxe from over there, then come over here.

As they complied, he pulled a cloth from off a round steel grate, about five feet in diameter. "Take a hold of this. You'll have to carry it where we're going."

They struggled for a moment trying to work out the best way to carry a pickaxe in one hand and hold the grate with the other, until Holoran suggested that one of them carry all the pickaxes and the other four carry the grate.

With a satisfied grunt, the Taskmaster said, "All right, let's be going then."

"Taskmaster Ulinor," asked Geradin, "where are we going?

"Why, to the sewers, milord." He chuckled. "To the sewers."

Chapter Eight

Allonna

There were books everywhere. As she looked around Omnimancer Selima's study, she realized there must be more books in this room than in all of Glicken. The bookcases lined the walls from floor to ceiling, interspersed with closed wooden cabinets. Allonna read the labels on some of the nearby shelves and was surprised to find that the subjects had little to do with mancy: History of the Age of Light, History of the Age of Dark, Modern History, Biography, Strategy and Tactics of Warfare.

While the number of books was overwhelming, she had expected an omnimancer's study to have books. The tellers were right about that much, at least. But she had also expected it to be filled with glowing artifacts and pungently bubbling potions, with piles of scrolls detailing mysterious spells strewn over a workbench along with vials of ground dragonscale or jellied snake-tongue.

Instead, Omnimancer Selima's study was about ten paces square with a wooden desk at its center. On the desk were few neat stacks of papers and a few objects which did not appear to glow in the least. No potions, no scrolls, no vials. Except for all the books, it was not much different from the accounting office in Lord Hilsakut's castle. After the crowds and bustle of the city, the excesses of the Midsummer's Eve festivities, and the shock of meeting the great Selima herself, this room was disappointingly ordinary.

Still, perhaps the truly magical items were kept in the cabinets. Selima had opened up one cabinet door and was moving objects around inside it. She removed what looked like a metal disk, closed the cabinet and turned to Allonna. "As I told you yesterday, I want you to be my apprentice, but I want you to make that decision fairly. Which means I have some things I need to tell you. However, some of these things are secrets which must not be revealed to anyone who might pass the information on so that it could eventually reach the ear of the High Priestess of the Dark God."

"I can keep a secret, milady."

"Can you really? What if one of the Soulless threatened to kill you if you did not reveal what you knew?"

"I...I would not tell it anything." There was a queasy feeling in the pit of her stomach, but she drew in a deep breath and continued. "I would rather die than help the Dark Priestess."

"That's good to know." Selima smiled, then suddenly frowned. "What if they threatened to kill your father and brother? Or what if they tortured you with worms that burrowed into your flesh? Could you guarantee that you would not let something slip?"

Allonna shrank back in her chair. What was she getting herself into? She felt sure she would rather die than betray the Light, but what if dying was not a choice? How could she know what she would do if she was tortured? The High Priestess of the Dark God was known for her cruelty. Could she really promise Omnimancer Selima that she would never reveal what she was told?

Tears stung her eyes as she shook her head. "I'm sorry, milady. I don't know if I could. I'm sorry to disappoint you."

"You do not disappoint me, Allonna. You impress me greatly. You recognize your own weakness." Selima walked over and handed her the metallic disk. "Take this."

Allonna held it gingerly; despite looking and feeling like metal, it seemed no heavier than a swatch of cotton cloth.

Unfamiliar symbols in golden script stood out from the silvery surface. She looked up at Selima. "What is it?"

"You remember when you entered the Keep yesterday, you put your hand on a stone and declared that you followed the Light and did not wish any harm to King Aumekor?"

Allonna nodded. She'd been told to do it and she'd obeyed, without really understanding what it was for.

"If you had been lying, that stone would instantly have turned white-hot and burned your hand. And the Protectors at the gate would probably have killed you before you had time to scream."

Allonna swallowed dryly.

"That stone is an artifact that was created in the Age of Light. It allows us to know if someone is telling the truth. Now, if you were to promise to keep a secret while your hand was upon it, and you were sincere in your promise, it would not harm you. But if you later decided to break that promise, whether under torture or for some other reason, you would be able to do so." Omnimancer Selima paused and looked at her expectantly.

"Is that because the magic only works while you have your hand on the stone?" Her voice was hesitant.

"Exactly. Now, the artifact you are holding is also from the Age of Light, and it also can be used to ensure that someone is telling the truth, but it is far more powerful than the stone. In fact, it was created by one of the gods, and it has power to bind free will."

Allonna's mouth opened slightly in awe as she looked down at the metal disk. She was actually holding something created by one of the gods? Then the last thing Omnimancer Selima had said registered. "Bind free will? But...But that's magic of the Dark God! Only he would do such a thing." She desperately wanted to no longer be touching the artifact, but didn't know what to do with it.

"No, Allonna. This object is not evil. The magic is not evil. Let me explain what it does. It can only be used by someone to bind his or her own free will, and the choice to do that must, in itself, be taken freely. If you choose to swear an oath while holding that plate, there is no power short of the gods themselves that can make you take any action to break that oath."

Selima's explanation made sense to her, but Allonna did not respond immediately. She began thinking about the implications of such a device. "But what if..." She let her words trail off, realizing that she was questioning what Selima had told her.

"Go on, child. Finish your question."

"What if I swore to never die? Would I become immortal? Or what if I swore to kill the Dark Priestess? Would the magic of the disk help me do it?"

"What do you think?" Selima looked at her with an amused smile.

"Well...If it really worked like that, someone would have done it already. I think...I think the answer lies in what you said earlier, that it binds free will. The magic only binds my will, and does not affect events over which I have no control."

Selima nodded. "Now that you understand, would you be willing to swear an oath never to reveal to anyone the secrets that I reveal to you?"

She was about to agree, but something about Selima's almost casual tone made her hesitate. It was the way a merchant spoke when he thought you couldn't tell brass from gold. Until now she had thought of Selima as being very open and honest. She should have known better—all that talk about not wanting to deceive her, wanting her to make her own decision. *Beware the merchant who tells you he's honest.*

Past experience in dealing with merchants had taught Allonna to control her expression, so her face did not reflect her suspicion. "How does it work? Does it need magic to activate it?"

"Yes. Just focus on it and send a small amount of power into it."

"How will I know it's activated?"

"The gold symbols will become transparent."

Putting a tremble in her voice, Allonna said, "I...I'm too nervous to do it. Could you activate it for me?" She watched Selima carefully. If activating the device was dangerous, Selima would insist she do it herself.

Selima let out an almost inaudible sigh, then stretched out her right hand. Allonna could sense the power flowing from Selima into the disk. The gold characters glowed blue, then turned transparent, so she could see bits of her palm through the disk.

"So now, any oath sworn while holding this disk cannot be broken?"

"Yes."

"Good." Allonna suddenly tossed the disk to Selima, who reached out and caught it instinctively.

"What do you think you're doing, child? You're supposed to —"

"I may not have my majority, but I'm not a child." She took a deep breath. "You think I'm just a naïve little girl from a backward village and that I'll do whatever you want. But even though I may have heard your name in countless tales, I really don't know you. I don't know what your real plans are for me. Before I swear an oath not to reveal your secrets, whatever they may be, I need to know that I can trust you. So, as you hold that disk, I want you to swear an oath that you will not harm me in any way."

"That's preposterous. I couldn't possibly—"

"Why not, if you mean me no harm?"

Selima slowly set the disk down on her desk. "If I meant to harm you, Allonna, don't you think I would have done so by now?"

"That's a question, not an answer. And just because you haven't harmed me in the past is no guarantee you won't in the future."

"True." Selima let out an exasperated breath. "Here's your

answer: It is impossible for me to swear not to harm you because my highest priority is to help the Heir of the Line to defeat the Dark Priestess. If harming you, or even killing you, will help me toward that goal, then I will do it. I may not enjoy it, but I will do it."

Allonna pursed her lips for a moment, to give Selima the impression she was thinking about her response. "There seem to be few limits to what you would do to accomplish your goal."

"Yes."

"Yesterday, you said that you thought I might be able to help you. Do you still believe that?"

"I do. You are a very powerful mancer. With training, you could become a valuable ally."

It was hard for Allonna to keep herself from smiling. Selima had walked into the trap; now it was time to close it around her. "I find it very puzzling, then…" She let her voice trail off.

"Yes?"

"If you are willing to do anything to defeat the Dark Priestess, and you believe I could help you do that, shouldn't you be willing to do anything to get me to help you?"

Selima stared at her for a moment, then walked around her desk and sat down. She set the disk down and traced its edge with a finger. Finally, she looked up and met Allonna's eyes.

"It appears I have underestimated you. Perhaps I took your ignorance regarding magic as indicative of a general lack of knowledge. I apologize for my condescension; I will not make that mistake again. You still have much to learn, but I shall not treat you as a child."

Allonna said nothing. She didn't want to give Selima any excuse to avoid answering the question.

"You were right to be suspicious. I was planning to teach you a lesson about the careless use of enchanted items by letting you swear an oath that was overly broad. I would have let you use this"—she tapped on the disk – "to release yourself from that oath, but I guess that won't be necessary." Selima gave her a slight smile.

Allonna refused to smile back. Let Selima think she wasn't getting anywhere.

"Very well. It is you that has taught me a lesson about underestimating an adversary. I—"

"So, you admit you are my adversary?"

"No! That was merely a figure of speech."

It was time to raise the stakes. Shaking her head, Allonna said, "You've been talking for a while now, and you still haven't answered my question. I think I'll go get my father and brother and find an honest inn to stay at." She started to rise.

"Please, Allonna. Stay. I'll explain everything. I know I've mishandled things, but please stay."

There was no mistaking the edge of desperation in Selima's voice. Allonna suddenly felt ashamed that she'd pressed Selima so hard. She'd been caught up in the contest of wills, focusing more on winning the point than on the effect it might have on Selima. She nodded to Selima and sat back in her chair.

Selima closed her eyes a moment. "I'm going to trust you. After I've told you what I have to say, I will leave it up to you to decide whether to take an oath never to reveal it to anyone outside the Inner Keep. And," she said, raising her palm to forestall any objection from Allonna," I will swear to tell you the truth."

Raising the disk with both hands, she said, "I swear that, until I leave this room, I will not say anything I do not believe to be true." The raised letters on the disk glowed green, then faded to gold.

"Allonna, I need your help to protect the Heir of the Line, at least until he has produced an heir of his own. King Aumekor has been crippled since the day he was born, too weak to even stand on his own, let alone wield his father's sword to fight the Dark Priestess. Only those of us who dwell or work in the Inner Keep are privy to this secret, which we are all sworn to keep."

This was not what Allonna had expected; she had thought Selima intended to pass on hidden secrets of mancy. She tried to absorb this new information and see its consequences.

"I can understand why you keep this hidden. If the Dark Priestess were to find out that King Aumekor is crippled, she would know he could not harm her."

Selima nodded. "She only dares to leave the protection of her sanctuary when the Heir of the Line is too young and weak to be a threat. When that happened eighty years ago, the last Free Kingdoms north of the Barrier Mountains fell before her armies. It is only because she expended so much of her magical power in attacking King Ordil sixteen years ago that she did not lead her armies forth during King Aumekor's childhood. The fates of kingdoms rest on this secret being kept."

Feeling a chill on the back of her neck, Allonna knew what she had to do. She stood up and sent out small burst of power. The characters turned transparent as she reached for the disk.

Chapter Nine

Geradin

The pain between Geradin's shoulder blades when he tried to stand up straight was not the worst of it. No one could train with Swordmaster Ytanor and not get used to feeling pain. Nor was it the sewer-smell that had wrinkled the noses of people they passed on their way back to the arena. Having spent half the day steeped in the stench, Geradin was no longer bothered by it. The brown-green grime that clung to his clothing did not bother him, although the laundry-maids would certainly have some harsh words for him. No, the worst of it was the muck in his boots that swished between his toes every step. Somehow it had not been so bad when he was knee-deep in the filthy water, but now that he was walking on dry ground it seemed wrong.

Geradin snorted and shook his head. There were more important things to think about than a little water in his boots. He and his companions in the sewers had rejoined the other two at the Gate of the Petitioners and they were now being led into the arena by the Lord Proctor. The stands were full of people now; the Oath of Citizenship would be administered during a break in the action of the Midsummer Tournament.

He had planned to compete in the tournament, but his detour to the sewers had prevented him from being there at the start of competition.

"Perhaps we should request a chance to compete in the

tourney," said Geradin. "I believe our stink is powerful enough to knock our opponents to their knees at five paces."

The others laughed, except for Holoran. Geradin still could not understand what was bothering him. During their labors, the big man had done more than his fair share, but other than suggestions on how best to do their work he had remained silent as the rest of them had talked.

"That would hardly be fair, Geradin," said Kilsun, an apprentice baker who hated baking and planned to go north to join the Barrier Guard once he had his majority. "Whatever happened to chivalry?"

Working side by side, hunching under a five-and-a-half-foot ceiling, soaking in sewage, Geradin had managed to cure the others of calling him "milord" every other sentence.

"Nothing is more important than chivalrous conduct...by an opponent. That's why you will always hear men complain about the propriety of their opponents' actions, but never their own."

Their laughs were cut short by the Lord Proctor raising his palm to silence them and the crowd. "Having passed the Test of Mind, the Test of Spirit, and the Test of Body, you have proven yourselves worthy to take upon you the privileges and responsibilities of adults and citizens. You will now each swear the Oath of Citizenship, and then you will be free to leave through the Gate of the Citizens." He waved his hand toward an arch in the south wall of the arena.

Geradin was fourth in line, and as the Lord Proctor administered the oath to those before him, he recited along with them in his mind just to be positive he had the words right. Finally it was his turn, and the Lord Proctor held out the massive iron key to the South Gate of the city. He dropped to his left knee and put his right hand on the key.

"I, Geradin att'Balunor, do truly pledge my mind to obey the laws of the Kingdom of Aud Sapeer, my spirit to honor the Gods of Light and follow their will, and my body to serve the kingdom when called. And this I choose of my own free will to do until I let out my last breath."

That was it. He was an adult now. Tomorrow he would apply to become a Protector of the Line and begin his life's work protecting Mek.

He felt a pang of regret that Mek could not be there beside him taking the oath, or even come to the arena to see him take it. What Mek's weakened condition did not prohibit, security concerns did. Never in his life had Mek been outside the walls of the Outer Keep, and rarely was he allowed to leave the Inner Keep. All fifteen of the High Protectors were agreed that until Mek had produced an heir, they could not allow him to take any risks. The Line of Orcan had to continue until the prophecy was fulfilled, however inconvenient that might be for the person who happened to be the current heir.

So as they grew up, Mek had experienced the outside world vicariously through Geradin. He would lie in his bed with his eyes closed while Geradin recounted the day's adventures: a gallop outside the gates of the city, perhaps, or swimming in the reservoir, or just accompanying Selima as she did her business about the city. Later, when Geradin began his training in weapons and combat, he would demonstrate what he had learned and Mek's critical eye would help find the flaws in his technique. And when they were ten years old and he won his first tournament trophy, narrowly taking second place to a boy two years older in the children's division archery competition, Mek had been excited as he himself and for days after would demand to be given a detailed recap of how each arrow flew and where it struck. So now, rather than wanting to stay and watch the combat in the tournament, he was anxious to get back to the Keep and tell Mek all about the Tests of Majority, especially how he had come to choose the Test of Body by Labor.

Holoran finished his oath, and Geradin was glad he would now be able to marry his beloved. Perhaps Mek would have a theory as to why Holoran had reacted the way he had. The seven new adults followed the Lord Proctor to the Gate of the

Citizens as the crowd applauded them.

At the gate, Geradin turned to the Lord Proctor and said, "Might I have a word with you privately, My Lord Proctor?"

"Of course, Lord Geradin. If you would follow me?" He led them to one of the small armoring rooms on the inner side of the corridor that circled the arena.

"How may I be of service to you, Lord Geradin?"

"Actually, My Lord Proctor, I wanted to apologize for putting you in an awkward position this morning. I also wish to thank you for allowing me to speak."

The Lord Proctor smiled slightly. "You are too kind, milord. There is no need for an apology. In fact, I want to thank you for saying what you did. The other proctors and I have felt for some time that the Test of Body by Labor did not receive proper respect from the young men of the city."

"Well, I don't know if one speech today will do much to change that, milord, but I am happy to have been of service."

"If I might ask, milord, why did you choose to make a public stand on this issue?"

Geradin hesitated. He didn't want to lie to the Lord Proctor, but he didn't really want to say that he had only done it so that Holoran could avoid the Test of Body by Combat. "I don't suppose you would believe me, My Lord Proctor, if I said that I just wanted to spend a relaxing time in the sewers of our fair city?"

The Lord Proctor let out a bark of laughter. "If you told me that, milord, I would have no choice but to believe you. Whatever your reason was, I thank you."

"You are most welcome, My Lord Proctor. And now, I must be getting back to the Keep to report to King Aumekor. And remove myself from these clothes."

"One thing more, milord?"

"Yes, My Lord Proctor?"

"Are you well acquainted with that big young man, Holoran?"

Geradin's heart seemed to stop a moment. They had sworn

their oaths already. The Lord Proctor couldn't take away their majority now, could he? "No, My Lord Proctor. I met him for the first time this morning. Why?"

"I just wondered, milord. I was particularly pleased to see him achieve his majority today. After two failures, the other proctors and I despaired that he would ever pass the Test of Body by Combat. How fortunate a coincidence for him that he happened to be here on the day Lord Geradin decided to take a stand in favor of the Test of Body by Labor."

Then, to Geradin's astonishment, the Lord Proctor winked at him, then said, "Go with the Light, Lord Geradin."

"Stay in the Light, My Lord Proctor." Geradin's reply came automatically from his lips, and he turned and left the room. Relief that he was not in trouble mingled with chagrin at having been discovered in his scheme to help Holoran. But it had worked—the Lord Proctor even approved of it—so he decided to count it as a triumph.

He'd hoped Holoran might be waiting for him outside the arena, so he could ask him what was wrong, but all the others who had taken the tests with him were gone. The streets were very crowded, but the combination of smell and filth on his clothes encouraged people to clear out of his path as he walked back to the Keep. Instead of the usual four guards at the gate, there were twelve. Because of what had happened sixteen years ago while Mek's father was giving his traditional Midsummer Day speech, every Protector of the Line was on duty right now, and would be until after Mek had finished his speech and returned to the Inner Keep. So there were plenty of Protectors to rib him good-naturedly about the smell as they congratulated him on his majority.

Fortunately, Mek had given him the privilege of using the King's Baths whenever he wanted, so there was plenty of steaming water in which to rinse off the sewer scum and then take a quick soak to ease the aching in his back. He would have liked to stay in the water longer, but he didn't want to be late for Mek's speech.

Back in his bedroom, he quickly dressed in his finest court clothes. He debated whether to wear his practice sword or leave it behind. The wooden sword was a symbol of the childhood he had left behind today. He was now entitled to carry a steel blade, but he didn't possess one. Since he hadn't officially enlisted with the Protectors yet, they had not issued him a sword. After a moment's thought, he decided to forget vanity and strapped on the practice weapon. After all, he was used to the weight and would probably feel like there was something missing if he didn't wear it. Finally, he picked up the box containing his present for Mek.

After finding out from a servant that Mek had already been taken down to the Outer Keep, Geradin swiftly made his way to join him. As he walked through the hallway outside the room adjoining the Balcony of State, he came across a woman staring intently at a tapestry.

It took him a moment to recognize her as Allonna, for she was not dressed in the homespun she had been wearing when they first met. Instead, she wore a simple gown of blue silk. Since the latest fashions among the ladies of Aud Sapeer tended toward more elaborate concoctions, he guessed that the dress might have once belonged to her mother. Still, it fitted her well, and he was not one to deny a girl was pretty merely because she had not the latest fashion.

"Miss Allonna, how good to see you. May I say you look lovely in that dress?"

She turned toward him, and he could see her eyes were rimmed with red. "Oh, not you, too. Well, My Lord Geradin" — she spoke his name as if referring to street filth — "I'm sorry if my lack of fashion offends your eyes, but not all of us were lucky enough to be born both beautiful and rich, and you may live in a castle and only wear the latest fashions, but that doesn't mean you—"

Geradin took a step back. "Stop! Please, I meant no offense. I really do think you look lovely in that dress. Who said you didn't?"

Allonna's face colored. "I...I'm sorry, milord. I must go." Then she turned and hurried down the hall.

"Miss Allonna, wait!" He thought of going after her to see what was wrong, but knew he was running late for Mek's birthday celebration. Sighing, he opened the door and entered the room.

Chapter Ten

Aumekor

Only half-listening to one of the minor nobles from the far south of the kingdom, Aumekor sat on his throne and nodded as if in agreement with what the man was saying.

It was his own fault, he realized. His insistence on this one public appearance each year had made his Midsummer Day address one of the most important events in the kingdom. At least, the nobles seemed to think so, and every year since that first speech, the question of which nobles would be allowed to stand on the Balcony of State with him as he spoke had become more complicated.

The first year, it had just been the members of the Regency Council. The second year, the Lord Regent had invited some of his political allies to be there. Naturally, to bar them the next year would have been seen as a calculated insult, so the only choice was to invite even more nobles who supported him in opposition to Kindul. Then Selima had advised him about the political wisdom of inviting those who were only marginally supportive, as a way of drawing them closer to his side. By the fourth year, he and his advisors had concluded that it would be better to invite all the hereditary nobles rather than offend any by leaving them out.

Sixty-five nobles milling around on the balcony, trying to position themselves as best they could both physically and politically, would have been bad enough. But some of them had insisted on bringing their spouses that year, and from that point on, they all had to.

And now that he was of marriageable age, they'd starting bringing their daughters.

He couldn't really blame them, of course. While it was generally expected that he would marry a princess from another of the Free Kingdoms, any young woman from the nobility of Aud Sapeer would be an acceptable match. And because of the strictures placed upon him to ensure his security, this was really the only social occasion on which the marriageable young ladies of the nobility would have a chance to display themselves in hope of catching his eye.

It wasn't all bad; many did catch his eye and he wished he could actually get to know some of them, instead of just mouthing a few formalities. His opportunities for seeing pretty members of the opposite sex were severely limited in the Inner Keep. But since Selima was now talking about arranging his marriage, perhaps he could convince her that some new social activities were needed.

He looked around for Selima, then remembered she was in the next room, preparing the magic she would have to use to make him stand and walk so he could give his speech. But where was Geradin? He should have been back from the Tests of Majority long ago.

A sudden blare of horns quieted the crowd. Kindul came forward and bowed before him. "Your Majesty, on behalf of the people of Aud Sapeer, I, Kindul att'Jorup, Lord Regent of the Kingdom of Aud Sapeer, and your faithful servant, do congratulate you on your birthday. Long may you reign over our kingdom in peace and prosperity."

Nodding his head in gracious acknowledgement of Kindul's ritual formalities, he said, "I thank My Lord Regent for conveying the wishes of the people. As long as I reign, I hope that our people will find prosperity and peace."

"Your Majesty, it is with exceeding pleasure that I offer

you this gift, in token of my esteem for you." As one of the members of the Regency Council, Kindul was one of the few people entrusted to carry a sword on this occasion. He slowly drew it forth from the plain scabbard at his side, and a murmur of awe went through the crowd as they saw the blade was transparent crystal, a blade which must have been forged in the Age of Light. Laying the sword on the ground, he said, "I hope that Your Majesty will one day wield this blade in defense of our kingdom."

Refusing to show his annoyance, Aumekor smiled. Only a few people in the room knew he could never wield that sword. Kindul must have paid a fortune to be able to make this veiled insult. There was little he could do but accept it with good grace. "You are most generous, My Lord Regent. A blade such as this is worthy of a king. You have my thanks."

Kindul withdrew, and another noble stepped forward to present his gift. There was an informal competition between the nobles to see who could present the most valuable or exotic gift. Buying expensive items was a way of flaunting wealth. Nobles with smaller fortunes hunted for unique items from more distant kingdoms or trinkets from the Age of Light. But as the pile of presents grew, Aumekor knew that Kindul's gift, useless to him as it was, would be this year's winner.

Finally, he was surprised to see Ger at the end of the line. He was carrying a rough wooden crate which compared unfavorably to some of the richly inlaid boxes that had enclosed some of the gifts. A few of the nobles snickered; they knew that Geradin's title as a lord was solely the result of his father's heroic sacrifice, and that he had no lands and little money. For that reason, he and Ger usually exchanged gifts in a private, joint birthday celebration with Selima.

"Your Majesty," said Ger with a half-smile, "I know I am but the poorest and least worthy of our kingdom's nobility, but I offer this humble gift for your enjoyment." He carefully set down the box and stood back up.

Knowing Ger must be up to something, Aumekor decided to

play along. "Your generosity exceeds all bounds, Lord Geradin. Not one of my lords or ladies has been thoughtful enough to provide me with so large a box, wherein I might place several of the gifts I have received. You have my gratitude."

Several nobles laughed aloud, particularly among the younger ones who were less familiar with court customs and could not tell from Aumekor's tone that he was not mocking Geradin.

"I apologize, Your Majesty, but the box is not my gift to you. Although, if it pleases, you make keep it if you wish. No, my gift is inside the box." And with that, Ger began wriggling his fingers inside the chainmail gauntlet he was wearing on his right hand.

There was the clink of metal in motion inside the box, and suddenly front of the box fell away. Out came a knight two palmwidths tall, fully armored and armed with a tiny sword. It marched up to the pile of gifts, waving its tiny blade as if attacking what others had given.

Aumekor had never seen any artifact like it. "I love it."

"I knew you would. Here, try it." The little knight collapsed in a heap as Ger took off the gauntlet and traded it out for the one Aumekor was wearing. "Just wiggle your fingers."

The weight of the gauntlet caused his hand to sink to his lap, but he wiggled his fingers and the little knight sprang up and began to march unsteadily.

"It takes a little practice, but you'll soon have it marching around like a real soldier."

"Thanks, Ger." Suddenly remembering the assembled nobles who were now chattering in amazement at the little knight, he spoke more loudly. "My deepest thanks, Lord Geradin. This is truly a most unique and amazing gift."

Ger coughed. "Well, Your Majesty, while I do believe it to be amazing, it is not truly unique. This is no artifact from the Age of Light; this is the work of talented artisans from our own Kingdom and day, a young man who smithed it and his sister who enchanted it through potent ferromancy." A mischievous smile played across his lips. "In fact, that powerful mancer was in this very room earlier, but had to leave. You may have seen her—a young woman wearing a blue gown. When last I saw her, she was saying something about preparing a suitable vengeance for mocking tongues, whatever that means."

Aumekor didn't know what it meant, but some in the audience did, as he heard several people take sudden, anxious breaths. Ger's words had obviously hit their intended targets.

"In any case, Your Majesty, my gift to you is not unique because they have made a few more. With some difficulty, I convinced them to sell me this one for your amusement, and I am glad it gives you pleasure." Ger bowed with an exaggerated flourish, then stepped forward to remove the control gauntlet and replace Aumekor's gauntlet.

The young woman who had made the little knight must be the new apprentice Selima was hoping to enlist. She was powerful indeed, if she could enchant objects like this. He looked again at Ger's gift. It was small, but seemed somehow important. Perhaps it was just a sign that a time of great magics was coming again, that knowledge lost in the Age of Dark might be found once more.

"Your Majesty? Selima says she is ready now." Kuf had quietly appeared at his side.

He nodded. "My Lords and Ladies, I thank you all for your gifts, your kindness, and your loyalty to the throne. But now, the event you have been dreading draws nigh: it is almost time for me to give my speech."

Laughter—some genuine, some not—filled the room. Aumekor could feel a tingling in his back, then his legs. He felt his hands move, grasp the arms of the chair, and he suddenly rose to his feet.

"If you would all be so kind as to await me on the balcony as I go over a few last-moment preparations?"

The nobles filed out of the doors to the Balcony of State. Flanked by four Protectors, and Ger, he felt himself walk into the next room where Selima stood, along with the three other court mancers. She was holding the top of a crystal rod with her left hand, with her right hand stretched out before her. The other three held on to the rod with both hands.

His legs took him to a chair, and he lowered into it. Selima visibly relaxed and lowered her right hand.

"Where's Allonna? I told her she should follow you in here when the time came."

Aumekor looked at Ger.

"Well, she left just as I was arriving," said Ger.

"Why? Where was she going?"

"Ah...I think she might have been going...I'm not sure where."

"Geradin?" Selima's voice was ominous.

"I believe she was insulted by someone. About her dress."

Selima sighed. "I should have foreseen that. I should have just had her in here with me, but I thought it would be exciting for her to see all the nobility." Turning to Aumekor, she said, "You haven't changed the closing line of your speech again, have you?"

"No."

"Good. Then, when you're done, I'll keep you there a moment to acknowledge the applause. I'll wave your hand, then walk you back in."

He nodded.

"And keep it short. Stick to what you've memorized; don't start improvising. It's very hard work to keep you standing, even if that armor you're wearing is the lightest in the kingdom."

From what Ramil, the royal armorsmith, had told Aumekor, this was twelve-fold armor — twelve times the strength of ordinary steel the same thickness. It was a relic from the Age of Light, because nobody could enchant armor that strong any more. The knight for whom it had been crafted must have valued speed and lightness over protection, because it was one twelfth the thickness of standard plate mail, so it offered no better protection than unenchanted armor, but was much lighter. For the purposes of today, that was the best combination.

"Yes, Selima. No improvising," Aumekor said.

"Actually, Your Majesty," said Donaril, one of the mancers, "there may be a little improvising that you may wish to do."

Selima's eyebrows rose.

"What do you suggest, Donaril?" asked Aumekor.

"Well, I was on duty at the gate earlier, checking for unauthorized enchantments, when they were letting in the audience for your speech. There is a group of veterans returned from the Barrier—some of them maimed or crippled, Your Majesty. All of them were held captive by the enemy, some of them for ten years or more, until they managed to escape. I thought you might want to acknowledge their presence, since they have suffered so much for our kingdom."

Aumekor nodded, as he could not trust himself to speak at that moment. He was not the only one who suffered because of this endless war.

Selima frowned. "Did you detect any enchantments on them, Donaril? Any at all?"

"No." He shook his bald head. "I know what you're thinking. I considered it myself, that they might have been enchanted while they were prisoners. There was no magic among them. The alarms would have sounded as they entered if there had been, for I approved nothing on them. And, of course, the Protectors made sure they were unarmed after they swore the oath at the entrance. And...one of them is my brother, Fen. He's lost his right arm, but we thought he was dead these past five years."

"Thank you for telling me about them," Aumekor said. "I'd like to talk with your brother, sometime. Perhaps you could bring him to meet me when it's convenient."

"Yes, Your Majesty."

Aumekor turned to Selima. "Are you ready?"

"Yes." She stretched her right hand toward him.

"Then walk me out of here. I'm certain my audience

anxiously awaits the rubies of wisdom that will spit forth from my lips."

Again he felt the tingling, and the strange sensation of his body moving out of his control. He smiled. This must be what it was like for the little knight Ger had given him. His protectors led the way through the nobles who were crowded onto the balcony. The Balcony of State was really more of a terrace, and some of the lesser nobles had been forced onto the steps that curved down into the courtyard.

He looked at the sun, which was more than halfway down to the western horizon, then closed his eyes and felt its heat on his eyelids. He had to find a reason to get out of the Inner Keep more than once a year. Perhaps after he was married and had produced an heir, the Protectors would be more willing to let him take risks.

He turned his eyes from the sky to the city he could see outside the walls of the Outer Keep. His city, in which he had never been. Finally he looked down at the people who were gathered, cheering his name. His people. And he remembered the real reason his life was so protected: the only thing protecting his people—and all people—from enslavement was the Line of Orcan. If he must be a prisoner so his people could stay free, so be it.

His arm started raising itself, and he realized Selima wanted him to quiet the crowd so he could get on with his speech. The cheers subsided.

He took a deep breath, then began. "People of the kingdom of Aud Sapeer. Lords and ladies, freemen and freewomen alike. I, Aumekor att'Ordil, present myself before you this day. As King of Aud Sapeer, Heir of the Line of Orcan, it is my duty to report to you on the state of our Kingdom."

"Imposter!" The shout came from somewhere in the crowd. "You are not the rightful king! You are not the true Heir!"

Chapter Eleven

Geradin

Geradin scanned the crowd to spot who was shouting.

"Usurper! Where is the real Heir?"

There—members of the crowd were pulling away from the shouter as if he had the greenpox. He was a tall, emaciated man with respectable but ill-fitting clothes. His right arm was stretched out with his index finger pointed at Mek, who had stopped speaking.

"Creature of the Dark God! You'll destroy us all!"

The Protectors had already sprung into action. The six closest to Mek had formed a protective wall around him, while most of the others seemed to be converging on the accuser. Members of the crowd continued to pull away as best they could, some even starting up the stairs and craning their necks for a view of what was happening.

Geradin wondered who had slipped up to let this madman in through the gates. Whoever it was would be thoroughly reprimanded by the High Protectors. It was only a minor error, really, as the truth-stone would have revealed anyone who intended harm to the king, and all this man was doing was—

His practice sword was out of its scabbard in an instant. "Protect the king! It's an attack! Everyone protect the king!" His feet naturally moved to a defensive stance.

If there were others in the crowd who did not believe Mek was truly King Aumekor, then the truth-stone would not have detected any deceit. The man who was yelling could be just a distraction—yes, he could spot them easily now, as they pushed nobles out of their way on the stairs, coming up onto the balcony. Perhaps twenty in all, unarmed, but they outnumbered the Protectors on the balcony by three-to-one, and were approaching from both ends of the balcony.

The Protectors around Mek drew their swords. Three of them were High Protectors, and their enchanted blades glowed the sharp yellow that signaled danger to the Heir of the Line. The nobles nearest to the Protectors mostly drew back in fright, but the way off the balcony back inside was still blocked. Geradin saw Lord Regent Kindul reach instinctively for a sword and upon finding only an empty scabbard, tear it from his belt to use as a weapon.

He saw now that some of the attackers had obtained swords —probably stripping them from some of the trusted nobles who were panicking instead of defending their king. He must slow them enough so the other Protectors could arrive and change the odds back in their favor. Changing his stance to offensive, Geradin cleared his mind of all but the approaching enemy.

There is nothing but the fight.

His wooden blade parried the flat of a steel blade. Instantly reversing its path, he brought the sword backhand to strike the back of another man's neck. He used his momentum to carry him around, pivoting on his right foot. His left leg shot out, his heavy boot cracking the wrist of a hand that held a sword.

Strike. Parry. Attack. There is nothing but the fight.

He knocked one of them back into another, and the two enemies fell over the balcony railing in a tangle of flailing arms and legs. Geradin's next blow was of such force that the blunt wooden point of his sword jammed through the flesh and between the ribs of his target. Before he could withdraw his blade, it was sliced in two by an enemy sword. Closing inside the reach of that sword, he thrust the now-sharp end of his shortened blade into the solar plexus of the enemy.

Somewhere behind him he heard Mek cry out, but he pushed the thought aside.

There is nothing but the fight.

And then, there was no fight. The enemies before him suddenly fell to their knees, their eyes dazed, then slumped to the ground. Not just the enemies, he realized with confusion: the same thing was happening to the nobles around him.

Wheeling about, he looked for Mek. The circle of Protectors was still standing intact, but even though no attacker had made it within six feet of him, Mek was a crumpled heap on the floor. On the whole balcony, only Geradin, the Lord Regent, and the Protectors remained standing.

One of the High Protectors was yelling, "Get him inside! Get him inside!" Other Protectors were arriving now, some standing guard over the fallen enemies, others reaching to lift the king from the floor.

Geradin was relieved to hear Mek's voice saying, "I'm fine. I'm fine. Get me up." Two Protectors lifted the king from the ground and started to rush him inside despite his protests, stepping over the fallen bodies of the nobility that had been blocking the way. They entered through one of the doorways just as Selima and the other three mancers burst out of another onto the balcony.

"Mek's all right, isn't he?" he asked Selima.

"Yes," she said. "We had to set him down while we countered the attack, that's all. He's fine."

Selima and the other mancers each moved quickly from body to body. A touch and a murmured word seemed sufficient to revive a fallen noble, so apparently there was no permanent harm to them, either.

Now that the crisis had passed, Geradin took time to study the enemy. Their features did not betray any foreign origin, and most of them had the look of experienced soldiers. These must be the "veterans" that Donaril had admitted.

Geradin sprang behind Donaril, grabbing the bald head with his left hand, and placing the sharp point of his fractured wooden sword to the man's neck. The mancer gasped.

"Geradin, what are you doing?" Selima's voice was confused.

"He's the one who let them in. He said they were not enchanted, and we believed him."

Donaril cleared his throat. "They weren't. I swear it. I could detect no trace of magic on them. Please."

Bending over one of the unconscious attackers, Selima clapped her hand to the man's forehead and closed her eyes.

"He's right, Geradin. Let him go."

Geradin released the mancer, who immediately reached his hand up to rub the spot where the sword edge had pressed his throat.

"If they weren't enchanted, then how could they do this? Why would they do this?"

Kindul answered from behind him. "I have heard of something like this. If a man is tortured long enough, deprived of friends, without hope of rescue, he can lose himself. He becomes completely dependent on his captors, willing to believe what they say, do what they suggest."

"Yes." Selima nodded. "That is almost certainly what happened here. This plot by the Dark Priestess was years in the making, designed to take advantage of our routines. She convinced them Aumekor was not the Heir, allowing them to get past the truth-stone. Fortunately, she could not protect them against magic, for her wards would have set off the alarm spells at the entrance. A simple sleep spell was sufficient to end the threat, once we realized what was happening."

Looking down at the bloody stub of his sword, Geradin said, "So there was no need for me to fight. You would have stopped them all anyway." He was suddenly nauseated. He'd known that Protectors of the Line had to kill to protect the Heir, but he had never killed anyone before, and these men had been innocent game-pieces of the High Priestess of the Dark God.

Surprisingly, Selima seemed to be at a loss for words. She stepped toward him, but then he felt a hand on his shoulder and turned to find Kindul beside him.

"Lord Geradin, you did the right thing. What if one of these men had made it through to the king before Selima could stop him? Do not blame yourself for the death of these men. The fault lies entirely with the Dark Priestess. She is the one who took these men and twisted them into a weapon. She is the one to blame."

He knew the Lord Regent was right, but still…If he had known the attackers were innocent men, perhaps he could have used less than lethal force to slow them down. He shook his head. No, the Heir of the Line was too important. He must never hesitate. Nothing would stop him from protecting Mek. If regret and guilt were the price, he would pay. There is nothing but the fight.

"My Lord Regent," he said quietly, "I owe you an apology. In the past, I have expressed doubts about your loyalty to the king. But when others fled, you stood your ground to protect him with naught but an empty scabbard. I was wrong."

Kindul laughed. "I was more fortunate than you: none of my opponents managed to arm himself with a sword. But I thank you for your apology, although I am sure you will soon be entertaining doubts of my loyalty again, youngster. But make no mistake—whatever I may feel about Aumekor's fitness to rule, I would give my life to save his."

Geradin nodded in acknowledgement.

"And, let me say this, Geradin att'Balunor. I know your father would be proud of you. You fought well today." With that, Kindul clapped him twice on the shoulder, then went inside to join the revived members of the nobility.

Suddenly tired, Geradin was disgusted by the idea of facing a crowd of cowardly nobles. Instead, he walked down the steps into the now-deserted courtyard, and made his way to his quarters in the Inner Keep. The remains of his practice sword he placed on his desk, and then he cleaned the blood off his hands in the washbasin.

He sat on the edge of his bed, elbows on his knees, the fingertips of each hand touching their counterparts. He stared at the stone floor, thinking of nothing in particular.

How long he sat, before the knock on his door, he couldn't say.

"Come in."

It was Nikufed, Mek's manservant. "Lord Geradin, His Majesty sent me to summon you."

Geradin sprang to his feet. "He's not hurt, is he?"

"No, milord. He is unharmed."

"Good." He started out the door.

"Milord? I believe he will want to see this."

Turning back, he saw the servant holding up the stub of his sword. Geradin sighed. "Yes, I suppose he will. He likes the little details." He took the sword from Nikufed and headed toward Mek's chambers.

"Not that way, milord. He's in the Outer Keep, in the same room as earlier."

"He is? I thought the Protectors would have brought him back to his chambers." He followed the servant through the corridor.

"They did, but he insisted on being taken back down there." Nikufed shook his head. "You know him better than anyone, milord. Lady Selima wasn't too pleased about it, having to walk him through the room full of nobles and sit him on his throne. I can tell she'll give him a good talking-to when they've all gone home. Fortunately, that new apprentice of hers showed up to help. There's someone else who'll get a good talking-to, running off to her room like that without permission. I imagine there's a lot of folk going to be getting some talking-tos tonight."

"I imagine so."

When they reached the room, Nikufed opened the door for him. As he stepped into the room, he was shocked to find everyone staring toward him as if they had been awaiting his entrance. Which apparently they had, for they started applauding him. He stopped, uncertain about what to do. He looked to the end of the room, when Mek sat, and saw his friend motion him forward.

He strode across the floor and dropped to one knee before Mek, who raised his palm to silence the applause.

"Lord Geradin att'Balunor," said Mek, his voice strong and confident, "I have been informed that you achieved your majority today. Is that true?"

Of course Mek knew that he had. His friend was up to something—probably trying to demonstrate that he was in control despite the attempt on his life—so he played along. "Yes, Your Majesty. You have been well-informed."

"Today, in defending my life, you stood forth with nothing but a wooden practice sword against the metal of your foes. Is that it in your hand?"

"Yes, Your Majesty." He held the bloody remnant of his sword aloft for all to see.

"As an adult, you have the right to carry a sword of steel rather than of wood. Why then did you carry wood?"

What was it Mek wanted him to say? If it was something specific, Nikufed could have brought him a message. He decided the truth would be good enough. "I do not own a steel sword, Your Majesty. I plan to enlist with the Protectors of the Line tomorrow, and I expected they would issue me a sword."

Mek nodded. "And tell me truly, if such had not been your plan, would you have purchased yourself a steel sword?"

"No, Your Majesty."

"Why not?"

"Because..." Why was Mek doing this? He couldn't see the point of exposing exactly how poor he was, but he trusted Mek and answered, "Because I have not the money to buy a sword, Your Majesty."

"Would you have had the money if you had not bought me that marvelous gift for my birthday?"

"Yes, Your Majesty."

"Speaking of birthdays, I seem to recall that today is your birthday, too. Is it not?"

"Yes, Your Majesty."

"I thought so. I had planned to give you a sword for your birthday, but recent events have forced me to adjust my plans." He motioned to one of the High Protectors, who came forward with a long wooden box.

"Your father was a High Protector who sacrificed his life that I might live. It was decided long ago that, once you joined the Protectors of the Line and had proven yourself worthy—a process that was expected to take years, I might say—you would be elevated to High Protector and given the sword with which your father so ably defended me." He paused. "After discussing today's events with the High Protectors, they have agreed with me that you have proven yourself already. So, my friend Geradin, my protector, will you swear your oath before me and take the place that has been yours by right since the day we both were born?"

"I will, Your Majesty."

The High Protector opened the box and held it out to Geradin, who lifted out the scabbard and sword. Unsheathing the sword, he lifted it up above his head. The blade glowed the fiery blue that meant the Heir was safe. Placing his left hand over his heart, he said the words he had imagined saying so many times, "I swear upon my life that I will protect the line of Orcan att'Fenisak of Aud Sapeer from this day until I let my last breath out."

Mek was grinning broadly. "Thank you, Lord Geradin. And now, we come to another important matter. It seems that, in their decision to accept you as a Protector of the Line, the High Protectors have made the paltry sword I had planned as your birthday gift unnecessary. That means I am forced to improvise a gift."

His face grew suddenly stern, and he swept his gaze over the assembled nobles. "And I have decided on one. Lord Geradin, it is long past time that you had lands appropriate to your title. Now, such a grant normally requires the approval of two-thirds of the Assembly of Lords, but meetings of the Assembly usually involve such long debates that I fear that approval might not happen before your next birthday.

"Fortunately, we have here assembled almost the entire body of the Assembly. I will therefore take their assent for granted, unless any of them would care to speak against the idea of granting lands to a man who, while richer men fled—" Mek's voice was cold as he emphasized those words. "—risked his life to save mine. And not my life alone, but the lives of all those who love freedom and oppose the High Priestess of the Dark God. If anyone wishes to say that this man, the son of the heroic Balunor, does not deserve to have lands that will provide him with an income befitting his title, now is the time to speak."

Before anyone else could say anything, Kindul raised his palm and said, "Your Majesty, if I might speak?"

Mek scowled and turned to look at the Lord Regent. "Well, My Lord Regent, no one can deny your bravery as you stood for me today. Do you deny Lord Geradin's?"

"No, Your Majesty. I merely wished to voice my profound approval of Your Majesty's plan. I very much doubt that anyone will disapprove." He looked out over the silent nobles. "I thought not. Your Majesty, it appears your gift to Lord Geradin is approved unanimously."

The gathered nobles applauded, although Geradin knew that some of it was not very enthusiastic.

"Thank you, My Lord Regent," said Mek. "Thank you, lords and ladies of Aud Sapeer. And now, the time being late, I'm sure you all have things to attend to. Go with the Light."

As the nobles began filing out of the door, Geradin said quietly, "Thanks, Mek. Not sure exactly what I'm going to do with lands, but thanks."

"Happy birthday, Ger."

"Happy birthday, Mek."

"Now go to bed. That's an order. I know you've been up since before dawn. We'll talk tomorrow."

Smiling tiredly, Geradin said, "As Your Majesty commands."

Back in his quarters, he took the sword out from its

scabbard. The blue light filled the room. His sword, his father's sword. He held the blade before him. His father's hand had held that blade. He almost felt like his father's presence was in the room with him.

"Father, I did it. I'm a Protector of the Line, like you. But this I swear to you, Father: unlike you, I will not fail."

Chapter Twelve

Allonna

A llonna sighed and looked down again at the book Selima had assigned her to read: Before the World Was: A History of the Gods. When she'd taken the oath as Selima's apprentice ten days ago, she'd thought she would be learning the secrets and techniques of mancy. And Selima had taught her some things—mostly related to the wards that protected the Keep and the Heir. But the bulk of her studies involved reading historical works, and while they told of many incidents in which magic was used, they lacked any details about how the magic was done.

This latest book seemed even less relevant. The Dark God had disappeared over five hundred years ago, and the three Gods of Light more than sixteen hundred years ago. What did the gods matter, if they were no longer here? It was the Dark Priestess who was the enemy, and it was her power that needed to be defeated. But there was nothing about that in these books, as far as Allonna could see.

She sneaked a glance over at Geradin, who was carefully reading the book Selima had assigned him. It made sense for him to study the histories of wars and political intrigue, so he could better protect the Heir of the Line. But his studies also included things of a much more practical and deadly nature. She'd seen him in the courtyard of the Outer Keep practicing with his sword, its magical blade glowing visibly even in the sunlight, and though she had no experience with combat she could tell that he was an expert.

His head began to move, and she quickly turned her eyes back to her book. If he caught her looking at him, he might get the wrong impression. He wasn't the arrogant young lord she'd thought him to be when they first met, but still, she didn't want him to think she was attracted to him. Not that he wasn't handsome—

"Allonna?"

Geradin's voice was just above a whisper, as if he didn't want to disturb her, but it startled her and made her reply a little more rudely than she should have. "What?"

He raised his eyebrows. "I was just wondering if you'd had a chance to ask Selima," he said.

"No, not yet." The truth was, she'd been scared to ask Selima, because Selima might have said it was impossible. And she wanted to believe it was possible; that she could do something important to help King Aumekor.

The little knight she had enchanted had given the king an idea. He had sent Geradin to ask her if she could create a full-sized suit of armor that could be controlled the same way. If so, it would enable him to walk on his own whenever he wanted, instead of having Selima control him like a puppet on special occasions.

She was sure she could do it. After all, it was exactly the same principle as the little suits of armor, and she'd managed to do thirty of them at once, even if that had been a mistake.

In fact, this was something she could have done before becoming Selima's apprentice. So why did she need Selima's help or permission to do it?

She decided to do it. "Do you have a suit of armor we can use?"

Geradin raised his eyebrows. "I think the king wanted to use his father's armor." He paused with a frown. "But I've seen it, and I'm not sure it would be a good fit. His father had broader shoulders and was a lot more muscular in his arms and legs."

"If my brother Pag were still here, he could alter the armor to fit, since he's really good at smithing, and I know he would do a marvelous job, because you've seen how expertly he made those little knights, and I'm sure if we sent a message and asked him to..." Her cheeks flushed and she stopped talking when she realized that a large city like Aud Sapeer would have plenty of excellent armorsmiths. Many of them would be far more experienced at such work than her younger brother.

Geradin smiled. "Your brother is a very good smith. If he were here, I'm sure the king would ask him to do the work. But we can probably just use the armor he wore for his Midsummer Day speech."

"Yes." Allonna nodded. "Can you arrange that? I can do the spell as soon as the armor is ready."

"Really? You already have the necessary power gathered?"

Sighing in frustration, Allonna said, "Selima keeps trying to explain about how to gather my power, but I don't understand what she means by that, even though she gives me examples, like 'magical power is stored in a lake behind a dam,' and I understand the examples, but I don't understand how the examples are like magic."

"Selima likes to teach by analogy. But if understanding the analogies is difficult for you, I'm sure Selima can explain things in a simpler manner. Just tell her—"

Her face was hot. He thought she was stupid, did he? "Understanding the analogies is *not* difficult for me. Just because I didn't grow up in a palace doesn't mean I'm dumb."

"I'm sorry, I didn't mean—"

"If I were to give you analogy, like..." She paused, searching for something he could relate to. "...swordfighting is like swimming, what would you think?"

Geradin frowned a moment. "I can see that, I guess. In both, you must keep moving or you'll end up dead."

"No, that's not what I mean." She ran both hands through her hair. "What if I said, swordfighting is like a bouquet of flowers?"

Nodding, Geradin said, "Yes. I see. Both have different components, which when combined prop—"

"Stop!" She raised her palm and he fell silent. "You're not understanding what I'm trying to say." She took a deep breath, then let it out slowly. "What's something that has no similarity to swordfighting?"

That appeared to stump him. Finally he said, "What you're saying is that Selima's analogies about magic don't make sense when compared to your own experience of magic?"

"Yes." She felt a rush of gratitude toward him for understanding, even if he had been slow about it.

He frowned. "And what was Selima's response when you told her?"

Allonna dropped her eyes to the book on the table before her.

"You didn't tell her, did you?" He chuckled. "You pretended like you understood what she was saying."

She glared at him.

"I know how it is. I must have done that hundreds of times. Yes, Selima. I understand, Selima. All is clear to me, Selima. Your magnificent powers of instruction have revealed the truth of the universe to me, Selima." He smiled at her, and she realized he was trying to be friendly, not condescending.

"I...I don't want her to think she made a mistake, choosing me as her apprentice."

Geradin shook his head. "She won't think that. But she needs to know when you don't understand, so she can find another way to explain things." He rapped his knuckles on his forehead. "She always managed to get through even this thick skull eventually. You'll do fine."

Allonna nodded. "Thank you." She resolved to ask Selima to explain the concept again.

"Do you want to go with me to the armorsmith now and get the armor?"

Caught off guard by the sudden change of subject, she looked down at her book. "I think I should probably study."

"That book? I've read it. Fairly useless unless you plan on

encountering a god any time soon."

He was right. Why not go with him? Perhaps she could enchant the armor and the king would be able to walk today. She closed the book and said, "Let's go see the armorsmith."

She followed Geradin to the Outer Keep. As they approached the smithy, Allonna could hear the ringing clash of hammer and anvil. She found herself missing her home back in Glicken, where such sounds had been in the background of her life for as long as she could remember.

Before they reached the smithy door, however, a Protector of the Line intercepted them. "Lord Geradin, there's someone at the main gate who wishes to speak with you. He did not wish to give his name."

Turning to Allonna, Geradin frowned. "I suppose I should see what this is about. I'm not sure how long it will take, though."

"I understand. I know my way around a smithy, so I can go talk to the armorsmith about... about our project, and if you get done quickly you can find me there."

Geradin nodded, then he and the Protector walked toward the main gate. She watched them for a moment, then she strode to the smithy door and pulled it open.

The smithy was larger than her father's had been, of course, but the smoky air and heat were no different. As she closed the door behind herself, she looked around to see who was there. A young man — an apprentice, she decided — was working the bellows pump. The hammering she had heard earlier had ceased, and a stout, balding man in a leather apron was now holding something inside the forge's flames using long-handled tongs.

Not wanting to distract the smith, Allonna remained silent and watched him work. He withdrew the tongs from the fire and moved the orange-glowing item onto the anvil. From its size and current shape, Allonna decided it was most likely a half-finished bracer. The smith began meticulously working the metal with his ballpeen hammer, rhythmically striking with his right arm while making minor adjustments to the position of the item with his left. The sparks flew with each blow, and he looked much like her father had when she was a girl, before he'd lost his arm fighting at the Barrier.

He continued to shape the bracer for a short while, returning it to the heat of the forge whenever it cooled too much.

Then the smith did something her father had never done. She felt a trickle of magical power flow out from him into the metal. She couldn't see anything happening, but she could sense it nonetheless. What was he doing? Strengthening the metal? Enchanting it with some form of protective magic? Whatever it was, perhaps he could teach it to her.

The bracer had cooled to a deep red, and the smith took it from the anvil and plunged it into a barrel of water for tempering. Steam hissed for a few moments, and then he brought it back out, no longer glowing. He set it down on a workbench, then turned to face Allonna.

"What brings you here, Miss Allonna?"

His recognition surprised her, and his tone seemed a little annoyed, even though she had taken care not to interrupt his work. "You know who I am, Master…Smith?" She had to stop herself from wincing at the awkwardness. Silently she berated Geradin for not telling her the armorsmith's name.

The apprentice stopped working the bellows and turned to look at her, his eyes wide.

The armorsmith's tone was artificially awed. "Who in the Keep— No, who in all of Aud Sapeer does not know of Miss Allonna, the mancer who can enchant metal into toys?"

Allonna felt the blood rise in her face. Gone were her feelings of comfort from the familiar surroundings, replaced by a different familiarity. She wasn't sure why the armorsmith was hostile — perhaps resentment that she could do things with metal he couldn't — but she'd encountered hostility before. "Yes, Master Smith, and if you have heard that much, then you know metal is not all I can enchant."

Standing a little taller, the smith tensed his muscles. "Are you threatening me, Apprentice Allonna?"

"Why do you ask, Master Smith? Is a large, strong man such as you often threatened by the likes of me?"

"Come into my own shop and sass me, will you? What gives you the right—"

"What gives me the right?" She put her fists on her hips. "What gave you the right to insult me when we have never even met before? I am sorry that I did not know your name, but Lord Geradin was bringing me here and I expected that he would introduce us, except he was called away by one of the Protectors on the way here and I decided to come in alone. Other than that, I don't know how I could possibly have offered you any offense, so your insult caught me unawares. Now, either you can tell me your name and we can start again with the proper respect on both sides, or we can just wait for Lord Geradin to get here, and I assume he will tell me what your name is, although he will probably be annoyed that we have not already discussed how we can best help King Aumekor." She kept her eyes intently on his, and raised her left eyebrow.

"You've a strong mouth on you, Miss Allonna."

The words themselves were insulting, but Allonna felt there was some respect behind them. So she smiled and said, "Comes from being a blacksmith's daughter, I fear."

He looked her over from head to foot, then nodded. "Master Ramil."

"I am glad to meet you, Master Ramil." Now that she had his grudging acceptance, it was time for a little flattery. "That was some very skilled work you were doing with that bracer. No wonder Lord Geradin said you'd be able to help us."

"Help you with what?"

"We need a suit of armor for the king to—" Suddenly, her throat felt numb and she found herself unable to speak. She put her hand to her throat and mouthed emptily. What was happening to her?

Master Ramil frowned at her motions, but then he smiled.

"Don't worry, all will be well in a moment." He nodded at his apprentice. "Utek, go get yourself something to eat."

Startled, the apprentice made his way quickly to the door and closed it behind him.

To Allonna's relief, her voice worked again. "What was that? What just happened?"

"The oath."

"The oath?" As she said it, she figured it out. "The oath I took never to…" This time she stopped herself.

Chuckling, Master Ramil nodded his head. "Young Utek has not taken the oath and does not know about the king's condition. So the oath would not let you reveal it in front of him. I do know, so you are free to speak of it to me." He looked at her pensively. "You truly believe you can enchant a suit of armor so the king can walk?"

Allonna was impressed that the man had worked it out based on what she couldn't say. "Yes."

He sighed. "I would like to see you do it. I believe I have what you need. Yes, it should do very well. Come." He beckoned her to follow, and led her into a small storage room. Pulling a cloth from off a suit of armor, he said, "What do you think?"

The armor was burnished steel plate with gold inlaid decorations. Allonna's experienced eye could tell it was both functional and beautiful.

"Magnificent. You made this all yourself?"

"Every piece. Each year, as King Aumekor grew, I reworked it to fit. I kept hoping that one day, a cure would be found for his condition and he would be able to wear it. It's only five-fold steel, but…"

"Between the armor you've made and my enchantment, we may have the next best thing to a cure."

"I hope you are right, Miss Allonna. I hope you are right."

Chapter Thirteen

Geradin

As he followed Protector Falor to the main gate, Geradin wondered who would ask for him without being willing to give a name. Unlike the Lord Regent, he did not have a spy network that might want to deliver information to him—and if he did, surely none of his spies would be stupid enough to approach the main gate and ask to see him.

"What can you tell me about this man?" asked Geradin.

"It's a man and woman, actually. Locals, I'm pretty sure. I think I've seen the man around town. Big fellow; hard to miss him."

Geradin grinned. "Holoran. It's got to be him. Biggest man I've ever seen."

"Friend of yours? Wonder why he wouldn't give his name."

That part was still puzzling. "I don't know him all that well. We took our Tests of Majority together." Geradin remembered that Holoran had seemed strangely quiet during the Test of Body by Labor. Though, since they had only met that day, Geradin realized that he might not be the best judge of Holoran's character. Perhaps he was silent by nature, and only seemed talkative before the Tests because of nervousness.

Approaching the gate, Geradin could see the massive figure of Holoran beyond the steel bars. At his side was the comely young woman Geradin had seen cheering Holoran from the stands. She was holding his arm as if to keep him from leaving, though Geradin doubted that anything less than three grown men would have had the strength to stop Holoran should he decide to walk away.

"Holoran! Good to see you again." Geradin smiled broadly as he passed through the gate.

The big man ducked his head. "Milord. I am honored that you would—"

"I thought I'd cured you of the habit of calling me 'milord' when we were down in the sewers." Geradin turned to the young woman and bowed. "And you must be the lady of whom Holoran spoke so highly. I see now that he did not exaggerate."

She bowed. "Thank you, Lord Geradin."

"I regret, Miss, that Holoran's praise of you did not extend to telling me your name?"

"Telani, milord."

Glancing up at the sun, Geradin motioned toward the gatehouse. "Shall we step inside there, where we can talk in more comfort?"

Once the three of them were seated around the table in the gatehouse, Geradin looked at Holoran and then Telani, trying to decide which of them to ask about the reason they had come. He thought it might be to invite him to their wedding, but if that was not the reason it would be awkward for him to mention it. Before he had made up his mind, Holoran spoke.

"I wasn't sure you would want to see me, mi—Geradin."

"I told you he would," said Telani.

"Of course I would," said Geradin simultaneously.

Shifting his shoulders uncomfortably, the big man looked to Telani, then back to Geradin. When he finally spoke, his voice was small. "Telani says I need to apologize to you."

"For what?" Geradin rapidly reviewed his memories of the day they had met.

Holoran turned to Telani. "See, I told you he was not offended."

She gave him a playful swat on the arm. "That Lord Geradin was not offended speaks well of his tolerance, but does not excuse your rudeness."

"Miss Telani," said Geradin, "I do not know of anything that Holoran has done to me for which he should apologize."

"Did he thank you for what you did for him? Making it so he didn't have to take the Test of Body by Combat?"

Finally understanding what this was about, Geradin waved a hand dismissively. "The Test of Body by Labor has been disdained far too long—the Lord Proctor himself told me so. It is I who should thank Holoran for helping me understand the need for change."

She shook her head. "No, you are far too kind, milord. It is thanks to you that we are getting married at the end of the season. If not for your intervention, Holoran would have failed to achieve his majority yet again, and we would—"

Holoran pushed back his chair and stood. "You shame me. We should not have come."

Geradin was embarrassed to be witnessing what was obviously a disagreement between the lovers, but he had no idea what he could do or say to smooth things over.

Telani sighed. "I'm not telling him anything he didn't already know. Things you told him yourself. You know he helped you, and you owe him your thanks."

After standing silently for several seconds, Holoran said, "I do not owe him thanks for helping me dishonor myself."

This accusation caught Geradin by surprise. "Help you dishonor yourself? When did I do that?"

"I had planned to take the Test of Body by Combat, even knowing I would not pass. But, after your speech, when faced with the choice of taking the Test of Body by Combat or by Labor, I chose Labor."

"There is no dishonor in that. I tried to make that clear in my speech—performing the labor was a service to our city. It was an honorable thing to do."

"For you, it was honorable. For me it was not."

"Why?"

"You said it in your speech. Your own words: 'The easy path

is before me. But I will not take the easy path.' And you didn't. But I did. I chose the easy path. I took the coward's way. It was my choice to take it, but I will not thank you for helping me."

Geradin furrowed his brow, opened his mouth to say something and then closed it again. He had been about to say that he'd been making up his speech as he went along, and that it shouldn't be taken so seriously, but then he realized that would imply that he didn't mean what he'd said. And he *had* meant it, though not in the way Holoran had taken it. How could he convince the big man that he was mistaken?

The least Geradin felt he could do was apologize. "You are right. I have insulted your honor, and I—" He stopped as sudden inspiration came to him, then he continued, "I will not apologize for doing so."

"What?" Holoran straightened his back and stood even taller.

"I said I will not apologize for insulting your honor. And if you value your honor as much as you claim, there is but one response you can make."

Telani's eyes opened wide. "Please, milord. It is my fault we came here, and I beg you not to force the issue."

Holoran's voice was flat. "No, Telani. It is too late for that." Holoran looked squarely into Geradin's eyes. "Lord Geradin, as you have insulted my honor, I claim the right of duel in defense of that honor."

The Assembly of Lords had outlawed dueling between commoners over two hundred years before. Commoners were expected to settle matters between them through the courts of the noble ruling over them — or in cases between commoners from different fiefdoms, by the King's courts. The Assembly had also banned nobles from challenging commoners to duel. By right, a noble could bring a commoner before a court composed of other nobles, and this was deemed sufficient to serve the needs of honor and justice.

Duels between nobles were still legal, but rare. The flowery formality of court speech allowed the nobles to insult each other in fact while maintaining the fiction of courtesy. If dueling between nobles were causing problems, though, then the Assembly of Lords would probably have outlawed it as well.

But the right of a commoner to challenge a noble to a duel was an original part of the Charter of Aud Sapeer, and several attempts to amend the Charter to delete that provision had failed. Since nobles could only be tried at law by other nobles, the commoners saw the right to challenge as their last line of defense against tyrannical nobles.

Even so, the advantage in dueling lay with the nobles: The challenged party had the right to choose the method of the duel, to choose whether the duel would be to the death, to choose the place of the duel, and to choose the time of the duel, up to one year and one day after the challenge was issued.

If Holoran took the step of challenging Geradin to a duel, he would be risking his life. Should Geradin chose a duel with swords to the death, there could be no doubt who would die. Was Holoran's sense of honor strong enough to make him take that risk? Geradin was fairly sure that it was.

Geradin stood up slowly, then gave a small bow to Holoran. "I accept your challenge."

"As I have no sword with me, milord, I ask your leave to go obtain one. I will then stand ready to meet you at the time of your choice."

"That will not be necessary. I choose to meet you here and now. You will not need a sword, as we shall be arm-wrestling." Geradin sat down, placing his elbow on the table with his hand ready.

"You mock me again, Lord Geradin."

"Do I? How so?"

"Arm-wrestling is not a real duel."

"As the challenged party, I have the choice of method for the duel, do I not?"

"Yes, but..." Holoran's voice trailed off to silence and he stood frowning.

"But what?"

"You know I am no match for you with the sword. And you must know that my strength is greater than yours. So choosing to arm-wrestle is intentionally throwing the fight. It proves you do not think me worthy of a real duel."

Geradin rose to his feet so violently that his chair was thrown onto its back. "Now you have insulted *my* honor."

Holoran took a step back. "How, milord?"

"If I were intentionally throwing the fight, that would be dishonorable. Yet if I chose to duel you with the sword, that would be the easy path for me, would it not? And, as you have made clear, to choose the easy path is dishonorable. If you are correct, then I cannot act honorably."

After a few moments thought, Holoran said, "You could choose a method of dueling in which we were more evenly matched."

Geradin shook his head. "Any method that would be easier than arm-wrestling would be the easier path, and therefore dishonorable."

"But for me, arm-wrestling is the easier path, so I would be dishonored by—"

"No, there is no dishonor for you, because the choice of methods is not up to you." Geradin picked up his chair, sat down and readied his arm again. "Sit down, Master Holoran, and defend your honor," he said, putting the force of command into his voice.

Holoran sat. Slowly, he put out his arm and grasped Geradin's hand in his huge fist.

Turning to Telani, Geradin flashed a smile. "Miss Telani, if you would be so good as to give us the word to begin?"

She nodded. "All ready?"

When both men nodded, she said, "Go."

Knowing that his only chance was an instant burst of strength before the bigger man could react, Geradin pushed as hard as he could the moment Telani gave the signal.

Holoran's arm did not even move.

For a few seconds, their arms remained upright as Geradin

struggled. Then, Holoran smoothly forced Geradin's arm back until it rested on the table, then released it.

Geradin rose to his feet and bowed to Holoran. "I trust that your honor is satisfied?"

Holoran stood up. "It is, milord."

"I am glad."

"Milord? I've acted rather foolishly, haven't I?" His voice was sheepish.

"Yes, you have. And I've told you before, stop calling me 'milord.'"

Chapter Fourteen

Aumekor

Aumekor saw the hint of a smile around Lord Regent Kindul's eyes. He'd had it since he arrived for the Regency Council meeting. That meant he was saving some choice bit of information until the end, and that information would not be good news. Why couldn't Kindul ever be on his side?

That wasn't fair, Aumekor told himself. Kindul had stood bravely to defend him during the attack on Midsummer Day. For a short while he'd hoped that incident would lead to a change in Kindul's attitude, but it had not.

"Your Majesty," said Kindul, "There is one more important item. I've received word from our ambassador in Cirkepam." He paused to look at the Council members and finally at Aumekor.

Sometimes Aumekor wished he could respond with what he really felt, instead of engaging in the ritualized sparring. *Our* ambassador? he wanted say. You mean *your* ambassador. *I* never receive word from any ambassadors because they all report to *you*.

But that would just be another sign of his weakness as a ruler. He cast aside two possible flippant responses to Kindul's vague announcement and decided to be direct, so as to find out the bad news as soon as possible. "My Lord Regent, please tell us what our ambassador had to say."

"He informs me that Queen Onara has agreed that a Conclave of Monarchs is the best way to avoid difficulties in the succession for her kingdom."

There were smiles and murmurs of excitement around the table at the good news. Aumekor did not smile, though, because he could sense that Kindul had not finished. And in a flash, he knew what the rest of the news was: the Conclave of Monarchs would not be held here in Aud Sapeer. He wondered if the ambassador had even raised that possibility with Queen Onara.

Kindul would almost certainly insist on going to the Conclave to "represent" Aud Sapeer. That would give him the chance to meet the other monarchs of the Free Kingdoms and present himself as the real power in Aud Sapeer. Suddenly an additional possibility gave Aumekor a chill. What if the Conclave of Monarchs decided to make Kindul's regency permanent? He wasn't sure if there was precedent for such a thing; he'd have to ask Selima afterwards.

There was only one thing he could do. He raised his hand to silence the members of the Council. "My Lord Regent, this is good news indeed. It is vital to ensure the stability of our neighboring kingdom. And since I will be unable to travel there, I can think of no better person to represent me at the Conclave of Monarchs than you, My Lord Regent. How soon will you be leaving?"

Kindul's eyes had grown wider as Aumekor spoke, and he now seemed momentarily at a loss for words.

"Begging Your Majesty's pardon," said Lady Uwixa, "I thought the Conclave was to be held here."

"I'm sure the Lord Regent will correct me if I was misinformed."

By now Kindul had recovered his composure. "Your Majesty is correct; the Conclave will be hosted by Queen Onara. I was not aware that Your Majesty had been informed already."

Waving his hand dismissively took an effort, but Aumekor managed to put a little flourish into it. "Our ambassador is hardly the only source of information in Cirkepam." Let Kindul think he was developing his own network of spies. "In any case, if that is Queen Onara's decision, we must abide by it. But, My Lord Regent, you still have not answered my question about how soon you will leave us."

Kindul's eyes flickered. Aumekor realized now just how far he had thrown the Lord Regent off guard by anticipating him. Kindul had probably planned to ooze false sympathy while explaining that the Conclave would not be held here. Then one of his cronies on the Council would suggest that Kindul be sent to represent the kingdom. Kindul's opponents would object, there would be an acrimonious debate, but there could have been only one possible outcome: it really would not be proper to send anyone of less stature than the Lord Regent to meet with the other monarchs. Which would have meant Kindul had won another round.

Instead, Aumekor had stolen that victory. And by sounding almost eager to send Kindul away, he had made the Lord Regent wonder whether he was missing something. Aumekor suppressed a smile as he watched Kindul try to analyze the situation.

"Well, Your Majesty, the date has not yet been fixed, since word will not yet have reached all of the Free Kingdoms. I anticipate the Conclave will be held some time during the winter."

Aumekor nodded. "Very well. When the time comes, you shall go as my personal representative to the Conclave, with full power to act on my behalf." By virtue of the regency, the Lord Regent had that power anyway, so there was no harm in granting it to him. "Except in one matter, of course, in which you do not have my trust."

Kindul stiffened. "Loss of the Monarch's Trust" was grounds for a vote in the Assembly of Lords on whether Kindul should remain as Lord Regent. Given the current political alignment, mustering the two-thirds vote necessary to remove him was impossible, which is why his opponents had never tried.

When he finally spoke, Kindul's voice was wary. "And what is that matter, Your Majesty?"

"Omnimancer Selima tells me that the Conclave of Monarchs might be a good place to arrange my marriage. If this matter were left up to you, I have no doubt you would arrange the most politically advantageous marriage, no matter how shrewish my future bride might be. That is why I have decided that Omnimancer Selima will also go to the Conclave of Monarchs, charged with that mission."

Relieved laughter came from around the room. Aumekor purposely did not look at Selima, because he knew she'd be furious with him for having made such a decision without consulting her. But she would have to go, now: if she did not, it would weaken his appearance of authority.

Shortly thereafter the meeting finished, and the members of the Council left, except Selima. She waited for the guards to shut the door to the council room before speaking.

"It would do me great honor, Your Majesty, if you would deign to consult with me before making decisions about where I am to go."

Aumekor shook his head. "Selima, don't play that game with me. I know you're angry, so why don't you just say it?"

"I will. You made a major mistake, Mek. You should have chosen someone else to go arrange your marriage. Lady Uwixa, for instance. She's loyal to you."

"Yes, but I need someone there who's strong enough to make Kindul back down, if necessary, and you're the only one."

"Kindul won't interfere with the marriage arrangements."

"That's not what worries me. What if Kindul decides to get the Conclave of Monarchs to declare him Permanent Regent?"

"He couldn't."

"Why not?"

"Well, he's sworn on the oath disk not to reveal your weakness. He can't tell them about that, so they would have no reason to make his regency permanent."

"He hasn't sworn an oath not to lie about me, has he?

He could tell them that the 'real reason' I didn't come to the Conclave is that I'm simple-minded, or that I shirk my responsibilities, or that I spend all my time with dissolute women, or—"

Selima held up her palm. "Enough."

Aumekor waited.

"Even if he would try such a thing, I still cannot leave. The Dark Priestess could attack at any time. Protecting your life is more important than any political machinations—" She held up a finger to prevent him from interrupting. "—even if the result is a permanent regency."

Aumekor knew he was losing the argument, but he persisted. "If you went, Allonna would still be here, and you said she's stronger than you."

"She's untrained. She doesn't even know her own strength. She couldn't stand against the Dark Priestess. No, my leaving is out of the question."

Aumekor took a deep breath to continue his argument, but something Selima had just said seemed strange, so he changed subjects. "Why doesn't she know her own strength?"

"Because she hadn't received any formal training before coming here. She has no concept of—"

"No. She's been your apprentice since Midsummer. Why haven't you shown her how strong she is?"

Selima's eyes flickered. "I've got her studying some important books right now, to build up her base of knowledge."

He didn't smile, but he knew he was onto something because Selima was being evasive. "That's strange. I thought you always said mancy was best learned through doing, not from books."

"Yes, that's true. But there is still something to be gained from books, and I've been so busy with Regency Council business that I haven't had time to start training her properly."

Selima was jealous of Allonna's power, he realized—and possibly a little frightened by it. It wouldn't be a conscious decision on her part, but she was probably reluctant to train

Allonna because the younger woman would one day surpass her. This was a surprising weakness, something Aumekor had not expected to find in Selima – perhaps because he had never seen her confronted by anyone she considered more powerful.

Immediately he began analyzing how he could use this weakness against her, to get her to change her mind about going to the Conclave. And then he stopped that path of thought, ashamed of where his instincts were taking him. This was Selima, not some political opponent to be maneuvered.

He thought for a moment about how best to handle this. Should he tell Selima what he suspected about her fears, in order to force her to confront them? No, that would embarrass her; a more subtle approach would be better.

"I think it might be a good idea to accelerate her training," he said. "It will make things more difficult for me on the political front if you're not as involved there, but as you pointed out, the political considerations are secondary to the overall fight against the Dark Priestess. Allonna's power can help us, but only if she knows how to wield it."

At first, it seemed Selima was about to object, but she didn't. Instead, she sat still with her eyebrows slightly lowered. He'd seen that look before; she was trying to work out a complex problem. The two of them sat in silence for a short while.

Then Selima shook her head slightly, and looked at him with an amused smile. "You don't have any agents in Cirkepam."

The unexpected change of subject made him laugh. "I never said I did. But I hope Kindul thinks so, now."

"I guess I hadn't realized until now just how good you are at figuring out what other people are thinking. Sometimes things they don't even know they are thinking." She nodded slowly. "I don't think you need to fear Kindul, even without my help. You are strong in ways he cannot understand."

It was the first time he really felt that Selima saw him as an adult, despite his not having taken the Tests of Majority. Not sure what to say, he merely nodded.

She rose from her seat and headed toward the door, then

stopped and turned to look at him. "Thank you."
"For what?"
"For choosing to be kind."

Chapter Fifteen

Geradin

F ollowed closely by Allonna, Geradin led the way to Mek's quarters. Master Ramil and two servants followed, carrying the suit of armor and its stand. Seeing there were only two Protectors guarding the door, Geradin knew Mek was not yet back from his daily meeting with the Council of Regents.

A few words from Geradin gained the party's admittance to Mek's room. While Master Ramil and the servants set the armor on its stand, Geradin turned to Allonna.

"Is there anything you need in order to perform the spell?"

Allonna shook her head, but didn't say anything.

Geradin frowned slightly; it wasn't like her to be silent. "You have met King Aumekor already, haven't you?"

She bobbed her head. "Selima introduced me, but it was just for a moment." Her hands began smoothing the front of her skirt.

"Then she told you all about the rules, I suppose." Geradin kept his face straight.

"Which rules?"

"Don't look directly at his face, and so on."

"No, she didn't tell me."

He feigned surprise. "Really? Careless of her. She must have a lot on her mind."

"What are the rules? She didn't tell me about any rules, and

I looked directly at his face when we met. He wasn't offended, was he?"

"Oh, if he'd been offended, you would know." Geradin shook his head gravely. "His wrath is terrible to behold – when we were children, he used to have his guards beat me with the flat of their swords if I spoke to him without his permission, and I'm his best friend. No, if he'd been offended, you'd be keeping company with the rats in the dungeon right now awaiting his awful judgment. He must have liked your eyes. Very pretty eyes they are, so it's understandable." He stopped, suddenly uncertain of himself. What had led him to say that about her eyes?

Allonna's pretty eyes had opened wider as he spoke, then they narrowed. "You're lying."

There was nothing to do but carry on with the joke. Geradin drew himself up to his full height. "You dishonor me. I would never lie about a woman's eyes being pretty."

Her cheeks flushed. "I meant about the king. You're just trying to frighten me."

"It was just a joke." He felt foolish all of a sudden. After passing the Tests of Majority, he really ought to act like an adult, instead of playing jokes as he used to with Mek. He was about to apologize when the door to the chamber opened, and Mek was pushed into the room on his wheeled chair.

"Lord Geradin. Master Ramil. And Miss Allonna." He looked at each of them in turn. "What a surprise to find you here in my chambers." Mek's personal servant, Nikufed, moved the chair to the center of the room and then turned it so he could face his guests.

It was not a surprise at all, Geradin knew. The guards outside would have mentioned their presence. "Your Majesty," he said, using the formal mode because of the others in the room, "if you can spare us some of your time, we would like to attempt an experiment."

Mek's face broke into a grin. "The armor? We're ready to try it?"

Geradin turned to the armorsmith. "Master Ramil, would you care to show His Majesty the work of your hands?"

The armor was on its stand under a cloth, which the smith now pulled off with a flourish. The steel and gold gleamed in the light from the torches that lined the windowless walls.

"Oh." Mek stared at the armor without saying anything more.

Geradin remembered how, when they were children, Mek had so desperately wanted to be a heroic knight in armor, saving princesses from evil creatures. Mek had not spoken of such desires in the last few years, but part of that childhood dream obviously remained.

And Geradin suddenly realized that in his enthusiasm for the idea, he had blundered. What if Allonna could not enchant the armor as she claimed? He should have had her perform her mancy down in the smithy, so they could test that it really did work. If she had failed, Mek would have been disappointed to hear about it, but showing him the armor like this would make the disappointment far worse.

He moved to his friend's side and spoke softly. "Allonna is ready to try the enchantment, but we can't be certain it will work. I should have—"

Shaking his head, Mek said, "It is a work of art, Master Ramil. You made this for me?"

"Yes, Your Majesty. I've an eye for measurements; it should fit you just right."

"Why have you never shown it to me before?"

The armorsmith bowed his head, but did not say anything.

Mek nodded. "What faith it must have taken for you to fashion this armor for me, when no one else could believe that I would ever wear it. I understand why you kept it hidden, lest others think you were mocking me. This is a great gift you have given me – no matter what happens with Miss Allonna's spell, this is the armor I shall wear from now on in my dreams when I go to battle."

Geradin turned his head slightly away from the

armorsmith. He thought he had seen glistening on Master Ramil's cheeks, and did not want to embarrass him.

"Miss Allonna," said Mek, "did you see Omnimancer Selima as you were coming here?"

Allonna's hands twitched when he addressed her. "No, Your Majesty."

"She and I have agreed to make your training a priority. Do you think you need more training before you attempt this spell?"

Without hesitation she said, "No. I can do it, Your Majesty."

Mek nodded. "Very well. Please proceed."

Over the years, Geradin had watched Selima perform many major spells. Usually she would mutter to herself while either holding an artifact or moving her fingers in strange patterns. He was interested to see if Allonna's technique was different.

She approached the suit of armor, then stopped and turned uncertainly to face Mek. "Which glove should I use to control the movements of the armor? I was thinking the right, but you might want to have your sword in the right hand, so should I do the left, or would it be better to have you control it with the right and hold a sword in your left hand?"

Geradin realized Allonna must not be aware that Mek's left hand was completely useless. He would have to explain that to her later.

Mek said, "The right glove will be fine."

Allonna removed the right glove from the suit of armor and placed it on the floor, then stepped back three paces. Her brow furrowed slightly.

Geradin waited for her to begin muttering, but she merely stood silently.

After a short while, Mek said quietly, "Is there a problem?"

Allonna did not reply, or even acknowledge that she had heard anything.

"I think she's casting the spell," whispered Geradin. "I think she does magic differently from Selima. She was talking to me about it earlier."

Mek nodded.

One of the Inner Keep's alarm bells began to ring close by. A moment later, Master Ramil shouted, "Protect the King!" and started moving toward the suit of armor.

Geradin pulled his sword out of its scabbard and swiveled his head trying to find the threat. The two Protectors of the Line that had been standing almost unnoticed on either side of Mek drew their swords. Four more Protectors burst through the door into the room. More alarm bells began to ring.

Not seeing anything that seemed threatening, Geradin moved closer to Mek while watching Master Ramil. Allonna seemed to wake from her stupor as the armorsmith crashed into the suit of armor, knocking it to the floor. She looked around wide-eyed at the Protectors entering the room, then at Geradin and the Protectors surrounding Mek. She began muttering and moving her fingers the way Selima did when casting.

Growing up in the Keep of Aud Sapeer, the most protected place in the sixteen Free Kingdoms, Geradin was familiar with protective warding spells. The strongest ones always created a slight shimmer in the air at their boundary, and in the dark could be seen by their faint glow. From floor to ceiling there now appeared a ward that rippled in brilliant blue light. It completely surrounded him, Mek, and the other two Protectors. Geradin blinked not just from surprise but also from the sudden brightness. Even the glow of his sword paled in comparison. It was then that Geradin realized his sword had been glowing the blue of safety, not the yellow of danger, ever since he had drawn it. Unless the magic of the sword had somehow failed, the Heir of the Line had not been in danger.

Holding his sword up so all could see it, he said, "The King is safe. Everybody calm down. The King is safe."

The Protectors began lowering their swords.

Master Ramil rose to his feet. "No! There's something in this room. Something invisible that can work magic."

The Protectors swords rose again. Allonna began twisting

her head to look around.

Something invisible? Geradin wasn't sure if the magic of his sword would recognize an invisible threat; he had thought so, but perhaps he was wrong. What could it be?

More Protectors of the Line came into the room, including three of Geradin's fellow High Protectors. Their swords glowed blue as well.

Geradin felt relief when he heard Selima out in the hallway asking, "Is he safe? Is he safe?" Selima would be able to tell what this invisible thing was, if Master Ramil was not just imagining things.

Selima rushed through the door, then stopped and looked around the room, taking in the whole scene. "Well, that explains part of it," she said as she looked at the ward surrounding Mek and Geradin.

"Omnimancer Selima," said Master Ramil, "there is something invisible in this room. I saw it use ferromancy directed at the suit of armor, and I feared it was trying to enchant the armor to attack the King."

That made no sense to Geradin. "But it was Allonna who was enchanting the armor."

"No, milord." Master Ramil shook his head firmly. "I could see the flow of the magic, and it did not come from her. It came from over there." He pointed at a spot several feet to the right of where Allonna was standing."

Selima nodded. "And that explains the rest of it." She raised her voice. "The glow of the High Protectors' swords indicate that there is no danger. King Aumekor is safe, and you have done your duties well even if this was but a false alarm. You may return to your posts."

Most of the Protectors filed out of the room. The three High Protectors remained, as did the two who were still enclosed within the ward with Geradin and Mek.

Walking over to Allonna, Selima said, "You can undo the ward now. It is safe."

The glowing blue ripples in the air winked out of existence, leaving a dark red afterimage on Geradin's vision. The disappearance of the protective ward made Geradin feel safer; it meant there really was no threat.

"What were you trying to do by enchanting the armor?" Selima asked Allonna.

Allonna seemed to shrink a little, and she looked down at the floor. "I…"

"This is not your fault, child." Selima looked over at Geradin and Mek. Geradin could tell whose fault she thought it was.

"I was trying to enchant the armor so it could be controlled by a glove, like the little knights I made before, and when I began everything seemed fine, but then everything seemed to get harder and slower, and I didn't know why, and then Master Ramil knocked the armor over and there were Protectors all around, so I put up a ward around the King like you taught me, except I guess I was so nervous that I did it wrong and that's why it was so shiny."

Closing her eyes, Selima took in a deep breath and let it out. She turned to Master Ramil. "You were partly right: you did see magical power coming from something invisible. But it was not a threat, it was something Allonna created to help her enchant the armor."

Allonna sucked in a sudden breath. Master Ramil looked thoughtful.

Selima turned to the three High Protectors next. "This is my fault, as I had not yet explained to Allonna some of the magical traps I have set for anyone using a large amount of magical power within the Keep. That is what set off the original alarm. It will not happen again."

Selima then turned to Geradin and Mek. "You two should have known better."

Geradin thought about saying he had no idea Allonna would be using so much power she would set off the alarms, but decided that trying to make excuses would only make her more angry with him. He knew from past experience that Selima's wrath was terrible to behold.

Chapter Sixteen

Allonna

Allonna sat in her chair in Selima's study, waiting for the older woman to say something. She realized now it had been a mistake to try to cast such an important spell without discussing it with Selima first. She frowned – it was Lord Geradin's fault; he was the one who had talked her into doing it.

Immediately she realized that it was foolish to blame him. Papa always said she was stubborn as a lame mule. If she hadn't wanted to cast the spell, Lord Geradin couldn't have talked her into doing it even if he had two tongues.

Selima sat in her chair, leaning with her elbows on the desk and lightly massaging her forehead with her fingertips, as she had been since the two of them had arrived at her study. Then, just as Allonna was about to break the silence by apologizing for her folly, Selima sat up straight and looked at her.

"I am sorry, Allonna. I have been neglecting your training, and what happened today was the result."

"No, I—"

Holding up her palm to silence Allonna, Selima continued, "King Aumekor and I both agree that training you is my most important duty, now—more important than any affairs of state. And having seen what you did with your powers during an emergency, even if there was no real danger, I realize how mistaken I was not to devote myself to your training from the moment you became my apprentice."

Surprise at how important her training was gave way to embarrassment at her improper casting of the warding spell. No wonder King Aumekor wanted her trained as soon as possible; he didn't want her ignorance to cost him his life. "I'm sorry I didn't create the ward properly. I'll try to do it better in the future."

Smiling softly, Selima shook her head. "Child, I have never seen a simple ward better than that one. If you had not undone it, King Aumekor and Lord Geradin would still be inside, for it would have taken me the rest of the morning to bring it down."

Her thoughts whirling, Allonna said, "But why? You could just undo my spell."

"No. The flare of power you used in creating the ward was too high." Selima looked at her and raised an eyebrow.

Allonna knew that meant Selima was expecting her to reason something out. One of the first things—one of the few things—Selima had taught her was that a mancer could easily undo a spell cast by another mancer by using a brief flare of power higher than the highest level of power used for the original spell. That explained why, back in Glicken, she had been able to undo anyone else's spell, but sometimes they would fail to undo hers. So, if Selima could not undo her spell, that meant Selima could not create a flare higher than Allonna's. Allonna began shaking her head. "That can't be right. No. You're *Selima*. You're *Omnimancer* Selima."

"Yes, I am Selima. But as far as I can determine, your power exceeds mine in every dimension. I cannot know for sure, but you may be more powerful than the High Priestess of the Dark God."

Allonna had grown up thinking of Selima as the most powerful omnimancer in the world. To be told that she was more powerful sounded wrong; it was like saying wood was stronger than steel. Selima must be testing her, to see what she would do if she thought herself powerful. That was the only thing that made sense. As for the implication that the

Dark Priestess might be more powerful than Selima, Allonna knew enough history to recognize the flaw. "The Dark Priestess cannot be more powerful than you. You undid her spell at the Battle of Denoral's Pass. That's why she was defeated."

"Your reasoning is sound." Selima sighed and rose from her seat.

Allonna was relieved that she had passed Selima's test.

"But sound reasoning is not good enough to determine truth, when it is based on incomplete information." Selima held up her hands. "Do you see the rings I wear? The bracelets and necklaces? They are artifacts from the Age of Light. They allow me to use magical power beyond my natural abilities. This ring, for example, allows me to store up twice the magical power I could otherwise have. And this one adds one tenth to the level of power I can send in a flare." She shook her head. "I do not wear any jewelry for decoration. I have spent decades accumulating these artifacts, to allow me to better defend the Heir and the Free Kingdoms."

Staring wide-eyed at the multiple rings Selima wore, and the several bracelets and necklaces, there was nothing Allonna could think to say in response to this revelation. The tales she'd heard as a child mentioned such magical objects, but they were always spoken of as being so rare that mancers had killed each other just to obtain one. And now Selima was claiming to have fifteen or more.

"Yes, I undid the Dark Priestess's spell, just that once. I had no choice—it was sucking the air from the lungs of ten thousand men. If I had not undone it, they would have died and nothing would have stopped her armies from taking Denoral's Pass and then sweeping down into the Free Kingdoms." Her voice became quiet, and her eyes were distant. "I had to do it, but I was forced to use three priceless artifacts that could only work once. I can no longer match that flare, not with the artifacts I have now. In her natural strength, the High Priestess of the Dark God almost certainly exceeds my power considerably. And she has artifacts of her own to augment her abilities."

A sudden weight seemed to press down on Allonna's chest. Did Selima expect her to face the Dark Priestess?

Allonna saw herself in her mind's eye, beams of light extending from her fingertips toward a figure cloaked in darkness, and the darkness seemed to reach toward her as if to swallow her whole. Shaking her head rapidly, she said, "I can't be as powerful as you say. Please, this is one of your tests, right?"

Selima crossed over to her and laid a reassuring hand on her shoulder. "The prophecies do not say it will be you who goes with the Heir of the Line to confront the Dark Priestess. They do not say it will be me." She laughed sadly. "True prophecies are seldom clear before they prove themselves. But I can tell you this—until I have trained you to the point that you would be more effective in confronting her, I would be the one to do it, not you. And such training will take twenty, thirty years or more. By then, most likely, I will have to restrain you from charging off to attack her."

The fear Allonna had felt began to fade. Still, something Selima had said nagged at her. "If that day is decades in the future, why the rush to train me?"

Selima turned and walked back to her seat. "When I recruited you as my apprentice, I knew you had the potential to replace me someday as Royal Omnimancer."

"Replace you?" Allonna realized her hands had been clutching her skirt for some time, and she uncurled them slowly.

"That would be decades in the future. If you were to take over responsibility for protecting the Heir, I would be free to devote my time to research, trying to rediscover spells lost since the Dark God burned half the world, looking for artifacts from the Age of Light, anything that might help us defeat the Dark Priestess." Allonna shook her head. "When I saw that ward you cast, I realized I had been wrong. I thought I would have to train you for years in the casting of the most delicate, difficult spells before you would be of much use in protecting the Heir. But the vast power you have at your command can make even simple spells very effective."

"But you had seen me cast spells before."

"I had seen the height of your flare, but I did not realize the true extent of the other dimensions of your power."

Unfortunately, the confusion Allonna felt was familiar from Selima's previous lessons. But her conversation with Geradin earlier in the day gave her the courage to confess her ignorance. "I don't understand. I'm sorry, I should have told you before that I don't understand what you mean when you talk about dimensions of power or about gathering power, but I was scared you would think I was too ignorant to be your apprentice, and I really do want to be, even if I am scared sometimes, but I talked to Lord Geradin about it this morning and he said I should tell you that I didn't understand what you were talking about, and that you would find a way to explain it."

Selima blinked a few times in rapid succession, then nodded slowly. "You obviously understand the idea that to do anything with magic requires the use of magical power."

"Yes."

"And in order to cast a spell, a mancer must have sufficient power stored somewhere."

"Why?"

Selima frowned. "What do you mean, why? If the mancer doesn't have sufficient power, he can't cast the spell."

"Well, you've talked about how a mancer gathers power. I don't quite understand that, either, but why not just gather the power that is needed at the time of casting the spell?"

Selima tapped her lips a few times with her index finger. "Does your father's smithy have a cistern for collecting rainwater?"

"Yes." What did that have to do with mancy?

"So if he wanted water for quenching some metal, he would get that water from the cistern. But if the cistern were empty, he would either have to wait for more water to enter the cistern or else find water elsewhere. Only water that is already stored in the cistern is easily available; it would take time to gather water from elsewhere. Magical power must also be stored up."

"So what do I do to store up power?"

"You already do so. Otherwise, you would not be able to cast spells at all."

"And gathering power is like rain falling into the cistern?"

"Yes, if it were always raining a little. Your 'cistern' of power is always being slowly refilled. If you do not use that power for a while, the cistern becomes full. If you use all the power in the cistern, it will take some time for you to fill it up again."

"How long?"

"It varies between mancers. And that leads me to an explanation of the various dimensions of magical power. Imagine that your cistern has a spigot at the bottom. Now, if you are trying to fill a pail from the cistern, you can open the spigot. If you open the spigot all the way, the pail will fill quickly; if you open the spigot only partly, the pail will fill more slowly."

Allonna nodded.

"The total amount of power needed for a spell is like the amount of water needed to fill the pail. Some spells only require a cupful of power, while others require a barrel. Now, some mancers have a very wide spigot, and can fill a barrel in seconds. Others have a very small spigot, and it will take them half the day to fill a cup."

Smiling, Allonna said, "I understand. The flare of power is how much water can come out of the spigot at once. I have a very wide spigot."

"Exactly. Now, let us consider another dimension of the cistern. If the cistern is very large, it can fill several barrels before it needs to be refilled. If it is very small, it may not even be able to fill a cup before it needs to be refilled. This corresponds to the total amount of power a mancer can use before needing to spend time gathering power again."

"And I must have a large cistern, because I enchanted those thirty little knights?"

Selima nodded. "Which brings me to the next dimension. Imagine two cisterns that contain the same amount of water. But one cistern is tall with a narrow opening at the top, while the other is short with a wide opening. Which will refill more quickly?"

"The wide one, because it gathers more rain."

"Yes. Some mancers gather power quickly, and some more slowly. Now, it's important that you understand that these dimensions vary widely between mancers. And it's possible for a mancer to be able to gather power quickly, but only dispense it slowly."

"Wide cistern, narrow spigot." Allonna was excited—she finally felt like she understood what Selima had been trying to teach her.

"And it's important that you realize you have a very wide spigot, a very large cistern with a very wide opening."

"I understand."

"And I have a very wide spigot, but not as wide as yours. And my cistern is only of medium width, which means that I gather power slower than many other mancers, and nowhere near as quickly as you. But it is very large, which means I can perform spells that require more power than they can ever store in their cisterns."

"And the artifacts you wear make the cistern bigger, or wider, or make the spigot larger."

"Yes. Now, a word of caution. When we first met, you told me that your mother had warned you about 'flaring out.' In our cistern example, this would be like tearing out the spigot completely. The water would flow out of the cistern more quickly if you did that, but it would never again be able to fill up with water."

"So how do I avoid doing that?"

"You may have noticed that when you have opened a spigot

almost all the way, it can become harder to turn. As you reach the limit of the power you can safely use, it will become more difficult to increase it. In fact, it will become painful if you try to do so. That is the warning sign. You must promise me that if the level of power you are using is painful, you will not increase it. We cannot afford to have you flare out."

"I promise. But if the pain is a warning, why does anyone let themselves flare out?"

Selima let out a long sigh. "Those who flare themselves out are almost always those with very narrow spigots. They constantly push against the edges of their power. Having succeeded in a spell despite the pain, the next time they try for a little more. And they keep increasing through the pain until finally the pain stops, and they think they have achieved a new level of power. And they have—by breaking off the spigot. But once they have drained the cistern and their power is gone the pain returns and remains with them for the rest of their lives, and they are never able to cast another spell. It is a tragedy, and one that could be avoided if people would stop trying to cast beyond their abilities."

She could tell from Selima's voice that this was an issue the omnimancer cared deeply about. "I promise I won't let that happen to me. I won't ever increase my level of power when it's painful."

"Good. I'm glad you understand the seriousness of the matter." Selima leaned back in her chair. "Is there anything else that's been puzzling you?"

After thinking a moment, Allonna said, "What happened when I tried to enchant the armor in the king's quarters? And I'm sorry I did that, because I know now I should have asked you first, but I didn't think it was much different from what I had done with the little knights I had enchanted, even if it would take more power, and I wanted to help the King, and since Lord Geradin—" She hesitated, realizing she had been about to say Geradin had talked her into it, but she knew that wasn't right. "—did not know how much power it would take, you cannot blame him."

A half-smile formed on Selima's lips. "I will forgo the placing of blame. As for explaining what happened when you began casting the spell: there is a special ward set up to detect the use of mancy within the Inner Keep. If the total power being used for a spell exceeds a certain amount, and the ward does not recognize the spell, it will sound an alarm."

"I see." Allonna thought a moment. "But what prevents someone from undoing the ward, so they can then do a spell of great power?" Undoing might take a high flare, but the total amount of power used was minute.

"There is another spell that will sound an alarm if the detection ward is undone."

"But what if someone undoes that spell first?"

Selima nodded. "It is good that you see the possibilities. However, there are over thirty layers of such spells. It is possible to undo them all without sounding an alarm if one does it in the proper order, but it is not possible to determine by observation what that order is."

Allonna nodded. No one could guess correctly that many times in a row. But still didn't explain everything that had happened. "The spells aren't just an alarm, are they? Enchanting the armor got suddenly harder."

"That is a spell of my own invention," Selima said. "To stretch our analogy past all reason, I turn the water in the cistern to honey, so it flows much more slowly. That gives us more time to react in case the spell is an attack."

"There is one other thing that I don't understand," Allonna said. "Master Ramil said that there was something invisible casting a spell, but you said it was something I made. I don't know what I did."

"Ah," said Selima. "That is the key to omnimancy. Most mancers have a talent for only one aspect of magical power. Some have a talent for two or three, a few for as many as five. As a ferromancer, Master Ramil can only enchant metal, and he can only see flows of power that are being used for that purpose. So he could not see the power you were using to create the *umbrit*."

"Umbrit?"

"An *umbrit* is a special kind of spell only omnimancers can cast—being able to cast it is what makes one an omnimancer. You have a talent for healing, but you do not have a talent for ferromancy."

"But..." If she didn't have the talent to enchant metal, then how had she made the little knights? "But I have a talent to make an *umbrit*? That was the invisible thing that was using the power Master Ramil saw?"

"Yes. An *umbrit* is a special spell that can be created to control any aspect of mancy. So an omnimancer is capable of performing all types of magic, through an *umbrit*."

"Why have I never heard of an *umbrit* before?"

Selima gave a small shrug. "It's not something we omnimancers discuss much with others. And it doesn't make much difference in the end whether we cast spells directly or through an *umbrit*." She leaned forward in her chair. "Now, unless you have more questions, let's start reviewing the basic protective spells I've already taught you, and see how effective you can make them."

Chapter Seventeen

Geradin

Geradin switched his sword to his left hand in order to wipe the sweat from his right palm against his tunic. The midday sun was not a problem—the first day of autumn was but three days away, and cooler winds were already rising from the south—but he had been training under Swordmaster Ytanor's direction since dawn.

The swordmaster called it stamina training. It was obviously necessary, because Geradin could not remember having been so exhausted in his life. He held back a sigh—he had better uses for that breath—as he turned and continued his double-paced march back across the training yard. To keep his mind off the hot ache in his legs, he concentrated on keeping his sword tip up. The sword's blue glow was noticeable even in the daylight, and that reminded him his switch of hands would not have gone unnoticed. Ytanor might decide to take advantage of the moment to strike at him.

Nothing. The swordmaster did not attack, but merely watched from his post in the middle of the yard as Geradin continued past him.

That was part of the training, Geradin decided. Having no food, no water, and no breaks in the physical activity was merely physical endurance. But the tension of not knowing when an attack would come tested his mental stamina.

His mind drifted back to Midsummer's Eve, when he had

arrogantly assumed the old swordmaster had nothing left to teach him. His training program over the last half-season had proved him wrong.

Approaching the swordmaster again, Geradin brought his thoughts back to focus on what he was doing. He should not let his mind wander like that. In a real battle, any distraction could be fatal. But Ytanor did not take advantage of even that momentary lapse, but remained standing in nearly inhuman stillness, with his sword at his side. His only movements since they'd started were to occasionally shout new instructions as Geradin reached one end or the other of his route.

Even though he now realized there was much more to the training of a Protector than mere swordsmanship, Geradin allowed himself a small smile of satisfaction at his skills in that area. In sparring with other Protectors, no one had yet managed to land a touch on him. That, coupled with his actions during the attack on Mek, had quieted any objection to his direct elevation to the rank of High Protector.

Growing up, he'd always known he would become a Protector of the Line, as his father had been before him. First he had worried that he would be made a Protector only because his father had died saving Mek. Later he worried that others would think so. It felt good to know that nobody could doubt that he deserved to be where he was.

He was approaching Ytanor again, and he suddenly tensed as he noticed the swordmaster's hand begin to move. But the hand was empty, and it merely reached up to scratch the swordmaster's nose. Geradin continued past without incident.

Scratching his nose? Swordmaster Ytanor was human after

—

A flash of movement in front of him was the only warning he had, but it was too late, and the unexpected blow to his breastplate almost knocked him off his feet. Then he intentionally threw himself to the ground and rolled to the side. Geradin's thoughts reeled. Was it an invisible enemy? Some sort of magical attack? As he rolled, his eyes searched the spot where he had been, and then he spotted it: a blunted arrow. Someone had shot at him, but the blunted end meant it was just part of the training.

Dust exploded from the ground next to him, and he blinked furiously at the sudden grit in his eyes. Another shot. He rolled to a crouch, then began to run erratically toward the far side of the yard, opposite the place he instinctively felt was the origin of the arrows. Two more blunted arrows hit the ground nearby as he ran, but the increased distance made them less accurate. When he reached the far wall he turned to see if he could spot his attacker.

There was someone with a bow up on the wall. As Geradin watched, the man drew another arrow and loosed it toward him. From his vantage point across the yard, Geradin was able to anticipate the arrow's path and did not even have to move out of its way.

Now that he felt he was out of immediate danger, he glanced at Ytanor. The swordmaster was watching him from the center of the yard.

What did his teacher expect him to do? He couldn't continue marching back and forth across the yard without getting shot. He had no weapon that could reach the archer. There was no way to continue the exercise, was there?

"Did I say you could stop marching?" shouted Ytanor.

"No, Swordmaster." Geradin began to march along the wall, keeping an eye on the archer for any sign of a new attack.

"You can stop now."

Geradin slowed to a halt and waited as Ytanor walked over to him. When the swordmaster got close, Geradin raised his sword. "Is the training over?"

"It is."

Sheathing his sword, Geradin said, "What did I do wrong?"

"What do you think you did wrong?"

"Before we started you said you would attack me at some point during the training, so I was expecting that. But I did not anticipate an attack by an archer."

"I did not say that I would attack you. I said that I would begin an attack on you." Ytanor smiled, reached up and scratched his nose.

"A signal." Geradin nodded. "You started the attack by scratching your nose."

The swordmaster's smile widened to a grin. "It's not the way I normally do things during stamina training, but how else was I going to land a hit on you?" After a short while discussing additional training exercises to build up stamina, the swordmaster dismissed him.

Spending a good portion of the afternoon in the steaming water of the King's Baths helped wash the aches from his limbs. He felt almost back to normal as he returned to his room and began to dress. Holoran and Telani were getting married that afternoon, so Geradin chose a dark blue formal tunic—not overly ornate like some of his court clothes, but something that made it clear he was not a commoner.

Was he starting to become proud of his status as a lord? He frowned at himself. His title had never meant much to him before, but now that he had lands and income to go with it, was he beginning to turn into one of the arrogant nobles he disliked? Holoran and Telani were both commoners, even if Holoran was a laborer and Telani came from one of the middle tier of merchant families. Telani's family looked down on Holoran because of his low status, so why should Geradin highlight the difference in classes by dressing like a lord?

He began to remove the tunic to replace it with something more plain, when he realized that he was making the same mistake he had made by refusing to take the Tests of Majority in order to protect Mek's feelings: pretending to be less than he was instead of using what he had to help his friends.

Telani's family considered Holoran beneath them? Let them choke on seeing that Holoran had a friend in the famous Lord Geradin, favored friend of King Aumekor. He pulled the tunic back on, then pulled it off again and replaced it with his most ornate court tunic, crimson with gold brocade. There was no way they could miss seeing him in this one.

After stopping off in the kitchen for a hurried meal, Geradin left the Keep and walked to one of the nearby shops to purchase a wedding gift. Gifts of money were seen as impugning the new husband's ability to provide for his family, so tradition said the wedding gifts should be items that a couple could use in their new home. But from those traditions had evolved, at least among those who could afford it, the practice of giving household items made of gold or silver. Thus the husband's honor was left intact, and if some of the gifts ended up being sold after the wedding, everyone agreed not to notice.

Geradin purchased a set of six silver bowls of descending sizes. That would allow Holoran and Telani to either sell all at once or to just sell one bowl when needed. The storekeeper complimented him on his choice, and enclosed the bowls in a handsome wooden case.

Supplied with a gift, Geradin made his way through the city to the home of Telani's family. The house was in a prosperous neighborhood, and seemed well-kept. Telani's father owned several trading caravans, and was obviously doing well for himself.

A servant met him at the door and asked his name, then escorted him to the banquet hall and announced, "Lord Geradin att'Balunor."

There were already over a hundred people crowded into the hall, which was noisy with conversation. Some of the nearer groups stilled at the announcement, and people looked toward Geradin as he walked down the steps into the hall. He handed the box with the gift to a servant, who whisked it away to place with the others.

He recognized some of the guests, merchants with whom he'd dealt in the past. They were probably friends or business associates of Telani's father, his caravans helping them trade with the neighboring kingdoms of Cirkepam, Tantaur, Cabeska, and Wellston. Geradin greeted those he knew and exchanged a few friendly words with them as he made his way through the crowd toward the head of the room.

The families of the bride and groom were clumped in opposite corners. Holoran was talking with some members of his family with his back toward Geradin. As Geradin went to greet him, Telani spotted him from her family group and called out, "Lord Geradin! I'm so glad you could come." Her voice sounded almost relieved.

Holoran turned and bowed to him. "Milord, you honor us with your presence."

Sure that all attention from those nearby was on him, Geradin tried to decide the best way to handle this. Should he return the formality, emphasizing his status as a member of the nobility in order to make the point that Holoran had a high connection? No, anyone with wit enough to recognize his name already knew how high the connection was.

Geradin laughed. "'Milord?' Is that how you greet all your friends?" He reached out and clasped the big man's hand. "I'm glad I could make it." Having made sure Telani's family and friends got the message that Holoran was his friend, he lowered his voice. "These must be your family. I would love to meet them all."

Having pointedly been introduced to Holoran's mother and father, brothers and sisters, uncles and aunts, nephews and nieces, and cousins of varying degrees, Geradin then went over to see Telani and her family.

Telani's father, Master Piraporil, bowed in greeting. "You do us great honor, Lord Geradin. We did not expect you."

Geradin nodded, acknowledging the bow. They did not expect him? They must not have believed that he considered Holoran a friend. "The honor is mine, Master Piraporil, to be able to attend the wedding of two such fine people as Holoran and your daughter. The King was most gracious in giving me permission to be excused from my duties as a High Protector so that I might come."

That was not exactly true: he'd told Mek he was coming, and

Mek's only reply had been "Don't break your ankles dancing with all the pretty girls. At least one of us needs to be able to walk."

After being introduced to Telani's family, Geradin asked Master Piraporil about his business, and where his caravans were at the moment, and what he thought of the political situation in Cirkepam, and whether, in his expert opinion, the Conclave of Monarchs would succeed in preventing a struggle over succession in that kingdom. The merchant became less stiff as the conversation went on, and seemed to be intelligent and knowledgeable. Geradin decided there was hope that eventually Telani's father would warm to Holoran and accept him as a worthy son-in-law.

The conversation was interrupted by the arrival of a priest from the Temple of Light. The assembled crowd grew quiet as he took his place at the front of the room. He wore the traditional white hooded cloak of the Priests of Light.

The priest gave the blessings of the Gods of Light to the crowd, then called Telani and Holoran to stand before him. They both looked happy. Telani was beautiful in what was obviously an expensive custom-made white wedding robe. Holoran's white robe was plain, but it, too, must have been made especially for him, as it was doubtful any of the robe-renters had one that would fit those broad shoulders so well.

Instead of beginning the ceremony, though, the priest said, "I was asked by Telani and Holoran to perform the ceremony of marriage. However, I am but a common priest, and there is someone here who ranks above me. It is, therefore, fitting that he should perform the ceremony."

Geradin felt a flash of confusion. The priest didn't mean him, did he? As far as he knew, he was the only member of the nobility here, which did technically outrank a common priest. And as a lord, he was legally capable of performing marriages for the commoners who owed him fealty, but neither Holoran nor Telani was one of his subjects. Besides, he didn't really know the proper forms.

The priest was not looking at him, however. Another white-hooded figure was coming slowly through the crowd, followed by whispers of astonishment. As the priest drew closer Geradin recognized him as Kogyrinem, High Priest of the Gods of Light. Kogyrinem rarely left the temple grounds. What was he doing at the wedding of two commoners? The murmurs of astonishment from the other wedding guests confirmed that this was an unexpected honor.

Kogyrinem spoke softly to Holoran and Telani, and they nodded their heads. The other priest moved aside and Kogyrinem took his place. With his right hand he clasped Telani's left, and with his left he clasped Holoran's right.

"Who is the man descended of Attol, God of Light, who loves a daughter of Beska?" High Priest Kogyrinem was not a native of Aud Sapeer, and his voice had lingering traces of his Pamidauran accent, but it was strong and clear.

"It is I, Holoran att'Wesemor."

"Who is the woman descended of Beska, God of Light, who loves a son of Attol?"

"It is I, Telani beh'Kala."

"Who are the children of Clanni, who love each other in the Light?"

Holoran and Telani in unison said, "We are."

"May Attol bless your union with his strength. May Beska bless your union with her love. May Clanni bless your union with her wisdom."

Kogyrinem moved Telani's and Holoran's hands together, and said, "The three Gods have joined you in the Light. May you always follow the Light."

"We follow the Light."

Kogyrinem let go of their hands, which now held each other. Holoran and Telani turned to the crowd and a cheer went up. They were married.

After congratulating the couple, Geradin mingled among the guests. He danced with several pretty girls, if not all of them, and he did not break even one of his ankles. But even though he was enjoying himself, he couldn't help feeling that something strange was going on, something he did not understand.

Why had High Priest Kogyrinem come to this wedding?

Chapter Eighteen

Aumekor

The routine noises of Nikufed's morning preparations brought Aumekor out of his dream. Still only half-wakened, he resisted the intrusion of reality and tried to restore the threads of his dream. He had been riding a horse into battle against a dragon about to eat a young woman in a silvery dress. After defeating the beast – the details of the battle were fuzzy, but his arms were the ones swinging his father's sword – he was the one who lifted the young woman onto his horse. He could remember her shy, wide-eyed glance as she thanked him for saving her life. And then…

Then the dream had ended, and there really was no use trying to get back into it.

As he came fully awake, the memory of using his arms and legs in the dream connected with reality, and excitement mixed with fear of disappointment. Today Allonna would try again to enchant his armor, this time under Selima's supervision. Even if it succeeded, the spell would not enable him to become the great warrior he was in his dreams, but just to walk under his own control would be freeing.

"It would make your life easier, wouldn't it?" he asked Nikufed, who had just finished laying out Aumekor's clothes for the day.

"What would make my life easier, Majesty?"

"Sorry, Kuf. I was mostly thinking aloud. It would be easier for you if I could walk about on my own, rather than having you push me in that chair."

Nikufed lifted Aumekor into the chair. "I hope you were not considering reducing my pay on that account. My creditors would be very disappointed."

Aumekor smiled. "Nothing breaks the heart so much as a creditor's tears. For their sakes, I shall not reduce your salary."

"Your Majesty is most gracious." Nikufed wheeled the chair toward the King's Baths. "And if you wish to go further and actually see grins of delight on their faces, you could merely double my salary. Purely for their sakes, of course."

"Of course." Aumekor exaggerated a sigh. "I fear, however, that Lord Regent Kindul controls the purse strings of the kingdom, and he does not rejoice in the smiles of creditors."

"But the Lord Regent is away—a fact which of itself brings smiles to the faces of many."

Aumekor smiled at that for Nikufed's benefit. The Lord Regent had left to attend the Conclave of Monarchs fifteen days ago. Aumekor had not confided to anyone but Selima his fear that Kindul would use the Conclave to confirm the regency as permanent, so he pretended to be happy about Kindul's absence. In the past he would have talked to Geradin about it, but his friend's new position as a High Protector made other responsibilities his concern.

Still, with Kindul away it might be possible for Aumekor to persuade the Regency Council on some minor matters. As he lay in the steaming bath, his head held steady by Nikufed, Aumekor tried to devise an agenda for the day's Council meeting. But his thoughts kept drifting to the suit of armor. Would he stand and walk this afternoon?

Distracted by such thoughts, Aumekor passed the rest of the morning unable to focus on the affairs of state. His hope of wringing some minor concession from his opponents on the Council was not fulfilled, but that did not matter. Playing the political games seemed unimportant compared to the possibility of having real control over his own body.

After the Council meeting, Nikufed wheeled him back to his chambers to wait for Allonna, Selima and Master Ramil. He knew they were making their preparations, but wished he could do something to speed the process. If only there were something he could do other than merely wait, but his role in all this was passive.

Except that it wasn't. He would have an active part once the spell was finished—and he could begin to prepare for that now.

"Kuf, put the little knight on the floor over there and give me the glove."

After taking the tiny suit of armor from its box, Nikufed walked over and fitted the controlling gauntlet onto Aumekor's right hand. Wiggling his index and middle fingers within the chainmail, Aumekor made the miniature knight march across the fitted stones of the floor. The finger-length sword in its hand flashed right and left to the rhythm of its steps.

What would it be like to be inside the armor, rather than watching from outside? Aumekor closed his eyes and tried to imagine himself surrounded by the metal. All he would have to do was move his fingers, and the metal of the suit would press against his legs, moving them forward. His left arm would hold a sword and it would swing back and forth cutting down everything before him. In his mind he saw the dragon from his dream again, its slate-gray scales glistening as it charged across the grassy hillside toward the young woman in the silver dress. He would save—

"Your Majesty?"

Nikufed's voice startled Aumekor back to reality. "Yes?"

"I think the bedpost wishes to surrender."

The little knight was halfway across the room, its sword bumping against the carved wood bedpost. Aumekor stopped wriggling his fingers, and the little knight stood motionless, sword ready to strike again.

Aumekor smiled faintly. "A good thing, too, for I was about to render it to kindling." In fact, the sword's blade was so dull he doubted it had even scratched the wood.

There was a knock at the door. One of the Protectors poked his head in. "Your Majesty, Omnimancer Selima is here, accompanied by Lord Geradin and others."

Finally. "Show them in, Protector."

"Give us moment, Protector," countermanded Nikufed. He walked over to Aumekor, removed the controlling gauntlet from his hand, and straightened him in his chair. Nikufed hurried to the bedpost, scooped up the little knight, and placed it back in its box. He nodded to the Protector. "Proceed."

The little details that Nikufed always handled for him gave Aumekor sudden doubts about the armor idea. What good would it do to just walk in a straight line like the little knight? Would he be able to sit down in the armor? If he fell over, would he be able to get up? Or would his armor just thrash about as it tried to keep walking while horizontal?

Selima entered the room, followed by Geradin and Allonna. Master Ramil, assisted by two servants, carried the suit of armor on its wooden stand into the room. On seeing the burnished steel and gold, Aumekor again was touched by the devotion the armormaster had shown in crafting the armor for him through the years, even when he could not use it.

"Let's hope this goes more smoothly than last time," said Geradin with a wry smile as he walked over to stand beside Aumekor's chair.

"It will," Selima and Allonna said simultaneously.

The reminder of the failed attempt brought back the doubts Aumekor had been feeling moments before. Had Selima and Allonna thought through all the implications? Perhaps more discussion was needed before they expended so much magical power on such a dubious project.

"Perhaps we should—" he began, but then hesitated. These people had gone to great efforts, not because it was their duty to serve him as king or Heir of the Line, but because they cared about him. Now was not the time to express doubts. He searched for a new way to end the sentence he'd begun, and decided on a gentle tease. "—check the room for invisible intruders before we proceed?"

Master Ramil chuckled. "I won't be making that mistake again."

The sound of Geradin's sword exiting its sheath startled Aumekor, and he tilted his head to look at his friend.

Geradin merely held the sword up so all could see it glowed blue, not yellow. "The Heir of the Line is not in danger," said Geradin. His voice was solemn and formal, but his mouth was resisting a grin.

"We are ready, Your Majesty." Selima put an encouraging hand on Allonna's shoulder. Allonna's hands were at her side, clenching her dress.

There being no reason to delay further, Aumekor smiled and said, "Proceed."

As she had before her first attempt, Allonna took the right gauntlet from the suit of armor and placed it on the floor. She glanced at Selima, who nodded. Allonna took three paces back, then stood staring at the armor with a frown of concentration.

The room was silent. Nobody moved. After a few moments, Aumekor realized he was holding his breath, and let it out quietly.

Throughout his life, Aumekor had seen Selima cast more spells than he could remember. Even for small enchantments, she always seemed to have at least a hand gesture or a mumbled word to indicate that she was performing magic. And the larger the spell, the more intricate the signs of its casting would be. The other mancers he had seen all did the same—even Allonna had done so when casting the defensive ward around him during the mistaken alert over the nonexistent intruder.

But Allonna remained still as stone. Aumekor felt almost disappointed. Grand magics were being wielded on his behalf, and he couldn't see anything happening.

Did Selima and the other mancers actually need the gestures and mutterings in order to cast a spell or were those purely for show? He would have to ask Selima about that later.

Selima took a small, sharp breath. She often did that when she was surprised. She appeared to be looking into the air between Allonna and the suit of armor, as if examining the flows of power. But she made no attempt to stop Allonna.

After a short period of tense apparent uneventfulness, Allonna took another step back, let out a long breath, and said, "I think that should work."

Selima looked over at Master Ramil. "Could you see what she did?"

He shook his head. "Parts, only. But even if I had seen it all, the flows...I could not reproduce them."

Nodding, Selima said, "I could see it all, but I could not understand some of it. And you are right about the flows." She turned to Allonna. "How do you feel? Drained? There wasn't any pain, was there?"

"No, I'm a bit tired is all, because it took a lot longer than the little knights, and I haven't ever handled that much power for that long, so I was worried that perhaps I was wrong about whether I could do it."

As Selima began complimenting Allonna on how well she had done, Aumekor grew impatient. The intricacies of the spell might be very interesting to those who could actually see the flows of power, but not to him. "Did it *work*?"

Selima shot him a frown that told him he was being rude, so he immediately added, "Miss Allonna, I am grateful for your efforts on my behalf, whatever the outcome. But I am very curious as to what that outcome is."

Allonna's eyes opened wide. "Of course, Your Majesty." She stepped quickly over to the gauntlet, picked it up, and brought it toward him. Master Ramil motioned to the servants to help him move the armor next to Aumekor.

"Wait!" Aumekor tried to make his voice authoritative to hide the uncertainty he felt.

Allonna halted, as did Master Ramil and the servants. Everyone looked toward Aumekor.

"Before I actually wear the armor, shouldn't I make sure I know how to control it? Perhaps make it walk around like the little knight, without me in it?"

"It's very simple, Your Majesty," said Allonna. She looked over at Geradin, who nodded at her. "Ger—Lord Geradin had some suggestions on how we could give you more control than you have over the little knight, and we tested them on another little knight." Her cheeks flushed. "I guess we should have given you that one to practice with, Your Majesty, and I'm sorry I didn't think of that, but I was concentrating on how I was going to cast the spell on the larger suit of armor, and so I stopped thinking about the small ones." As she spoke, her left hand went to her side and began twisting a handful of her skirt.

He was not the only one who was nervous, Aumekor realized. "No need to apologize; I understand. Please continue."

She looked down at the gauntlet, shifted to hold it into her left hand, then raised her right hand. "The biggest change is you don't have to keep wiggling your fingers the whole time in order to walk." She bent her index and middle fingers for a moment, then straightened them. "That will start you walking. When you want to stop, just repeat the motion."

That was definitely an improvement. In playing with the little knight, Aumekor's fingers usually got tired within a short while. He nodded at her and said, "Go on."

"To turn to the left, hold your index finger down. To turn to the right, hold your middle finger down."

He smiled. "I was wondering how I would turn."

Under Allonna's direction, he learned the various signals that allowed him to sit, stand, move his arms, walk slowly or quickly—even run, although there wasn't much space for that in the room—and the rest of the motions she had added to the armor.

When she ran out of things to tell him, Aumekor asked, "And how do I draw my sword?"

Allonna glanced at Geradin, who answered him in a soft

voice. "You won't be drawing your sword, Your Majesty."

"I won't?" He tried to hide his disappointment, but his voice betrayed his feelings.

"The rudimentary control this gives you is not sufficient for even the most basic swordsmanship. I discussed this with the other High Protectors, and we have agreed that it is not a good idea." Geradin's voice was still soft, but he spoke with an air of finality.

Even though he knew Geradin was merely trying to protect him, Aumekor persisted. "Why? Surely even a slight ability to wave a sword around is better than nothing."

Geradin pressed his lips together before answering. "Not necessarily." He frowned at Aumekor as if trying to stop him from pressing the subject.

"Why not?"

After letting out a long breath, Geradin said, "Because if you were in danger you might be tempted to draw your sword and fight instead of getting yourself to safety."

Aumekor started to object that he would not act so rashly, but then realized Geradin knew him well enough that the protest was futile. "Very well. No swordplay." He looked back to Allonna. "Anything else I should know?"

She shook her head. "I think that's all."

"Then I guess it's time to try it."

Nikufed stepped to Allonna and held his hand out to take the gauntlet. "If I may, Miss Allonna?" She handed it to him. He came to Aumekor and gently slipped it onto his hand.

The servants and Master Ramil stepped back from the suit of armor.

Taking a deep breath, Aumekor bent his index and middle fingers to start the suit of armor walking.

Nothing happened. The spell must have failed somehow. Aumekor said, "It didn't—"

Allonna interrupted him. "Oh, I forgot to tell you about the activation, which is something I thought of since there will be times when you want to move your fingers without having the suit of armor react, and so you need to touch your thumb and middle finger together like this to activate the armor, and then if you repeat the gesture, it will ignore your signals until you activate it again. I'm sorry, I forgot about that."

"Like this?" He brought the thumb and middle finger together, then did the gesture to start walking.

The suit of armor lurched forward, dragging the wooden base of the armor stand behind it. Its legs bending only slightly at the knees, it staggered two small paces, then began to topple forward. Aumekor tried to signal it to stop walking. Master Ramil sprang forward to catch the armor, but only succeeded in slowing its fall. The armor clanged to the floor. The helmet came off and rolled, finally stopping about a pace away from the rest of the armor.

The silence in the room was complete until two Protectors burst in through the door to see what had happened.

Unable to think of anything else to do, Aumekor chuckled. "It's a good thing my head wasn't inside that helmet."

That broke the tension sufficiently that others began laughing as well. But Allonna's cheeks turned bright red, and she did not join in the laughter.

Neither did Geradin. Instead he walked over to the suit of armor and squatted down to look at it. He stood back up after a few moments, as the laughter quieted. "I think your spell worked fine, Miss Allonna. But a suit of armor on a stand can't walk very well because the stand doesn't bend in the right places. That's not your fault." He turned to Aumekor. "The armor is too small for me, but perhaps we can find someone else who can fit in it while you test it."

"No," Aumekor said. "I will wear it. I trust there are enough people here to catch me if I start to fall."

"Are you sure that's—"

"I will wear it." Aumekor put all the authority he could behind the words, and Geradin acquiesced.

It took a short while for Nikufed and Master Ramil, working together, to dress him in the armor. When the pulling and tightening was over, they stepped back from him slightly. Geradin stood beside him, and two more protectors waited close by.

"I'm standing up," Aumekor said when he realized nobody was holding him.

"Yes," said Geradin. "Do you want to try walking?"

Aumekor moved his fingers to activate the armor. He took a deep breath, then signaled it to start walking. His right leg took a step forward. Then his left moved forward. Right. Left. Right. Left.

He was unable to resist the urge to grin.

Thought he was still surrounded by people, they were not holding him up. For the first time in his life, he was the one in control of his own movements. He stopped, then pressed down with his index finger and the armor shuffled his feet to turn him until he faced Allonna.

"Thank you, Omnimancer Allonna." She might technically still be an apprentice, but she deserved the title.

Again Allonna's cheeks grew red, but this time a broad smile lit up her face.

Chapter Nineteen

Geradin

Geradin watched Mek pace the Council Room, turn, and pace back. Over the past four days Mek had worn the armor almost constantly. He might even have slept in it if Nikufed hadn't insisted on removing it. Not that Geradin wasn't happy to see his best friend able to walk, but the almost continuous movement was such a contrast to Mek's former condition that it was difficult to concentrate on what he was saying.

When Mek started making wild gestures with his left arm, Geradin decided that was too much. "You're going to make me dizzy with all that walking around. Can't you just sit down for a few heartbeats so I can think about what you're saying instead of wondering whether you'll topple?"

Mek walked over to his chair, turned, and sat. His face grinned out at Geradin from under the raised visor of the helm. "I thought it might work like that."

"Work like what?" They had been discussing Lady Uwixa's message about her arrival with the Lord Regent in Cirkepam. Or rather, Mek had been talking about it and Geradin had been trying to listen, but this seemed off the subject.

"You're so used to me sitting passively in this chair that to have me moving about is disconcerting. If Kindul were here, I'd disconcert him out of his boots."

"You mean you were *trying* to have that effect?"

Me grinned. "I'll have to do it at the next Council meeting. Walk about, stand directly behind recalcitrant Council members so they wonder what I'm doing, that sort of thing."

Shaking his head, Geradin smiled. "You're going to wear us all out."

"Isn't it amazing? I could walk all day without getting tired."

Remembering Swordmaster Ytanor's stamina training, Geradin said, "Perhaps I should ask Allonna to enchant my armor, just so I can keep up with you."

Mek looked pensive. "That might be a good idea. Image an army that could march for days without stopping."

"Outfitting an entire army with suits of plate armor, even unenchanted plate armor, just isn't possible. Too expensive."

"Well, perhaps not an entire army. But to have a group of soldiers capable of going much farther on foot than the enemy anticipates could have some tactical value."

"True," said Geradin. Being able to move his body obviously hadn't made Mek's mind any less nimble. "I'll talk to the other High Protectors about the possibility."

"Good. But getting back to Uwixa, I think she deliberately left three words out of her message—rather, one word is missing three times. That cannot be coincidence."

"What word?"

"She refers to Lord Kindul three times. Not Lord *Regent* Kindul. Lord Kindul."

It did sound a little strange to Geradin, but not beyond the bounds of court protocol. "He is a noble, so it's proper to refer to him as such."

"Yes, but Lady Uwixa is unfailing in her etiquette and always calls him 'Lord Regent Kindul.' Or she did until this message."

"So what do you think it means?"

"I'm not sure. Since the Lord Regent should be acting on my behalf, perhaps it means she thinks he's acting for himself rather than for me."

"But that's hardly news, is it?"

Mek let out an exasperated puff of air. "You're right, there's no reason to even send such a message, for she knows that I know Kindul is working for his own ambition."

"Perhaps it means Kindul has given up on his idea of being made permanent regent. After all, she's taken 'regent' out of his title." Geradin was joking when he said it, but then a darker interpretation came to mind.

"He's going to try to become king in his own right." Mek had obviously come to the same conclusion as Geradin. "He can't seriously believe that would work. The Conclave is made up of other monarchs, and I can't think any of them would like the idea of removing a king from his throne. And he's not the Heir of the Line of Orcan, so how dare he think of claiming Orcan's throne?"

"Perhaps we should ask Selima her thoughts." It occurred to Geradin that Selima often used to stay after the Council meetings to talk with Aumekor alone, but that she hadn't done so for some time. "Why didn't she stay after the meeting? You haven't had an argument with her, have you?"

"No, it's nothing like that. Training Allonna is more important than the internal politics of Aud Sapeer."

"She's known Kindul since before we were born. She would know whether this is something he might do."

"True." Mek stood up, a feat which still amazed Geradin every time he saw it. "Go find her and meet me back in my chambers to discuss this."

◆ ◆ ◆

Geradin made his way through the Inner Keep to Selima's study. He was surprised to find Allonna standing outside the door. "Miss Allonna," he said, nodding his head to acknowledge her.

"Milord." She bowed.

Why did he feel awkward meeting her like this? While preparing for the spell on Mek's armor, they had exchanged ideas easily, each of them building on what the other had proposed. But now that the project was finished, there really wasn't any reason for them to talk unless they happened to meet. And now that they had met, what did they have to talk about? "Is Omnimancer Selima in there?"

"Yes, but she has a visitor." Allonna's eyes almost glowed with excitement.

"Really? Who?"

"The High Priest of the Gods of Light." She pronounced the title as if it were a blessing.

"High Priest Kogyrinem is here, now?" This was the second time in five days that Kogyrinem had not only left the temple, but actually been in the same building as Geradin. "What does he want with Selima?"

Allonna shrugged. "Selima told me to wait outside while they spoke, but as I was leaving, do you know what he said to me? 'Go with the Light, Miss Allonna.' He said that to me."

"He says that to…" Geradin's brain caught up to his mouth before he could finish the sentence but it was too late.

"…to everybody?" Allonna finished for him. "Is that what you were going to say?"

"I didn't mean—"

"Yes, I'm sure it's all very commonplace to you, Lord Geradin, being raised in a palace and having lords and ladies and kings and high priests to converse with, but in Glicken, we didn't even have a priest who lived in the village—twice each season they would come to visit, and they would perform marriages for those who were waiting, bless the graves of the newly dead, and collect our deathday offerings to be taken and burned at the temple on the appropriate days, and I don't remember ever seeing the same priest more than once, and they never stayed more than one day, so I've never really had much interaction with them." Her eyes filled with tears. "So when the High Priest of the Gods of Light not only tells me to go with the Light, but knows *my name*, that means a great deal more to me than one like you could possibly understand." She turned her back on him.

Not sure what to say, Geradin remained silent.

The door opened and Selima poked her head out. "Allonna, can you go— Oh, you're already here, Geradin. Good. Can I speak with you a moment?" She return to the room before Geradin had a chance to answer.

He looked at the back of Allonna's head, whispered, "Sorry," and went into Selima's study.

Chapter Twenty

Allonna

Allonna frowned at the closed door of Selima's study. Whatever was happening behind those stout wood panels must be of great importance—the High Priest of the Gods of Light wouldn't come here just for a social visit with Royal Omnimancer Selima and then want to have a gossip with High Protector Geradin, best friend to King Aumekor. No, it must be a matter of some urgency, but she was left to stand in the hallway like a small child sent to bed to avoid disturbing the adults.

Was her opinion worth nothing? She might not be as knowledgeable or experienced as the High Priest and Selima, but she was older than Geradin. And even if she was only an apprentice, had not the king himself called her "Omnimancer Allonna"? At least the king respected her.

How was she supposed to learn to be a Royal Omnimancer if she couldn't hear what Selima was doing? If only she could hear what was being said in that room, but to press her ear against the door would make her look childish if she were caught. Omnimancers shouldn't be seen eavesdropping in doorways.

Surely omnimancers had better ways to eavesdrop, magical ways. She might not know how to do it, but perhaps her umbrit would. She allowed a small amount of power to flow from her, willing herself to be able to hear what was being said behind the door. She felt the stream of power separate into tendrils, and those tendrils began to penetrate the wood of the door.

She heard Selima's voice, but it didn't seem to be coming from the room. Instead, it came from behind her. "Just what do you think you are doing, Apprentice?"

Allonna cut of the stream of magic and whirled around to see nobody there. "Omnimancer Selima?"

"You didn't really think you could eavesdrop undetected through an *omnimancer's* door, did you, Apprentice?"

The voice seemed to come from her right, but when Allonna turned her head toward it, the sound came from her left. "I'm sorry. I was too curious."

"Every apprentice tries this at some point. I tried it on Jiltunok when I was his apprentice. His voice behind startled me so much I tripped over my own feet, fell into the door of his study, knocking it open so I could sprawl on his floor like a doormat."

The image of the great Selima blundering into her master's study almost made Allonna laugh, and she felt her panic at being caught fade. "You aren't angry with me?"

"I can only hope that you have not fared as poorly as I did."

Allonna frowned. Selima's response didn't quite make sense. "I apologize for interrupting your meeting. I will not attempt to eavesdrop again."

"One day, you will have an apprentice, and you will create special wards against eavesdropping, like this one. Try not to scare the poor child too much."

It was not really Selima speaking to her, Allonna realized. These were messages Selima had woven into the ward against eavesdropping. Since they did not refer to Allonna by name, the spell might even have been cast long ago.

Certainly the ward would have alerted Selima that someone was trying to eavesdrop, but the messages in the ward seemed almost playful, rather than scolding. The fact that Selima had not come out of the room to punish her for what she had done gave Allonna a nearly giddy sense of relief.

Focusing her thoughts on the door and wall before her, she tried to sense the ward that had been placed around Selima's study. At first she could detect nothing, then suddenly it was as if the rest of her surroundings dimmed and she saw layer upon layer of shimmering gossamer inside the stone of the wall and the wood of the door. It was not just one spell, but dozens. She recalled Selima's explanation of how spells could be built up in layers, so that if someone tried to undo one it would set off the alarm of another. Some of these spells might ward against eavesdropping, others might provide different forms of protection, and still more might be there for the sole purpose of guarding the other spells. Had she wanted to, Allonna knew she had the ability to use her burst to undo every one of those spells, but it would take time to do that, and it couldn't be done without sounding the alarm. It was, she decided, a clever use of mancy to counter the ability of more powerful mancers to undo spells.

Again she was startled by a voice from behind her, this time a man's. "Are you quite all right, Miss Allonna?"

Her view of the webs of magic faded and the rest of the world seemed to brighten. Allonna turned to see the king's manservant standing there. "Yes, I'm fine, thank you..." She struggled to remember the man's name. Niku-something.

"Have you seen Lord Geradin or Lady Selima?"

She pointed to the door. "They're meeting with the High Priest of the Gods of Light."

"Ah, that explains it."

"Explains what?"

"His Majesty sent Lord Geradin to get Lady Selima in order to discuss something, and then sent me to find both of them. There are few people capable of delaying Lord Geradin and Lady Selima from seeing His Majesty. The High Priest is one of them."

"It must be something very urgent." Perhaps this servant could tell her something. "Do you know what it is about?"

"It is not my place to say." His face showed no emotion as he spoke.

"Of course."

"I want to thank you for enchanting that armor for His Majesty. I'm sure there's no harm in telling you that he was putting it to good use when I left him pacing back and forth across his chambers."

She felt a small fire of pride inside. She had done something important, something that would be remembered. Perhaps one day the storytellers would spin tales about the Enchanted Armor of Aumekor. "Thank you," she said.

"I had best return to His Majesty and inform him of the reason for Lord Geradin and Lady Selima's delay, before he decides to brave the stairs and come look for them himself. Good day, Miss Allonna." He turned to leave.

"Brave the stairs?"

He turned back. "Yesterday His Majesty tried to go down some stairs—just a short staircase, fortunately."

Allonna gasped. "He didn't fall, did he? It's all my fault because I didn't think about stairs."

"No, he didn't fall, although he hit the wall at the end of the stairwell. The armor kept him upright, but it started going faster and faster down the steps, even though he signaled it to stop walking."

After thinking a few moments, Allonna said, "Going down stairs must make the armor seem like it's falling forward, so it tries to keep upright by bringing the other foot forward."

"That was His Majesty's speculation. Do not concern yourself, though. He said the armor will do fine for now, and that he is confident you would be able to find a way to overcome the problem and enchant the armor again once you had fully recovered your powers."

"Fully recovered my powers? But I'm fine." Though she understood that some mancers needed time to replenish their store of power, she had never felt such a need, and the idea did not seem natural to her. "I can do it right now." She began walking toward the king's chambers.

"Are you sure that's wise, Miss Allonna?" The servant trailed her along the corridor. "Perhaps we should wait for Lady Selima?"

Allonna halted. She couldn't cast the spell to enchant the armor again without Selima there to prevent the alarms from sounding, and who knew how long Selima would be talking with the High Priest and Geradin in her study—the study that was surrounded by *layered* spells. Perhaps layering spells would not work for this, but there would be no harm in trying. She would only use a low level of power so as to avoid setting off the alarms.

When they arrived at King Aumekor's chambers, the servant told her to wait outside, then went through the door one of the Protectors on guard had opened for him.

Allonna smoothed the front of her skirt. This was the first time she would see the king without either Selima or Geradin there. Suddenly she felt very alone. The only support she had was from a servant whose name she couldn't even remember.

The door opened again, and a Protector from inside said, "His Majesty will see you now."

Consciously keeping her hands away from her sides so she wouldn't clutch her skirt, Allonna walked into the room. King Aumekor was standing off to the right in his armor, so she approached to a respectful distance and bowed.

"Omnimancer Allonna, it is a pleasure to see you again so soon. Nikufed tells me you may be able to fix the problem of the stairs without too much trouble?"

Nikufed—that was his name. She promised herself she would not forget it again. "It may be possible, Your Majesty, because I was thinking another spell laid on top of the previous one may be all that is needed, and if so there is no need to remove the prior spell and do the enchantment again."

The king nodded. "Are you ready now?"

"Yes, Your Majesty." She hoped she was.

"Then proceed." He raised an eyebrow. "You wouldn't be able to add on some swordsmanship while you're at it, could you?"

She did not know if that was possible, and even if it was, Geradin had said the High Protectors had decided against it. "I —"

"I am only jesting. Please feel free to frown disapprovingly at me when I do that. That's how Selima usually reacts."

Unsure of how the king expected her to respond to such banter, Allonna decided it was best to simply proceed with the spell. She concentrated on the armor and felt a great relief as the rest of the world seemed to dim and quiet around her. The enchantment in the armor did not look like gossamer; rather, it seemed as if the armor itself were made of green fire. As she looked carefully, she could barely see other, far weaker spells on the various pieces of armor. Those must be the ferromancy spells cast by Master Ramil as he forged the armor, spells to make the metal harder or better able to absorb blows.

Focusing her mind on her task, she imagined the armor being able to recognize that it was going down a step, and that it would bend whichever leg was behind in order to keep the armor upright rather than tilt forward. When she had the concept fully-formed in her mind, she let a stream of power out toward the armor. Now that she knew about it, she could sense the umbrit form beside her, guiding her power, splitting it into smaller streams that wrapped around the armor. Though her power always seemed to be a bluish-white when it left her, the umbrit changed the colors of individual streams as they passed.

Without knowing how she knew, she knew she was done with the spell and stopped the flow of power. The glow of the spells faded and the room around her came back into focus. "I think that will do, Your Majesty."

"Shall we try it?"

The eagerness in his voice reminded her of her brother Pag whenever he'd learned a new smithing technique. She felt suddenly guilty for not missing her brother enough. There had just been so much new here—and Selima had kept her so busy training—that she had not spent much time thinking of her family. Even now she could not spare time to reminisce. "If you are ready, Your Majesty."

Two Protectors led the way and two more walked right behind the king. Allonna and Nikufed followed the procession to the nearest stairway, which consisted of ten steps down to a landing, from which more steps descended to the right.

King Aumekor's arm came up somewhat awkwardly and knocked the visor of his helmet down to cover his face. "Just in case," he said.

With two protectors waiting down on the landing to catch him, and one on either side, the king took a step forward onto the first step and stopped.

"Is something wrong?" Allonna asked.

"No, I wanted to see if I could stop. Last time, I couldn't. Now, to see if I can take several steps in succession." He moved down the stairs at a stately pace, reached the landing and stopped. He turned to face up the stairs and opened the visor of his helmet, revealing a wide grin. "It appears you have succeeded again, Omnimancer Allonna." He took a step forward, the toe of his armor clanged as it hit the front of the first step, and he wobbled. Four pairs of arms reached out to stop him from falling.

"Oh, no," said Allonna. "I forgot about going up."

Chapter Twenty-One

Geradin

High Priest Kogyrinem rose from his seat when Geradin entered.

Geradin bowed. "Your Grace, I am honored to see you again so soon."

Acknowledging the greeting with a nod, Kogyrinem said, "Lord Geradin, I came here to consult with Lady Selima, and now I have some questions to ask you, if I may."

"Does this have something to do with why you were at Holoran and Telani's wedding?"

"It does. Sit, please." Kogyrinem gestured toward one of the chairs. Geradin sat down as Selima walked around her desk to sit in her own chair.

Kogyrinem stared directly into Geradin's eyes for a long moment. Puzzled as to what this meeting was about, Geradin started wondering if he had done something wrong. He had upset Allonna, but it couldn't be that.

Finally Kogyrinem spoke. "I need you to tell me about this Holoran. Is it true you met at the Tests of Majority?"

Geradin frowned. "We met that morning." This was about Holoran?

"Is he as strong as he looks?" asked the High Priest.

"I've never seen anyone with such strength." The course of the conversation puzzled Geradin.

Kogyrinem glanced at Selima, then looked back at Geradin.

"Now, think carefully on this. I know you consider him stronger than anyone else you know. Is this difference merely a matter of degree, or is his strength of a different magnitude?"

"I have seen him easily carry double a load that would be difficult for me. When we arm-wrestled, I was unable to even move his arm with all my strength, and was powerless to resist him when he moved."

Leaning forward, Kogyrinem asked, "You think it possible that he is the strongest man in all the world?"

"It's possible."

Kogyrinem turned to Selima. "It is it too much to be ordinary coincidence. It is prophetic coincidence."

"I was hoping against it," she said. "It is far too soon. We need another generation at least."

"Would you mind telling what you are talking about?" Geradin looked back and forth between the other two. "If it please Your Grace and milady," he added in a more respectful tone.

Selima looked at the High Priest. He nodded, so she began to explain. "There is a prophecy about those who will go forth in the company of the Heir in order to confront the Dark Priestess. One line of that prophecy says, The strongest of all men and..." Selima took a deep breath. "...the weakest. And now we find that there's a tremendously strong man who was born on the very same day as Aumekor. When it comes to the fulfillment of prophecy, coincidences like that—"

"It can't be Aumekor," Geradin said. "You may be experts at interpreting prophecy, but perhaps you're so caught up in prophecies that you try to force events to fit their words. You see that Aumekor is weak, and so you think he might fit your prophecies as the weakest man. You see that Holoran is strong, so you try to fit him into your prophecies as the strongest man. But here's a question for you: who's the oldest man in the world?"

Kogyrinem frowned. "I suppose it would be either Omnimancer Istubik or Omnimancer Pel."

"It's Pel," said Selima. "What is the meaning of this, Geradin?" Her glare told Geradin he had not been showing the proper respect to the High Priest.

Geradin looked back at her innocently. "So when Omnimancer Pel dies, there will no longer be an oldest man in the world, right?"

"Don't be absurd," said Selima. "Istubik would—Oh. Of course." She laughed. "Geradin is right: we are the ones who are absurd. Before Holoran, somebody was the strongest man in the world, and after him someone else will be."

High Priest Kogyrinem frowned. "But still, the coincidence—"

"—is not as great as you think," said Geradin. "Holoran may have been born on Midsummer Day, but he is a good four or five years older than Aumekor and me."

"Perhaps I have spent too long among the prophecies," said the High Priest. "When I was young, I hoped I would live to see the Heir of the Line confront the Dark Priestess. Now my greatest fear is that I will live to see the confrontation come when the Heir of the Line is weak. I mean no offense to King Aumekor, but defeating the Dark Priestess will take strength he does not have. I thought Aumekor's father was the one—Ordil was a warrior of great skill and power. In fact, he came to me in the temple the day before he died, and told me that after his son was born, he planned to gather the armies of the Free Kingdoms, march to the City of the Dark God, and kill the Dark Priestess."

"You never told me that," said Selima.

"I never told anyone. He wanted to ask me whether the prophecies supported his plan. I knew of nothing in the prophecies that could not apply to him, so I told him they did. And he was killed the next day. May the Light forgive me, the very next day." He leaned forward, placing his elbows on his knees and covering his eyes with his palms.

"It was not your fault," said Selima.

"Of course not," said Geradin. "How could it be? Veratur

did not turn traitor overnight. The Dark Priestess's plan was already in place before King Ordil talked to you."

Kogyrinem looked up and smiled sadly. "Prophecy is like a living creature, a thinking being. I tried to force it to happen before its time, and so it killed Ordil to prevent him from attempting to fulfill it."

Geradin wanted to say that was nonsense—the blame for King Ordil's death lay with Veratur and the Dark Priestess. But he glanced at Selima to see her reaction, and she looked him in the eye and gave a slight shake of her head. Best to just let it pass, she seemed to be saying.

Perhaps it would be a good time to change the subject. "Your Grace, King Aumekor sent me to ask Omnimancer Selima to advise him on something, but since you are here, possibly you could offer your insight as well."

Kogyrinem straightened in his chair. "What is this other matter?"

Geradin quickly explained about Lady Uwixa's note, the three missing words, and the possible interpretation that Kindul was trying to usurp the kingdom. "Can you think of another, more reasonable explanation? Lord Regent Kindul is ambitious, but can he believe the other monarchs would accede to removing Aumekor from the throne?"

"Making the regency permanent I could understand," said Selima, "but Kindul is a realist. He knows that the other monarchs would not want to set a precedent that allowed a Conclave to remove someone from the throne. And despite his ambition, I don't believe he would do something he thought was against the interests of Aud Sapeer."

"There is a possibility," said Kogyrinem. "Sometimes we have a priest who presents certain difficulties for the other priests in his area. Understand, he is not evil, just difficult, and so removing him from the priesthood is not something we would do. We do not punish him, we promote him to a position that sounds impressive but offers limited opportunity for meddling in the affairs of other priests."

"Are you saying we should promote Lord Regent Kindul to something to keep him from causing trouble?" Geradin couldn't think of any position above Lord Regent, other than king.

"No. You must understand the relationship between the sixteen free Kingdoms. Because the line of Orcan rules Aud Sapeer, and the Heir to the Line is the only one who can defeat the Dark Priestess, that puts this kingdom in a position of primacy among the Free Kingdoms. That's why the other kingdoms send talented warriors, like your father, to be Protectors of the Line. By the terms of treaties signed in the days of King Orcan, troops under the flag of Aud Sapeer can enter any kingdom without asking permission first. That's why the Barrier Guard is always commanded by men of Aud Sapeer. Though we haven't done this in recent years, there were times when the army of Aud Sapeer freely gave protection throughout the Free Kingdoms to our own trade caravans, while charging other trade caravans for that same protection. We are not the largest kingdom, nor the richest, but we are the most powerful, and that causes some envy from the other monarchs.

"And that gives Kindul an opening. Having the Heir of the Line of Orcan as king gives Aud Sapeer an advantage over other kingdoms. But what if the Heir of the Line were 'promoted': given a fancy title such as Overseer of the Free Kingdoms and charged only with protecting the kingdoms against the forces of the Dark Priestess? Kindul could suggest this as a way to lessen the burden on the Heir, so he does not have to deal with the ordinary matters of running a kingdom. The Heir would belong to all kingdoms, not just one. And who better to take over as the new king of Aud Sapeer than the man who has been leading it for the past sixteen years? In return, Kindul could promise the other monarchs that he would relinquish the right to send Aud Sapeer troops into other kingdoms. And they could all ensure that the position of Overseer had little power to do anything to interfere in their kingdoms."

High Priest Kogyrinem shrugged. "Now, I cannot know that this is what Kindul has in mind. But it's what I would do if I wanted to become king of Aud Sapeer."

Geradin jumped up from his chair. "Kindul must be stopped!"

Slowly, Selima stood as well. "We don't know what Kindul plans, but I fear you may be right. Interference with the Heir of the Line's proper inheritance cannot be tolerated. We must speak with Aumekor and decide what to do."

Nodding his head, High Priest Kogyrinem rose from his seat.

As they exited Selima's study, she said, "Where has that girl gone off to?"

Geradin looked around, and there was no sign of Allonna. "I may have offended her."

Selima merely shook her head.

The three of them proceeded toward Mek's chambers. To Geradin's surprise, they encountered Mek and four Protectors on a landing of the stairway closest to Mek's chambers.

"We were just coming to see you, Your Majesty," said Selima.

"Thank you. I will be happy to see you in my chambers in just a moment, Lady Selima, High Priest Kogyrinem." Raising his voice, he said, "We will have to fix upstairs later, Omnimancer Allonna." Then, to the Protectors around him, he said, "If you would be so good as to carry me up the stairs?"

Allonna was here? Geradin looked up the stairs to see her at the top. What was she doing? What did Mek mean by "fix upstairs"?

As Mek was lifted up by the Protectors, Kogyrinem shook his head and said, "It is truly a wonder to see him standing like that."

Once the entire group, Allonna included, had returned to Mek's chambers, Kogyrinem explained his speculation about Kindul's plan.

Mek's response was immediate and decisive: "I have no choice but to go to the Conclave of Monarchs myself."

Chapter Twenty-Two

Aumekor

Two beats of stunned silence followed Aumekor's announcement. He refrained from smiling—he could not allow them to treat this as a joke.

Geradin, Selima, and Kogyrinem began speaking almost simultaneously, then stuttered to a stop as each tried to let the other speak.

"I know you have objections," said Aumekor. "I know there have been good reasons for confining me in the Inner Keep all my life, and I agree that it was necessary. However, circumstances have changed. It is now not only possible for me to leave, it is necessary."

"The High Protectors will never allow it," said Geradin flatly.

"Are you speaking for yourself as a High Protector or as a representative of their collective will? Or are you merely making an observation as *my friend* about the likely reaction of the High Protectors as a whole?" Aumekor didn't like playing on his friendship like that, but he had to get past Geradin's habitual overprotectiveness.

Geradin took a deep breath as if to launch into an argument, but then he remained silent.

"I thought we had covered this already," said Selima. "You are losing sight of the ultimate goal. Protecting your life is more important than anything Kindul can do."

"The ultimate goal is not to protect my life—it is to have

the Heir of the Line defeat the Dark Priestess. If Kindul does as Kogyrinem has speculated, he will hamstring not just me, but all my successors. I could live with Kindul as Lord Regent for all my days, but I cannot allow the Line of Orcan to be removed from the throne of Aud Sapeer."

"The Dark Priestess will undoubtedly try to kill you if you leave the protection of the Keep," said Selima. "This place is the most secure—"

"Allonna!" Aumekor spoke with all the force of command. "A protective ward—now!"

Allonna's eyes opened wide, but she reacted almost instantly. A blue-white shimmer appeared in the air surrounding him, its glare so bright Aumekor had to squint to see through it.

He could see Geradin already had his sword out while the other Protectors were still drawing theirs. The power of Allonna's ward set the alarm bells ringing. The Protectors from just outside the door burst into the room. Selima was glancing quickly about her, while Kogyrinem stood still, seeming quite unconcerned.

"Selima, if you would be so good as to silence the alarm bells. As you can see from Geradin's sword, I am in no danger." He ordered the Protectors back outside and told them to notify everyone that it was a false alarm.

"Should I take down the ward, Your Majesty?" asked Allonna.

"Not yet, thank you." He squinted at Selima. "As I said earlier, circumstances have changed. I was referring not just to Kindul's threat to the continued power of the Line of Orcan, nor my newly acquired ability to walk, but also to the changes that Allonna brings to the balance of power we have had with the Dark Priestess. Tell me, Selima, given Allonna's abilities, can I not be as safe outside the Keep as I was inside it before she arrived?"

"You would be safer still remaining inside the Keep with Allonna here," said Selima, with furrowed brow, "but I see your point." She turned to Allonna. "You may undo the ward now."

Allonna looked to Aumekor. He nodded, and the blue shimmer surrounding him disappeared. The fact that she had looked to him before following Selima's instruction meant he had undermined Selima's authority over her apprentice. He would have to correct that later, if possible.

"If I may, Your Majesty," said Kogyrinem. "I agree with you that Kindul must be stopped, and if that means you must travel to Cirkepam, you have my support and my blessing. But if it can be done without your leaving the Keep, that would be preferable. I am certain the monarchs at the Conclave would listen to me, as High Priest of the Gods of Light, and I could persuade them to oppose Kindul's plan."

This was not a suggestion Aumekor had been anticipating. Much as he wanted to have good reason to leave the Keep, he had to consider other options. There was some merit to Kogyrinem's suggestion—the other monarchs of the Free Kingdoms would at least listen to the High Priest of Light.

But even here in Aud Sapeer, lit by the glow of the temple the Gods of Light had built, worship of the Gods had long been in decline. A large segment of the population held the opinion that all the Gods, both of Light and Dark, had vanished from the world and would not return. Some even claimed there never had been any gods. If such thoughts were common here, they were even more prevalent in the other kingdoms. Many of the monarchs might no longer consider the High Priest relevant, while Kindul would be offering tangible concessions for their support. But how could he make that point to Kogyrinem without slighting the High Priest's authority?

Geradin replied to Kogyrinem before Aumekor could. "Your Grace's plan is a worthy one, and I would suggest we follow it if the High Protectors determine that the Heir of the Line must remain here. But consider the timing: Kindul already has fifteen to twenty days before you could arrive at the Conclave, and if you somehow failed to dissuade the monarchs from following Kindul's plan, it would then be another fifteen to twenty days for His Majesty to make the trip. The more time Kindul has, the more likely he will have gained the support he needs among the monarchs. We must move quickly, and strike our hardest blow first."

"There is no point in discussing this further right now," said Selima. Before Aumekor could protest, she continued, "This matter must be brought before the High Protectors and the rest of the Regency Council, at which point any arguments can be fully explored."

"No," said Aumekor. "The High Protectors I agree to, but there are members of the council whose loyalty is to Kindul, not me. They cannot be informed of what we are planning."

Selima considered that for a moment, then nodded.

"Ger," said Aumekor, deliberately using the nickname despite the formality of the situation, "would you summon an immediate meeting of the High Protectors in the Council room?"

"At once, Your Majesty." Geradin bowed formally, then left the room. Selima excused herself, taking Allonna with her, and Kogyrinem followed.

There was no question that Geradin's formality had been intentional. Aumekor hoped he had not pushed too hard in reminding Geradin of their friendship. Geradin took his duties as a Protector very seriously—he served actual guard duty more often than any four other High Protectors combined. He must feel trapped between his responsibilities as a Protector and his loyalty as a friend.

Convincing the High Protectors that it was necessary for Aumekor to leave the Keep would be a challenge. Though all of them were sworn to protect him, all but two were technically not his subjects. There were sixteen High Protectors, one from each of the Free Kingdoms—except for the Kingdom of Bosperan. Veratur had been from Bosperan, and after his treachery sixteen years ago the rest of the High Protectors had refused to accept a replacement for him, saving that position until Balunor's son was old enough to take it.

But as Protectors of the Line, their oath was not just to him. He whispered the words to himself: "...I will protect the line of Orcan att'Fenisak of Aud Sapeer from this day until I let my last breath out." Protect the *line*, not just the person who happened to be heir to it at any one moment. All he would have to do is show them that their oaths required them to let him go to the Conclave. He snorted—that should be about as simple as falling up a hill.

◆ ◆ ◆

The debate had been going on for most of the afternoon. Aumekor was fairly certain he had eight of the sixteen on his side, but that wasn't enough. According to the rules laid out generations before, it took an actual majority of the High Protectors to change an existing policy. There had originally been twenty High Protectors, but the four free kingdoms north of the Barrier Mountains had been impossible to defend for long and had been conquered by the Dark Priestess over three hundred years ago, thus reducing the number of High Protectors to sixteen. The refusal to accept Veratur's replacement had taken the number down to fifteen, so during those years eight votes had been sufficient, but now there were sixteen members again.

There was no use wishing Geradin had not yet joined the High Protectors, because Aumekor counted Geradin among the eight votes he had.

Which of the others could he convince? He focused on Wyran, one of only three remaining who had served as a High Protector to Aumekor's father. "High Protector Wyran, you have stated several times that the Heir of the Line must remain in the Keep because it is the safest place. Yet I know you went into battle with my father and served heroically at his side. Did you argue against him going into battle?"

"Most strenuously. I did not think he should be risking his life like that. Only one battle matters for the Heir, and that is the final battle against the Dark Priestess."

Apparently Wyran had been overly cautious even before he became old. Aumekor didn't like to strike at the man's scars, but there didn't seem to be many options left. "But my father did not die in battle, did he? I know you did your best to save him, but he was killed *in the Keep*. You insist the Keep is the safest place, yet more Heirs of the line have been killed inside it than out." His father was the only Heir who had ever been killed, and those who had been Protectors at that time still felt the shame of it.

Wyran merely stared at the center of the table.

"There is a strategic point behind His Majesty's words," said Geradin. "The attack sixteen years ago took several seasons of preparation. The attack last Midsummer took years to prepare, and it was carefully planned to take advantage of an exact knowledge of our routines. Perhaps because of her long life, the Dark Priestess is accustomed to planning on a long-term basis."

"Geradin's right," said High Protector Otunvol, whom Aumekor already counted as a strong yes. "Surely the Dark Priestess has noticed that the Heir *never* leaves the Keep. She may be planning some way to destroy the Keep itself. Predictability is our greatest weakness. Leaving the Keep may throw some of her plans into disarray."

This touched off another round of arguing among the High Protectors, until finally High Protector Ianik called for order. The High Protectors rotated nominal leadership among the whole group, changing the leader every season, and this autumn it was Ianik's turn.

Ianik looked around the table. "I do not believe further discussion will be productive. I call for a vote on whether to allow the Heir of the Line to attend the Conclave of Monarchs."

Aumekor still only counted eight supporters, but he did not know what else could be done to convince any of the opponents. Perhaps these last arguments had convinced someone who was hiding his support, or perhaps someone who was not actively in opposition would abstain.

By rule, a vote was taken by order of seniority, starting with the longest-serving High Protector.

"No." Wyran. Not a surprise there.

"Yes." As expected.

Three noes followed, but Aumekor had not counted on their support. Two yeses, a no, two more yeses and they were tied at five apiece.

"Yes."

"No."

"Yes." That was a surprise. Uollop had spoken vigorously against the idea near the beginning of the meeting. But he had been silent later on. As long as there were no more surprises, Aumekor had won.

"No."

"Yes." That was eight votes in favor.

Geradin's voice was calm as he cast the final vote. "No."

Chapter Twenty-Three

Geradin

Geradin sat still in his chair, waiting for people to react. High Protector Ianik, after blinking a few times in rapid succession, said, "The votes stand eight to eight. I am sorry, Your Majesty, but the High Protectors cannot accede to your request."

Out of the corner of his eye, Geradin looked at Selima. During the course of the debate, he had decided to vote yes. But then he had felt an itch on the back of his neck. In reaching back to scratch it, his hand had found a scrap of paper.

Careful not to show his surprise, he had brought the paper down, hiding it in the palm of his hand, and then surreptitiously read the note on it.

Trust me on this. Vote no. I'll explain.

It was Selima's handwriting. Since she had not come near him during the meeting, she must have placed the note there by magic. He had looked at her and raised an eyebrow. She had nodded ever so slightly, then looked away.

Geradin could not recall ever having been put in such a difficult situation. Mek and Selima were the two most important people in his life, and both had pressured him to do what they wanted, rather than simply encouraging him to do his duty.

It was not until there had been eight votes in favor that he had been able to decide how to vote. By voting no and allowing a tie, he would give Selima a chance to explain herself. Under the rules, a proposal that lost could be reconsidered after three days at the request of someone who voted against it. There was no guarantee that a yes vote might not change to a no during that time, but at least he had left open the possibility of reversing the outcome.

Now that the vote was over, some of the High Protectors scraped their chairs back in order to stand.

"High Protector Ianik," said Selima, "I believe there has been a mistake."

Ianik tilted his head slightly. "What kind of mistake?"

"Over the past ninety-four years, I have been a guest at many meetings of the High Protectors, and have been impressed by the rules that govern your procedures. I even studied those rules carefully at one time, hoping to make the Regency Council run as smoothly, though I must confess I failed."

There were a few chuckles at that. Geradin wondered what Selima was up to, but he felt relieved that she was up to something.

"During my study, I noticed that the drafters had wisely chosen to make all the High Protectors equal. One example is the way they rotated leadership through all the High Protectors, each having a turn."

"That is true, Omnimancer Selima." Ianik smiled. "I now find myself wishing I had studied up on those rules before my turn began, because I fear I am about to be taught a lesson."

"The High Protectors were created to demonstrate the unity of the Free Kingdoms in supporting the Heir of the Line. The High Protectors are equal in order to show that the Kingdoms are equal. And under the rules, the vote of a High Protector is the vote of the Kingdom he is from."

"Yes," said Ianik.

"But as you voted just now, I noticed that High Protector Telar voted no, as did High Protector Geradin. Yet both are from Aud Sapeer, and Aud Sapeer is not entitled to two votes. One of their votes must be declared invalid."

As Selima finished, High Protectors began murmuring to each other, trying to decide if she was correct. Geradin knew she was—Selima was meticulous about details like that.

There was only one thing he could do now. "High Protector Ianik, if I may speak?"

Ianik nodded, and Geradin rose to his feet as everyone else quieted. "My fellow High Protectors, it has been a pleasure serving with you. But given the irregularity of my position, as pointed out by Omnimancer Selima, I feel I must—"

"Stop." High Protector Telar held up his palm to silence Geradin. "You will not resign from the High Protectors. Neither will I, at this time. We shall share one vote between us, that all the kingdoms may be equal." He looked at Selima. "I trust that does not violate the rules, Selima."

"I do not believe so," she said.

"Does anyone object?" asked Ianik. "If not, it is agreed that Telar and Geradin shall share their vote, by whatever manner they shall agree upon."

No one objected.

Geradin sat down, relieved that he was still one of the High Protectors. But he found himself growing angry with Selima for nearly forcing his resignation. She had asked him to trust her, and in return his vote was now shared with Telar, rather than being his own.

"If there is no further business," said Ianik, "then—"

"Wait," said Otunvol. "If Telar and Geradin's votes only count as one, then the vote to allow the Heir to go to the Conclave of Monarchs is eight to seven in favor."

Ianik blinked. "I guess that's true." He looked doubtful.

Before Ianik could say another word, Selima said, "In that case, we must not delay any further." She stood. "I must begin preparations for the journey, and I'm sure you have plans to make about how to undertake it."

She turned and left the room.

Mek spoke before anyone else. "If I leave tomorrow at dawn with a small group of Protectors, traveling light and fast, we could arrive in Cirkepam in fifteen days, perhaps even less."

"Impossible!" said Wyran. "Such a journey requires more than just fast horses and a good map. If you leave the Keep, every Protector must go with you. We are not Protectors of the Keep."

"Has Your Majesty even ridden a horse?" asked someone.

With that, the arguing began again. But now it was about how to carry out such an expedition, not whether to do so.

Mek had done it. Geradin tried to catch his friend's eye to share a smile, but Mek seemed to intentionally avoid looking at him. Selima must not have informed him about the note she had sent Geradin. Mek probably believed that Geradin had wanted to stop him, and that he had won only through Selima's intervention. Geradin hoped he would get a chance to straighten it all out soon.

Over the course of discussion, a plan began to emerge. One hundred and twenty Protectors would go along to protect Mek, leaving thirty to guard the Keep against any attempt to infiltrate it.

Something had been nagging at Geradin's mind during the discussion, and finally he realized what it was. "Secrecy. We need secrecy. We can't march a hundred and twenty Protectors out the front gates without everyone knowing the Heir is taking a journey."

"Is it that important?" Ianik frowned. "The news will come out once we reach Cirkepam in any event."

"Perhaps if Kindul hears Aumekor is coming, he'll abandon his plan," said Otunvol.

Geradin shrugged. "Who knows what Kindul will do? But I say the longer it is before the Dark Priestess hears about it, the better."

There was a long pause before Wyran finally spoke. "A small group may be more easily concealed, but there are too many possible dangers on the road. We need the strength of numbers."

"Bandits," said Geradin, suddenly remembering what

Allonna's father had mentioned about bandits. "That's the solution."

"Surely you don't mean we should pose as a band of bandits," said Otunvol.

"No. But if we announce that a group of soldiers is being sent to deal with the bandit problem, our party could be seen leaving the city without arousing suspicion. We'll have to disguise our armor in order to appear as normal soldiers, but if we trickle out of the Keep in ones and twos, nobody will notice that most of us have left."

"And if we're very lucky," said Otunvol, "we'll run into a bandit or two along the way." He grinned.

Chapter Twenty-Four

Allonna

"How much do you know about riding horses?" asked Selima as she entered her study.

Allonna looked up from the book she was reading, *Using Your Umbrit*. Before going to the meeting of the High Protectors, Selima had instructed her to wait here. Allonna had been dreading Selima's arrival, expecting to be scolded for her attempted eavesdropping. This question came as a relief. "We had a cart horse named Muddy, because of her brown color, and I used to ride her sometimes when the delivery was only something small, like a box of nails. Why? Will I need to ride a horse?"

"Yes. We're going to Cirkepam." Selima's voice was distracted.

"You and me?" Aud Sapeer was the first great city Allonna had ever seen. Now she would get to see another—in a different kingdom, even.

"Not just us." Selima began selecting various items out of one of her cabinets. "The king, plus whomever the High Protectors decide should accompany him. Which means Aumekor will have to learn to ride a horse."

"I'm sure there are far more experienced riders who can teach him."

"What? Oh, you won't be the one to teach him. But he'll need to be able to mount a horse with his armor on. I noticed the overlay this afternoon. What does it do?"

Overlay? "You mean the extra layer of spell on the armor? It's so he can go down stairs."

"Good." Selima hunted around in a desk drawer, drew out what appeared to be some entangled chain necklaces, and began tugging to disentangle them. "I was planning to teach you about overlays, but it appears you figured them out on your own."

Guilty at being praised for something she had learned by trying to eavesdrop, Allonna squirmed in her seat. Selima must know anyway, so she might as well confess. "I tried to eavesdrop on you and the High Priest, so it was those wards that gave me the idea, and I still have to fix it so the king can walk up stairs."

"There." Selima held up a silver necklace. "You'll have to use this because I will be busy with the oath disk elsewhere, and... well, I don't like to use that unless necessary, anyway."

"What is it?" If Selima didn't want to talk about the propriety of eavesdropping, Allonna would not press the subject.

"Horsemaster Isserod has never been informed of the king's condition, since we didn't think the king would need to ride. Have him put this on before he sees the king, and then after he has given what training he can, have him remove it. He will forget all that happened while he was wearing it."

Allonna rose and took the necklace. It seemed too ordinary to be enchanted. "So you want me to overlay the armor so the king can mount a horse?"

"Yes, and so he can guide his mount."

"Why not just have him ride in a carriage?"

Selima paused in her rifling through the desk drawers. Then she shook her head. "It's been so long since I've thought in these terms that I'd almost forgotten the reasons. A carriage presents an easier target. That reminds me, you'll have to get with Master Ramil as well, to have him disguise the king's armor. It's too distinctive right now."

Allonna nodded. It would be a shame, but she understood. "Anything else I can do?"

"That will do for a start. No, wait." Selima looked around the bookshelves, found a clothbound volume, and handed it to Allonna. "When you get a chance, read the chapter on mobile wards, for background. The techniques involved are rather different from the wards you've been casting. I'll have to find time to practice with you before we leave."

Tucking the book under her arm, Allonna said, "Is everything all right? You seem..." Allonna shrugged—she wasn't quite sure what Selima seemed, but she didn't seem like Selima.

Selima wiped her palm across her forehead. "The idea of Aumekor leaving the Keep just takes some getting used to. There's so much to do. Now, go on and take care of those errands."

Allonna nodded and left the study. As she closed the door, she heard Selima say, "How will I ever be able to carry enough?"

◆ ◆ ◆

Scheduling riding lessons for King Aumekor turned out to be a lot easier than getting him to give up his armor so it could be disguised. Finally the king agreed that she and Master Ramil could take the armor to work on during the night, so long as he could have it back in the morning.

With all the preparations for the journey, Allonna had not gone to bed until nearly dawn, but fortunately the king's riding lesson was not until shortly before noon. She arrived early for the lesson, because she had to get Horsemaster Isserod to wear the necklace.

"What is it for?" the horsemaster asked. He seemed a rather cheerful man of about thirty years. The horse that stood calmly beside him was far larger than old Muddy had been, with a glossy black coat and three white stockings.

What was the proper way to explain to someone that

they've been excluded from a tremendous secret, and that they will not be trusted to keep it? "It's for protection," said Allonna, carefully avoiding saying whose protection it was for. "Omnimancer Selima said it is very important that you wear it during the king's lesson."

He took it from her and passed it over his head. "Doesn't feel like it's enchanted."

She leaned toward him and whispered conspiratorially, "The best artifacts never do."

"The king has never taken an interest in horses before. This journey must be very important."

"It is."

"I've worked here for fifteen years. Never met him, only seen him give his Midsummer speeches." Suddenly he stiffened, then bowed. "Your Majesty."

Allonna turned to see King Aumekor and four Protectors standing at the entrance to the training yard. Normally, this yard was used for the Protectors' combat training, not for horsemanship lessons, but it was safer from prying eyes than the stable yard.

From ten paces, the king's armor looked good even in broad daylight. Or rather, it looked bad. Gray paint as a base, with patches of slightly differing shades, made it look like a suit that had been banged around in battle and repaired by a smith of below-average skill. Traces of red clay looked like a patina of rust in some of the more awkward spots to polish. It would not hold up under close inspection, but at a distance no one would think that was the armor of a king.

"Have you explained it to him yet?" asked Aumekor.

Allonna shook her head. "I was about to." Last night, Selima had used the oath disk to modify the oath Allonna had taken, so that she could explain the king's condition to the horsemaster.

The king paced forward and came to a halt before the horsemaster, who bowed deeply.

"Your Majesty," he said, "I am greatly honored."

"Is this my horse?"

Isserod nodded. "Her name is Whirlwind of Clanni, but we usually just call her Windy. She should serve you well. Very strong, very quick, but good-tempered."

"She?" Aumekor raised his eyebrows and smiled wryly. "Somehow, I thought a king would ride a stallion."

The horsemaster bit his lower lip. "Why don't we see how you ride, and then perhaps we can find another mount."

"No, you were right to choose Windy. It would be difficult for me to control an unruly horse. I was born so weak I have never been able to even stand on my own. It is only through the magic of Omnimancer Allonna here that I'm able to walk right now."

Eyes wide, Isserod flashed a glance at Allonna.

She explained how the armor worked, then added, "I'm here to enchant the armor so he can use it to control the horse. And so he can mount."

Tapping two fingers against his lips, Isserod didn't speak for a long moment. "This will be more difficult than I thought. Forgive me, Your Majesty, but I believed I was only dealing with someone who was inexperienced and lacked interest in horses. I had no idea…"

"You can understand why we keep it a secret," said Aumekor.

"Of course." Isserod reached out and caught hold of Windy's bridle. He led the horse to position her so the king could mount from the left side.

◆ ◆ ◆

It had taken over a dozen tries before Allonna managed to create an overlay spell that would get the armor's left boot to rise unerringly into the stirrup, then boost the king up and swing his right leg over the horse to land in the other stirrup. Though she had almost cried in frustration at her failure, the king did nothing but encourage her, even though the quick reactions of his Protectors were all that kept him from crashing to the ground several times.

Now, as the king rode around the training yard on Windy's back, Allonna felt her confidence return. Creating overlays to allow the king to pull on the reins, give pressure with his knees, or give the horse slight kicks would be a lot closer to what she had done before.

"What is the name of the village you're from?" asked the king.

"My village? It's called Glicken."

"Did you leave behind a best friend in Glicken, in order to become Selima's apprentice?"

Allonna immediately thought of Lisira, with whom she had spent countless days at play. But a year ago Lisira had married Sinog, a farmer who lived outside the village, and they hadn't seen each other much since. Even before that, Allonna's growing responsibilities in her father's business had left little time for her childhood friends. "Not as such, Your Majesty."

He snorted. "Don't tell me you had no friends."

"No, I had friends. A best friend, even, when we were children. But I guess as we grew older, things changed."

The king did not reply.

Allonna pushed away all thoughts of Glicken and concentrated on her next spell. She felt the power flow out of her and into the armor. "Now, try the signal to turn Windy to the left."

◆ ◆ ◆

The spell for dismounting had been much easier than the one for mounting. Isserod had declared the King knew as much about the basics of riding as could be taught in one day, and King Aumekor had decided that was enough. Only Allonna and Isserod—and Windy—now remained in the training yard.

"You have done well, Horsemaster Isserod," said Allonna. "I shall always remember your service this day."

"As I shall always remember the amazing enchantments you

cast on the king's armor. I had never imagined such a thing to be possible."

Allonna shook her head. "No. You understand, of course, that it is essential you never reveal the king's condition to anyone."

"I would never betray my king."

"You will not. Once you return that necklace to me, you will have no memory of what happened here."

He reached up to his neck and rubbed the chain between his fingers. "Am I so mistrusted?"

"It is not a matter of trust. I, myself, am bound under a magical oath. But what you do not remember, you cannot be magically tricked into revealing."

He looked at her for a long time. "I know I shall not remember this conversation, but I thank you for telling me the truth before taking back the necklace." He reached up and took off the necklace. Suddenly uncertain, he looked down at the chain in his hand.

"I'll take that," said Allonna.

He handed it to her, then rubbed his forehead. "I'm sorry, I felt a bit dizzy for a moment. Is the king going to be here soon?" He looked up at the sky and frowned.

"I'm sorry, the king won't be coming," said Allonna. "He has much to do before the journey."

Isserod sighed. "I should very much like to meet him someday."

Chapter Twenty-Five

Geradin

As the sun set behind the plains to the west of the city, ninety of the Protectors of the Line were already disguised as an "army encampment" just outside the city walls. Twelve of the sixteen High Protectors were there as well. Geradin stood at the edge of the camp, watching the last sliver of sun vanish.

High Protector Wyran walked up to stand beside him. "I think we're about ready," said Wyran. "The only thing we don't have is the Heir." The final thirty Protectors to make up the expedition would arrive before dawn, escorting Mek from the Keep.

"I can't believe you organized all of this in two days." Because Geradin lacked any experience with troop movements—or travel of any kind, since he had never even been a half-day's journey away from Aud Sapeer—he had spent most of the past two days as a glorified courier between the High Protectors. It had been very educational: rather than just give him messages to carry, most of the High Protectors had taken the time to explain to him the reasons behind what they were doing.

"Organizing this? Pah! That was not the challenge. Maintaining security was. If it hadn't been for Omnimancer Selima binding half the merchants of Aud Sapeer to secrecy, the city would already be abuzz with rumors that the Heir was on the move. As it is, I think people will start to suspect something fairly quickly, when the guards at the gates of the Keep do not maintain their usual rotation."

"Perhaps Telar's plan to deal with the Regency Council could be extended to handle that," said Geradin.

"What plan?"

"After we leave, he will send the members of the council a message about a threat to the Heir, explaining that the Inner Keep must be sealed until the danger has passed. If word were to spread that most of the Protectors were sealed in the Inner Keep, it would explain the change in rotation."

"No, he mustn't do that," said Wyran. "He has the right concept, but explicitly mentioning a threat is wrong. Rather, he should say it is a drill, to test our ability to withstand a siege. Some people will consider that an obvious lie, meant to conceal the fact that there is a real threat, but the rumors will be more uncertain about the reality of the threat. Citizens will be less likely to panic."

Geradin sighed. He was already wearied to the marrow. "I will go back to the Keep and give Telar your message."

"After that, go to bed. We've a long day ahead."

"I was planning on sleeping here in the camp."

Wyran snorted. "Why?"

"It didn't seem right that I should sleep on a bed while so many Protectors sleep on the ground tonight."

"Very noble of you. But you've been back and forth more than any three of us. The days ahead will afford you sufficient opportunity to sleep on the ground. Sleep well, and come tomorrow with His Majesty."

Geradin nodded. It would be good to sleep in his own bed. And perhaps he would have a chance to speak with Mek. They had not spoken privately since Geradin voted against him.

After delivering his final message, Geradin went to Mek's quarters.

"I'm sorry," said Nikufed, "but His Majesty is already asleep. And based on the way your eyelids are drooping, I would suggest the same for you."

Recognizing that he had pushed himself to the limits of weariness, Geradin went back to his room. He removed his armor, but stretched out on his bed fully clothed and shut his eyes.

Moments later, there was a knock on his door. Sighing, Geradin rose from the bed. He hoped it wasn't another message of the "highest priority" that needed to be delivered immediately. It seemed he had done nothing else for the past two days. He opened to door to find Selima there.

"May I speak with you?" she said. Her face sagged with exhaustion.

Too tired to be angry, he waved her in. She sat in his chair and he sat down hard on the edge of his bed.

"I haven't had a chance to explain yet."

He shook his head. "It's done. Go get some rest. You look like you need it more than I do."

"No, I must explain because I still need your trust. Just as you need to explain to Aumekor, because you need to trust each other. We should have time on the journey to sort everything out, but in case something happens before that, I need you to trust me so you'll do as I say even if you don't understand why."

"Very well. You demand my blind trust again. Fine. I trust you, Selima. Now will you let me get some sleep?" Despite the tiredness, he was starting to get irritated.

"Listen to me." Her voice grew sharp. "In the wake of the attack on Midsummer Day, Aumekor pushed you into the High Protectors before they were ready for you. They always meant for you to join them, but no one had ever been made a High Protector before the age of twenty. Many of them felt you were not ready for the responsibility, and that you would let your friendship with Aumekor come before your duties as a Protector. They decided you were Aumekor's puppet Protector, and did not take you seriously. They respect your fighting ability, but they did not respect you."

He had not felt treated as an equal by many of the other

High Protectors, but he had attributed that to his youth and inexperience. "They would have grown to respect me eventually."

"You need them to respect and trust you now, not in a few years."

"And your plan was to almost force me to resign, then instead have them consider me worth only half a vote? Brilliant, Selima. Now they really consider me an equal."

"Have you not noticed the change? You've been so busy. By voting against what Aumekor clearly wanted, you showed them that you were not his puppet. Already your suggestions carry more weight than they did before. And your willingness to resign certainly impressed them."

"What if they'd let me resign?"

Selima shrugged. "It would not have been for long. Telar is getting on in years, and will most likely resign before spring, at which time you would have been reinstated. But your half-vote status will not even last that long: since Telar is remaining here, your vote will have full weight while we are on this journey."

"And you had foreseen all of this when you asked me to vote no?"

"I have been playing games of power since before any of the High Protectors were born."

"Did you foresee that if I trusted you and voted no, Aumekor would believe I had betrayed him?"

Selima hesitated. "Yes. But there wasn't time to explain it beforehand, and I could hardly confer with both of you without making it all seem staged. But I will explain it to him as soon as I can, and I'm sure he will forgive you when he understands."

"Thank you." Geradin nodded to reassure Selima.

After they bid each other goodnight, she left.

Geradin lay back down on his bed. He knew Mek would forgive him. But would Mek ever forget that when Geradin had been forced to choose, he had sided with Selima?

Chapter Twenty-Six

Aumekor

There was a bustle of activity in the pre-dawn darkness: men loading supplies into saddlebags, horses being formed into a line. With Nikufed trailing behind, Aumekor followed Selima into the courtyard of the Outer Keep. The only light seemed to be from torches on the walls of the courtyard, plus a few here and there carried by some of the men. Aumekor looked up at the sky, expecting to see the Nightglow he had read about, but the sky seemed a featureless slate.

"Where's the Nightglow?" he asked Selima.

"Clouds are covering it," she answered. "That's good—it means even fewer people will be out in the streets. I just hope it doesn't rain."

Despite that disappointment, Aumekor found it hard to stop smiling. Even rain would be a new experience. He was leaving the Keep. He was riding off on an adventure, to save his crown. It was like something out of a teller's story, the sort of thing he had only dreamed of doing all his life. The excitement was enough to mostly take his mind off the pain of some sores caused by the rubbing of the armor against his skin. Eventually, he supposed, calluses would form and he would be able to wear the armor without pain. Until then, he would just have to keep finding excitement.

Unfortunately, there was no one to share that excitement

with. A year ago, Ger would have been excited, too, but it seemed all High Protector Geradin cared about now was safety.

That wasn't a fair assessment, Aumekor knew. After all, he was the one who had pushed to get Geradin made a High Protector, and with that position came the duty to protect the Heir of the Line, something Geradin had taken seriously ever since he had learned how his father died. But it still rankled that Geradin had voted against him.

"Your Majesty! Over here." Allonna beckoned to him from beside a horse.

His horse. Aumekor's grin widened. He walked over to where Windy stood with Horsemaster Isserod holding her reins.

"Your Majesty, may I present to you Horsemaster Isserod," said Allonna. "I asked him to come this morning and personally present you with this horse."

It took a moment before Aumekor understood. Selima had mentioned that they would remove Isserod's memories of yesterday's training session. "Horsemaster Isserod, I know you have served me faithfully for many years. Thank you."

"Thank you, Your Majesty." The horsemaster bowed deeply. "I am greatly honored."

"Is this my horse?" Aumekor held back a smile at the thought of repeating this conversation.

Isserod nodded. "Her name is Whirlwind of Clanni, but we call her Windy for short. She's quick and strong, but good-tempered. She'll serve you well, Your Majesty."

"I could not ask for a better horse. You have done well."

"I do wish you had been able to come for some training—" The horsemaster stopped speaking as Aumekor moved into position and activated the magic of the armor to mount the horse. His legs moved, his arms reached out, and after a moment of smooth motion he found himself sitting in Windy's saddle.

"Well done, Your Majesty," said the horsemaster. "You must have inherited your father's abilities. I hear he was a fearless rider."

Aumekor decided that after returning from Cirkepam, he would have Selima take this man's oath on the disk so he could be told the truth. All Aumekor could do for now was say, "Thank you." The horsemaster would think the thanks were for the compliment, but they were really for the help he had given yesterday.

Someone on horseback pulled up beside him. "Ready to ride, Mek?" said Geradin.

"I am prepared, High Protector Geradin." Aumekor couldn't resist countering the use of his nickname with formality. If you want to be treated like a friend, you need to act like one.

Geradin sighed. "You, Selima, and Allonna will ride in the center of the formation. With me. We will join up with fifteen protectors who are already outside the Keep, making sure all is secure. We'll meet the rest outside the city."

"Give the word, then."

"I'm not in charge of the group; High Protector Loruquaf is. He wanted me to 'liaise' with you because I'm your friend."

"Tell him to give the word when he is ready."

Geradin flicked the reins of his horse and moved off.

Trying not to let the encounter with Geradin spoil his good mood, Aumekor searched for more novelty, but the darkness made it difficult to see anything. He looked again at the sky, and noticed a faint bluish light. "Is that the Nightglow?" he wondered aloud. Perhaps there was a break in the clouds.

"What did you say, Your Majesty?" said a Protector who was checking Nikufed's mount.

Aumekor hesitated. It was foolish to feel embarrassed about his lack of knowledge, since the Protectors all knew he had never been outside Inner Keep at night. "The light in the sky, over to the left. Is that the Nightglow?"

"No. And it's too early for dawn, so I'm not sure…Oh, it's the Temple of Light reflecting off the clouds. Look to your left when we cross Temple Street, and you'll be able to see the temple itself."

Though he had studied maps of the city, Aumekor was not sure he would know which street was Temple Street, but he kept silent. He would just have to look left at every cross street.

A faint shimmer appeared in the air surrounding him.

"Too strong," said Selima from behind him, and the shimmer disappeared. "There are two problems with a moving ward that strong. One is that it clearly signals the target of most value. The second is that it acts almost like a kite, catching the wind as he travels and either slowing him down or tiring his horse too quickly. Yes, that one is much better."

Squinting, Aumekor tried to spot the telltale shimmer of a ward. He signaled Windy to turn so he could see Selima and Allonna. "Are you sure there's a ward around me? I can't see anything."

"There is," said Selima. "A traveling ward cannot be like a wall. Its effects must be more subtle. The primary danger to you on this journey will be from spells or distance weapons, so the ward is specifically designed for those threats. We will count on your Protectors to keep away swords. Any unrecognized magic is repelled completely, and anything traveling too fast—such as an arrow or spear—is slowed sufficiently that even if it does manage to strike you, it will be unable to do any real damage."

"Are there any other differences?"

"Moving wards fade much sooner than a stationary ward, so they must be recast periodically." She waved her hand at one of the two court mancers who had just joined her. "If it were just Donaril and I, we would have to stop periodically to regain sufficient power to—"

"Protectors of the Line! Prepare to move out!" High Protector Loruquaf's voice echoed in the courtyard.

"—power to refresh the ward. However, Allonna's exceptional power means we will not have to do that."

Geradin returned, maneuvering his horse next to Aumekor. "Just follow that horse there," Geradin said, pointing to one of the Protector's horses. More Protectors formed a protective wall surrounding Aumekor and the mancers. Then the whole formation moved toward the gates of the Outer Keep at a walking pace.

The large iron grilles parted so silently that Aumekor decided they must be well oiled—or else mancy of some sort was used to keep them quiet. The party moved between the gates onto Keep Street.

He was outside the Keep. Excitement mixed with sudden trepidation. He wanted to look back at the walls that had protected and confined him all his life, but he couldn't turn his head sufficiently in his armor to look back even out of the corner of his eye.

The horses' shoes clattered on the cobblestones of the street. Aumekor expected people to open their windows to see what was causing such a racket, but if anyone did, he did not see them. As they passed various side streets, figures on horseback melded into the party. Since no one seemed alarmed by this, he assumed they were the additional Protectors who had been scouting ahead.

"Look off to the left," said Geradin.

They were approaching a large crossroad with an indistinct statue in the middle. As they entered the crossroad, Aumekor looked up the road to the left. He instantly recognized the Temple of Light, though no painting he had ever seen had truly conveyed the way it glowed. Triple spires that resembled crystallized blue-white flames rose toward the clouds.

A lump rose in Aumekor's throat. He had always believed in the Gods of Light, just because Selima believed. But how could anyone see this temple and not believe it built by the Gods? "I follow the Light," he said quietly. "May the Gods of Light grant that I serve their purpose with this journey."

Chapter Twenty-Seven

Geradin

The fourth day of riding wasn't as bad. Though Geradin had plenty of experience on horseback, it had never been for more than a short while at a time. Riding from sunrise to sundown with only a few breaks in between, day after day, had left him sore. It must have been far worse for Mek, but he never uttered a word of complaint, so Geradin wouldn't either.

He reached forward and patted Gristle's neck. A powerfully built warhorse, Gristle was not the fastest of mounts, but had strength and endurance to spare. "You probably wonder why we have to stop so often," said Geradin.

"I didn't catch what you said, Ger." Mek pulled his horse up even with Gristle.

"Just talking to my horse." Geradin was relieved that Mek was treating him like a friend again. Selima had spoken to Mek privately after the expedition had made camp on the first night, and after that things had returned to normal—as normal as they could be, considering they were farther from the Keep than either of them had ever been.

"I hope you don't bore him to death. It's a long walk to Cirkepam."

"Gristle's tough. I recited him one of your Midsummer Day speeches and he didn't keel over."

"I've misjudged him," said Mek. "Gristle is obviously an

equine of superior wit and taste."

Geradin shook his head. "If we run out of food while trapped by an early blizzard, we'll see whose mount is of superior taste. I'm guessing it's that cow you're riding."

Mek's tone became eager. "You don't think we'll see a snowstorm, do you?"

"It's possible." Before he could add that he hoped they didn't see one until they were safely back in Aud Sapeer for the winter, Geradin's attention was caught by one of the scouts returning to the party at a full gallop. "Looks like there may be trouble up ahead."

It was a likely spot. This portion of the road to Cirkepam ran alongside the Sel River, which was too deep to ford safely along this stretch. The river and road ran along the bottom of a valley between two rather steep hills. Not so steep that riders could not come charging down to attack travelers, but too steep to allow for an easy escape except by racing along the road in either direction.

The company came to a halt and set up a defensive formation around Mek. The scout rode straight to High Protector Wyran.

"There's a caravan around the next bend," the scout said, breathing heavily. "They're surrounded by a band of raiders—at least seventy, split into two groups, mostly armed with swords and staves. The caravan has perhaps twenty guards, plus whatever merchant can carry a sword. The fight seems to have stopped for now—the bandit leader is offering to let the merchants live if they surrender."

Seventy men was far larger than any group of road bandits Geradin recalled hearing about. But since the caravanners had begun hiring more guards, it was natural that bandits would start forming larger forces.

"Any chance we can circle around them by going up over the side?" asked Wyran.

Before the scout could answer, Mek had stirred his horse into motion, trotting toward Wyran and the scout. "Did you just ask this man if we could *avoid* these raiders?" Mek's voice was contemptuous.

"Our mission is to get you safely to Cirkepam, not rescue caravans."

"The people of that caravan are either my subjects or foreign merchants entitled to the protection of my government."

"Unnecessary combat puts your life at risk," Wyran said.

"Defending the innocent is not unnecessary combat." Mek's voice was firm. "If you, as commander of this force, feel incapable of destroying these bandits, I will replace you with someone who is."

Geradin knew Mek usually judged the character of others accurately, but perhaps due to pain and fatigue he was pushing the old High Protector too hard. Wyran would not react well to such an insulting challenge to his command. If it came to a vote of the High Protectors, either Wyran's leadership would be shattered or else Mek would be furious with the Protectors. Either outcome could be disastrous.

As respectfully as he could, Geradin said, "With your permission, High Protector Wyran, I believe we can save the caravan without risking the Heir's life."

Wyran must have realized where the confrontation was headed, because he took a deep breath and let it out slowly before responding. "What do you suggest, Geradin?"

"We outnumber these bandits, and bandits are not known for their willingness to fight against a superior force. If we approach slowly, in formation, I'm sure they will abandon their plans and flee rather than face us in battle."

Otunvol said, "It makes sense. There would be no combat, so the Heir would not be in any danger."

"I suppose it—" began Wyran.

"No," said Mek. "Scaring off the bandits leaves them free to prey on someone else. I want at least some of them killed, as a lesson to the others."

"Please, Your Majesty," said Wyran. "I swear by the Light I have no desire to spare these bandits. But I must protect you, and I cannot afford to split our forces by sending sufficient men to fight these bandits. If we can rescue this caravan without loss of life, that is sufficient victory for now."

Mek didn't reply.

Geradin leaned toward Mek and spoke in hushed tones. "An expedition needs one commander, not two."

Mek sighed. "Rescue the caravan. Killing the bandits will have to wait for another time."

"However, this may be a trap meant to lure us into the valley," said Wyran. "I don't like the idea of taking the entire force down there, but splitting our force seems just as risky."

"What about one man, under flag of truce?" said Geradin. "We stop within sight of them. If they don't flee at our appearance, I'll go down and convince their leader it's in his best interest to leave."

"What would you say?" asked Mek.

"I'll think of something."

There was some more half-hearted debate, but no one came up with a better plan. High Protector Wyran gave the order, and the whole company moved down the road in the direction of the caravan.

Soon the road turned and sloped downward more steeply. Geradin spotted the wagons of the caravan about two hundred paces away. Raiders formed a ragged semicircle about ten paces from the close side of the caravan, with another group similarly situated on the far side. Only about ten of the raiders seemed to have mounts; the rest were on foot.

"Company, halt!" Wyran's voice was loud enough that some of the bandits turned and looked uphill.

There was a shout of alarm. A handful of the bandits began to flee, but were called back by a sharp voice.

"I was afraid of that," said Wyran. "A company of bandits that large could not be maintained without some leadership." He looked at Geradin. "We are committed now. It's your turn."

"Let's go, Gristle," Geradin said, and urged the horse into motion. In his left hand, he carried a white banner of truce.

♦ ♦ ♦

The bandits on the near side had turned away from the caravan. Some looked behind Geradin trying to gauge the strength of his troops. Others watched him suspiciously, weapons at the ready.

At five paces from the line of raiders, Geradin halted Gristle. "I come under flag of truce to speak to your leader."

"Say your piece, then." The speaker was one of the few raiders on a horse, and the sword he carried was held in a practiced grip.

"As you can see, our force outnumbers yours. There is no question that we would defeat you if it comes to battle. However, such a battle might entail losses on our side, and since our strength is needed elsewhere, my commander would prefer to avoid doing battle with you. If you depart now, you have my word we will not pursue."

"Well, that's astonishingly generous of you," said the leader. "But seeing as how we have taken some losses ourselves here, it would taste bitter for us to leave without plundering these wagons. However, since I have no desire to hinder your journey, tell your commander that he's free to go around us, at a safe distance of course."

Grimacing, Geradin shook his head. "If it were up to me, I'd do it. We're supposed to be preventing border incursions by the Cirkepamians, not tangling with bandits. But my commander feels it his duty to rescue this caravan. And you know how some officers get about duty and honor."

"He's bluffing," said one of the other bandits. "If they really had the strength to take us, they would have attacked."

"There are a lot of them," said another.

More bandits began voicing opinions. "We've taken on soldiers and won before."

"Perhaps they've already been through a battle, and most of them are injured."

"Be nice to get some more horses."

As they spoke, six raiders with crossbows moved to take up positions on either side of him.

This was not going the way Geradin had hoped. He knew that even a small group of Protectors could easily defeat this band of raiders, but the raiders did not know they were facing the king's elite guard rather than common soldiers.

The leader held up his hand to silence his men. "Take this one's horse and send him walking back to give his commander the bad news. No, better yet, just kill him. That will send the message clear enough."

If the raiders wanted a fight, they would get one. The men with crossbows were ready to shoot him down if he tried to turn Gristle around and flee.

Geradin cleared his mind of all distractions. There is nothing but the fight.

He kicked Gristle forward toward the men between him and the caravan. Geradin whipped out his sword and took one raider's head off as he passed through their line, then turned to the right. Gristle's motion kept his sword going to cut through a second raider at shoulder level and slice a palmwidth deep through the chest of a third.

Gristle carried him close to the caravan wagons, where Geradin swung down to the ground. He wasn't used to fighting on horseback, and here he could use the wagons to protect his back.

He knew his skill plus the advantage his enchanted sword gave him was enough that he could kill several of the raiders without too much trouble—at Midsummer he had killed two men with only his blunt wooden practice sword. But his only hope lay in whether taking such losses from just one man would be enough to scare off the raiders. If they chose to attack in mass he could not survive for long.

Then he noticed that his sword did not glow blue—it glowed yellow. Mek was in danger. Had this all been a trap from the beginning? He would have to trust his fellow Protectors to handle the threat. For now, there was nothing but the fight.

The closest bandit swung at him with a sword. Geradin's stroke cut through the man's blade, and the man had time to widen his eyes in disbelief before he died. Five more raiders died in rapid succession without even touching Geradin, and suddenly there was nobody within reach of his sword.

He looked for the next raider to kill, and saw most of them were fleeing to the hills on either side of the road.

"Look out!" a man shouted from the caravan.

Geradin spun to see a raider ten paces away, aiming a crossbow at him. Knowing that a bolt at such short range could easily penetrate plate armor, Geradin instinctively began to dive to the ground, but the man had already been pulling the trigger, and Geradin's reactions just were not quick enough.

The bolt struck him in the chest.

Chapter Twenty-Eight

Allonna

Allonna thought High Protector Wyran was being very unreasonable in his refusal to save the caravan. One hundred and twenty Protectors of the Line, and all the use she'd seen for them so far was in putting up tents when the company stopped for the night. The tents were of good quality, and she wasn't ungrateful for the work the Protectors did in setting up the tent she shared with Selima, but there certainly did not seem to be much threat to King Aumekor so far. Why not send sixty or so Protectors to deal with the bandits, especially since the king was ordering it?

But nobody asked her opinion.

"Stay close to the king," said Selima. "If this is a trap of some sort, I don't know yet whether we're better off running or standing our ground. Be ready to cast a stationary ward around him, strong as you can make it, if I decide we stay."

Allonna nodded. "What do I do if we run?"

"You concentrate on running. I haven't taught you any offensive spells yet, and they are far too dangerous to be used without experience." Selima smiled coldly. "I will do my best to make whoever follows us regret that course of action."

"Company, forward!"

High Protector Wyran's command came as somewhat of a surprise to Allonna, but obviously the decision was made to rescue the caravan. She flicked the reins of her horse, Crescent, and began to move with the rest. Crescent was bigger and faster than Muddy had been, but Allonna had no trouble controlling the mare.

The company halted within sight of the bandits.

But Geradin continued down the road alone. Was he going to scout the situation? No—he carried a flag of truce. He was going to try to *reason* with such men?

Three days of frequent practice had made casting a traveling ward almost natural to Allonna, although this was the first time she had done it from farther than a few paces. "Light protect him," she said when she finished. It was all she could do for Geradin.

She watched apprehensively as he halted before the line of raiders. He spoke, but at this distance she could not make out the words. Suddenly men with swords moved toward Geradin, and he began fighting.

"Wyran, you must send men to support Geradin, now." Selima's voice sounded nearly choked. "You must."

"And if these bandits are a distraction meant to split our force?" Wyran's voice was unsteady. "On my oath, I cannot weaken the protection of the Heir."

"Please, Wyran," said King Aumekor. "Save Geradin, and I will give you no more trouble."

Allonna looked at High Protector Wyran, who had closed his eyes as the king spoke.

After a beat of silence, he opened his eyes. "We ride to battle!" He pointed at the king. "You, stay in the middle of the formation."

The Protectors at the front of the formation spurred their horses into a gallop. Allonna gave her horse free rein and followed. Let them not be too late.

As she approached the caravan, she prepared herself for the sight of Geradin lying injured on the ground.

Not dead, he mustn't be dead.

She knew what she would do: cast a stationary ward around him to prevent further injury, and while the Protectors fought off the raiders she would heal his wounds.

The Protectors in front of her slowed to a halt. It took her a moment to comprehend the scene. Geradin stood by the wagons of the caravan. His sword was raised, glowing yellow.

"Protect him!" Geradin shouted. Behind him, some of the caravanners began to peek out from behind the wagons.

Allonna realized she had gotten ahead of the king in her concern over Geradin. She wheeled her horse around to look at King Aumekor. He did not seem to be in any danger, surrounded by Protectors.

Wyran looked at the people of the caravan, who were now emerging from hiding. He said to Aumekor, "Sir, I believe we need to take you elsewhere immediately."

The king did not respond. Because his helmet visor was down, it was impossible to see what expression was on his face.

"Sir?" asked Wyran.

Still the king did not respond.

Allonna wondered if something had happened to the enchantment on the armor, somehow freezing the king inside. She concentrated on the spell. The sunlight seemed to darken, and the weave of her enchantments glowed inside the armor. They seemed normal. But in trying to sense the enchantments she also felt something more, something familiar from her days as a healer in Glicken. "He's ill! The ki—commander is unconscious."

"Quick, get him down from there," said Selima. "Set up a tent."

Several Protectors jumped into action, and soon the king was lying on a cot in a large tent. With Selima's help, Nikufed began removing the king's armor.

Allonna bit her lower lip when she saw the bloodstains on the king's shirt and breeches. "How? How was he injured? There was no attack."

"He made me swear not to tell anyone," said Nikufed. "It wasn't too bad back at the Keep. They were starting to heal, but all this time riding.... He made me swear."

Selima's voice was cold but rushed. "Tell me."

Nikufed hesitated, glancing at Allonna. "It's the armor. It rubs his skin raw until it bleeds."

Allonna let out a sob. She had done this to him? The armor was making him bleed in pain and he had treated her with nothing but respect and kindness.

"It's not your fault," said Selima. "Apparently Geradin isn't the only one who feels the need to be stupidly brave." Selima winced as she peeled back the king's shirt to reveal several swollen abrasions leaking pus and blood. "Do you know how to heal these or will I need to show you?"

Squatting down beside the king, Allonna held her hand a thumbwidth away from one of the sores. She felt power flow out of her, stopping the bleeding, seeking the infection and destroying its potency. Unlike casting wards or enchanting armor, this was a kind of mancy she had been practicing for years. She took her hand away. The swelling already seemed to be lessening, and the abrasion no longer leaked.

"Well done," said Selima. "I could not have improved on that."

One by one, Allonna used her power on the abrasions. When she finished, she stood and concentrated on him as a whole. As she suspected, the infection had spread from his sores into his bloodstream. Left untreated for much longer, the infection could have killed him. She spread out her hands and let her power wash over his body. Finally, she could sense no more of the infection.

"He needs rest now," she said, "but he will recover."

"Thank you." Selima's voice was quiet.

Allonna nodded. "What will we do now? If the king can't ride?"

"I don't know. I must consult with Wyran and the others." Selima rose to her feet and went out of the tent.

"Miss Allonna?" said Nikufed.

"Yes?"

"He cannot go back."

"To the Keep? But it's the best place for him to recover. "

The manservant shook his head. "He cannot go back to the way he was before the armor."

All those sores being scraped as he moved—Allonna shuddered just thinking of it. "I don't know how he was able to bear the constant pain."

Nikufed gave her a sad smile. "In some ways, His Majesty is the strongest man I know."

Chapter Twenty-Nine

Geradin

The Nightglow was bright enough that Geradin did not need a torch to walk through the camp. Nodding to the Protectors standing guard, he pushed aside the flap of Mek's tent and entered. Mek lay on his cot, staring at the roof of the tent, dimly lit by an oil lamp.

"So, what was decided?" Mek's voice was resigned. He did not even look at Geradin.

With as formal a tone as he could muster, Geradin said, "The High Protectors of the Line, after due consideration of their oaths, have voted that we should…continue the journey to Cirkepam."

Mek turned his head and frowned. "You're serious?"

"Believe it, because it's true. We'll travel more slowly—we'll probably continue with this caravan the rest of the way—and you will not be wearing your armor until we can have it padded properly. But we are continuing."

"Wyran must have been annoyed at losing the vote," said Mek. "He won't be happy, especially with the slower pace."

Shaking his head, Geradin said, "Actually, the vote was unanimous, and it was Wyran whose argument won the day."

Mek closed his eyes. "Obviously I've misjudged him somehow. I've misjudged most of the High Protectors. I was sure you were going to pack me up and scurry back to the safety of the Keep." He opened his eyes and squinted at

Geradin. "*Wyran* argued in favor of continuing? What did he say?"

"He pointed out that you had endured terrible discomfort and even endangered your life to go on this journey, and hid that information from us. 'The Heir of the Line almost died,' he said, 'because he felt he could not trust us. The only way we can regain his trust is to get him safely to Cirkepam.'"

After a long silence, Mek said, "Tell Wyran he has regained it already."

◆ ◆ ◆

The next morning, Otunvol came to get Geradin. "Wyran's trying to get a wagon to carry the, uh, commander in, but apparently the head of the caravan won't negotiate with anyone but 'the hero who single-handedly defeated those ruffians.'" Otunvol grinned and clapped Geradin on the shoulder. "I haven't had a chance to say it yet, but that was nice work."

"Thanks." Geradin was grateful for the praise, but felt he didn't quite deserve it because things hadn't gone as he had planned. "But I guess I overestimated the fear they would have of ordinary soldiers."

"No, no, no. That's not how you do it."

"Not how I do what?"

"When you are accepting praise from a teacher, like Swordmaster Ytanor, you must always acknowledge your mistakes. But when the praise is from a fellow soldier, it's your chance to brag." Otunvol puffed out his chest and began speaking in an exaggeratedly confident tone. "It was hardly a fair fight. There was one of me, and only seventy of them. I had to let most of them go just because I hate cleaning blood off my sword."

Geradin snorted. "I would have left some for you to kill, but I wasn't sure if anybody else was coming."

"That's the spirit."

They arrived next to the lead wagon, where Wyran stood stiffly next to a balding merchant wearing an embroidered tunic.

The balding man bowed. "Thank you for coming, Lord Geradin. And thank you for saving our caravan."

The merchant had recognized him, or at least was testing to see if he had. Geradin said, "What did you call me?"

"It's no use pretending, milord," said the merchant. "I saw you at the wedding of Piraporil's daughter. You made yourself rather visible there. And there aren't many men who carry a sword such as yours."

There wasn't much point in trying to hide his identity from this man any longer. "You have found me out, Master…?"

"Exil, milord."

"A pleasure, Master Exil. Have you already told others of my identity?"

Exil shook his head. "You seemed to be traveling under pretense of being a common soldier, so I did not feel it was my place to say anything."

Geradin thought quickly. He needed a plausible story. "As you may have guessed, I am on a secret diplomatic mission for the king. I will trust in your discretion."

"Of course, mil— I suppose I should not call you milord or Lord Geradin. Even the name Geradin may cause unwanted speculation."

Geradin had never thought about the need for a false name. "There are plenty of people named Geradin."

Shrugging, Exil said, "Plenty of Geradins so expert with the sword as to kill twenty men on their own? Plenty of Geradins wielding an enchanted sword?"

"I only killed nine. But your point is made. What should I call myself?"

"Humble?" said Otunvol, grinning.

"I suggest something like Kiriden," said Wyran. "It sounds close enough to Geradin that it will be easy for you to answer to it, and if anyone slips up and calls you by your real name, it may not be noticed."

"Kiriden it is," said Geradin.

The negotiation that had required Geradin's presence turned out to be very simple: protection on the road to Cirkepam in exchange for the use of one of the carts to carry Mek. If Exil suspected the true identity of the "gravely ill commanding officer," he had sense enough to give no sign of it.

After a great deal of bustle by the traders to empty one wagon while not overloading the rest, Mek was moved into his new traveling accommodations. Geradin heaved a sigh of relief when the combined party finally got underway shortly before noon.

Geradin pulled his horse alongside Allonna, reached over and handed her a crossbow bolt.

She looked at it. "What's this?"

"It's a crossbow bolt."

She rolled her eyes. "I know that. I mean, why did you give this to me? I don't have a crossbow."

"I thought you might like it as a souvenir of my epic battle." Geradin grinned.

Allonna stared at him. "Thank you," she said, but she wore a puzzled look.

"I know, you think I'm being a braggart but are too polite to say it. There's a reason I'm giving this to you. That bolt you're holding was fired at me from no more than ten paces, and it hit me square in the chest. But thanks to someone's magic, I'm still alive to brag about it."

He looked directly into her eyes. "My life is in debt to you."

◆ ◆ ◆

Twenty days of journeying with the caravan had passed uneventfully, but the slower pace meant they were still six days from Cirkepam. Geradin was eating a breakfast of honey-sweetened bread prepared by one of the young unmarried women of the caravan and watching Mek walk around in his newly padded armor.

"It still feels a little tight," said Mek.

"Perhaps we can find a smith in one of these villages to adjust the armor," said Allonna.

"No," said Mek. "That can wait until we get to Cirkepam, don't you agree, Kiriden?"

Geradin had a mouthful of bread, so he just nodded.

"Of course, the way all the women around here keep stuffing food into your mouth, I'm surprised your armor isn't tight, too," said Mek.

Trying to swallow quickly so he could deny Mek's allegation, a sticky lump of bread lodged in Geradin's throat until a choking cough cleared it.

"Careful." Mek's voice was amused. "Had you fainted, the maidens in camp might have trampled me in their rush to breathe life back into you."

Geradin recovered his breath. "I don't know what you're talking about." While many of the young women did seem to take extra care to ensure he kept up his strength by bringing him food, that was just because they had seen him fight to save their caravan.

Allonna muttered something Geradin couldn't quite hear, except for the words "above their station."

"What was that?" he asked her.

She frowned. "I'm sorry. It's not really my place to say anything."

Waving a hand to dismiss her objection, Geradin said, "There are no lords or kings here; just a couple of common soldiers."

"Well, that's just it," she said. She glanced around, lowering her voice. "You are a lord, but they don't know that, and it's not fair for you to dally with the affections of a common girl looking for a husband when you are far above her station."

"I wasn't dallying!" Geradin paused. "What do you mean, 'looking for a husband?'"

"You don't think the young women keep asking you to eat

their cooking just because they think you're hungry?" Allonna began to speak in a sing-song voice. "Oh, Kiriden, I cooked you some fish with my own special recipe of spices. Have some of this frycake I made for you, Kiriden. A strong man like you needs to eat."

Not sure whether she was mocking him or the young women—or both—Geradin said, "What am I supposed to do, tell them I don't want the food they went to the trouble of making? I don't want to offend anybody."

"You don't need to offend anyone," said Allonna. "But there's —"

Mek let out a sigh of exasperation. "I'm such a fool. I can't believe I didn't see it earlier."

"Just because a woman offers me food—" Geradin began.

"Go ahead and marry her if you like her cooking," said Mek. "I'm not talking about that. I'm talking about offending the other monarchs, Queen Onara in particular. We're about to play right into Kindul's hands."

"How?" asked Geradin and Allonna simultaneously.

"If Kindul's fueling resentment of Aud Sapeer's right to march its troops through any kingdom without permission, how will it look if I march to the gates of Cirkepam with over a hundred soldiers?"

◆ ◆ ◆

The hastily convened meeting of the High Protectors was crowded into a tent, and Geradin found he had to keep his head lowered to avoid having the canvas bump against his head as gusts of wind blew outside. Because Selima had cast a spell to prevent eavesdropping, the exchange of views had been frank and sometimes heated.

"Absolutely not," said Wyran. "A bodyguard of fifteen Protectors may have been sufficient while slipping out of the Keep into deserted streets, but it is not sufficient in a strange city."

"I am willing to take suggestions," said Mek, "but taking a substantial number of Protectors may only inflame the situation."

"Perhaps we could all dress as traders and go in as part of the caravan," said Ianik.

"Yes." Mek's tone was sarcastic. "I'm sure Queen Onara would be far less offended if I *secretly* bring troops into her capital than if I do it openly." He sighed. "I'm sorry, Ianik. I feel the fool for not having seen this problem sooner, and I'm venting my frustrations on all of you. Perhaps we should spend some time thinking on it and meet later today."

Geradin was not sure what triggered the idea, but suddenly the solution seemed clear. "Permission," he said.

Mek frowned. "What?"

"That's what we need: permission. It's not the troops themselves that would offend Queen Onara—it's your bringing them to her capital city without asking. We send someone ahead to ask her permission."

Mek thought for a moment. "What if she refuses?"

"Then we consider other measures," said Selima. "Geradin's solution is the simplest, and certainly has a good chance of success."

"I agree," said Wyran.

Turning to Geradin, Mek said, "What are you waiting for? Hop on that overgrown dog you call a horse and go get permission."

"Me?" said Geradin. "My place is here, to defend you."

"I have over a hundred swords here to protect me. Who else can I send who has sufficient standing to get an immediate audience with Queen Onara? You and Selima are the only nobles in our party, and she cannot be spared."

Reluctantly, Geradin acknowledged the logic. "I will leave as soon as I can." He turned to leave the tent.

"Ger," said Mek, "unlike your last negotiation, try not to kill anyone."

◆ ◆ ◆

Nearly two days of hard riding brought Geradin and one of the traders, acting as his guide, to the gates of Cirkepam long after sunset. Upon telling the city guards who he was—and promising that Lady Uwixa could vouch for his identity—he was escorted to the palace. Six guards marched him through the palace toward Lady Uwixa's chambers, led by a polite silk-clad manservant. Geradin could not help noticing along the way that the tapestries and other luxurious furnishings contrasted sharply with the solid stone and bare utilitarian trappings of the Keep.

One of Lady Uwixa's chambermaids answered the door to her room.

"My apologies for disturbing her ladyship," said the manservant, "but this man claims to be Lord Geradin, of your lady's acquaintance."

Lady Uwixa immediately came to the door, still wrapping a robe around herself. Strands of gray hair fell from beneath her sleeping-cap.

"Lord Geradin! Thank the Light you've come, and so quickly. The Conclave of Monarchs seems to have lost all reason—they won't even listen to me."

"I'm sorry for our delay," said Geradin. He looked pointedly at the people surrounding him.

"I vouch that this is Lord Geradin," she told the manservant. "Please see that a room is prepared for him." She ushered Geradin into the room.

"King Aumekor should be here within days," said Geradin. "I came in advance to get Queen Onara's permission to bring the Protectors of the Line into the city."

"The King is coming? That is wonderful news. Surely the monarchs will delay the trial until he gets here."

"Trial? What trial?"

Lady Uwixa frowned. "You didn't get my letter?"

"Nothing about a trial."

"It's terrible. Lord Kindul has been arrested for treason against the Free Kingdoms. The monarchs plan to try him. If he's found guilty, they'll execute him."

Chapter Thirty

Aumekor

Aumekor rode in the center of the procession as it entered through the Northern Gate of Cirkepam. That morning, Allonna had removed the paint from his armor, which now gleamed in the afternoon sunlight. The Protectors of the Line also had restored their suits of armor to undisguised splendor. At the front and rear of the procession marched the soldiers of Cirkepam who had escorted them for the last two days of the journey.

To Aumekor's surprise, the street by which they entered the city was lined with cheering people. He could see the Protectors warily eyeing the throngs. "Why are these people here?" he asked Centurion Tilber, a Cirkepam commander.

"They are here to welcome you to our city."

"Yes, but so many?" Aumekor had never seen so many people; the crowds admitted to the Outer Keep for his Midsummer speech were tiny by comparison. He had now been seen by more of Queen Onara's subjects than his own. "I'm not even their king."

"If you are the prophesied Heir of the Line who will defeat the Dark Priestess—" Tilber turned his head and spat on the ground. "—then they will tell their children and grandchildren that they saw you." He waved a hand at the Protectors of the Line. "Besides, it's a spectacle, and the public loves spectacle. Queen Onara proclaimed today a feast day in your honor. After the sun goes down there will be fireworks and dancing."

"I shall have to thank Her Majesty when I see her." Though it seemed excessive, it was much better than the greeting he had dreaded. But apparently Kindul had not swayed the other monarchs against him. Geradin's note, brought by Centurion Tilber, had been maddeningly lacking in detail: *Mek, the monarchs welcome your arrival. There is but a minor trouble which need not concern you. Even priests are fallible. Ger.*

If High Priest Kogyrinem's speculation had been wrong, then Aumekor had forced this whole expedition by mistake. That would make it very difficult to convince the High Protectors to follow his reasoning in the future.

So he might as well enjoy this time out of the Keep, since it was likely to be his last. He activated the right arm of his armor and began waving to the crowd. The cheers intensified. Perhaps the High Protectors would allow an occasional parade in Aud Sapeer. It didn't seem fair that most of his own subjects never saw him.

Eventually the procession reached the palace. Tilber quickly explained that Queen Onara was the woman in the center at the top of the broad stairway, and that she was flanked on both sides by the other monarchs.

Holding his breath, Aumekor gave his armor the dismount command. Once he was firmly on the ground, he nervously set the armor walking up the stairway, hoping he would not fall flat in front of all the monarchs—not that the High Protectors around him would let him hit the ground. But Allonna had done her job well, and he made it to the top of the stairs without incident. A twitch of the correct finger combination even allowed him to make a regal bow before Queen Onara.

"Welcome to Cirkepam, King Aumekor att'Ordil, Heir of the Line of Orcan," she said. "On behalf of the Conclave of Monarchs, I bid you join us for a feast in your honor."

"I thank you and my fellow monarchs for your hospitality," said Aumekor. "The honor will be mine to join you in feasting." He had hoped to speak privately with Geradin, whom he had spotted standing with Lady Uwixa, but that would have to wait. It seemed strange that Kindul was not there.

Surrounded by a core of eight High Protectors, he followed Queen Onara through the ornate doors of her palace into a large hall. Once they were far enough inside that they could no longer be seen from outside, she stopped and turned to look at him.

"Well, dear boy, you certainly know how to make an appearance. I'm so glad you were able to break free and join us. My subjects will be talking about this for days. Your Protectors of the Line are very impressive—do you ever have them compete in tournaments?"

Careful not to let his face betray his surprise at the turn of conversation, Aumekor said, "No, Your Majesty. That would allow our enemies to gauge their fighting abilities, looking for weaknesses."

"A pity." She sighed. "As for calling me 'Your Majesty,' we decided on the fifth day of the Conclave that we couldn't all be our majesties while we were here. We're all old friends by now, except you—I guess you're the new friend. So call me Nara." She began pointing to the other monarchs, who were now inside. "That's Weyl and Jorak and Toli and Supa. Paskolyik there refuses to answer to Paskol, but sometimes we call him that anyway when he's being particularly outrageous."

"Beh!" King Paskolyik's voice boomed in the hall. "A true friend's nickname be longer than real name. My finest friends name me Paskolyikor-Tumis."

Without acknowledging Paskolyik's interjection, the queen continued her introductions. "And Lita and Kesik and Den and Urquon and Lom and Techil and Gwee and Irrop and Norpit. As for you…" she said as she faced Aumekor squarely.

This was definitely a lot less formal than he had expected. It seemed the monarchs were reveling in their equality. Aumekor grinned and said, "Call me Mekor. Except for you, Paskolyikor-Tumis—you may call me Aumekorin-Lerid." He was suddenly glad Selima had made him study Aldamundian naming conventions. If he remembered correctly, he had just given himself a nickname that indicated a small or humble follower of the Light.

"A civilized man be you, Aumekorek-Lerid," said Paskolyik, changing the suffix to mean a great follower of the Light. "Unlike some short-names I could tell you."

"Be mindful of letting him tell you anything, young Mekor," said Onara. "Paskol could talk the ears off a mule with the epic saga of what he ate for breakfast. And speaking of eating, the dinner feast will begin soon. But I'm sure you need time to refresh yourself after your journey and get out of that armor. I will have someone show you to your chambers." She waved a manservant over.

Aumekor had long been anticipating the suggestion that he remove his armor. "Thank you, Nara. I could use some time to refresh. But I mean no offense to your palace security by the fact I will continue to wear my armor. I wear it constantly even in the Keep of Aud Sapeer, surrounded by the Protectors of the Line." That was true enough.

Fortunately, Onara nodded in understanding. "Go, then. You will be notified when the feast is ready." She leaned close. "And if you change your mind about sending your Protectors to fight in the arena, we could charge a premium for admission and split the proceeds." She turned to the other monarchs and said, "Go do what you will. The feast will begin later."

The manservant led Aumekor down three long corridors to some gilded double doors. The manservant opened the doors. "Your chambers, Your Majesty."

Aumekor could see a sitting-room with several well-stuffed couches atop thickly woven carpets. Beyond that room were more doors, open so he could see a massive bed. Two High Protectors went inside to confirm the rooms were secure.

Geradin, Selima, Allonna and Lady Uwixa arrived before the Protectors had finished their inspection.

"How wonderful to see you like this, Your Majesty," said Lady Uwixa. Her tone left no doubt she was amazed and happy to see him walking. Geradin must have explained the enchanted armor to her.

"It is good to see you again, Lady Uwixa." He frowned. "But why is Lord Regent Kindul not here to greet me?" What was Kindul up to?

Geradin coughed like he sometimes did when trying not to laugh. "He was...detained."

"This matter is no joke, Lord Geradin," said Uwixa.

With the Protectors' approval, they moved into the sitting-room so they could converse privately.

"Kindul's been accused of treason against the Free Kingdoms," said Geradin.

"Treason? How?" Treason against the Free Kingdoms went beyond maneuvering to take the throne of Aud Sapeer; it would mean Kindul was working for the Dark Priestess. That didn't make sense—Kindul had saved his life at Midsummer, and probably could have killed him at almost any time over the past sixteen years.

"I'm certain the charges must be false," said Lady Uwixa. "But he is accused of sending secret messages to the Dark Priestess and...and imprisoning the Heir of the Line." She seemed embarrassed by the second charge. "When Kindul refused to decode the message he sent, the monarchs decided that was sufficient evidence of his guilt to arrest him."

"He's sitting in Queen Onara's dungeon right now," said Geradin. "And, I might add, his cell is larger and more comfortably furnished than my room back home."

Aumekor tried to work out the implications. "If he refused to decode the message, how do they know it was to the Dark Priestess? And why did they think I was imprisoned?"

Uwixa bowed her head. "That latter charge is my fault, I'm afraid. Kindul never said outright that you didn't come to the Conclave because you were a coward, but his manner and tone always suggested it. 'It is not for me to criticize my king if he chooses to remain in the safety of the Keep,' he would say. It was starting to have an effect—I heard some of the monarchs asking what the point of supporting the Heir of the Line was, if he wouldn't come out to fight if the Priestess attacked."

Uwixa leaned forward. "So one night I had a servant take me to Onara's quarters, and I pretended I was frightened of Kindul. 'He has abused his powers as Regent to keep poor King Aumekor away from the Conclave,' I told her. 'It's supposedly for the king's own protection, but he's practically a prisoner in his own Keep. Why, Kindul only allows him outside to breathe fresh air but once a year.' I told her more along those lines, and Onara promised to do what she could to counter Kindul's influence with the other monarchs."

"So that explains part of it," Aumekor said. But what's this about sending a message to the Dark Priestess?"

"After we got here, Kindul began sending messages back to Aud Sapeer by messenger bird. I even sent you some messages that way myself. You did receive them?"

Aumekor nodded.

"Then one day, King Pivalom noticed that Kindul released two birds. One bird flew to the northeast, toward Aud Sapeer. But the second flew north."

Geradin said, "I've asked Kindul about that, and he claims the bird was going to an agent of his in Aldamun. From here, it would be impossible to distinguish a bird heading to Aldamun from one headed to the City of the Dark God. But there's no way of proving it."

Uwixa continued, "Having heard what Onara had to say about Kindul, Pivalom was suspicious. So he waited until Kindul again was preparing two birds, and then seized them. The messages are written in some form of code, and while Kindul maintains there is nothing in them that is treasonous, he refuses to divulge their contents. And that refusal may cost him his life."

For a moment, Aumekor wondered if Kindul could somehow be an agent of the Dark Priestess. Then he realized the logical explanation for Kindul's refusal to decode the messages. "I've always believed that Kindul was loyal to Aud

Sapeer, even if he was not loyal to me personally. He cannot prove the contents of the messages are harmless because the only way to do so would be to reveal how to decode the messages—and thereby enable the decoding of any other messages sent by agents of our kingdom. He is willing to die rather than betray Aud Sapeer."

"It was much more fun to think of Kindul as a traitor," said Geradin. He sighed. "Now I supposed we have to keep the other monarchs from beheading him."

◆ ◆ ◆

Kindul's eyes bulged when he saw Aumekor walk into the cell. "Your Majesty? How…?"

"Lord Regent Kindul, you have been charged with serious crimes." Aumekor couldn't help feeling a bit of a thrill at seeing his long-time adversary humbled like this—although Geradin was right, the cell was spacious and well-furnished. It even had a window overlooking the palace gardens. *I've never had a window in my chambers*, thought Aumekor.

Closing his eyes, Kindul said, "And now you've come to see me executed. Fair enough. I never did give you cause to want me alive." His voice was resigned.

"Kindul, you're a fool."

"Obviously, or I would not have let myself get trapped like this."

"No. What I mean is only a fool would engage in playing games of power with an adversary he did not understand. You could never see past my disappointing weak body to find out what kind of man I am."

Kindul opened his eyes. He seemed puzzled.

"I know you're loyal to Aud Sapeer. I do not want you convicted of treason, nor executed. But you will have to reveal to me the method for decoding the messages, so that I may tell the other monarchs I have read them, and they do not contain treason against the Free Kingdoms. They will have no choice but to take my word on it."

Looking Aumekor up and down, Kindul said, "You have been cured?"

"No, this armor is enchanted. Inside, I am still the same weakling you've despised. But I am your king, and as such I have a duty to make sure you are dealt with justly. And as your king, I command you to explain how to decode the messages."

"As Your Majesty commands."

Kindul had said that countless times over the years, but this was the first time Aumekor sensed respect behind the words.

◆ ◆ ◆

The coded messages consisted of groups of three to five letters. At the first level of deciphering, each letter was converted to the number based the order in which the letters first appeared in the *Book of Walira*, one of the more popular of the books purporting to explain what had happened to the gods. At the next level, the first number in each group was the number of a chapter in the book. The middle numbers in the group indicated a word in that chapter, and the final number indicated a letter in that word. If the final number was greater than the length of the word, then the whole word was meant.

It was not until after the feast in his honor that Aumekor was able to work on decoding the messages. It was a laborious process, and Nikufed had to request extra candles to replace the ones that had burned down all the way.

The first message, to one of Kindul's men in Aud Sapeer, merely contained a report on the progress of the Conclave was making toward deciding on an heir for Queen Onara. Apparently the progress was slow because various nobles of Cirkepam were quite adept at currying favor with one monarch or another, and Kindul speculated that the Conclave would take a long time to come to a conclusion because the monarchs were enjoying each other's company.

The second message was much shorter and more cryptic:

Biyeskalya beh'Denori. Report immediately. The name Biyeskalya sounded Aldamundian, so it was plausible that this message was intended for an agent in Aldamun. He would have to ask Kindul about the purpose of this message later, but now Aumekor felt confident he could convince the other monarchs to drop the charges against the Lord Regent.

❖ ❖ ❖

King Pivalom was the only one who caused any difficulty. "I saw the bird with my own eyes, flying north to the City of the Dark One."

Aumekor was sitting in a chair in Pivalom's quarters. "But Lom, it could also have been flying to Aldamun. I have seen the contents of the messages you seized—there is no treason in them."

"As you say." Pivalom nodded. "But you did not see the contents of the first message. There could have been treason in that one."

Were all Bosperanians so stubborn they could not admit to making a mistake? Aumekor paused, searching for another way to approach the problem.

"We must have no tolerance for treason," said Pivalom. His voice was quiet and earnest. "It must be found before it takes root. This man Kindul is plotting against you, and it is better to kill him now even if he has not yet betrayed you. If he were my subject, he would be dead, and his children also."

Aumekor knew that some monarchs could be ruthless in maintaining their power, but he was shocked by Pivalom's suggestion. In Aud Sapeer, children were never held responsible for the deeds of their parents. "You would kill a man and his family if you suspected he was plotting against you?"

Pivalom raised his eyebrows. "Plotting against me? Of course not. I'd have to kill half my nobles, and that would leave only the stupid ones."

Aumekor's confusion must have shown, because Pivalom raised his index finger and said, "Ah, I see the problem. The worst that could happen if someone plots against me is I am deposed, perhaps killed, and someone new sits on the throne of Bosperan. Such things happen." He shrugged, then pointed at Aumekor. "But if someone plots against you, the High Priestess of the Dark One will rule the world until it ends, and such cannot be allowed to happen. To even think of treason against the Heir of the Line is worthy of death in my kingdom."

"I see." It was suddenly all clear to Aumekor. Veratur the Betrayer was probably the most-remembered Bosperanian name in all the Free Kingdoms. Since Veratur, the High Protectors had refused to let any Bosperanians serve as Protectors of the Line, for fear they might also turn out to be traitors. Pivalom refused to back down in his accusation against Kindul because he wanted to remove the stain of treason from his kingdom. What better way to do that than have a Bosperanian save the Heir of the Line from treachery?

"Lom, I appreciate that you are trying to protect me. But Kindul's plotting against me is just games of power, not treason against the Free Kingdoms." Aumekor felt the irony of defending Kindul for the same actions that had been so frustrating in the past. "Please do not pursue this matter any farther."

Remaining silent, Pivalom nodded after a few moments.

"Thank you." Aumekor rose to leave, but then realized he had more to say. Under the laws of Aud Sapeer, children were not responsible for the acts of their parents. Did it make sense for an entire kingdom to be held responsible for the acts of Veratur? "I was but a baby when the High Protectors refused to seat the Bosperanian replacement, and I never thought to question that decision. They were wrong then, and they are still wrong. If Bosperan is still willing to send of its best young men to serve as Protectors of the Line, I will insist they be treated as the equal of those from any other kingdom."

Pivalom rose to his feet and bowed to Aumekor. "Thank you

for restoring my people's honor. We shall not fail you again."

◆ ◆ ◆

Although he had been released from his cell, Kindul did not join the monarchs and nobles at dinner that evening. Aumekor could not blame him, as the Lord Regent probably wanted little to do with the people who had been calling for his head the day before.

"I'm curious, Your Majesty," said Uwixa, who was seated to Aumekor's left. "You left Aud Sapeer before I sent my message that Kindul had been arrested. Why?"

"It was the hidden message you sent me earlier, about Kindul trying to take the throne."

Her voice was shocked. "I didn't send any such message!"

"Yes, you…" Aumekor paused, trying to remember. It was barely half a season, but already life back at the Keep seemed long ago. "We interpreted your message about arriving in Cirkepam to mean that Kindul was trying to take the throne. High Priest Kogyrinem figured out how it was possible." He frowned. "That wasn't what you meant?"

"How could anything I said possibly have been construed that way?"

"You referred to Lord Regent Kindul as Lord Kindul. Three times. You deliberately omitted the word 'regent.' What else could you mean by that, but that Kindul was trying to take the throne?"

She stared at him and then laughed. Turning to Selima, she said, "And you went along with that?"

Selima looked uncomfortable. "It made sense at the time. You always called him Lord Regent Kindul. The omission did seem deliberate."

Uwixa laughed again and kept laughing until everyone in the room was staring at her. She wiped her eyes and said, "I'm sorry, but I can't believe you mounted this whole expedition based on my leaving out a word."

"Three times," Aumekor said. He started to feel foolish. "Why did you leave it out then, if not to send a message?"

Uwixa looked at him. "I guess I was trying to send a message, but not that one. During the journey to Cirkepam, as I thought about my mission to arrange your marriage, it occurred to me that you are no longer the child you were when I took my husband's place on the Regency Council. I decided that as far as I was concerned, you had no need of a regent, so I decided to stop calling Kindul the Lord Regent." She shook her head and laughed again. "I suppose it's Lord Kindul's good fortune you were so suspicious of him, else he might have been executed before you arrived."

◆ ◆ ◆

Nikufed had already removed most of Aumekor's armor in preparation for bed when one of the Protectors entered the bedroom and said, "Lord Kindul is here, asking permission to see you."

The story of the missing "Regent" had obviously spread to the Protectors of the Line. Aumekor smiled faintly.

"Shall I put your armor back on," said Nikufed, "or do you want him to come back in the morning?"

"No," said Aumekor. "Let him see me as I am."

When Kindul saw Aumekor lying on the bed, he said, "Forgive me, Your Majesty. I will return tomorrow."

"Now is fine. What did you wish to speak to me about?"

Kindul went down on one knee. "I have come to offer my resignation. Lady Uwixa or Lady Selima can serve in my stead until we return to Aud Sapeer and the Assembly of Lords can either appoint a permanent replacement or dissolve the regency entirely. Tomorrow I shall return to my estate, and from there I shall trouble you no more. My eldest daughter will represent me in the Assembly, and as long as I live she will vote as you wish."

Kindul was giving up. Yet the moment of triumph seemed

hollow. He didn't want a disgraced and defeated Kindul—he wanted a strong Lord Kindul on his side.

"Lord Regent Kindul," said Aumekor. He waited until Kindul lifted his eyes to look at him. "You served my father well as his Lord Chamberlain. You were loyal to him personally, not just as his subject. Is that not so?"

"It is."

"If you will swear fealty to me personally, I would have you as my Lord Regent, and later as my Lord Chamberlain, that you might serve our kingdom as you did in the days of my father."

After a pause, Kindul said, "I cannot swear to always agree with your decisions. I cannot swear never to argue against you."

"As long as your arguments come from a desire to help me do what is best for our kingdom, I cannot fault you."

"Then I will swear my fealty to you."

Kindul came forward and, clasping Aumekor's hand, swore his oath.

◆ ◆ ◆

Before falling asleep that night, Aumekor thanked each of the Gods of Light for the foolish mistake that made possible the greatest victory of his life.

Chapter Thirty-One

Geradin

Geradin furrowed his brow. "You're sending him back to run the kingdom while you're gone?"

"That's what I just said." Mek smiled.

"Did you leave your brain back in Aud Sapeer? This is Kindul we're talking about. It's got to be a trick. He's plotting something."

"He gave me his oath of fealty."

"Did he swear it on Selima's oath disk?"

Sighing, Mek looked away. "Sometimes I wish she'd never found that thing. In my father's day, men used to trust a simple oath. Now anything less than the oath disk is suspect."

"If he's really become your loyal servant, he won't object to swearing on the disk." Geradin sat back and folded his arms. If Mek didn't want to take proper precautions, it was up to Geradin to make sure he did.

"Did you swear your oath as a Protector on the disk?"

"No, but I haven't been plotting behind your back all your life."

Mek started to say something, then stopped.

Geradin's memory jumped to his vote against allowing Mek to leave the Keep. Did Mek have doubts about his loyalty?

Mek shook his head. "I won't ask that of him. Kindul needs to feel that I trust—"

One of the Protectors standing guard outside Mek's

chambers opened the door. "Excuse me, Your Majesty, but you're being summoned to an emergency meeting of the Conclave of Monarchs."

Nikufed hurried over and began strapping on the rest of Mek's armor.

Geradin rose from his seat. He drew his sword just to confirm its blade glowed a safe blue. "I'll see if I can find out what this is about."

"Yes, go," said Mek.

Geradin went.

In the hall, Selima was the omnimancer on duty maintaining the wards around Mek's chambers.

"Aumekor will be following shortly," said Geradin. "Any idea what this emergency meeting is about?"

Selima shook her head. "Lady Uwixa may know more; she was supposed to meet with King Paskolyik this morning." There was an odd tone to her voice, as if she disapproved of the Aldamundian monarch.

"I'll see." He began trotting down the corridor, his armored boots making only a muffled thump on the carpet rather than the clang he was used to hearing back in the Keep. After almost bowling over a couple of servants, he slowed his pace to a brisk walk.

Lady Uwixa was not in her chambers, but he met her in the corridor as he headed toward the council room. He turned and walked with her back toward her rooms. "Do you know what this emergency meeting is about?"

"Only that King Paskolyik is the one who has called for it. It's hard to tell with him. It could be something serious, or it may just be that his wife has given birth to yet another baby."

"Yet another? How many children does he have?"

"Five by his first wife, three by his second, five by his third and one by his fourth."

"He has four wives?" Geradin didn't remember hearing that Aldamundians had more than one wife, but from what he'd read about them, they weren't very civilized.

"No. His first three wives were killed."

"By who?" Geradin felt a pang of sympathy for all those children who had lost their mothers.

"Raiders." Uwixa motioned him to follow her into her chambers. "From over the Barrier Mountains. They were all valiant warriors, though."

Geradin was caught off guard by the seeming change of subject. She couldn't mean the raiders were valiant. "Who?"

"Paskol's first three wives. Particularly Denori, his second wife. I met her years ago, when my husband was sent to inspect the Barrier Wall. She was a bit shorter than you, and of course not as proficient with the sword, but she was a fine warrior."

The storytellers told legends of barbarian female warriors, but every army Geradin had ever seen used only men for physical combat. "I'd always heard Aldamundians were fierce warriors, so why don't the men protect their women instead of sending them into battle?"

"Spoken like a bold and true man of Aud Sapeer," said Uwixa. Her tone left no doubt he was being foolish.

"What do you mean by that?"

"Why don't you protect Allonna and Selima instead of sending them into battle?" Uwixa gathered up some papers and began to walk out of the room.

Geradin followed. "That's different. Physical strength is important for manual combat, and men are generally stronger than women. But there is no difference between the sexes in magical strength."

"Still, you could keep the women mancers safe at home and only use male mancers in combat."

Geradin shook his head. "We need every mancer capable of combat. We can't afford to leave out the women."

"The Aldamundians live in a state of almost constant battle against raiders. No large army can come through the Barrier Mountains anywhere except Denoral's Pass, but bands of raiders can make it along trails too treacherous for horses.

The Aldamundian women fight because they must. And some of them are very good at it. That's why I've been working to arrange a match between Aumekor and Paskol's daughter Biyeskalya."

Geradin's mouth hung open for a moment. "You want M—Aumekor to marry a barbarian warrior-woman?"

"It is an excellent match. Aumekor comes from a line of great warriors. Biyeskalya not only comes from a line of great warriors, she is one herself. Their child will naturally be a great warrior, perhaps the prophesied Heir of the Line who will go on to defeat the Dark Priestess."

"You're not breeding horses. What if he doesn't even like her?" Geradin had known Lady Uwixa was arranging a marriage for Mek, but he'd expected her choice to be from one of the nearby, civilized kingdoms—a princess who would know how to act her role in Aud Sapeer society.

Uwixa stopped and put her hand on Geradin's arm. "Please don't ever talk like that around Aumekor. You are free to choose whom you will marry, so it matters if you love her. With kings, particularly this king, there are far more important matters at stake than love. Don't make things difficult for him."

Before Geradin could respond, Mek and Selima appeared from an adjoining corridor.

"Did you find out what going on?" Mek asked.

"Only that King Paskolyik called the meeting," said Geradin.

Mek frowned. "That could mean trouble at the Barrier Wall."

"Or it could merely be the birth of his next child," said Uwixa. "He told me his wife was well along in pregnancy."

Mek's brow wrinkled for a moment before he said, "Reskara. That's his wife's name, right?"

"His fourth wife," said Geradin.

Mek raised his eyebrows. "He has four wives?"

"That's exactly what I said." Geradin was glad he wasn't the only one to make that mistake. "The first three are dead. Did you know they have women warriors?"

"Geradin," said Selima. "I think that's a conversation that can wait until after the meeting."

◆ ◆ ◆

About half the monarchs were already in the meeting room, along with various advisers and servants. Geradin took his place next to Selima and Uwixa in chairs behind Aumekor's seat at a large semicircular table.

King Paskolyik stood at the focus of the table. He wore leather armor, not plate, and it had been dyed blood-red. The Aldamundian king waited silently until the last of the monarchs arrived.

"Friends," he said, "it be not an accident we gather at this time. It be not an accident Aumekorek-Lerid arrive in time to hear my news." He paused and looked around the table. "My wife write to tell me a great army make camp in sight of the Wall. They number larger than counting."

A wave of surprised mutterings went through the assembly.

"In years ago, we beat such numbers." Paskolyik bowed his head to Selima. "The Wall be strong, and be never broken."

Off to Geradin's left a couple of people clapped, but Paskolyik sharply waved a hand to silence them.

"This army of the Shadow be not trying to break the Wall. But day upon day, they bring rocks with their carts and their giant beasts. Rocks and dirt, which they pile before them."

"A fortress?" someone said.

"A ramp," said Geradin, simultaneously with King Noraweyl of Pamidaur.

"Impossible," said King Pivalom. "There's no way they can build a ramp that big. And even if they tried, our archers would pick off the builders long before they could complete it."

"Wards," said Geradin. "I was hit in the chest from ten paces with a crossbow bolt, and it didn't even dent my armor."

Mek rose from his chair. All eyes looked to him.

He's the youngest and least experienced of all the monarchs, thought Geradin, and yet they all expect him to lead the armies of the Free Kingdoms into battle.

"Paskolyikor-Tumis," said Mek, his voice firm, "as your friend, I will use what little strength is in this arm to defend your kingdom, even if no one else will stand with me." He raised his right arm. "But as King Aumekor att'Ordil, Heir to the Line of Orcan, I call upon all the Free Kingdoms to muster their armies and send them to the Barrier Wall. If the armies of the Dark Priestess wish to fill Denoral's Pass, they shall do so—with their dead."

King Pivalom jumped to his feet and called out, "I stand with the Heir."

Other monarchs stood and added their support.

In the tumult, Selima leaned over to Geradin. "You must gather the High Protectors. You must stop him from going. He cannot lead them into battle; it's too risky."

Geradin looked into Selima's eyes. They glistened as if she were about to cry. He shook his head. "Not even the High Protectors can hold him back now. Even if I could, I would not. It's his destiny to lead, and he will. All we can do is our best to make sure he lives."

I will not fail him. Light help me, I must not fail him.

Chapter Thirty-Two

Allonna

On the tenth day of the journey to Aldamun, Allonna watched Geradin practicing with his sword, his fluid motions causing stretched shadows to dance in the early morning sunlight. She had been awake a while; it had been her turn to be the mancer on alert during the second half of the night.

Now she sat by a cookfire, sipping a mug of tea to stave off the autumn chill. She would have to ask Selima if there were a magical way to stay warm. Draping herself with blankets while keeping watch seemed awkward, so she had abandoned them as the sun came up.

"Is that tea?" said Lady Uwixa.

Her arrival had gone unnoticed by Allonna. "Yes, milady." She instinctively began to stand, but Lady Uwixa motioned her to stay seated.

Lady Uwixa served herself from the pot on the edge of the fire, then sat down on the ground next to Allonna. "At least it will start to get warmer farther north, until we have to go up into the mountains."

Geradin continued to practice, his enchanted blade moving so fast that Allonna couldn't follow its motion, even with its blue glow.

Lady Uwixa said, "He's a handsome one, isn't he?"

Allonna started. "I was just admiring his swordsmanship is

all."

"Oh, of course." Lady Uwixa's voice was amused.

Allonna's face felt suddenly warm despite the cold air. "I don't deny Lord Geradin is handsome, but not any more so than some of the young men in my village and so his handsomeness is not so great as to fascinate me, while as a swordsman he is the best I have ever seen, so to see him wield a sword is worth watching."

"I see." Lady Uwixa sipped her tea.

Allonna's eyes went back to Geradin.

"What do you think of High Protector Wyran's abilities with the sword?" asked Lady Uwixa.

"I...I don't believe I've really seen enough to form an opinion."

"And High Protector Ianik?"

Feeling suddenly wary, Allonna said, "Likewise."

"You must forgive an old lady like me for prying. Although..." Lady Uwixa raised an eyebrow. "I suppose it is merely coincidence that for the past several mornings you've been watching Lord Geradin practice, but have missed seeing any of the others."

"I always sit at the fire closest to my tent. It's not my fault if Lord Geradin happens to practice nearby while the others practice elsewhere."

Smiling, Lady Uwixa said, "But you are wrong: it is your fault."

"How?"

Lady Uwixa winked. "I think he's trying to impress you."

"Impress me?"

"Why not? You're a fine-looking young woman. And I hear you saved his life—that must have made you look very good in his eyes."

Allonna shook her head. It was ridiculous. Geradin was a noble; he wouldn't be attracted to a commoner like her. Then she remembered the annoying way he had flirted with the caravan girls, and suddenly it didn't seem so ridiculous.

Tightening her lips, she said, "He'll try to impress any young woman, so there's nothing particular about his attentions to me. I just happen to be the only young woman in our party."

Geradin sheathed his sword and strode over to the cookfire. He pointed at the pot. "Any tea left?" His breath made puffs of mist that blew away in the chill breeze.

Allonna nodded, and Geradin rummaged in a leather bag on the ground, finally bringing out a tin cup. He poured himself some tea, but did not sit down. Instead, he took a couple of paces from the fire and stood looking out over the plains.

She thought back to the day they first met. How wrong she had been to think he was no more than an arrogant lordling. He might be arrogant in some ways, true, yet his arrogance was based on skill and confidence, not noble birth. He was the youngest of the High Protectors, but already his advice and leadership were sought by the others.

Surely she was not the only one whose opinion of the other had changed. He must have seen her as a naïve country girl the day they met. Since then they had worked together to plan the enchantment of the king's armor. He had seen the power of her magic; it had even saved his life. He respected her power, and more than that, it seemed he respected her for who she was.

And he really was quite handsome.

He turned around and looked at her, as if sensing she was thinking about him. Allonna quickly turned her eyes to look at the fire.

"Good tea," he said. "Thank you, Allonna. You did make this, right?"

"Yes," she said, "although I cannot really take credit for the quality, because it's just tea, and it's not as if I have various herbs to flavor it, like I did back in Glicken."

"I like it. Some people make it too weak. I'm sure you must be a good cook."

A good cook? He was complimenting her on her cooking? Did he think she was one of those caravan girls, trying to gain a husband by winning his stomach? "Would you like some warm, fresh bread, flavored with honey?" she asked, her voice dangerously sweet.

He raised his eyebrows. "That does sound good."

Allonna stood and splashed the remains of her tea in the fire. "Make it yourself, then." She stalked back to her tent, wishing it had a door she could slam behind her.

◆ ◆ ◆

Allonna rode beside Selima. There was a cold wind, but at least it was from the south so it blew at their backs, not their faces. Red and yellow leaves whirled past occasionally, stripped from the trees that lined the road.

"So you don't think we're going to confront the Dark Priestess," said Allonna. The sudden memory of the figure cloaked in darkness she had seen in her mind a season ago made her shudder. The darkness had seemed like a living thing reaching for her.

"Most likely she has sent her armies, but is not with them," said Selima. "She does not like to put herself where the Heir of the Line might come at her with a sword. But that does not mean there is no danger. According to prophecy, the Dark Priestess cannot be harmed by anyone but the Heir of the Line. The Heir has no such promise. He could be struck down by arrow, by sword, even an accident. That's why I think this journey is foolishness—Aumekor could command the armies from Aud Sapeer. He does not have to lead them physically into battle. Especially not..."

They traveled on in silence. Allonna could see Selima's point, yet she could also understand the effect seeing King Aumekor would have on the troops at the Barrier Wall. Her father had served in the Barrier Guard. In telling tales of what he had seen he had shown nothing but contempt for officers who stayed as far as they could from combat. What did the soldiers of the Dark Priestess think of her, hiding in her temple while sending them out to fight?

A sudden curiosity made Allonna ask, "What's her name?"

"Who?"

"The High Priestess of the Dark God. What's her name?" Allonna knew the Dark God's name was Zerul, even if she respected the tradition of not saying it aloud lest it call him back from whither he had disappeared. But no one had ever told her the name of the Dark Priestess.

"I don't know," said Selima. "It's possible no one in the Free Kingdoms knows. Perhaps she has forgotten it herself. Some sources say she was actually born in the Age of Light, which would make her more than a thousand years older than anybody else now living. Others say she is the second Dark Priestess, chosen by the Dark God to replace his first when she displeased him. That would make her only about nine hundred years old."

Only nine hundred. Allonna still found it hard to believe that her own life might last four or five hundred years. "Why hasn't she just died of old age?" Realizing that sounded a little foolish, she added, "I know she's an omnimancer, but even you are growing older. Does the prophecy that she can only be killed by the Heir of the Line keep her alive?"

"There is a foul subject." Selima didn't speak for a few beats. "It's not the prophecy that keeps her alive, it's necromancy."

Allonna had heard of death magic before, but knew little about it. "So you could extend your life that way, too, if you wanted?"

"Don't even talk that way, child. Necromancy is a thing of evil. It was created by the Dark God, and its workings are very different from regular mancy. Its source of power is life itself, and it can be invoked only through the taking of life. The Dark Priestess extends her life by giving birth to a child and then killing it—sacrificing her own child to force the demigod Death to do her bidding."

A queasiness in her stomach made Allonna wish she had not asked. She took several deep breaths until the feeling passed. "Why is this not widely known? It would make people even more willing to help defeat her."

Selima sighed. "Because there is too much of evil, even among the Free Kingdoms. The less people know about necromancy, the better. Most parents would not kill their children even to extend their own lives. But some would, and that is a horror I would rather not see."

"Are there that many people with a talent for necromancy?" asked Allonna.

"Necromancy requires no talent, only knowledge and the willingness to kill. Fortunately, most necromancers are selfish enough not to teach the use of their power to others—perhaps because a pupil who kills his teacher is granted great necromantic power."

Allonna could think of nothing to say. Thinking of the helpless babies she had attended as a healer back in Glicken, she could not understand how anyone could want to kill them. Somewhere within she felt herself harden in resolve. If it was her fate to stand beside the Heir of the Line to confront the Dark Priestess, then it was a fate she no longer feared.

Chapter Thirty-Three

Geradin

Geradin and Mek lay on their backs, looking up at the shapes of the Nightglow. The weather in the kingdom of Cabeska was pleasantly warm for late autumn, although it was starting to cool now that the sun had gone down.

"It doesn't look like a snake," said Mek. "I mean, which end is which? There are no eyes, no mouth. And it has bulges in it."

"It's long and winding, and that's close enough," said Geradin. "The Snake is very useful, because its head points to the Mushroom."

"How can you tell which end is its head?"

"Its head is the end pointing to the Mushroom. See, over there?" Geradin pointed to a portion of the Nightglow that formed a semicircle with a stem coming out.

"The Mushroom is upside down."

Geradin sighed. "It is now, but by morning it will rotate to be almost right side up. The important thing is that the Mushroom is always directly south, no matter where you are. And even if it's hard to spot at first because it's turned at a strange angle, the Snake always points to it."

Mek didn't say anything for a while. "I feel like that, sometimes."

"Like what?"

"Like the Mushroom. No matter which way I turn, the Dark

Priestess is always pointing straight at me."

It had been a long time since Mek had confided in him like this. Ever since the armor—no, ever since Geradin had passed the Tests of Majority—Mek had been acting as if he were completely confident in himself. But for some reason, tonight felt like those childhood nights when Geradin would sneak out of his room and, abetted by the Protectors standing watch, slip into Mek's room so they could talk long after Selima had put them to bed.

"You've got it wrong," said Geradin. "Perhaps before, but now she's the Mushroom, you're the Snake."

"Why do you say that?"

"The Mushroom stays in one spot, while the Snake moves around. She's hiding in her temple, while you're moving about."

"Selima thinks it's a mistake."

"The High Protectors, me included, disagree. If that army gets past the Barrier Wall, there is nothing to stop it from sweeping down all the way to Aud Sapeer, and even the Keep would not stand for long. Therefore, the Wall must be held, and your being there increases our chances. You made the right decision."

"Thanks," said Mek. "Now it's your turn."

"For what?"

"To unload something that's bothering you."

"There's nothing." Nothing Mek could do anything about, in any case.

"Ger." Mek's voice held an edge of warning.

Reluctantly, Geradin decided to let Mek in on his secret. "Allonna's been avoiding me. I don't think she wants me to like her."

"Why wouldn't she—oh." Mek paused. "So, how long have you liked her that way?"

"I'm not even sure. After we left Cirkepam, I guess. It wasn't even until she started avoiding me that I figured it out. And every time I try to be nice to her, she turns away."

"I think it started before that," said Mek. "I wondered why you continued your studies with Selima after you passed the Tests of Majority. Was it because there was someone attractive to study with?"

"I..." Could it have been developing as long as that? How could he not have noticed? "We didn't study together. It was more like we just happened to be studying in the same room."

"Ah." Mek's tone was amused.

"That's history, in any case. The problem is she doesn't seem to like me now."

"She is a few years older than you. Perhaps she just prefers someone older, so she's trying to discourage you."

Geradin snorted. "Oh, that's extremely helpful to me. Thank you so much."

"What am I supposed to say? I can't order her to fall in love with you."

"You could try. No, I suppose not." Geradin thought of what Uwixa had said about Mek not having much choice in marriage. Here was a chance to make Mek feel better about that. "You're lucky not to have to worry about that sort of thing. Arranged marriages have their advantages."

"Yes. But I suppose the arranging was disarranged by the arrival of the...Could the Dark Priestess have planned this to delay my getting married? Getting me involved in a prolonged siege far from home could be her way of distracting me."

Geradin chuckled. "May all her plans go so well."

"What? It looks like she's succeeding."

Had Uwixa not told Mek about the barbarian princess at their destination? Perhaps she had been worried about Mek's reaction at being betrothed to a barbarian. Or perhaps there had been a problem coming to a final agreement.

Whatever the reason, Geradin decided it was not his right to tell Mek about his possible bride, so he said, "Lady Uwixa may be more resourceful than the Dark Priestess could predict."

"You know something you're not telling me."

"If I do know something, perhaps I'm not supposed to say

anything. You must ask Lady Uwixa about that."

Mek let out an exasperated breath. "I have. She won't tell me anything except that I must be patient."

Geradin spoke with mock gravity. "Wise advice indeed."

After a pause, Mek said, "Then perhaps you should follow it." His voice was serious.

"Me?"

"With Allonna. Be patient."

"You think she might grow to like me?" Perhaps in a year or two, she wouldn't consider their age difference too great. He hoped she wouldn't fall in love with someone else first.

"All is possible, given enough time," said Mek. "And I'll promise you this: if she still doesn't like you fifty years from now, *then* I'll order her to fall in love with you."

◆ ◆ ◆

The fastest route from Cirkepam to Aldamun had been the trade road to the city of Wellston and from there to the city of Cabeska. Though the party had passed through the northwest reaches of the Kingdom of Aud Sapeer, they had not been within even twenty days' journey of home. But near the northeastern border of Cabeska, the trade road from Aud Sapeer merged with the one they were on. To Geradin's surprise, after less than a half day's journey they encountered an army of three hundred footsoldiers from Aud Sapeer.

"They're mostly untrained volunteers," General Opattol reported to Mek and the High Protectors. "The main body of our regular forces are ahead of us by several days now, I wager. I've been going slower to give my men some time to train each day. Once we arrive, we'll integrate them with the veterans."

Mek's voice was filled with wonder. "How did you get here so quickly? And the rest of the army before you?"

"We heard about the Army of the Dark massing at the Barrier Wall before you, since the messenger birds had less distance to travel. So our army was ready to march when word came from Lord Kindul." The general shrugged. "By then we had all these volunteers, so we had to organize them somehow."

Geradin was impressed, both by the general's organizational skill and by the patriotism of the volunteers.

Apparently Mek was also impressed, because he said, "Well done, General. Would it help if I spoke to your men?"

"I'm sure they would be honored, Your Majesty."

◆ ◆ ◆

The volunteers stood in ranks for inspection. Geradin noticed that few of them had even leather armor, to say nothing of chain or plate mail. A handful had swords, many had bows, but most of them carried only wooden cudgels or staves as weapons. They were all commoners, Geradin realized, and from the lower half of that class.

Suddenly, Geradin saw one soldier who stood a head taller than the men around him. There was no mistaking that tremendous bulk. "Holoran?"

Holoran grinned. "Lord Geradin, it's good to see you."

"What are you doing here?"

"Same as everyone else. I'm here to fight for the Heir against the Dark Priestess."

At the words, all the men around Holoran gave a cheer.

It took effort for Geradin to avoid showing any disapproval. After all Geradin had done to keep Holoran out of the mock combat during the Tests of Majority, here he was volunteering to go into real battle. Strong as he was, his slowness made him vulnerable. "We'll talk later, and you can tell me how things are with Telani."

Holoran's grin faltered. "As it pleases you, milord."

Geradin had suspected Telani was not happy about Holoran's decision, and the big man's reaction confirmed it. Perhaps once they reached the Barrier Wall, Holoran could be assigned to some labor duty, rather than combat—unless, of course, Holoran's over-developed sense of honor forced him to go running at the enemy armed with nothing more than his fists.

Chapter Thirty-Four

Aumekor

"There it is," said Uwixa, pointing to a distant smudge on the mountains directly ahead.

Squinting, Aumekor tried to make out some detail, but the city was still too far away. "Will we make the city before nightfall?" Since leaving the Keep, he had become reasonably adept at judging the time of day by the position of the sun, but the mountain heights on both sides of this stretch of the road to Aldamun made that impossible.

"No," said Wyran. "The last part is very steep, and the altitude makes it harder to breathe, so we will have to move slowly. We'll make camp and start fresh tomorrow."

Aumekor had hoped to sleep in a real bed tonight. Wyran insisted on avoiding inns as too confining and difficult to defend. In the half season after leaving Cirkepam, he had slept on a cot every night except for two: the nights they had spent in the palaces at Wellston and Cabeska. The padding in his armor—and the calluses on his flesh—now allowed him to ride a horse without abrasions, but he still ended each day with pain in his joints. He had hoped his body would adjust over time, but Selima theorized that the stiffness of the enchanted armor prevented his body from moving in proper rhythm with his horse. Allonna's efforts to compensate had so far been futile.

"It's not your fault, Windy," he said. She really was a good horse, always willing to follow the commands he gave her.

"Did you say something?" asked Uwixa, who had pulled her horse alongside his.

"Nothing of import."

"What is your assessment of King Paskolyik?"

After thinking a moment, Aumekor said, "I like him. He seems competent as a leader, and I understand he's a ferocious warrior. He seems to care about his people." He wasn't sure exactly what Uwixa was looking for.

"You realize his people are not as civilized as ours."

Frowning, Aumekor said, "His lands are less productive and his people live permanently on the edge of battle, so it is natural they lack some of the comforts we have in Aud Sapeer. That doesn't mean they are less civilized any more than the luxuries of the Cirkepamians mean they are more civilized."

"I am glad to hear it. I feared you might share Lord Geradin's opinion that the Aldamundians are barbarians."

He smiled. "I did when I was younger. As children, Geradin and I used to listen raptly to stories of the barbarian warriors in the Barrier Mountains. But Selima required me to read much concerning the different kingdoms, including Aldamun. I'm afraid Geradin may have been learning to use a sword, though, instead of reading those books."

"I suppose that served him well enough," she said.

"You want me to talk to Geradin, to make sure he does nothing to offend the Aldamundians?"

"Oh, I don't think that's necessary. He's polite enough not to call them barbarians to their faces. I brought up the subject for another reason."

Surely she didn't think Geradin was more politic than Aumekor. So why would she be concerned whether he thought the Aldamundians barbaric? A flash of insight gave him the answer. "You have arranged my marriage to an Aldamundian." That's what Geradin had been hinting.

"Geradin told you, I suppose."

"No, he refused. What's her name?"

"Biyeskalya beh'Denori. When we arrive tomorrow, Paskolyik will make the announcement of your betrothal. She's his eldest surviving unmarried daughter, by his second wife."

"Biyeskalya." He had heard that name before. His brow furrowed until he remembered. Kindul's second coded message had mentioned her. Aumekor had meant to ask why, but then Paskolyik's news threw everything into an uproar, and Kindul had returned to Aud Sapeer.

"One cannot always take a father's word on such things, but Paskolyik assured me she is considered beautiful. If she's anything like her mother, he isn't exaggerating." Uwixa paused. "She's also reputed to be an excellent warrior."

Uwixa probably feared that he would resent having a wife capable of combat when he was not. "Unlike Geradin, I knew the Aldamundians had women warriors. Besides, if I objected to having a wife stronger than me, I would not be left with a wide selection of possible mates."

◆ ◆ ◆

In a way, it was like coming home. Like the Inner Keep of Aud Sapeer, the entire city of Aldamun had been carved from the mountainside. Unlike the Inner Keep, though, it had large portions open to the sky, and many narrow window-slits through which arrows could be fired at invaders.

As the party passed through the massive doors into the city, their reception was far different from the triumphal entry they had received in Cirkepam. There were no cheering crowds lining the winding narrow streets. The people who stopped to stare were mostly older women and young children.

On approaching the king's palace, Aumekor was relieved to see Paskolyik standing at the top of the steps awaiting their arrival, surrounded by several of his guards.

"You come at last, Aumekorek-Lerid," shouted Paskolyik. "My city be at your feet."

"You honor me too much, Paskolyikor-Tumis," shouted Aumekor in return. He dismounted and began walking up the steps.

Followed by one of his guards, Paskolyik met him halfway down and clasped his arm. "Fear not, you ben't late for the battle," he said quietly, then shouted, "The Heir of the Line stand with us against the Dark!"

A cheer came from above and Aumekor looked to see armed men high upon the walls of the city. After a moment, he realized there were women there as well. When the cheering died down, Aumekor felt it was his turn to shout something. "Citizens of Aldamun, your bravery is well known even in my kingdom far to the south. With you at my side, we cannot fail."

The soldiers cheered again. Paskolyik waited for silence to return before speaking again. "The Line of Orcan be the hope of all Free Kingdoms. From the days of my ancestor Tetchniyol att'Garolyik, the blood of Orcan flow in the Heir of the Line. My people, I make now a glad announcement: for the first time, the blood of Tetchniyol join with the blood of Orcan. The Heir of the Line be betrothed to my daughter Biyeskalya."

A roar of approval came from the walls above. Aumekor had expected to at least see his intended bride before the announcement of their betrothal, and he began to wonder if Paskolyik was trying to hide something.

"Here." Paskolyik grabbed Aumekor's hand and brought it together with the hand of the guard that had followed him down the steps.

Surprised, Aumekor looked at the guard's face, which was mostly hidden by the horizontal bars of a visor. This was Biyeskalya? He should have remembered that she was a warrior—and a mere guard would not be wearing such finely crafted plate mail. Its metal was polished so well it almost seemed to have no color of its own, just reflections of its surroundings.

"It is a pleasure to meet you," Aumekor said quietly through the cheering.

He couldn't hear her response clearly, but it sounded something like "Soon be over with."

"Biyeskalya," said Paskolyik, his sharp tone belying the grin he wore on his face as he looked up at the celebrating soldiers. "Show to your husband-to-be proper respect."

Apparently Aumekor's betrothed was not overly fond of the prospect of marrying him. Winning her over would be a challenge. His life had been full of challenges, so what did one more matter? Aumekor signaled his armor, and bowed before her, saying, "No, it is I who must show proper respect for her."

She wrenched her hand free from where her father clasped it to Aumekor's. Then she turned and stalked up the steps toward the palace. The cheers died down as she left.

Paskolyik sighed. "She be angry I call her back from patrol for meeting you. Temper be hot but short. You see." Raising his voice, he said, "Now it be time for the welcome feast for our guests. Come inside, come inside." He beckoned the rest of Aumekor's party to follow him.

As Aumekor reached the top of the steps, Geradin caught up with him.

"Perhaps she prefers someone older," said Geradin with mock sympathy, "and so she's trying to discourage you."

"I suppose I deserved that." Aumekor smiled wryly. "I don't think ordering her to fall in love with me will work, though. I'm certain her father already tried."

◆ ◆ ◆

"I don't know what Uwixa was thinking," said Selima as she paced across Aumekor's room. "I gave her a list of twenty-three potential matches before she left for Cirkepam, and this Princess Biyeskalya was definitely not on it."

"Why didn't you say something earlier?" Aumekor was amused to see Selima so upset about this. He would try to win Biyeskalya's acceptance of the match, but if that didn't work, the marriage could be called off and surely one of Selima's twenty-three potential matches would be amenable.

"She assured me she knew the girl's mother, and that it would be a great match. But this is unacceptable."

"It's your own fault, of course."

Selima stopped pacing and looked at him. "My fault?"

"If you recall, I wanted to send *you* to the Conclave to arrange my marriage, but you insisted on staying behind. This is obviously your punishment for not obeying your king. I know it's gravely insulting to *you* that someone doesn't want to marry me, but I suppose that is a burden you will have to bear."

She sighed, looked around for a chair and sat down. "I'm sorry. This must be difficult for you."

Aumekor smiled. "I must admit, I tended to assume my betrothed would consider it an honor to marry the Heir of the Line, but I'm not—" He stopped as the door opened and a Protector came inside.

"Your Majesty, the Princess Biyeskalya and her escort are here, asking permission to speak with you."

"Show them in, please." Perhaps her father had been right, and her temper had not lasted. If they could talk for a while, Aumekor was confident he could win her over.

Two Aldamundian guards entered. When Aumekor saw the tall young woman who followed them into the room, it took him a moment to remember to breathe. Had he dreamed of her face before, or did it only seem like he must have? He tried to collect his thoughts so he could say something, but nothing intelligible came to mind.

She strode past her guards to the chair farthest from Aumekor. Her long neck held her head high as she sat stiffly, back straight and arms folded. She stared straight ahead rather than look at him. "My father has instructed me to hold a conversation with you."

Her careful enunciation had only a trace of the Aldamundian accent. Aumekor's mind began working again. She must have been sent elsewhere for her education while young—perhaps Bargas or Crez Pecui. She was wearing a patterned silk dress in the latest Cirkepam style—her father had probably brought it back and ordered her to wear it. The way she folded her arms indicated she was not comfortable with it, and that gave Aumekor his opening.

"As you see," he said, "I am wearing my armor. I know that you might be needed in battle at any time, so perhaps you would prefer to wear your armor as well. That way we will both be prepared if there is some emergency. I will wait for you to change; we can converse when you return."

She looked at him suspiciously.

"I'm serious. I want to see you dressed as a warrior should be."

She rose from her seat and followed her guards out of the room.

Aumekor let out a long breath. He looked at Selima and said, "That went well, don't you think?"

"We'll see." Selima pressed her lips together for a moment. "Perhaps you can make this work. Playing her off against her father like that is risky, though."

"I think she's worth risking for. Would any of your twenty-three matches be better able to protect me, or more likely to produce a great warrior as an heir?"

"You sound like your father," Selima said. "He came up with very sound political and strategic reasons for why his marriage should be arranged to your mother." She sighed. "He loved her very much."

◆ ◆ ◆

When Biyeskalya returned in her armor, Selima excused herself and left. Aumekor had no doubt she would be right outside, eavesdropping magically on the conversation, but he hoped Biyeskalya might feel more open about talking if it was just the two of them. Well, their guards and Nikufed would also be there, but over the years Aumekor had become accustomed to ignoring the presence of guards and servants, and she probably had a similar attitude.

Again, she sat in the farthest chair. Removing her helmet, she handed it to one of her guards. "We may now converse as my father instructed." As she had before, she stared straight ahead instead of looking at him.

Aumekor tried to gather his thoughts, which had once again scattered when he saw her face. "What would you like to talk about?"

"Nothing."

No help there. She was a warrior, so he would ask her about the war. "Biyeskalya, what is your—"

"Please call me Kalya."

"Kalya." In any other culture of the Free Kingdoms, that would have been an invitation to familiarity. In Aldamun, it meant she did not think he had earned the right to address her by her full name, let alone one of the extended nicknames friends used for each other. "What is your opinion of the Dark Priestess's current strategy for attacking the Free Kingdoms—Aldamun in particular?"

She looked at him, and it felt like his heart did a somersault in his chest when their eyes met. "It be— It is very wasteful, but if she is able to take such losses, it may be successful."

"Do you think our defenses are properly organized?"

"Mostly, yes."

"Mostly?"

She launched into an explanation of troop dispositions and the possibility of sending raiding parties to harass the supply lines of the enemy. Every time she stopped, Aumekor asked another question to get her talking again. Her grasp of military strategy and tactics was better than Aumekor's, which was not surprising since it turned out she had fought in her first battle at age twelve. His only participation in battles had been as a target.

As she told how she and several soldiers under her command had tracked down a band of raiders who had stolen some valuable furs, she stopped and frowned. "You ben't like the other soft southern men I meet." Sometime during the conversation, as her speech had flowed more freely, her Aldamundian accent and speech patterns had returned. "They all talk of my beauty. Be I not beautiful to you?"

Aumekor knew he was in dangerous territory. Denying her beauty would be both offensive and a lie. But extolling her beauty would put him in the same category as the soft southern men she was used to. She had set a trap, allowing her to take offense either way. He could see only one way out. "That's very clever of you, changing the subject suddenly to catch me off guard. Do you find that tactic usually works?"

"Now it be you who change the subject."

"Yes, and I've often been quite successful in doing so. Am I as horrid a southerner as you imagined I would be?"

"That be not the question."

"Would it make it easier for you to hate me if I recited you some soft southern poetry?"

"I do not hate you," Kalya said.

Aumekor raised an eyebrow. "Despise? Loathe? Detest? Abhor?"

She shook her head. "Stop."

He stopped.

"It be not your fault," said Kalya. "It be my father's. He force me to forswear myself on account of you."

"How?"

"In order to be rid of a man's unwanted attention, I swear I only marry a man who best me in battle. Several try, but none succeed."

"I see." Aumekor winced inwardly. He had thought he was making progress by getting her to talk about the reasons for her hostility, but there was no way he could meet her expectations.

"My father say you be a great leader, but that you be little talented with the sword. On the strength of my fealty to him, he require me to forswear my oath and marry you. This be true, you be not strong with the sword?"

"It is true," he said. Silently he cursed his frail body. "I did not know of your oath."

She shrugged. "My father not tell you, of course. But by my fealty to him, I need marry you."

She would marry him. He could have her as his wife despite his weakness. Desire and honor struggled within him. Honor won. "There is something I must tell you, Kalya, if we are to be married."

Suddenly he had hope again. He would tell her the truth—she would have to respect him for that. Perhaps she would even see it as her calling to protect him. He would force the High Protectors to accept her as the first female Protector of the Line. And at some point she might grow to love him.

Selima rushed into the room. "Your Majesty, I must speak with you."

He ignored her. All he had to do was get Kalya to understand. "My mother was poisoned before I was born. Because of that, I—"

"No!" shouted Selima.

"—was born with no strength in my limbs." He signaled his armor to stand him up. "I cannot even stand on my own: this armor is enchanted. I have no talent for the sword because I cannot even draw the sword I have at my side. If you marry me, Kalya, I will rely on your strength. I need you at my side, to be my sword."

Looking him up and down, Kalya asked, "Do my father know of this?"

He looked to Selima, who shook her head. Aumekor said "No, he does not. I told you because I did not want to marry you under false pretenses."

"For that I be ever thankful," said Kalya, but there was no warmth in her voice. She rose to her feet. "Even if my father do not renounce the betrothal, marriage to you never be but a pretense. Weakling." She strode quickly out of the room, followed by her guards.

Aumekor felt a tightness in his chest and he had difficulty catching his breath. He had been so sure he was making the right decision. Kalya was supposed to understand. He sat down in his chair. She should not have reacted like that. How could he have been so wrong?

In a moment, Selima was at his side. "Are you all right?"

"Altitude," he lied between gasping breaths. "I'll be fine."

Chapter Thirty-Five

Geradin

"I knew they were barbarians," said Geradin. He drew his sword partway out of its scabbard and slammed it back in. "Oh, they're brave warriors, all right, but they have no honor."

"That's not fair," said Mek.

"I can't believe you're defending them. According to them you should be dead: left out on a mountainside to starve if you weren't eaten by wild animals first. Honor comes from protecting the weak, not killing them." Or insulting them for their weakness. If only he had been present at the time, he would have tested just how good a warrior this barbarian princess was.

"They don't do that anymore. They haven't for over a hundred years. I just wish I had known that part of their history before I blundered with Kalya."

"I say you're lucky you found out before you married her that she's a savage, vicious—"

"Stop!" Mek rose from his chair. "Not one more word against Kalya, no matter what your opinion of her. She is my betrothed and any insult to her is an insult to me."

Taken aback, Geradin nodded.

Mek sighed. "I know you want to defend me, but attacking Kalya is not the way. I want to win her, not beat her."

"What's your plan, then?"

"I haven't quite come up with one yet."

"Perhaps Selima and Lady Uwixa could help?"

"Not Selima. She'd rather I forgot about Kalya and married someone on her list. Lady Uwixa might be useful—she must want it to work out to prove she was right to arrange the marriage in the first place."

"If you would permit me to suggest something," said Nikufed, who had been unobtrusively standing by, "Miss Allonna is closer to Princess Biyeskalya's age."

"Yes," said Mek. "She and Uwixa together may be helpful."

Nikufed said, "Shall I fetch them?"

"No," said Geradin. "I'll go." It would be interesting to hear Allonna's recommendations for winning a woman's affections. Perhaps both he and Mek would learn something.

◆ ◆ ◆

Geradin ushered Allonna and Lady Uwixa into Mek's room.

"Lady Uwixa, Omnimancer Allonna, I thank you for coming," said Mek. He pointed them toward the seats closest to his chair.

"I must apologize, Your Majesty," said Lady Uwixa as she sat. "Princess Biyeskalya's behavior—"

Mek raised an armored hand to stop her. "That's the past. We are here to discuss what can be done."

As Geradin moved toward a chair facing Allonna, Mek said, "Geradin, I have another assignment for you. Please gain an audience with King Paskolyik and find out what his attitude is concerning this."

"Me? Lady Uwixa knows him best." Geradin had been looking forward to spending some time with Allonna, even if it was in the company of others. When she was involved in discussion, she sometimes forgot to snub him.

"I intend no insult to Lady Uwixa when I say this, but I think these circumstances call for someone whose strength as a warrior cannot be questioned."

"I agree, Your Majesty," said Lady Uwixa.

Geradin couldn't argue with that. "I'll do my best."

◆ ◆ ◆

A servant guided Geradin to King Paskolyik, who was standing on the roof of the palace looking out over his city. Geradin was surprised see that the king was alone. The Protectors of the Line would never willingly leave Mek unguarded.

"Your Majesty," said Geradin, "might I have a word with you?"

Paskolyik did not turn to face him. "What see you when you look at this?" The king waved his arm across the view before him.

Geradin walked over and stood beside the king. Below them, a few scattered people made their way through the narrow, winding streets of the city. Even though it was only late afternoon, the city was already in the shadow of the mountain it was built on. Unsure of what Paskolyik wanted him to see, Geradin said, "I see your city and your people."

"My people." Paskolyik sighed. "Yes, my people. It be my duty as king to protect them."

"Of course."

"A king need be strong to protect his people."

Geradin winced inwardly. "What exactly did your daughter tell you?"

"That the Heir be too weak to even stand." Paskolyik raised a palm as if to forestall Geradin from objecting. "She tell me, but tell no one else. She be not a fool. The secret be safe still."

Geradin nodded, but he knew Mek would not be happy about the course of the conversation. How could he convince Paskolyik to look beyond physical strength?

"Does that mean the strongest man deserves to be king?" asked Geradin, repressing a sudden urge to smile at the idea of Holoran being chosen as king of Aldamun.

"No, you be right. Strength be not all."

Perhaps the king could still be persuaded. "Do you know who my father was, Your Majesty?"

"You be Lord Geradin att'Balunor. Yes, I know. Your father, he be a great hero."

"My father failed."

Paskolyik turned to look at Geradin.

"My father's duty was to protect King Ordil, and King Ordil was killed. My father's duty was to protect Queen Anutia, and Queen Anutia was killed. Above all else, my father's duty was to protect the Heir of the Line. Because my father was not strong enough to prevent it, King Aumekor was born weak. You may blame the Dark Priestess for sending the attack, you may blame Veratur for his betrayal, and you may blame Balunor for his failure, but you cannot blame Aumekor for what happened before he was born."

"There be truth in what you say. But still it be truth that Aumekor be weak. It be folly to join to weakness, even if there be no blame."

What could Geradin say to that? He looked out over the city again. He missed Aud Sapeer, with its wide streets filled with people going about their business. The streets of Aldamun were relatively empty. As the implications began to work their way into his thoughts, Geradin said, "Your population is declining."

Paskolyik said nothing.

"It's the constant battles, isn't it? The women killed while still in their childbearing years?"

The king's voice was bitter. "And the Barrier Guard do nothing but protect the wall, while my people be dying. Small raids be not their concern, they say."

"So you wanted to marry your daughter to the Heir of the Line, because he is ultimately in command of the Barrier Guard and could order them to protect your people."

"It be only option."

"No," said Geradin. "All you had to do was ask. Aumekor

would have ordered the Barrier Guard to protect your people."

"It be a weak king who need beg for help to protect his own people."

"A strong king will do what he must to protect his people, even if he will appear weak."

Paskolyik's face broke into a huge grin. "You be good advisor. Be there chance I hire you away from Aumekor?"

Geradin smiled. "How much is the pay for a king's advisor in Aldamun?"

"It be like the wealth of the greediest man." Paskolyik laughed. "It never be enough."

"Then I must sadly decline your offer," said Geradin.

"Come, we go talk to your king about protecting my people. We forget about the betrothal and my daughter bother him no more."

Geradin winced. "About the betrothal…King Aumekor is quite smitten with your daughter. He would not force her to marry against her will, but he would like to have a chance to win her affections."

"My daughter be strong-willed and prideful. It be nigh impossible to change her mind. But if Aumekorek-Lerid wish, I not cancel betrothal."

"He wishes," said Geradin. If Mek could bring Kindul to his side after their long antagonism, perhaps he could persuade Biyeskalya. Geradin just hoped it wouldn't take sixteen years.

Chapter Thirty-Six

Allonna

Two seasons ago, Allonna had never even seen a royal person. Now she was assigned by a king to plead his love to a princess. King Aumekor was one of the nicest people she had ever met—she was only a commoner, but he always treated her with more respect than she got from the average shopkeeper. This Princess Biyeskalya who had insulted him deserved to be rolled down a hill in a barrel full of skunks, but instead Allonna was supposed to help convince her to marry him.

She shook her head as she walked down a narrow stone hallway toward the room she shared with Selima. The things men would put up with for the sake of a pretty face.

Before confronting the princess, though, Allonna needed to change out of her new dress. It was a pity—this was the first chance she'd had to wear it since Selima had bought it for her just before leaving Cirkepam. The dress was made of fine silk, and its cut flattered her figure. But from what King Aumekor had said, the princess had no fondness for southern fashions. Allonna had no armor, but she thought that her riding breeches and tunic would present a more warrior-like appearance than anything else she owned.

"Allonna!" Geradin's voice echoed in the hall behind her.

She turned to face him. "Yes, Lord Geradin?"

He looked around the empty hallway. "It's just us. You don't have to call me 'Lord.'"

"But I may do so if I choose," she replied. He kept trying to press familiarity on her, as if he did not understand she was trying to maintain the distance between them. Storytellers claimed love could cross the barrier between noble and commoner, and as a child she had believed them. But now she knew of too many young women who had only caught the eye of a lord, not his heart. Such tales never ended happily.

"I wish I'd been able to hear your advice on how a young man can win the affections of a woman who spurns him. I'm sure I would have found the information useful." He grinned.

Allonna steeled herself against the attraction of his smile. "Was there a reason you stopped me? I'm on assignment for the king."

"It's not enough that I just wanted to talk with you?" He gave an exaggerated sigh. "Aumekor sent me to tell you that Princess Biyeskalya's father is not going to call off the betrothal. He thought you should know that before you meet with the princess."

Allonna nodded and turned to go.

"And he wanted me to tell you that you look lovely in that dress," said Geradin.

Allonna frowned and turned back to Geradin. The king had hinted that this dress would not do for meeting with the princess. Was this his way of apologizing in case she had been offended? "Tell him I thank him for his compliment."

Geradin's brow furrowed. "No, wait. He didn't say that at all. It was *me* who wanted to tell you that you look lovely."

Would he never give up? "Goodbye, Lord Geradin." She spun on her heel and walked away. Without looking back, she knew his eyes followed her.

◆ ◆ ◆

"No," said Selima. "I think you should wear that dress."

Allonna hesitated. "Are you sure? Princess Biyeskalya—"

"Princess Biyeskalya is a warrior, so she dresses as a warrior. You are an omnimancer, so dress as an omnimancer."

"And omnimancers wear dresses like this?" In picking out this dress, Allonna had thought only of how it looked, not whether it was appropriate wear for an omnimancer.

Selima flashed her a fierce grin. "Omnimancers wear *whatever they want.* You are not a blacksmith's daughter hoping to have an audience at the pleasure of the exalted Princess Biyeskalya. You are a powerful court omnimancer assigned to discuss diplomatic issues with the princess. She won't object to the way you dress—it isn't wise to annoy someone who can melt her armor just by thinking about it."

"I can't do that!" said Allonna. "Can I?"

Selima shrugged. "Your umbrit seem to have a talent for ferromancy, so it's possible you could. But I suppose it would have unpleasant diplomatic repercussions if you actually did. That doesn't mean you shouldn't go in with an attitude that makes her think you'd do it. Aldamundians respect strength—you show your strength by acting like who you are: an omnimancer."

The advice felt right to Allonna, but there was something that didn't fit. "King Aumekor says you oppose his match to the princess, so why are you helping me help him?"

With a sigh, Selima sat on the edge of her bed. "If you're going to be Royal Omnimancer one day, you need to start acting the part. Teaching you is of more consequence than which young woman Aumekor ends up marrying. And, though the most important thing is that he produce an heir, I want to see him happy. I don't know that this princess can make him happy, but he seems to think so. If he is right, I will rejoice with him. If he is wrong, I do not want him blaming me for my interference. So I will help where I can."

"I will let him know that," said Allonna. Suddenly she felt awkward. It wasn't right that King Aumekor seemed to have more confidence in her than in Selima, who had raised and protected him all his life.

"Thank you," said Selima. "Now, show the princess that we southerners are not quite so soft as she imagines."

◆ ◆ ◆

"Her Highness be ready to see you now," said the guard.

Allonna let out a slow breath and tried to curb her annoyance. It had been late afternoon when she arrived, and it was now long after sunset. Being forced to wait was an obvious insult, but Allonna knew there was no point in being angry at the servants and guards.

During her wait, several people had come to see the princess, been admitted, and then left. Servants had brought the princess food for her supper, then carried away the remnants.

Now that she was being admitted to Princess Biyeskalya's presence, Allonna reminded herself that acting out of anger would accomplish nothing. It was time to be calm and logical, like Selima.

Seated on a chair next to a fireplace, Princess Biyeskalya was polishing a sword. She still wore her armor, and its surface reflected the flickering flames. A small table next to the princess still held a plate with a half-eaten piece of cake, which reminded Allonna that she was hungry.

The nearest chair was set well away from the fire, but Allonna decided that it would be better to sit like an equal than to stand like a servant in attendance.

Princess Biyeskalya didn't even look at Allonna. She held up the sword, turning the blade in the light of the fire.

Allonna suppressed a snort. Was this show of armor and weapons supposed to intimidate her? She had grown up in a smithy—she probably knew more about looking for defects in metalwork than the princess. "If you're checking for flaws, you need more light than that. Allow me." Allonna cast a simple spell to create a globe of light over her own head, but made it powerful enough to light up the room like the noonday sun.

The sudden change in brightness made the two female

guards behind Biyeskalya shield their eyes, and Allonna saw them grip their swords. The princess seemed to freeze for a beat. Then she brought her sword down and sheathed it.

"So you be a mancer," the princess said. She turned to face Allonna and had to squint because of the light. "Your tricks not impress me."

For a moment, Allonna wished she could melt Biyeskalya's armor, just to see whether that "trick" would impress her. The idea of melting armor triggered a memory of her encounter with Master Ramil. He had initially resented her, but she had gained his friendship by focusing on what they had in common. And what they had in common was *armor*.

Allonna turned her attention to Biyeskalya's armor, and despite the bright light, everything else seemed to dim. Under dozens of layers of spells to protect the enchantment Allonna could see the embedded spell to enhance the armor's strength, allowing it to be thin and light while protecting as well as normal steel about three or four times as thick.

Allonna smiled. "I see your armor is enchanted. How strong is it?"

Holding up an armored arm, Biyeskalya said, "Six-fold stronger than steel."

Raising an eyebrow, Allonna said, "Is that all?" Either the princess was exaggerating or she had been lied to— the strengthening enchantment was not nearly as powerful as Master Ramil's, and his best efforts could only make a piece five times stronger.

"Your mocking be in ignorance. Six-fold armor be the strongest forged today. Only armor forge in the ages of old be stronger. My eldest brother, Istenyubak, wear ten-fold armor that belong to my family for twenty generations."

Spotting a fork on the plate next to the leftover cake, Allonna rose and walked over to the table. She picked up the fork, and with a little effort bent its handle to a right angle. "I know you think of us southerners as weak," she said as she began to enchant a strengthening spell into the fork. "But we do have strengths in our own way." Without heating the metal in a forge, the enchantment would not be as strong, and she had not yet learned how to embed it permanently in the metal, but it would do. "This is proof of how strong I am." She handed the fork to Biyeskalya.

The princess looked at the fork and laughed. "You think you be strong because you bend a fork?"

"What a weak southerner can bend, a northerner should be able to unbend. Unless she's a weakling." Allonna hoped she hadn't gone too far with that last part.

Scowling, Princess Biyeskalya grabbed the fork with both hands and tried to straighten it. Her eyes widened and she tightened her grip. Soon her arms were vibrating with effort, but the fork did not change. "You enchant the fork," she said accusingly.

Allonna said, "You hold in your hands a fork that has been strengthened twelve-fold." She yawned. "I had hoped we would have more time to talk, but it is now so late that I must retire to my room for the night. It was a pleasure meeting you, Your Highness."

"Wait! You can do this to armor?"

"If you have time to come see me tomorrow, we can discuss that," said Allonna. She could not repress a grin as she walked out the door.

◆ ◆ ◆

The Aldamundian armorsmith could not stop staring at Allonna, even as he spoke to the princess. "I did not think it be possible, Your Highness, but it be true. The omnimancer here —" He bowed his head quickly to Allonna. "—strengthen metal fifteen-fold."

"Fifteen-fold armor," said Biyeskalya. She nodded to the armorsmith. "Leave us."

He bowed and withdrew from his own smithy.

"So," said the princess, "that be why your king choose you as his emissary: to bribe me with enchanted armor."

Allonna shook her head. "No. My studies with the armorsmith in Aud Sapeer were cut short, so I cannot embed the strength enchantments permanently. The effect lasts a few days at most." Despite her abilities with ferromancy, she did not have a talent for strength enchantments—they were something she would have to learn by study and practice.

"Still, it be a useful thing to do before battle."

"Yes and no. It replaces any permanent strength enchantment, so while it might be good for a short-term advantage, it does not make sense to enchant armor like yours until I can do it permanently."

"Pah! Then why your king choose you, if not to bribe me?"

Allonna paused. Honesty had not worked for King Aumekor, but she felt it was the only way to get past Biyeskalya's suspicions. "Because I'm a young woman close to your age, and he hoped we might become friends, and then I could plead his case with you."

The princess furrowed her brow. "You be a mighty woman in magic. Why serve a weakling?"

"His body may be weak, but he is strong in other ways. He is a leader, and strong men and women follow him because they recognize that."

"Men like Lord Geradin."

"Exactly." Perhaps she could get through to the princess that it was possible to be a great warrior while still respecting King Aumekor. "Despite being young, Lord Geradin is the best swordsman among the Protectors of the Line—possibly the best in all the Free Kingdoms, or even the world. Yet he chooses to wield that sword at the orders of King Aumekor."

"That be the type of man I like to marry. My father say Lord Geradin charge into battle alone against twenty raiders and kill them all."

"It was only nine. And he didn't charge them; it was supposed to be a parley."

"Nine, twenty." Biyeskalya shrugged. "Be he married?"

"Lord Geradin? No." How had they gotten onto the subject of Geradin?

"Good. He be fine husband for me."

"You can't marry Lord Geradin!" Allonna tried to think of how to bring the conversation back under control.

"He be good warrior and handsome, too."

"You're betrothed to King Aumekor. Your father—"

"My father tell me your weakling king not force marriage. Let him marry soft southern princess. I marry Lord Geradin."

Allonna knew she had to stop this foolishness right now. "No, you will not marry Lord Geradin."

Biyeskalya raised her eyebrows. "Why not?"

Finally admitting the truth to herself, Allonna said, "Because I'm in love with him, that's why."

Chapter Thirty-Seven

Geradin

"If we leave tomorrow shortly after dawn," said Geradin, "we should reach the Barrier Wall by late afternoon. We can perform an inspection, you and King Paskolyik can speak to the troops, and then we can have a strategy meeting with the generals. We camp overnight and return the next morning. It should be safe enough—the ramp they are building is still a half-season from completion, even if we weren't harrying them."

Mek nodded, then glanced at Selima. "What do you think?"

"I don't like spending the night so close to the border. Raiding parties do come across."

Geradin said, "And that's exactly why we should spend the night there. We'll be camped in the midst of thousands of soldiers. No raiding party will come anywhere near us."

As Geradin spoke, one of the Protectors entered and gave Nikufed a piece of paper. The manservant broke its seal and held it out for Mek to read.

Geradin was relieved to see a smile grow on Mek's face as he read the note.

Mek looked up from the paper. "It appears my cause is not entirely lost with Princess Kalya. I have been invited to walk with her this afternoon to see some of the sights of her city."

Geradin frowned. It seemed too easy a change in the princess. "Perhaps her father ordered it?"

Mek's smile faded a bit. "It looks like a feminine hand, so I think she at least wrote it herself."

"Even if her father ordered it," said Selima, "it is still a good sign. The way she stormed out yesterday had me convinced she would disobey her father on this."

Geradin rose from his chair. "I'd better talk with the other High Protectors. We'll have to arrange a suitable escort and coordinate with her guards."

"No," said Mek. "As to the last part, I mean. It says right here in her note that 'if your most expert swordsman be present, I need not my own guards.'"

◆ ◆ ◆

After making the necessary preparations to guard Mek and Biyeskalya on their walk, Geradin returned to Mek's chambers. Allonna had taken over as the mancer on duty outside the door, so he stopped to talk to her before going inside.

"Are you the one responsible for Princess Biyeskalya's change of heart?" he asked.

A frustrated sigh burst from her. "It's not my fault. I don't know how she got that idea into her head, and I did my best to talk her out of it, but she is the most stubborn person I've ever met, and she—"

Geradin held up a palm to silence her. "It's fine, really. The High Protectors have agreed to it."

Allonna's eyes opened wide and she began to say something, then stopped and frowned. "What have the High Protectors agreed to?"

"The walk." Seeing Allonna's puzzlement, Geradin said, "Princess Biyeskalya and King Aumekor are going for a walk in the city. You didn't have anything to do with her invitation?"

"No." Allonna's voice was incredulous. "She invited His Majesty to go on a walk?"

"I was as surprised as you." Geradin wrinkled his brow. "What did you think I was talking about?"

Allonna blushed. "I was confused. It was nothing."

Deciding not to press the point if she was embarrassed about it, Geradin said, "We'll be leaving soon. Do you want to come with us? I'm sure Selima won't mind. And there's no point in guarding an empty room."

"You're going?" said Allonna. "Of course—you're a Protector."

Geradin chuckled. "It's a bit funny, actually. The princess mentioned in her note that as long as I came along, she wouldn't need her own guards."

"The conniving snake!" Allonna's eyes flashed.

"What?" Geradin's suspicions toward the princess returned.

"She wants to meet you. It's *you* she wants to marry."

Geradin couldn't recall ever seeing Allonna so angry. Then the meaning of what she had said sank in. "Me? She wants to marry me?"

"She told me this morning. I said it was impossible, because..." Allonna blushed again. "...because King Aumekor is your friend and you would never betray his trust."

"You're right about that," said Geradin. "But she obviously didn't believe you. What do we do now?"

"Call off the walk."

Geradin considered it, then shook his head. "Aumekor is looking forward to it. What happened yesterday was a blow to him. I'd rather avoid having his hopes dashed again so soon."

"I suppose you're right. But what do we do about her? She'll be trying to attract you."

A perfect plan formed suddenly in Geradin's mind. "Allonna, I know that you're not interested in me. But for the sake of King Aumekor, could you pretend that you and I are romantically involved? If it appears I'm attached to you, surely the princess will abandon her quest for me."

"I wouldn't be so sure," she said. She cocked her head and looked at him. "Pretend that we are in love? It might be possible."

Geradin couldn't help grinning. Perhaps in pretending

affection, Allonna would gain some.

"But this doesn't mean you may take any liberties."

Holding up both hands as if to protest his innocence, Geradin said, "Any liberties will be up to you."

♦ ♦ ♦

Geradin stood at the top of the palace steps with Mek to his right and Allonna to his left. Selima was behind them as they stood facing the doors. Forty Protectors of the Line formed a two-deep circle around them, leaving only a gap through which Princess Biyeskalya could join the others.

Other than her brief, fully armored appearance when the party had first arrived in Aldamun, Geradin had not seen the princess. He was curious to see if she was as beautiful as Mek claimed.

"She *would* make us wait for her," said Allonna quietly.

"Did you say something, Allonna?" asked Mek.

Geradin said, "She said she can hardly wait to see the city." If Mek was going to take offense at any slight to the princess, it was best not to let him hear anything offensive.

One of the palace doors opened and Princess Biyeskalya came out. At least, Geradin assumed that was who the beautiful woman in the gold-embroidered dress was. She would have been the focus of attention at any noble's ball in Aud Sapeer. No wonder Mek was so determined to marry her.

"Geradin." Allonna's voice was an annoyed whisper.

He moved his eyes away, as if to check for possible threats from the walls of the palace.

"Princess Kalya," said Mek, "you are not wearing your armor?"

"That's unnecessary, if such a man as Lord Geradin protects me." Her voice held little trace of the Aldamundian accent. She walked toward the spot between Geradin and Mek.

Obviously, the princess wanted to position herself next to him. A good tactical move, but only if he hadn't known her motives. Geradin stepped out of her way so she could stand beside Mek. "Your Highness, as I bear responsibility for your safety, I have decided that Omnimancer Allonna and I will walk ahead of you and King Aumekor, to protect against threats both of steel and of magic." He caught Allonna's eye and gestured with his head for her to move around the royal couple and meet him on the down side of the steps.

He couldn't see Biyeskalya's expression, but he hoped she was annoyed.

◆ ◆ ◆

They had not gone far from the palace before Princess Biyeskalya seemed ready to go back. Geradin felt sure that meant she had decided her plan for him wasn't going to work. Unfortunately, Allonna hadn't really done anything to demonstrate her pretended affection for him. He had positioned her to his left so she could do something like put her arm through his, without compromising his sword hand.

Geradin tensed suddenly. The Protectors at the front of the formation were slowing. One of them called out, "Make way! Make way!"

"I need see them. I need talk to them," said a man's voice, which seemed to tremble with age.

Geradin ordered the company to halt. He moved forward a few paces and saw an old beggar kneeling in the middle of the almost deserted street.

"Move aside," the Protector nearest the beggar said to him.

Rather than have the Protectors forcibly move the man out of the way, Geradin decided the quickest course was to give the beggar something. He fumbled into the purse tied to his belt, and drew out a gold dinar. "Here," he said, and flung it to the man, who caught it with surprising agility. "Now move aside."

"Thank you, milord," said the beggar as he made the gold coin disappear into his clothing. "But as you pay me, I need prophesy your fates."

"He be a crazy beggar, pay him no mind," said Biyeskalya. "He think he be a prophet."

"Wait," said Selima. "True prophets are often mistaken for insane—often because they speak of things so far in the future they make no sense at the time. Let us hear what he has to say."

"Very wise," said the beggar. "Now be a crux of history. My prophecies be all that stand between the Dark and the Light."

Geradin began looking up at the walls and buildings around them. Could this beggar be a distraction while some sort of trap was sprung? "Be ready, just in case," he said quietly to Allonna.

She nodded.

The beggar pointed a wiry arm at the princess. "I see you in a vision," he said. "You proudly tell all around you that within your womb be the next Heir of the Line."

Biyeskalya stamped her foot. "You be no prophet. That never happen."

Geradin couldn't help smiling for Mek's sake. If this man really was a prophet, Mek and Biyeskalya would get married, and she would be proud to carry his child.

"You," said the beggar, moving his finger to point at Geradin. "You will succeed where your father failed." His accent had shifted to that of Aud Sapeer.

The man's words jolted Geradin. He had told almost no one that he thought his father a failure. He must be a prophet—and Geradin felt an overwhelming sense of relief that his success in protecting Mek had just been prophesied.

"And you will fail where your father succeeded," said the beggar.

"What?" said Geradin. "What do you mean by that?"

The beggar moved his finger to Allonna. "Your friends here will all leave you behind—"

"Answer me!" shouted Geradin.

"—and you will leave all of them behind." The beggar then pointed to Selima. "You wish to be remembered for seeking the truth, but shall be remembered best for the lies you have told."

Geradin started toward the man. He had to know what the prophecy meant.

"Leave him," said Selima. "Her Highness is right, this man is no prophet. His phrases are but emptiness made to sound profound. He is either a madman or a charlatan."

Geradin paused. "You're sure?"

"Yes," said Selima and Biyeskalya simultaneously.

"Believe what you will," said the beggar, and he began to scurry off the road.

"Wait," said Mek. "Don't I get a turn at this game?"

The beggar paused. He looked Aumekor over from head to foot. "I'm sorry, milord. I see no future for you."

Chapter Thirty-Eight

Aumekor

The sky seemed to be growing lighter outside the windows of Aumekor's bedchamber. The party would leave soon after dawn, so Nikufed was already busy dressing Aumekor in his armor.

"I don't understand how you can be so calm about it," said Geradin.

"And I don't see why you're so upset," said Mek. "Selima said the man wasn't a prophet."

"But what if he was? I mean, Selima could be lying—he even said she was a liar."

Aumekor sighed. "So you're going to take the word of a street beggar you've seen once over the word of Selima?"

Geradin glanced at the floor. "What if she's…mistaken?"

"What if she is? What do you plan to do about it? You don't even know what the prophecies refer to. I actually hope they are true prophecies."

"You do?" Geradin stared at him.

"Out of the prophecies, there's only one that wasn't a word game, and that was Princess Kalya's. Yours could mean almost anything—that you succeed in living to the age of ninety, but fail to die heroically in battle; that you succeed in having daughter, but fail in having a son. Anything fits, as long as your father was the other way around. Allonna's prophecy can be fulfilled if we take a trip somewhere without her, and then she goes somewhere without us. In fact, perhaps we should do that soon, to fulfill the prophecy and show it doesn't mean anything significant. As for Selima's..."

"Yes?"

"Well, I don't know. Perhaps it just means we'll remember her more for the stories she told us at bedtime when we were children than for anything else. My point is, if the man was a true prophet, then Kalya's going to marry me and we're going to have a child. So I'm going to hope it's true." After the way the walk had gone yesterday, the prophecy was one of the few strands of hope left for his chances with Kalya.

"What about your prophecy? That you have no future?"

"Word games again. Did he actually prophesy that I have no future, or did he just say that he could not see it?"

Geradin frowned. "I'm not sure."

"Exactly," said Aumekor. Since Nikufed had finished putting the armor on him, Aumekor rose from his chair. "Just forget about—"

A bell began clanging from somewhere high above. Other bells quickly joined in

Aumekor looked at Geradin. "Is it some sort of ritual or—"

Geradin's sword was already out and its blue glow was a welcome sight. "I don't know, but I'm not leaving you to go check."

The door opened and several Protectors came inside, followed by Selima.

"Is it an attack?" asked Aumekor.

"I don't know," said Selima. "I don't sense any significant magical power being used nearby, but that doesn't rule out raiders or other non-magical threats."

Geradin ordered one of the Protectors to see if he could find out what was happening.

"Let's hope it's just a false alarm," said Selima.

Aumekor grinned. "Allonna's not here. Perhaps she's enchanting someone else's armor?"

♦ ♦ ♦

King Paskolyik strode into Aumekor's chamber. "Know you where my daughter be?"

"I thought she was coming with us to the Barrier Wall," said Aumekor. Was she going somewhere else? He had hoped that if she saw him inspiring the troops, she might realize he could lead despite his weakness.

"She be gone."

"Where? When?"

Paskolyik shook his head. "She take two guards and leave the palace last night. We check if she leave the city."

An Aldamundian guard rushed in and began to speak to his king in hushed tones.

Aumekor could only think of one likely reason Kalya would leave like that: to escape from marrying him. If she were hurt or killed, it would be his fault. He had bungled everything from the time they first met.

"Call every man and woman of arms," Paskolyik ordered his man. "Send them out in twenties as they gather."

The man ran from the room.

"What has happened?" asked Aumekor.

"One of Biyeskalya's guards came back to the city gate. Wounded. They be ambushed by raiders. She be captured or dead."

A moment of despair was replaced by furious hope. She could not be dead, if the prophecy were true. And if Aumekor rescued her from the raiders, she would start seeing him differently. "Geradin, get whatever Protectors are ready. We leave immediately." He looked at Paskolyik. "If you can spare us one man who knows these mountains, my men and I will do our best to get your daughter back."

"Aumekorek-Lerid!" said Paskolyik. "That be how a man acts when his betrothed be threatened. March your men to the gate. I send a tracker to meet you." He turned and exited the room.

Before anyone else could say anything, Aumekor said, "Let us assume you have all made your objections and I have noted them. This is no more dangerous than my predecessors riding to battle. The mother of the next Heir of the Line has been captured. It is imperative that she be rescued and, if possible, that *I* be the one to lead the rescue. Understood?"

No one said anything for a moment.

"I understand, Your Majesty," said Geradin. He turned to Otunvol and Wyran, the only two other High Protectors in the room. "If you escort the king to the gate of the city, I will join you with as many men as I can muster."

They both nodded.

"Get Allonna as well," said Selima.

Aumekor had expected resistance to his plan, especially from Wyran and Selima. But despite Selima's discounting of the prophet, the prophecy about Kalya carrying the next Heir of the Line must be forcing everyone to think beyond his current personal safety to the continuation of the line.

◆ ◆ ◆

Dawn was breaking when they reached the city gate. A short, stocky Aldamundian greeted Aumekor. "I be Serilyon. Once your men be ready, I guide you into the mountains."

"How much of a start do you think they have?" asked Aumekor.

Serilyon shrugged. "Could be a quarter-day, perhaps more. If they have prisoner, they be slower. We catch them before dark if we find the trail."

A group of about forty Protectors came down the road, marching double time. Aumekor caught sight of Allonna in their midst as they approached.

"Where's Geradin?" Aumekor asked.

"He can't come," said Allonna. "When he came to get me he...tripped and injured his ankle. He said to go on without him, as he would only slow you down."

Allonna's hesitation meant she was hiding something. Geradin's injury must be severe, if it would hold him back from being there to protect Aumekor. But there was nothing to be done about that now; rescuing Kalya was the priority.

He nodded at the guide. "Serilyon, lead the way."

◆ ◆ ◆

Serilyon smiled. "We gain on them, Your Majesty. And I be certain the princess be with them, and alive."

Relief flooded through Aumekor's body. In the early morning they had found the spot where the princess had been ambushed, and though the body of one of her guards was there, hers was not. But though Serilyon had followed the six raiders' tracks throughout most of the day, there had been no sign of Kalya, other than Serilyon's estimation that two of the men were carrying something heavy enough to be her armored form. Now that they were above the snow line, even Aumekor could follow the trail of the raiders, but he had no way of telling whether Serilyon was right.

"How do you know?" asked Aumekor.

"Impressions in the snow up ahead." He pointed toward a spot on the trail. "She struggle enough to force them to drop her. She then roll off the trail to try to get away, but since she be tied up, they capture her again."

"You can tell all that from marks in the snow?"

"Armor leave a mark in the snow." Serilyon shrugged. "Tell person's size. See impressions from ropes. All this point to princess be alive."

"I did not mean to doubt you," said Aumekor. "I was merely curious."

"Come," said Serilyon. "Best if we find them before nightfall. Storm come, wipe out all tracks by morning."

◆ ◆ ◆

"Stop," said Serilyon.

The company came to a halt. The sun had passed behind the peaks to the west, and the overcast sky made it darker, but it was still daylight.

"We be very close. Over that ridge. But raiders be stupid. There be good cave there for shelter, which be smart when storm comes, but they build fire, which be stupid before dark. Cave hide light from flames, but not hide smoke. See?" He pointed to an almost invisible thread of smoke rising to dissipate in the sky.

"What now?" said Aumekor.

"Be very simple. There be no back way out of cave. It be small. We surround, we offer gold and freedom to the raiders if the princess be unharmed."

"Do we have enough gold?" Aumekor realized he should have thought of that before leaving the city.

"Be no matter. Raiders' word not be trusted. Aldamundians' word be trusted. We make promise, we take them back to Aldamun and give them gold, then we let them go."

Aumekor had read convincing arguments that paying for hostages only increased the incentive for the taking of more hostages. But for this hostage, right now, he would pay whatever the raiders asked. Even though his force outnumbered the raiders ten to one, if they fought their way into the cave, Kalya might get killed. "Very well, let's surround the cave."

Serilyon and Wyran took half the men to go downhill a bit and come up on the other side of the cave.

Aumekor hoped they were not too late. She had to still be alive. The prophecy had to be true.

◆ ◆ ◆

"Serilyon's right," said Otunvol. "They are stupid. It doesn't even look like they've posted a guard."

"Perhaps he's inside the cave far enough that we can't see him," said Aumekor.

"Perhaps. But then he can't see us, either, and since there's no way out of the cave, they would need to run at the first sign of trouble."

"The smart thing to do," said Allonna, "would have been to light a fire in the cave and just keep going, in order to distract us."

There was a moment of stunned silence.

"And we fell for it," said Otunvol.

"We can't wait for Serilyon to get in position. We need to find out right now if they are in that cave," said Aumekor. "If not, we're losing time."

"If they are there, they may run before we can encircle the entrance," said Otunvol.

"But they will be close enough for us to see and follow. We can catch them." Aumekor knew he could not keep up on a run, but it was more important that Kalya be saved.

Selima said, "If we get close enough before they run, I can seal the cave entrance with a ward."

Otunvol nodded. "Then let's go." He signaled the Protectors to proceed over the ridge.

They charged downhill toward the cave mouth. No one came out before Selima yelled, "It's sealed. It's sealed."

After they surrounded the entrance, Aumekor said, "There may not be anyone in there. But we can't—"

"There is someone in there," said Selima. "I can sense at least one person, but there's something strange..." She gasped. "Someone is in great pain."

"No time for negotiations, then," said Aumekor. I'm coming, Kalya. I'll save you. "Bring down the ward. Otunvol, take as many men as you need, and I'll follow behind."

Otunvol drew his sword, which glowed blue in the fading daylight. He quietly pointed for five men to join him, and then they rushed into the cave.

Aumekor followed as fast as his suit would take him. He had

no doubt that Otunvol with his enchanted sword and five well-trained Protectors could easily defeat any six raiders. As he turned the corner to the main cavern, he almost ran into all six of his men, who had stopped right at the entrance. They parted to let him through.

"There was nothing for us to do," said Otunvol.

Looking at the scene in the middle of the cavern, Aumekor realized he had arrived too late to save Kalya.

She had saved herself.

Five raiders' bodies lay scattered close to the fire. Kalya was kneeling over a sixth, holding with both hands the sword stuck in the man's chest. She was chanting something with her eyes closed, blood on her face. The man's body jerked strangely.

"Princess Kalya, are you all right?" asked Aumekor. "We came to rescue you."

She continued chanting.

"What's she doing?" he asked Otunvol.

"No idea."

"What is going on here?" asked Selima from behind him. "Is she alive? Is she safe?"

"She's alive. She's—"

Selima burst past him and ran toward the princess. "What are you doing? Stop! Stop at once!"

Kalya's eyes opened. "Stay back."

"No. It is forbidden." Selima grabbed at Kalya's hands and tore them away from the sword. "It is evil. Who taught you this?"

"I be questioning him, to protect my people. That be not evil." Kalya rose to her feet, her armor glinting red in the firelight. "I be done here." She marched toward the exit.

As she came to where Aumekor stood, she stopped. "The day I need a weakling such as you to rescue me, I consent to be your wife."

Chapter Thirty-Nine

Geradin

Geradin felt relieved when the mountain trail widened and leveled off. Even though the combined company of Protectors of the Line and Aldamundian soldiers could fight off any ordinary band of raiders, traveling in single file made Mek seem too exposed, despite Allonna's wards to protect him.

Urging Gristle forward, Geradin brought his horse even alongside Mek's.

"How's the ankle?" asked Mek.

"It's doing better," Geradin answered. He hated lying to Mek, but faking an injury had been the only excuse he could think of to put himself out of the way so Biyeskalya wouldn't be able to give him any credit for her rescue. And it had all been for nothing: Biyeskalya still despised Mek, and Geradin's foot was sore from walking around with a pebble in his boot to remind himself to limp.

Mek sighed. "I suppose even those born to be heroes have their non-heroic days."

"I think those days generally don't make it into the storytellers' rhymes."

They rode on in silence for a while.

"You were, you know," said Mek.

"What?"

"Born to be a hero. The first time you cried, you saved my

life. As for me, I was born to be rescued, not to rescue. My destiny lies in the hands of others."

"Don't be ridiculous." Geradin tried to think of a way to cheer up his friend.

"I'm serious. I was *born* being rescued. All my life I've been protected and rescued from harm—you did it on Midsummer Day. For once in my life I had the chance to rescue someone. Since we were children I've dreamed of being a hero like those in the tales, and then the opportunity came to rescue, not just anyone, but a beautiful princess. It was my perfect moment. And I failed."

"She's alive, isn't she? You protected her all the way back home, didn't you?"

"Not heroic, and rather boring. No teller will rhyme about it."

Geradin thought a moment. "But you have rescued someone. Kindul would have been put to death if you hadn't arrived in time to defend him."

"Yes, and I'm sure many a child will get a thrill hearing how brave King Aumekor boldly talked people into submission, and will go to sleep dreaming that one day, he too may give a fine speech. No, I may come from a long line of heroic kings, but the only purpose I serve is to produce a heroic descendant who can defeat the Dark Priestess. And so far, I'm making a mess of that, too."

"Perhaps you are right," said Geradin. "You were not born to be a hero. Does Kindul regret he is still alive, because you rescued him with words and not a sword? Are the merchants of the caravan worse off because you ordered your Protectors to rescue them, instead of you heroically doing it yourself? Will the people of Aldamun curse the day you ordered the Barrier Guard to defend them, because you were not born hero enough to guard them personally? You say that your destiny lies in the hands of others, but whose idea was it to leave the safety of the Keep and ride off to Cirkepam? Not the High Protectors'. Not Selima's. Not mine. Yours. Who decided we would come here to Aldamun? Not the High Protectors. Not Selima. Not the Conclave of Monarchs. You did. Born hero or not, your hands hold our fates, not the other way round."

Mek waited a few beats before speaking. "Thanks. I suppose I needed that lecture."

"That's what heroic best friends are for."

They rode on in silence for a while.

"How's the ankle?" asked Mek.

"Slightly better than the last time you asked."

◆ ◆ ◆

"That's it?" asked Allonna.

"That's it," said Geradin. The company was now on a meadow that narrowed to an end at the Barrier Wall. Camps of soldiers were scattered around on the flat ground between the mountainous sides of the valley.

"I thought the wall would be taller," Allonna said. "My pa was in the Barrier Guard, and he said the wall was the largest thing ever built. But I can see men walking around in front of it, and it's hardly three times their height, and it's not that long."

"From the other side, you would see how tall it really is—about twenty times the height you can see. But height is only part of it. In a way, we're already on top of the wall. This valley used to be much deeper and narrower, but it was filled in with rocks and dirt behind the stonework of the wall. Look up to the sides and you can see the scars on the mountains where mancers blasted off rock to fill this whole space."

Geradin had read a book about the construction of the Barrier Wall. He decided Allonna didn't need to know the details about the dozens of workers who had been killed by accidents during its construction. Their numbers were small compared to the thousands of soldiers who had died fighting the armies of the Dark Priestess as she conquered the three Free Kingdoms which had existed beyond the Barrier

Mountains, sacrificing themselves so there would be time to seal this pass and protect the kingdoms to the south.

Allonna looked up at the mountainsides. "The power it must have taken. I could never match that."

Selima's voice came from behind them. "The mancers who did this were old, come to full maturity in their powers before the Dark God burned the world. Mancers born after have generally been far weaker—as if the burning took much of the magic out of the world."

"Is it possible the magic is coming back?" asked Geradin. "I mean, Allonna's young, but she's very powerful."

"Perhaps. I hope it is so," said Selima. "There is more to it, of course. Talents are often passed from parent to child, and the most powerful mancers and their descendants were killed in the burning. We tend to talk of the Free Kingdoms as the center of civilization, and we are. But five hundred years ago, we were a rather insignificant part of the world. When the Dark God caused the sun to flare up and burn away his enemies, he did not even bother to destroy us."

To Geradin, Aud Sapeer had always been the center of civilization. He knew that much knowledge had been lost, but had never thought that the nations of the East might have been more advanced than Aud Sapeer before their destruction. "I guess there are advantages to being insignificant."

"We're significant now," said Selima. "The Dark Priestess has decided to send her armies against us."

"You defeated her last time," said Geradin confidently. "Even if they complete the ramp, which I doubt, we still hold the high ground, and they cannot bring their full force to bear."

"Last time the Dark Priestess had a spell prepared that could have killed ten thousand soldiers," said Selima.

"On which she wasted a tremendous amount of power for no result," said Geradin. "As long as you're around to undo her spells, she won't even bother."

"But—" said Allonna, then she pressed her lips together.

Geradin looked at her. "What?"

"Nothing. I shouldn't have said anything."

"So, Geradin," said Selima, "I can see you've been giving the strategic situation much thought."

Geradin recognized Selima's tone of voice—she was about to help him talk himself into a trap. The less he said, the lesser fool he would prove to be. "Yes."

"Assuming the Dark Priestess has generals who are familiar with the same principles of war as you, they should reach the same conclusion about our superior position."

"Probably."

"So why have they chosen to mount this offensive?"

"I don't know," he admitted. He should have seen that. The enemy must have a hidden weapon they planned to unleash when they attacked. He looked out at the enemy camps. He had thought there were already more than enough troops here to repel an invasion. Now he was glad more were on the way.

◆ ◆ ◆

Geradin stood with Mek, Allonna and Selima behind the parapet of the Barrier Wall. It was a long way to the rocky ground below. About two hundred and fifty paces from the base of the wall, a pile of rocks and dirt rose up ten times the height of a man.

"Their building progress has slowed a little since they got into longbow range," said General Menaren of the Barrier Guard. "At this distance, of course, it's not very effective, but we have arrows to spare. And the closer they get, the more casualties they'll take."

Beyond the ramp were clusters of tents with men moving about between them. Geradin tried to estimate their number, but gave up as he realized an unknown number of camps were hidden by mists farther out in the valley. The domain of the Dark Priestess had a population almost twice that of the Free Kingdoms, so her army could be correspondingly larger.

"So many," whispered Allonna.

"Fear not, milady," said the general. "We're quite safe here."
Geradin wished he still believed that.

Chapter Forty

Allonna

Allonna was glad to be back in Aldamun, and not just because a bed in the palace was more comfortable than a cot in a tent. Being so close to the seemingly endless army of the Dark Priestess had given her dreams of soldiers sweeping down upon Glicken, burning her childhood home and killing her father and brother. As she put on her nightdress, she hoped the dreams had not followed her here.

"What is your estimation of Princess Biyeskalya?" asked Selima, who was sitting next to the fireplace in the room they shared.

Allonna considered being diplomatic, but only for a moment. "She is the most arrogant, willful, inconsiderate, annoying, nasty, spiteful, treacherous, frustrating… arrogant…"

Selima smiled slightly. "You said arrogant already."

"It deserved to be said again, because there aren't enough words to describe how awful she is."

"Any qualities that are perhaps not quite so awful?"

"She is a skilled warrior." Allonna had to admit that, since the princess had not only managed to escape her captors, but kill them.

"Is that all?"

Allonna sat on her bed. "Some might think her beautiful."

Selima sighed. "Yes, there is that. Both Aumekor and

Geradin seem quite taken by her."

Allonna unsuccessfully tried to suppress a snort. "Geradin's not taken by her."

"I see the signs," said Selima. "He avoids looking at her, tries to avoid being near her. It's clear as rainwater he's attracted to her and feels guilty because she's intended for Aumekor."

"You think Geradin is falling in love with Biyeskalya?" Allonna almost laughed.

Frowning, Selima said, "I thought you suspected the same thing. You've been acting jealously around Geradin, as if trying to draw his attention back to you. You spurned his advances during our journey here, and now of a sudden you start walking by his side, spending every spare moment with him."

"That was Geradin's idea: pretend we're in love to keep Biyeskalya away from him. She is attracted to him—she told me Geradin would make her a fine husband."

Selima looked up at the ceiling and shook her head. "Of course. That makes even more sense than what I had worked out. Well, if I needn't fear Geradin running off with Biyeskalya, that does make things easier."

"What things?"

"Lady Uwixa and I will be sending a message to Kindul and the Regency Council. She had authority to arrange the betrothal, but we will now need authority to cancel it officially."

Allonna was surprised. She did not like Biyeskalya, but she had thought Aumekor was willing to wait in the hope that the princess would soften. "King Paskolyik won't cancel it on his own? His daughter would be happy."

"Paskolyik likes Aumekor, and won't go against his wishes on this."

"You mean you're canceling the betrothal against King Aumekor's wishes?"

Selima nodded. "This is the kind of thing you will have to do when you become a Royal Omnimancer. Biyeskalya must never be allowed to marry Aumekor."

"But why? What about the prophecy?"

"That madman was no prophet. As to the reason why—Biyeskalya is a necromancer. When we found her in that cave, she had trapped the soul of a dead raider in order to question him. And Aumekor is still so besotted that he only makes excuses for her."

Her mouth hanging open, Allonna could not think of what to say. She had thought the princess to be a horrid person, but a necromancer like the Dark Priestess? An image of Biyeskalya killing a baby flashed in her mind. Tonight's dreams would not be pleasant.

◆ ◆ ◆

Heat.

Allonna concentrated on the fist-sized rock. Magical energy flowed from her into the stone.

Heat.

It was hard to see the rock itself through the shimmer of her power. Was it beginning to turn red now?

"Stop," said Selima. She reached down and picked up the rock, shaking her head. "With the amount of power you're using, this rock should have been reduced to a glowing little puddle if you had any talent for heating stone. It's not even warm."

Allonna's shoulders sagged. "I'm sorry."

"No, it's fine. I have no talent for heating stone, either." Selima dropped the rock. "It's something you can learn eventually. Quite useful for cooking, really, when you don't want to have a fire that might be spotted." She walked over to a nearby tree, snapped off a small branch and tossed it to the ground a pace from Allonna. "Try that."

Concentrating on the branch, Allonna tried to heat it. She imagined it bursting into flame. Wouldn't that be useful, being able to start a fire by magic?

Heat.

"Never mind," said Selima. "Let's try something different. Try to make the rock move."

Allonna let out a long breath. Focusing her mind on the rock, she willed it to move. She felt power flow out from her to the rock. It wobbled. Had she imagined it? No—it began rocking back and forth, slowly edging farther from her. It looked like a very fat little man waddling away. "I did it!"

"Yes," said Selima. Her voice was amused. "That's not quite what I had in mind, but you did make the rock move." She reached out her hand, and the rock jumped in the air, then flew faster than Allonna's eye could track to shatter against the mountainside.

"Oh," said Allonna. "I can see how that would be a bit more useful in a battle." She might be more powerful than Selima in many ways, but so far they had not discovered any talent that would be useful offensively.

"Don't be discouraged. You can't expect to become an expert everything at once. We just need to learn what talents you have and build from there. You have a talent for wards, I do not. It took me two seasons to learn to cast protective wards properly. At first, I could only cast them around myself."

"Really?"

"I thought I'd never learn to cast them around other people or objects. I was younger than you—barely fourteen—and Omnimancer Jiltunok kept showing me how to cast a ward around a flowerpot he kept near a window. I would try, but the ward always surrounded me."

"Did you finally do it?"

Selima grimaced. "I thought perhaps distance was the problem, so I stood closer to the flowerpot and cast a ward. The ward was still around me, but the edge of the ward curved through the place where the flowerpot was, and repelled it right out the window. And Jiltunok's study was on the third floor. After that, no more casting wards around flowerpots."

The image of Selima as bumbling apprentice forced a smile to Allonna's lips. "How long were you his apprentice?"

"Twenty-two years."

Allonna's eyes widened.

"Oh, technically I was no longer his apprentice after five years, but it took me that long to master all that Jiltunok could teach me. After that, Pel and I moved back to Aud Sapeer, and I took on an apprentice of my own."

"Who is Pel?"

"Pelorin was my husband."

"You were married?" Allonna did not recall any of the storytellers' tales mentioning Selima's husband. "Was he an omnimancer, too?"

"No, he was a historian. That's how we met, actually. He was writing a history of the war against the Dark God, so he came to Crez Pecui to interview Jiltunok. Since Pel and I were both from Aud Sapeer, we spent time talking of home, and one step followed another. We were married the summer of my twenty-fifth year." Selima stopped talking and seemed lost in memory.

When she could bear the silence no more, Allonna said, "So what happened?"

Selima started. "Oh, we lived very happily for many years, although we never did have children. Eventually Pel died." Her tone was matter-of-fact.

"How?"

"He grew old. We had barely celebrated his seventy-third birthday. Then one morning he just didn't wake up."

Although Allonna had thought about the possibility that, as a mancer, she would live to be hundreds of years old, she had not truly considered the implications. Everyone she knew who did not use magic would grow old and pass away while she still looked young. Here was yet another reason to refuse Geradin's advances—he would age and die and leave her alone. "Is that why so few mancers seem to be married? Their spouses died?"

Shrugging, Selima said, "That's true for some. Some marry other mancers, some marry many times." She looked at Allonna and raised an eyebrow. "Is there perhaps some truth behind your pretending to be in love with Geradin?"

Allonna felt heat rise in her face. "Perhaps."

"If you want my advice...?"

"Please."

"If you think you can make each other happy, don't waste any more time."

It was good advice, though not entirely helpful. Allonna wished Selima could tell her whether she and Geradin would make each other happy.

"Now, back to your training. Don't fret—even if we don't find an offensive talent, your power will still be valuable in the coming war. Your wards may save the lives of countless soldiers." Then she smiled and said, "And who can say that an army of marching rocks might not cause the enemy to flee in terror?"

Chapter Forty-One

Geradin

Geradin tried to calculate how long this meeting had been dragging on by looking at the angle of sunlight coming through the western windows of Paskolyik's council room. They had started long before noon, and more than half the afternoon was now gone.

When Aumekor had asked Geradin to attend this meeting with him, Geradin had been excited to hear strategy for the war being discussed at the highest level. The discussion was not irrelevant—but with nine generals, three kings and one queen in attendance, between them representing ten of the Free Kingdoms, everything tended to be repeated from slightly different points of view.

"Enemy ships? My people fear no attack from the sea," said General Drisken, commander of the Bargasian troop contingent that had arrived in Aldamun yesterday. "No warship has a shallow enough draft to cross the Western Shoals, and the Bargasian navy will feed the fish with the enemy should they come in lighter vessels. I can only wish that the Dark Priestess would send us her troops to be slaughtered wholesale like that."

"My point was not to diminish the prowess of Bargasian sailors," said King Nelurquon of the Desoli. "I merely wondered whether the gathering of troops at the wall could be meant to divert us from an invasion by sea."

Drisken bobbed his head. "No offense taken, Your Majesty. Let me add that we have sent small ships to spy along the enemy coast and there is no sign of the shipbuilding activity that would be necessary. No, the northerners are not men of the sea. Even their merchant ships are far inferior to those of the Free Kingdoms. They have never attacked us from the sea, and as long as we maintain naval superiority, they cannot hope to succeed."

"This be the only place to bring armies through the mountains. And there be too many troops here for a diversion," said Paskolyik. "All the armies of the Shadow be here, except for those who guard the Priestess in the City of the Dark God. Perhaps they be confident in their numbers, but I think there be some magical weapon they rely on."

"Selima thinks that's likely," said Mek. "And while she undid the spell used by the Dark Priestess the last time Denali's Pass was attacked, there is no guarantee she can do so again. If, for example, this new attack is based on an artifact created by the Dark God, it cannot be easily countered."

Geradin had wondered why Selima did not seem confident of defeating the magic of the Dark Priestess. There were legends about various weapons made by the Gods—some even attributed the High Protectors' swords to the Gods of Light, although the swords had clearly been made after the Gods of Light had disappeared. Even unlikely objects were rumored to be powerful—one persistent myth claimed extraordinary power for the three legs of a stool the Dark God had sat on, though the powers attributed to the legs and the claimed locations of their hiding places varied with the teller.

Did Selima know something she wasn't telling, or at least not telling him? Such an artifact might pose a special risk to Mek, and therefore the High Protectors needed to know whatever she knew. He would have to talk to her about it when this meeting ended.

If it ever did.

◆ ◆ ◆

Late that evening, Geradin and Selima met with Mek in his quarters.

"I have no knowledge of a particular threat," said Selima in response to Geradin's question. "It is just speculation, but the Dark Priestess must have something new if she thinks she can successfully invade us."

"What if the troops are a diversion," said Geradin, "but not the way King Nelurquon was thinking?"

"What do you mean?" asked Selima.

"Perhaps she cannot invade. But since we cannot know that for sure, we had to react as if she could," Geradin said. "We've gathered a large army, with more on the way. The monarchs of several of the kingdoms are here, and all of them will arrive within the next half-season."

"You're thinking of uprisings in the kingdoms?" said Mek. "If certain nobles were under her influence, knowingly or not, they might take advantage of the situation to seize the thrones of their kingdoms."

"Unlikely," said Selima. "The rightful monarchs might be absent, but they are absent with large armies. They could easily reclaim their places."

Shaking his head, Geradin said, "No, I'm thinking of one particular monarch." He looked at Mek. "You. Something as complicated as this must have been planned before we left the Keep. Perhaps it was her way of luring you out into the open, since her attempts to kill you in the Keep were unsuccessful. And while our attention is focused on the massive army at the wall, she will send a much smaller group aimed at attacking you."

"We discussed this before we left the Keep," said Mek. "You yourself made the point that the Dark Priestess uses long-term plans, and that by leaving we could…Oh. She might not have expected us to go to Cirkepam, but if it was her plan to draw me to Aldamun, I've put myself in place."

Selima stood up from her chair by the fire. "We must leave for home at once, then."

"If that was her plan, why haven't I been attacked yet? There have been opportunities: when the prophet stopped us—"

"The madman," said Selima.

"—and when I went out to rescue Kalya. Geradin's theory may be true, but there are many possibilities. Perhaps the plans of the Dark Priestess involved my absence from the front, counting on my youth and the, ah, enthusiastic protectiveness of those around me to keep me away."

Selima frowned.

"He's right, Selima," said Geradin. He was a little surprised at her overreaction. "Constant second-guessing only leads to confused action. We need to look at the possibilities and take precautions, but Mek's proper place is here, leading the Free Kingdoms."

"She knows that," said Mek. "She just wants an excuse to get me away from Kalya."

"You cannot marry her," Selima said. "Necromancy is an evil practice."

"Necromancy?" said Geradin.

Mek raised his eyebrows. "Selima didn't tell you?"

Geradin shook his head.

"When we managed to not rescue Kalya," Mek continued, "she was questioning one of the men she had killed."

"She's a necromancer?" Geradin tried to work out the implications. Was she a servant of the Dark Priestess? If so, why had she not tried to kill Mek when she had the chance? Geradin recalled how he had let her walk right alongside Mek.

"Followers of the Light should not engage in such filth," said Selima.

"Some say followers of the Light should not kill," said Mek, "yet you have done so on my behalf. Kalya did not kill that man in order to gain power through necromancy; she killed him because he was an enemy who had captured her. If, after he was dead, she used necromancy to question him for information to help protect her people, is that evil?"

"And if you marry her, and word gets out that the Queen of Aud Sapeer uses necromancy, you don't think others will take up the practice? People killing others to gain power and beauty and longevity? Is that what you want for your kingdom? For all the Free Kingdoms?"

Mek looked down.

"I thought not," said Selima. "She may believe she is doing right for her people, but it is not worth the cost."

Geradin could understand if Biyeskalya believed she was using necromancy to help her people, even though it was wrong. But was that all she used it for? Or did it explain why she was so beautiful she had captured Mek's heart?

◆ ◆ ◆

Allonna was waiting for him outside his room. "I need to speak to you."

"Of course," Geradin said. "Is there a problem?"

"Yes."

"What?"

"It's about pretending we're in love. I don't want to do that anymore."

It had seemed like such a wonderful plan at the time. "I understand. I don't think it matters any more—I think Aumekor may finally be turning away from his plan to marry the princess."

She smiled crookedly. "No, you don't understand. You are a lord and I am but a commoner. I have seen before that a lord may pretend to be in love with a common girl, but he really is not."

Geradin's mouth fell open. "You think that I would do such a thing? That I would dishonor myself by lying to you for my own pleasure?"

"No. I have decided that you would not do that. So I ask you,

Lord Geradin, do you believe we could make each other happy, despite our different stations?"

Hope made him feel suddenly warm. He grinned at her. "What different stations? I was born a commoner, to common parents, as were you. Selima was born no more noble than you and me. But she is Lady Selima now because powerful omnimancers are always granted titles of nobility. So there is no question you will be Lady Allonna."

"Really? Lady Allonna?"

"Yes, and it makes sense for the nobles, because they don't want an omnimancer siding with the commoners, and why am I explaining politics to you when I should be saying, yes, I believe we can make each other happy."

She laughed. "I thought I was the one who babbled when nervous."

"So does this mean you will allow me to court you?"

"Yes, Lord Geradin. You may court me."

"Good." Geradin was uncertain what to do next. He had pursued her all this time without really knowing what to do if he caught her. "Perhaps we could go for a walk tomorrow? Together?"

She raised an eyebrow. "We could do that, yes."

"Good." He felt awkward. Why hadn't Selima given him lessons on courting? "Then I guess I will see you tomorrow."

"Geradin. Ger." She smiled and shook her head. "I shall consider this conversation quite a waste of time if you do not take me in your arms and kiss me right now."

"Oh."

So he did.

Chapter Forty-Two

Aumekor

Aumekor was eating breakfast cakes in his chambers when a Protector came in and announced that Princess Biyeskalya wanted to see him. He put down his fork as Nikufed moved the plate out of his way.

"Please tell her I will be ready for her shortly," Aumekor said. He was dressed in his armor, except for the right arm. Though he could use the armor's enchantment to move that arm, but he didn't have sufficient control to eat that way. But without magic, the vambrace was too heavy for the muscles in his arm.

So he always ate in his room, using what little strength he had to lift the pre-cut food to his mouth. It had made things a little awkward, especially when his hosts tended to throw feasts in his honor. Selima always intervened by claiming that, meaning no offense to the cooks or the host, the safety of the Heir of the Line required all food and drink to be subjected to special magical examination, and she would order that his meal be sent to his chambers to be consumed when her examinations were complete.

Nikufed put the vambrace on Aumekor's right arm, then slipped the gauntlet onto his hand.

"Show her in," Aumekor said. Despite what Selima had said about Kalya's necromancy, he still felt like her strength and determination would make her a wonderful queen. And, he admitted, he was still very attracted to her.

Nikufed went to the door and returned leading Kalya, two guards, and a brown-robed man that Aumekor recognized as Paskolyik's Royal Omnimancer.

Aumekor rose to his feet. "Princess Kalya, it is a pleasure to see you again. Omnimancer Tobalich, I am honored by your visit. Please, sit down." Why was the omnimancer here?

"I stand, as I be not staying," said Kalya.

Tobalich looked at her and then chose a chair near Aumekor.

"I'm sorry you must go so quickly," said Aumekor, "but I thank you for escorting the omnimancer here."

She smiled fiercely. "You not thank me later. Under our law, it be possible for a noble who be betrothed to demand the potential spouse be examined as to his or her fitness for matrimony. Refusal be grounds for canceling the betrothal. Omnimancer Tobalich has agreed to perform the examination—unless, of course, you refuse."

She had found a way out of the betrothal—the omnimancer could not fail to discover Aumekor's weakness.

Aumekor almost refused the examination, but decided not to give her the satisfaction of seeing his defeat. "Very well. I will allow Omnimancer Tobalich to do his duty."

Kalya frowned. Aumekor allowed himself one last appreciation of her beauty before she turned and stalked from the room.

"If you do not mind, Omnimancer Tobalich, I would like my own omnimancer here to observe."

"Of course, Your Majesty." Tobalich's Aldamundian accent was mild.

Aumekor nodded to Nikufed, who left to summon Selima.

"I apologize for the indignity, Your Majesty," said Tobalich. "This is a very unusual case."

"How so?"

"The law invoked by the Princess Biyeskalya is an archaic one." The omnimancer's voice was apologetic. "I've never seen it used. It took me a while to find the necessary artifacts. She must have had people poring through the scrolls in our library to find a way out of the betrothal."

"You do not think I will pass?"

"Though she did not say why, the princess led me to believe that was the case."

Aumekor debated whether to tell Tobalich, but decided to wait for Selima. "How long have you been the Royal Omnimancer here?"

"About sixty of the last two hundred years." He grinned. "I haven't always found favor when a new monarch took the throne."

Selima swept into the room. "Bal, what are you doing here?"

Tobalich stood. "Sorry, Lima, I didn't have time to talk to you first. Princess Biyeskalya can be most insistent."

Aumekor hadn't realized the two omnimancers knew each that well. And he had never heard anyone call Selima by her nickname. Shortened names might be an insult in Aldamun, but judging by the friendly tone, Tobalich was obviously familiar with nicknaming customs elsewhere. "I guess formal introductions are unnecessary."

Selima nodded. "Back before your great-grandmother asked me to be her Royal Omnimancer, I did some research at the Great Library of Ostilya. Tobalich was teaching there—"

"During one of my out-of-favor periods," said Tobalich.

"—and he helped me quite a bit with my research. He's an expert on magical artifacts from the Age of Light."

Aumekor nodded. "I am glad to know I am in good hands, then."

Selima frowned. "Good hands?"

"Omnimancer Tobalich is here to perform an examination to determine if I am fit for matrimony."

"I see." She turned to Tobalich. "Is that really necessary?"

He nodded gravely. "Princess Biyeskalya has insisted on it. An archaic legal provision."

"Oh, well in that case, I guess you are obligated to proceed." Her tone was not as reluctant as it could have been. "But I might as well tell you what you will find. The scorpik poison that killed his mother also infected him. His legs and left arm are paralyzed, his right arm is only partly useful, and his neck can barely hold up his head."

During Selima's list, Tobalich stared at Aumekor and his eyes grew wider. He remained silent for a few beats, then said, "Your Majesty is most fortunate to be alive."

"Yes, I am."

Tobalich tugged at his beard. "Your armor—very remarkable." He turned to Selima. "Where did you find it? It's in wonderful condition."

Selima grinned. "You won't believe me."

"Where?"

"This armor is not an artifact of the Age of Light. My apprentice, Allonna, enchanted it."

Tobalich walked over to Aumekor and peered at the armor. "You're serious? She wields that level of power?"

"She does."

Aumekor coughed. "I'm sure you two have plenty to talk about regarding Allonna, but could you wait until after the examination?" It was time to be done with Kalya.

"Oh, yes," said Tobalich. "Won't take long." He fished around in a pocket of his robe and pulled out a dark green ball about two thumbwidths in diameter. He reached in the pocket again and pulled out a maroon ball the same size. He hesitated. "I need you to hold these directly in your hand. Can you do that?"

"Yes."

Nikufed came over and removed the right gauntlet.

Aumekor opened his hand to receive the balls, and Tobalich placed them side by side on his palm.

Selima looked at the artifacts curiously. "What kind of examination is this?"

"An archaic one," said Tobalich. "The law Princess Biyeskalya is using was intended to allow a man to confirm that his potential bride was a fertile virgin. But the language is vague enough that it can be used by her to check the potential husband."

"That's all it does?" said Aumekor. If it wasn't checking his strength, then he could pass it.

"Yes. Quite remarkable artifacts, those. The maroon one checks for virginity—and there. See?"

The maroon color swirled and then faded to white.

Tobalich cleared his throat. "Yes, well, I suppose, in your condition..."

The dark green of the other ball swirled and faded to black.

"What does that mean?" asked Aumekor.

Tobalich wiped his palm across his forehead. "It means you are infertile."

Selima grabbed Tobalich's arm. "You are sure? Could the artifact be mistaken?"

"Yes. No. I mean, yes, I'm sure that's what it means, and no, if the artifact were broken, it would cease to work completely. I'm sorry, Your Majesty, but it is a certainty you are incapable of fathering children."

◆ ◆ ◆

After Tobalich left, Selima pulled her chair close to Aumekor's. "You must not blame yourself. You have done more than I ever imagined you would."

Aumekor bit hard onto his lower lip, letting the physical pain focus his mind away from the gaping emptiness he felt. He must not cry. He must not appear weak. After a long pause, he said, "Do the prophecies say anything about this?"

Selima shook her head.

"Perhaps there's a cure out there—an artifact from the Age of Light that can either take away my weakness or make me able to have children."

"Perhaps." Selima's voice held no hope.

"That's what we'll do." He forced his voice to be cheerful. "A quest to find such an artifact. We'll summon the Protectors and ride out to find it. It will be quite an adventure, just like in the tales: long and difficult, with monsters to defeat and challenges to overcome, but in the end we'll find it because the heroes always do."

"Oh, Mekor," she said. A tear left a wet line down her cheek. "If there were even rumors of an artifact to heal your weakness, you know I would have tracked it down long ago. And a cure for infertility is just as unlikely."

"Then what is the plan, Selima? All my life, I've known my role was to stay alive and father an heir. I longed to be the hero, the Heir of the Line who would defeat the Dark Priestess, but even though I could not do that, at least my life had a purpose. What purpose is there for me now? What good is it that I was even born?"

"Every life has a purpose—"

"Don't. I don't need platitudes. I need to know what I am supposed to do." He wiggled the fingers of his right hand. "Am I supposed to take my father's sword in this hand and go fight her? Isn't that what the prophecies say I am fated to do? The prophecies never said the Heir would win that fight, and now I guess we know why. Hundreds of years of protecting the Line of Orcan to produce the hero, only to get me at the end of the line. Fate has been playing a fine joke on us all, and I am the punchline."

"We go on," said Selima.

"What?"

"You wanted to have a plan? We go on doing the best we can, for as long as we can. You ask what good it was that you were born? I'll tell you. Without you, the Dark Priestess would have no fear. She would have invaded the Free Kingdoms long ago. All the world would be under her dominion. For sixteen years, people have lived free because you were born. Even if you cannot save the world from her, you have made a difference, and you must go on doing so."

Aumekor thought about it. "Go on." He smiled sadly. "Why not? What else am I to do? At the very least, my presence may foil her current plan, and that's good for something."

The door to Aumekor's chambers opened, and Geradin

strode into the room. His face was grim. "A messenger bird just arrived from Bargas. The city is under attack by a large army that came down from the north, destroying all in its path. No one knows yet how they crossed the mountains, but they didn't come by sea."

There had been one purpose left to him, and now fate had snatched it away just as he had grasped it. Aumekor couldn't help himself: he began to laugh. He laughed until the tears flowed freely down his face.

Geradin stared at him. "This is not a joke."

"Yes, it is," said Aumekor. "Fate is laughing at me right now, so I might as well join in. What else am I to do?"

Chapter Forty-Three

Geradin

"There must be a cure," said Geradin after Selima explained the results of Tobalich's test. "Why would the prophets have bothered to write down all those prophecies, if they knew it would end like this?"

Selima shook her head. "Prophecies don't work like that. Prophets don't see all of the future. Even they do not always know how their own prophecies will be fulfilled."

"He was right." Mek sat limply in his chair, and his face was expressionless.

"Who?" asked Selima.

"The prophet. He said I had no future. My life is nothing but an end."

"The prophet! That's it!" Geradin said. "He prophesied that Biyeskalya would be pregnant with your child. He may know something about how to restore your fertility."

Selima sighed. "How many times do I have to explain that madman was not a prophet? Nothing he said can be relied upon, either as saying you have no future or as predicting Biyeskalya's pregnancy. The two contradict each other, even."

"You are right, Selima," said Mek. "I have a future. But if the news of the invasion of Bargas is true, it is likely to be neither long nor happy. If the Dark Priestess has found a way for her armies to cross the Barrier Mountains, then it is only a matter of five, ten years at the most before she conquers all of the Free

Kingdoms. Perhaps Ostilya will hold out longer, especially if the Bargasian fleet makes its home there when Bargas falls, but this is a war we cannot win. And everyone knows it. Soldiers will desert to go back to their families. Nobles will surrender in the hopes of maintaining some position within the new order. Even some of the monarchs may—"

"Enough," said Selima. "We have been attacked before, and that did not happen."

"Didn't it?" Geradin could not recall ever having heard Mek sound so bitter. "Surely you've read about what happened in the Free Kingdoms north of the Barrier Wall when the rest of the Kingdoms abandoned them? Oh, yes, there were many who fought bravely to the end, and we owe them our thanks. But they at least thought they were dying to protect a future in which the Dark Priestess would be defeated. Why bother to fight to the end when all hope is gone?"

"Because all hope is not gone," said Geradin. "As long as you live it is possible the Dark Priestess will be killed. As long as the Heir of the Line is alive our soldiers will fight and our nobles will not surrender."

"You would have them fight and die for a false hope?" asked Mek.

"It is not a false hope. I know you don't think you can do it. I know Selima doesn't believe a cure is out there waiting to be found. But neither of you is a prophet. Neither of you knows for certain what the future holds. So I will hope you are both wrong."

Mek closed his eyes for a few beats, then opened them to look at Geradin. "Perhaps I wasted all my hope on Kalya. I haven't the strength to hope for myself. Yours will have to be strong enough for both of us."

"All my strength is at your command." A sudden thought came to mind, and Geradin turned to Selima. "Is there a way to do that? Transfer strength from one person to another?"

"No," said Selima. "Not in that way. If there were, there are many who would have volunteered years ago."

"Thank you," said Mek. "You are a true friend for being willing." He frowned. "I wonder what that makes me, since, if it were possible, I would have taken your strength."

Geradin smiled. "It makes you my king."

◆ ◆ ◆

"The princess will see you now," said the guard. She motioned for Geradin to follow her.

"Lord Geradin," said Biyeskalya, "it is a pleasure to welcome a great warrior like you to my chamber." Her Aldamundian accent was faint, and she wore a silky gown that clung to her figure. Geradin had no doubt the reason he had been forced to wait outside was so she could change into that dress.

"I want to ask you a question, Your Highness."

"If it is in my power to answer, I shall."

"It is power that I want to ask you about. I understand you are a necromancer."

Her brow wrinkled. "It is not a crime in my kingdom. Do not judge what you do not know."

"I'm not here to condemn you. I'm here to ask you about it. Could necromancy make King Aumekor—" Geradin's breath seemed to freeze in his throat and he found himself unable to say another word. For a moment he wondered what was going on, and then he realized it was the binding of the oath disk. Even though Biyeskalya knew Aumekor's condition, her guards apparently did not, and the magic would not allow him to reveal it. After a moment, he could breathe again, and he said, "We must discuss this privately, without your guards."

She tilted her head and looked at him, then ordered her guards to wait outside.

"What I meant to ask was this," said Geradin. "Could necromancy make King Aumekor strong?"

"Did he send you to ask this?"

"No. This is my own idea."

"You are aware that necromancy requires the killing of a

person?"

"I know. I am willing to give my life in order to give his body strength," said Geradin. That would erase his father's failure.

Biyeskalya stared at him and didn't speak for a long time. "You respect him so much?"

"I do."

"The most powerful necromancy be when the necromancer offer his own life to cast the spell," she said. "But even with such power, I do not think it be accomplished. Necromancy be not for healing."

Geradin felt a mixture of disappointment, relief and guilt. "I thank Your Highness for having answered my question." He bowed, turned and walked out.

◆ ◆ ◆

It was two more days before confirmation of the initial message arrived. "Three messenger birds have arrived from Bargas," General Drisken told the assembled generals and monarchs. "There is good news among the bad. The city gates have held. Apparently the invaders do not have siege engines with them."

Geradin joined in the general sigh of relief that swept the room, but he wondered what the bad news was. He looked at Mek, who nodded. In discussing the possibilities, Mek and Geradin had concluded that the enemy troops had been infiltrating for a few seasons in small groups through narrow passes—a theory supported by the fact the enemy had no siege engines.

"Having failed to break into the city, the invaders have not settled in for a siege," said Dresken. "Instead, they are roaming the countryside, ravaging unprotected villages. Most commoners are fleeing to their respective lords' castles. For now, though, the enemy remains mostly unopposed in the field. Therefore, I must take my troops and return immediately to defend my kingdom."

No one objected.

"Be there any estimate on the number of the enemy?" asked Paskolyik.

"At least ten thousand, half of them Soulless—scorpiks and leonaks, mainly, with a few of the other types mixed in."

Ten thousand? Geradin looked at Mek, who looked back with a frown of puzzlement. They had been expecting no more than a thousand. Ten thousand was too many for the infiltration scenario.

"Impossible," said Paskolyik. "The Dark Priestess does not have another ten thousand troops."

"Is it possible your source is overestimating?" another general asked. "How could such a large army have made it over the mountains without anyone noticing?"

"It could not," said Drisken. "We had a spy within their army, who was unable to warn us before the attack, but as soon as he could he escaped and reported two key pieces of information. The army did not come over the mountains. It came under them—through a tunnel the Dark Priestess built over the last thirty years."

Various people began talking excitedly. Geradin silently tried to analyze the implications. The Dark Priestess had planned well. By placing most of her troops near the Barrier Wall, she had diverted the armies of the Free Kingdoms so her forces could establish a foothold in Bargas. There was no doubt the exit of the tunnel was well-guarded, and it would be very difficult to attack it and seal it off. The enemy troops stationed beyond the Barrier Wall were probably already preparing to march west to the tunnel and join the invasion of the Free Kingdoms. Meanwhile, the armies of the Free Kingdoms would have to march around the spur of mountains to the southwest, making their route longer. The only course of action seemed to be to leave a small force here to defend the Barrier Wall and march with all speed to Bargas.

"General Drisken," said Mek, "you said there were two key pieces of information. I take it the other piece is that the troops that have invaded Bargas are the forces that normally defend the City of the Dark God?"

Drisken's head jerked up. "Yes, Your Majesty. How did you know?"

"It's the only place that many Soulless could have come from," said Mek. He rose from his chair. "General Drisken, I know you must get your men back to your homeland as soon as possible. I can promise you that reinforcements will not be far behind—Bargas does not stand alone."

Drisken bowed his head. "Thank you, Your Majesty."

◆ ◆ ◆

In Mek's chambers, Geradin and Selima sat while Mek stood at a window, looking out into the fading light. "She knows, Selima."

"Who knows what?" asked Selima.

"The Dark Priestess. She knows about my weakness. It's the only rational explanation as to why she would feel safe in stripping her city of its troops."

"How could she have found out?"

Geradin sprang from his chair. "Biyeskalya. She was not under oath not to reveal your secret. And she's a necromancer, like—"

"No," said Mek. "The troops must have left the City of the Dark God before we even arrived here. The plan was put into effect even before we arrived at Cirkepam, because the massing of troops here was part of it."

"Midsummer," said Selima. "We were holding you up with magic, and then dropped you to put the attackers to sleep. Someone with a good perception of magical flows could have figured out what we were doing."

"Midsummer." Mek nodded. "The timing would be about right. I should never have insisted on speaking at Midsummer."

"It's not your fault," said Geradin. "This plan has been going for thirty years. It would have happened whether you spoke or not."

"Perhaps. No, you're right. It would have happened. But what really bothers me is that we cannot take advantage of the fact that she's left her city unprotected. If I could fight like Geradin, I would lead a force there to confront her."

"If you could fight like Geradin, she would not have left her city unprotected," said Selima. "Such circular reasoning is not worth pursuing."

Geradin suddenly felt like something significant had been said, but he didn't know what. As Mek said something else to Selima, Geradin sat in his chair and tried to figure out what he was missing. If Mek could fight like him, all their problems would be solved. But that was impossible as long as Mek was weak, so it all came back to finding a cure for Mek's weakness. Which was the same problem they had always had. Nothing new there.

Mek walked from the window to a chair and sat down across from him.

It was as if the mists cleared from Geradin's mind and the solution sat in front of him. "Allonna!" he said.

Mek and Selima both stared at him. "What about Allonna?" asked Selima.

"I don't know if it's possible," said Geradin, "but she might be able to do it. What if, instead of you controlling your armor with that gauntlet, my entire suit of armor controlled yours?"

Chapter Forty-Four

Allonna

Omnimancer Tobalich's study was quite different from Selima's. The shelves were not filled with books, but rather with a strange assortment of items in no logical arrangement Allonna could determine. A jewel-encrusted dagger hilt caught her eye. On the same shelf she could see what looked like a plain pewter goblet, a rather worn woolen blanket, and a bone that she hoped was not human. She concentrated a moment, and as the rest of the room seemed to dim, she could see the enchantment in the objects all around the room. Some merely seemed to have a faded glow, while others shone steadily and a few blazed like miniature suns.

"Were the brightest ones made by the gods?" she asked.

"Taking a peek, were you? Most of them were, yes. Two were made by great mancers of the Age of Light."

Allonna stopped looking at the magic. "What do all these things do?" she said, waving an arm around the room. Selima had some magical artifacts in her study, but Allonna estimated there must be ten times as many here.

Tobalich grinned at her. "All of them? That would take quite a long time to explain. But the truth is, even I do not know what all of them do. Take this, for example." He reached to his table and picked up a fist-sized hemisphere of stone that had held one of the brightest magical glows. "It was created by one of the gods—Clanni, I believe—and has more power in it than I have used in my lifetime."

"What is it?"

"Right now, a paperweight. I haven't found any other use for it. There's a similar problem with many of these items—they were created so long ago that their purposes have been forgotten. Sometimes in studying an item I discover that purpose." He looked around the room for a moment, then reached over and grabbed a pottery mug. "This, for example." He handed it to her.

Allonna took it. It seemed an ordinary empty mug. "What does it do?"

"Put it to your lips, as if to drink from it."

Warily, she raised the mug to her mouth. It seemed to grow a bit heavier and suddenly a cold liquid touched her upper lip. She jerked the mug away and clear liquid spilled from it, wetting her dress and splashing on the floor.

"I'm sorry," she said.

"It's only water. I should have warned you, but I do love a surprise."

Allonna looked in the mug, which was still half-full. "Where did the water come from?"

Tobalich shrugged. "I don't know. It can fill up with water up to five times a day. It must have been a wondrously useful item for someone who spent a lot of time traveling in a desert. There is so much the ancients could do that we have neither the power nor the knowledge to recreate. Which is why I asked Selima if I could speak with you. The enchantment on King Aumekor's armor is remarkable. I have not seen anything like it made since the burning of the world. You have quite the talent."

Allonna blushed. "I don't really know how I do it."

"That doesn't matter. But you have a level of power available to you that allows you to create artifacts like these." He pointed at his shelves. "After this war is over, if you'd like, you can come spend a season or two here studying these artifacts, to see what you can learn from them."

"Could I?" Except when Selima had specifically told her to use an artifact, Allonna had not had a chance to examine such items. She was quite curious about how they were made and what they could do. She wondered if Selima would allow her to take time off from her apprenticeship to study with Tobalich.

"Of course. Let me show you something I think you'll find fascinating. It was discovered—"

There was a knock at the door.

"Come," said Tobalich.

Geradin opened the door and entered. "Sorry to disturb you, Omnimancer Tobalich, but we need Allonna to try something. Selima said you may come, too, if you wish."

What could they want her to try? Allonna turned to Tobalich. "I guess we'll have to leave the fascinating for later."

He tugged at his beard. "To the contrary. I think we'll be seeing something fascinating soon."

◆ ◆ ◆

"So, do you think you can do it?" Geradin asked, after he explained his idea.

"I don't know," said Allonna. It didn't seem too different in principle from having the gauntlet control the armor, but judging by the hopeful looks she was getting from Aumekor and Geradin, it was better not to promise something and then find out there were problems she hadn't foreseen. "In some ways, it seems easier, because the enchantment would not need to specify how to make motions for walking or turning— it only needs to mimic the movement of Geradin's armor. But in other ways it's more difficult. The connection would have to work both ways, I think."

"Why?" asked Selima.

"Because Geradin's armor must always be in the same position as Aumekor's armor," said Allonna. "If they were not synchronized, then what might seem a normal movement to Geradin could force the king's armor into a contorted position."

"Wait," said Aumekor. "I can't always be in the same position as Geradin. It would look very strange."

Geradin laughed. "That would be funny. We'd be like twins. But there must be a way around that." He looked at Allonna. "Could you make my control of his armor something that is switched on and off, like his arm movements?"

"Possibly. As I said, I don't know if I can do it. I need time to plan. Perhaps we could practice on another suit of armor first, because I don't know whether I can do this as an overlay or whether I'll have to replace the current enchantment." Her mind was already thinking of the possible approaches to the problem.

Aumekor said, "Why don't you and Geradin go work out the details?" He glanced over at Tobalich and smiled. "I assume that with Omnimancer Tobalich's assistance, you can enchant armor for practice without setting off alarm bells?"

Allonna wondered briefly if that incident would ever be forgotten.

◆ ◆ ◆

"It's never going to work." Allonna dropped into a chair and stared at the armored forms of Geradin and Otunvol, who had volunteered to help test the enchantment. The two of them were lying on the ground with their right legs up in the air.

"You've got most of it, Allonna." Geradin's voice was encouraging, if a little weak. "You'll figure it out."

Allonna winced. Falling on his back like that must have knocked some wind out of him, even on the soft soil of this palace garden, yet he was still trying to encourage her. "I'm sorry."

"I vote that we conduct further tests from this position," said Otunvol. "I think I can handle a fall from this height without too much difficulty."

"I'm going to try lowering my leg," said Geradin.

"Ready," said Otunvol.

Geradin's armored leg began slowly to move down. Otunvol's raised leg mirrored the action. Both legs began moving faster until they thudded into the ground with an impact Allonna could feel.

"I'm going to unlink the armor," said Geradin. After a moment, he rolled onto his stomach and laboriously climbed to his feet. He reached down and gave Otunvol a hand in standing up.

Allonna considered the problem. Enchanting one suit of armor to control the other had been so easy that it had worked perfectly the first time she tried it. But, as she had anticipated, any obstacle encountered by the controlled armor meant the two suits were no longer synchronized in their motions. And simply doing a similar enchantment to allow the second suit of armor to control the first had resulted in disaster. Any movement Geradin made was exaggerated by both suits. Trying to take a small step forward was what had left them flat on their backs.

She turned to Tobalich. "You're the expert on enchanted objects. Do you have any ideas on why this isn't working?"

He unwrapped a lock of beard that he had twisted around a finger. "I'm an expert on objects that have already been enchanted, not how to enchant them. But even simple enchantments can interfere with each other. If you cast a spell for heat and a spell for cold on the same object, the effects can be unpredictable. Casting spells for a suit of armor to both control and be controlled may be similar."

So it might be impossible to do what King Aumekor wanted. Allonna looked at Geradin. "Why does the king need this, anyway? I thought the High Protectors didn't want him using a sword."

Geradin said, "Omnimancer Tobalich, are we safe from eavesdropping here?"

Tobalich nodded.

"The Dark Priestess knows about the king's weakness. That's

why she used the troops that normally defend her city to invade Bargas. She feels safe because the only one who can kill her is Aumekor, using his father's sword." Geradin's voice grew quieter, even though no one could spy on what he was saying. "Our military situation is precarious. We have been caught out of position, and as long as the Dark Priestess can send troops through that tunnel, we will eventually be overwhelmed. It may already be impossible for our armies to get to the mouth of the tunnel to close it off. So our best hope may be to send a party into the City of the Dark God—which the Dark Priestess has so kindly stripped of its defending army—and have Aumekor kill the Dark Priestess. And for that, he must wield a sword."

Allonna's heart thudded within her chest. They were going to confront the Dark Priestess? "Selima has agreed to this plan?"

"If you can enchant the armor. It's either this, or go back to the Keep to prepare for a siege. It's possible that someone will find a cure for Aumekor's condition. But by then the Dark Priestess will be expecting an attack, and we would have to fight through thousands of troops to get to her. And most of the Free Kingdoms will have already been devastated."

Geradin walked over to her chair and squatted so he could look her directly in the eyes. "No one will blame you if you can't enchant the armor. All it would mean is that going back to the Keep is what we are supposed to do. The Keep of Aud Sapeer has never fallen to an enemy in the two thousand years since it was built. We can live there safely for many, many years."

Allonna could see the concern for her on Geradin's face. The Free Kingdoms might be destroyed if she failed, and he was trying to make sure her feelings would not be hurt. "I'll find a way," she said.

◆ ◆ ◆

The mud squished beneath her. Allonna got up and twisted the *new dress Mama had made for her to see the huge stain on the back.* "Look what you did!" *she shouted at Pag.* "It's ruined!"

He laughed, then singsonged, "Lonna's got a dirty bum. Lonna's got a dirty bum."

Angry, she rushed toward him. He started to run, but she was two years older and caught him easily. She gave him a shove and he fell face-first into the mud.

Pag got up and spit mud out of his mouth at her. "I'm telling Mama you pushed me."

"You pushed me first," *she said.*

His quickness surprised her, and she found herself sitting in the mud again.

"Pag, stop pushing me!" *She rose to her feet and charged forward, knocking him back into the mud.*

"No, you stop pushing me!"

Allonna awoke suddenly from her dream. "Stop pushing me," she whispered. It all made sense.

Chapter Forty-Five

Geradin

Geradin's tailbone still hurt from his fall the day before, but he wasn't inclined to tell Allonna about it. If the enchantment went crazy today, he would just have to turn it off more quickly so he could react to the fall properly. He looked over at Otunvol, who had been crazy enough to volunteer again. "Are you ready?"

"Always."

"I'm going to take a step forward now." Geradin gingerly lifted his right foot and saw Otunvol do the same. His leg did not suddenly accelerate into a wild kick; it completed a cautious step. He tried another, then another, until he found himself face to face with Otunvol. Geradin reached out to place a hand on Otunvol's shoulder, but his gauntlet stopped two thumbwidths away at the same moment Otunvol's gauntlet pressed against Geradin's shoulder. Geradin took a step back and Otunvol did the same.

"I feel like a puppet," said Otunvol.

Geradin turned to face Allonna. "You did it!"

She was already grinning. "I told you I'd find a way."

Geradin suddenly felt his right arm move. His hand came up and then waved to Allonna. Why was it doing that?

"Hello, Allonna," said Otunvol. "Just wanted Geradin to know what being a puppet felt like."

"Very funny," said Geradin. He brought his arm down and

gave the hand signal that disabled the link between the armor.

Omnimancer Tobalich stood up from the bench he was sitting on, walked over to Otunvol and peered closely at the armor. "Impressive. After what happened yesterday, I admit I did not think you would succeed; at least, not so soon."

"Last night I realized what the problem was. Geradin's armor made Otunvol's armor start to move, which is how it was supposed to work. But because Otunvol's armor was moving, the enchantment made Geradin's armor move in reaction. And the enchantment in Geradin's armor then made Otunvol's armor move some more, which made Geradin's move even more. It was as if they kept pushing each other."

It made sense to Geradin. He had read of historical parallels, where nations got caught in a cycle of retaliation that started with minor grievances and spiraled out of control into full war. "How did you fix it?"

"I made it so that movements caused by the enchantment don't get sent to the other suit of armor."

"An elegant solution," said Tobalich. "And doing all this enchantment hasn't drained you too much?"

As Allonna and Tobalich began talking about omnimancer subjects, Geradin watched Allonna's face without really listening to her words. The flash of her smile and the brightness of her eyes made her seem so full of life. Geradin felt a pang of guilt at having come up with this plan. He had been telling the truth when he said striking now was probably the best hope for the Free Kingdoms. But from what he had heard of the prophecies concerning those who would go with the Heir of the Line to confront the Dark Priestess, it was quite possible that most or possibly all of them would be killed—even if they succeeded in defeating the Dark Priestess.

Geradin had always known he might be killed in protecting Mek. He did not fear that fate. He feared for Allonna's safety, though, and he was not used to that. Allonna had, of course, been at risk since becoming Selima's apprentice, but now they would be heading deliberately into danger, not hoping to avoid it.

"What's wrong, Geradin?" asked Allonna.

Geradin blinked, then smiled. "Nothing," he lied. "Should we go enchant the king's armor now?"

◆ ◆ ◆

"I'm ready," said Mek.

Geradin reached for his sword. Mek's armor followed the movement, but his sword was not in the right place. Geradin tried various movements until he finally got Mek's hand around the hilt. But now Geradin's hand was out of position for his own sword. He realized suddenly that he didn't need it—through the enchantment, he could feel Mek's sword in his grip. He pulled it from its scabbard and raised it. He was actually holding nothing, but he could still feel the sword's weight.

"This is fantastic." Mek's voice held all the excitement of a child with a new puppy. "Do some slashes or something. I want to see how it looks."

Geradin obliged by beginning some of his routine sword exercises. "Let me know if I do anything that hurts." He watched as Mek's armor smoothly moved the sword up and down, back and forth.

"Faster, Ger," said Mek.

"Not too fast," said Selima. "The armor may be able to take it, but I think it's best not to push too hard at first. There will be plenty of time on the journey for you to get accustomed, Aumekor."

"Fine, fine," said Mek. "But how does it look? It's smooth, isn't it? Like I'm an expert swordsman?"

"Your armor seems to follow my moves perfectly," said Geradin. "I didn't think it would be this easy."

"Practice moves may be easy," said Otunvol. "Have you considered what it will be like to actually fight?"

Geradin finished a swing and stopped. He had not

considered the actual mechanics of fighting someone by controlling Mek. He would be looking at the fight from a distance. His view might even be blocked as Mek and his opponent circled each other. How could Geradin react to the enemy's swordplay if he couldn't see it properly?

"Watching you two, another problem occurs to me," said Selima. "Anyone who sees both of you will quickly figure out that your armor is linked. So they might attack Geradin in order to disable Aumekor."

Geradin's heart sank. His brilliant idea was turning out not to be so brilliant after all. Despite the effort Allonna had put into finding a solution, perhaps they would have to abandon the idea and retreat to the Keep after all. There had to be a way around this.

"This may be good enough," said Mek. "I only need to fight once, and though the Dark Priestess is a formidable foe, that's not because she is known for her cunning with the sword. As long as I can get near her, Geradin can probably control the armor well enough to strike her. Someone will just have to protect Geradin while he's controlling my armor."

Geradin could tell Mek was using his falsely confident tone. It was probably apparent to the others, too, but nobody said anything.

◆ ◆ ◆

As Geradin was walking Allonna back to her room, he spotted someone in a white-hooded robe walking toward them. He was startled to recognize the man. "High Priest Kogyrinem? What are you doing here?"

Kogyrinem smiled. "Lord Geradin, it is good to see you again, too. And you also, Miss Allonna."

Geradin bowed his head. "Forgive my rudeness, Your Grace. I did not expect to find you so far from the temple."

"I concluded that if the armies of Light and Dark were about to clash, my place was here." Kogyrinem let out a mock sigh.

"Apparently I was wrong, though, and my place is actually in Bargas. I'm surprised to find you still here."

"There have been...developments. It's good that you have come. We need your advice about how to proceed." Geradin felt a little more confident. Kogyrinem knew many of the prophecies about how Mek was supposed to confront the Dark Priestess. His advice might increase their chances of success.

"I will do all within my power to assist you," said the High Priest. "Now, if I might ask your assistance, I wanted to speak with Omnimancer Selima, but she was not in her room. Do you know where I might find her?"

"She was headed to Omnimancer Tobalich's study. If you need someone to show you the way..." Geradin glanced at Allonna, who nodded. "...Allonna could take you there. I have to meet with His Majesty now, but I'll inform him of your arrival."

◆ ◆ ◆

Nodding to the Protectors on duty outside Mek's chambers, Geradin slipped through the door.

"—will require that you stay here a few more days at the most, as we may have a special mission for you," said Mek to the generals of Aud Sapeer's army. They had brought their troops from the Barrier Wall and stopped here before continuing on to Bargas.

"What sort of mission?" asked one of the generals.

"I cannot discuss that yet," said Mek. "But if your men are needed, your input will be appreciated in finalizing the plans. Go back to your troops now, and I shall send word when the time comes."

The generals began to leave, but one of them paused. Geradin recognized him as Opattol, whom they had met on the road to Aldamun.

"Pardon, milord," said Opattol, "but I just thought I'd tell you that I did as you asked. Your friend won't be in any close combat—I've placed Holoran with a catapult team, and a fine job he does there. Worth any three men."

Geradin opened his mouth to thank the man, when suddenly he recalled the prophecy Selima had thought applied to Holoran. The strongest man in the world was supposed to go with the Heir of the Line to confront the Dark Priestess. Geradin had hoped to keep Holoran out of harm's way, but that was no longer possible. "I thank you for that, General Opattol. If you could send Holoran to see me as soon as possible, I would appreciate it."

"Of course, milord."

◆ ◆ ◆

"Do I have you to thank for my being on a catapult team?" Holoran's voice was gruff.

Geradin had known Holoran might take it as an insult to his honor. "It's a very important part of fighting, and General Opattol says you're very good at it."

Holoran's mouth opened into a giant grin. "Well, I thank you, then. For the first time, I feel like I can really be worth my pay as a soldier. I get along great with the others on my team, and we're the fastest catapult team from Aud Sapeer. When we get to Bargas, we'll be knocking holes in the Dark Army so fast they'll think it's raining mountains."

Hearing Holoran's enthusiasm, Geradin felt the burden of what he had to do grow heavier. "Holoran, you remember that day we first met?"

"Midsummer, of course."

"Did you ever feel like we were meant to meet that day?"

Holoran frowned. "Strange you should say that. Telani told me it must have been fate that you met me that morning, so I could marry her without waiting another year."

"There's something called prophetic coincidence. It means that sometimes coincidences happen in order to help fulfill a prophecy. It's almost as if the universe is trying to help the prophecy along."

"And my meeting you was like that?"

"Yes. As is your presence here now. And it means you won't be going on to Bargas with your team." That was the most Geradin could say for now. Selima would have to swear Holoran to secrecy on the oath disk before he could be told any more.

"Wait," said Holoran. "You're not just trying to keep me out of battle again, are you?"

"I wish I were," said Geradin. "Light, I wish I were."

Chapter Forty-Six

Aumekor

Surrounded by Geradin, Wyran and two other Protectors, Aumekor walked into the meeting hall. Including Selima, fourteen Royal Omnimancers rose from their seats around the table, watching him as he made his way to sit in the chair at the head. High Priest Kogyrinem stood also, even though etiquette did not require him to do so.

After everyone was seated again, Selima introduced all of the omnimancers Aumekor had not yet met. She concluded by saying, "I believe this is the largest gathering of Royal Omnimancers in over fifty years. It is a pleasure to see so many of you again."

"Get to the point, Selima," said Istubik, a bald and hunched old man. The Royal Omnimancer from Crez Pecui was over four hundred and seventy years old, but according to Selima he would probably not live to his five hundredth birthday. "Why is the Heir lollygagging in Aldamun with his troops when he should be marching to Bargas?"

Since Crez Pecui's status as a wealthy kingdom bordering Bargas made it most likely the next kingdom to be attacked by the enemy, Aumekor understood Istubik's anxiety.

Selima took a deep breath. "We believe the Heir can best serve the Free Kingdoms by killing the Dark Priestess, in accordance with the prophecies."

During the silence that followed Selima's announcement,

Aumekor looked at the faces around the table. Most of them were successful at hiding any surprise—like Selima, the other Royal Omnimancers were adept at the games of power played out in most courts.

"Why?" said Jebasta, of the nomadic Desoli. At a little over a hundred years old, she was the youngest of the Royal Omnimancers, and looked like a woman in her thirties.

"Because fear of the Dark Priestess is all that keeps her domain together," said Selima. "If she is killed, her army would return home and split into factions as provinces revolted and various people tried to take power."

"No, I meant why do you believe that this Heir is the one who can succeed? Do you have a prophecy that points to him specifically?"

"All the prophecies point to him specifically," said Selima. "King Aumekor is infertile. Unless one of you knows of a cure for that, he is the last of the Line of Orcan."

Several people began speaking at once.

Selima raised her palm to silence them. "There is more you must know. King Aumekor has been mostly paralyzed since birth. Only by means of his enchanted armor is he able to walk and wield a sword."

As Aumekor and Selima had planned for this meeting, Selima had been reluctant to let the other omnimancers know the full truth. Aumekor had convinced her that the only way to ensure the others gave the best possible help was to let them know the real situation.

But that did not mean there would be no negative reactions from her peers.

"How could you let this happen to the Heir?" said Istubik. "Bad enough that you let Ordil die, but to allow the last Heir to be neutered and crippled is inexcusable."

Neutered? Activating his right arm, Aumekor brought it down with a resounding thump on the table. "We are not here to discuss the past. But I must point out that I do not blame Selima for my condition. In fact, it is that very condition that has opened the door for us to attack the Dark Priestess: she has stripped her city of its army because she does not fear an attack from me."

"Of course!" said Kalik, from Tantaur. "You've all read Disen's prophecies. I always thought of his contradictions as being figurative, but 'The powerless strong man and the powerful weak man' obviously applies here."

Istubik said, "But you're forgetting Tisuri: 'The strongest of all men and the weakest.' In the original Godstongue, the words for strongest and weakest used by Tisuri only apply to physical strength. You're not claiming Tisuri is figurative?"

To Aumekor's surprise, Geradin spoke up. "If you will pardon my interruption, there is a soldier here who is by far the strongest man I know. And he is a commoner, which makes him a 'powerless strong man,' in contrast to King Aumekor as a 'powerful weak man.' Would that satisfy both prophecies?"

Istubik nodded slowly. "That would." He turned to Selima. "I suppose you want us all to share any additional prophecies we know of regarding the Heir of the Line, beyond the common ones?"

"Every piece of information may help," said Selima.

◆ ◆ ◆

Aumekor looked at the list Selima had written on a piece of paper:

    Heir of the Line
    Protectors of the Line
    Weakest man—Aumekor
    Strongest man—Holoran
    Most powerful omnimancer—Allonna
    Expert omnimancer—Selima
    Unlearned omnimancer—Allonna
    The swordsman—Geradin
    The archer—?
    The guide—?

The general—?
The soldier—? Holoran?
Teacher who is below the student—Selima
Student who is above the teacher—Allonna
One who goes before—Same as guide?
One who comes after—?
Leader who follows—Same as guide? Or Aumekor following guide?
Follower who leads—Same as guide? Or Aumekor following guide?
One who watches from afar—?
The rich—Aumekor
The poor—Allonna, Holoran
The noble—Geradin
The commoner—Holoran
The old—Selima
The young—Geradin, Aumekor
Young crone—Selima?
Old child—No majority? Allonna?

It had caused quite a stir when Selima had announced that she had an apprentice who was more powerful than she was. There had also been some dispute over who fit the "expert omnimancer" title, but once it was clear that the prophecy did not say "most expert," no one objected to Selima in that role.

"I've got one that I'm not sure of," said Mirai, from Cirkepam. "It contains Godstongue words that were not in any reference I have: *yepeto* and *yepetik*."

"Ah," said Istubik. "At least the party will be entertained on their journey." He shook his head. "You must have the words wrong."

"I do not," Mirai said. "What do they mean?"

"They mean puppeteer and puppet."

Aumekor laughed. "Omnimancer Mirai has the words right. And they are the best news yet, because they prove we fit the prophecies." He commanded his armor to synchronize with Geradin's. The armor immediately stood him up into the same watchful pose Geradin was in. "Lord Geradin, if you would be so kind as to demonstrate your puppeteering skills?"

His right arm reached over, drew his sword and lifted it high over his head. Out of the corner of his eye, Aumekor could see Geradin in the same position, but not holding a sword. "I suppose that makes me the puppet, but I trust Lord Geradin as my puppeteer."

The sword came down and slid back into its sheath. Aumekor took control of his armor again and sat down. "I believe that sword is mentioned in the prophecies as well."

"'Only with his father's sword shall he have power to kill her,'" quoted Jebasta.

"That's strange," said High Priest Kogyrinem.

"Do you know something about the sword prophecy?" asked Selima.

"What? No, I was looking at your list," he said. "I had the impression from reading the prophecies there would be a lot of people in the company of the Heir. Passages like, "Rich and poor, noble and common, old and young— all shall go with him," gave me the impression of a large crowd. But the way you're doing this list, I see only five different names there: Aumekor, Geradin, Selima, Allonna and Holoran. If you find a general who's an archer with good eyesight to be your guide, that would complete the party with only six people."

"It does say 'Protectors of the Line,'" said Geradin. "That's over a hundred people right there."

"We're just establishing the minimum," said Selima. "We need to make sure we have all the people we need, but I don't know of anything that says we're limited to one person that fits each category. Having several expert omnimancers along would make victory that much easier."

Kalik coughed. "Does anyone else have the prophecies of Sisnak?"

"I've read Sisnak," said Istubik, "but never saw anything to do with the Heir of the Line. His prophecies are all about lights in the sky."

"I'm sorry," said Kalik. "I meant his son, Sisnak att'Sisnak. Anyone else have his prophecies?"

Nobody spoke.

"As far as I remember," Kalik said, "he only made one prophecy about the Heir of the Line, but it was quite clear: 'Before the Heir of the Line meets the Dark One, all but four shall be lost along the way. Four alone shall enter the Dark One's temple.' I remember it clearly because it's such a dire contrast to the other prophecies that seem to call for large numbers of people going with the Heir."

The plan Aumekor, Geradin and Selima had made called for taking the Protectors of the Line plus whichever omnimancers wanted to join the expedition, and making the dangerous trek on foot over the mountains. That would have been around two hundred people—but now prophecy said only four would reach the destination. Aumekor knew enough about prophecy to know that the phrase "lost along the way" could mean anything from death to merely getting lost, but the prophecy was clear as rainwater that only four would be left, no matter what the reason.

"You're certain this is a valid prophecy?" asked Selima.

High Priest Kogyrinem spoke before Kalik could answer. "'Four shall be their number, and upon their heads lie heavy the fates of the free.' A prophecy of Jaridolim, my great-grandfather. I didn't know what it applied to until now."

Istubik said, "I've always wondered about the passage in Tisuri where she says, 'Where shall they be who confront her. May they suffice.' It makes no sense, so I thought it might be a transcription error, since we have no originals of her prophecies. In Godstongue, the words 'four' and 'where' are only one letter different. 'Four shall they be who confront her. May they suffice.'"

Resolve built within Aumekor. If the prophecies decreed only four people would make it, then he would take as few people as possible to be lost along the way. "So we have our party. Selima. Allonna. Holoran. Geradin, plus one more

Protector of the Line, so we have plural Protectors. If we can find Kogyrinem's sharp-eyed archer-general to guide us, that will make seven. Three will be lost, but we need not lose any more."

Wyran spoke for the first time during the meeting. "Our oaths require us to protect you, Your Majesty. We cannot stay here in safety while you go into battle."

"You will be protecting me, Wyran. You will find someone my size among our troops, dress him in this armor, and act as if he were me." Seeing Selima about to object, Aumekor said, "Allonna can easily enchant some other armor for my use. Thanks to Master Ramil's craftsmanship, this armor is distinctive. Everyone will believe I am traveling to Bargas to take command against the enemy. If the Protectors of the Line are here in the Free Kingdoms, the Dark Priestess will not suspect I am coming after her, and that is my best protection."

Selima looked around the table. "Does anyone know of any more prophecies that are relevant?"

The omnimancers glanced at each other, but no one volunteered any more information.

"In that case, I thank you all for your help," she said.

"There is one more thing," said Istubik. He reached up to his neck and removed a medallion. "This artifact increases your maximum flow of power by one part in ten. It is not much, but it may make the difference."

Aumekor knew such artifacts were highly coveted. For an omnimancer to willingly give one up was remarkable.

Jebasta removed two rings from her fingers. "This one allows you to gather power more quickly. And this one is for a doubled flare, but it only has two uses remaining."

Selima remained speechless as one by one, the other omnimancers offered artifacts to her. Aumekor could see her eyes filling with tears.

As the last one placed a bracelet on the pile in front of Selima, Aumekor said, "Thank you all. May you walk forever in the Light."

"We follow the Light," they replied in near unison before filing out of the room.

◆ ◆ ◆

As they sat by the fire in Aumekor's chambers that evening, Kogyrinem said, "When will I get to meet your betrothed, Your Majesty? I've heard she's a great beauty."

Aumekor gave Kogyrinem a twisted smile. "I'm afraid that's something that did not work out too well." How mistaken he had been about Kalya. He had been so sure she was part of his destiny.

"And just as well," said Selima. "The girl practices necromancy."

"What?" Kogyrinem's eyebrows rose. "Are you certain?"

"I saw her myself," said Selima, the disgust clear in her tone.

Kogyrinem shook his head slowly. "And I was so sure it had to be a mistake. It made no sense when applied to the Dark Priestess."

Selima's brow furrowed. "What are you talking about?"

"A prophecy by my great-grandfather about the battle between the Heir and the Dark Priestess: 'The princess with the magic of death is needed for the Heir to live.'"

Aumekor's heart seemed to jump in his chest. Kalya was supposed to come with them? Perhaps if she saw him defeat the Dark Priestess, she would finally be willing to marry him.

His momentary happiness shattered when he realized Kalya's presence meant one more person to be lost along the way.

Chapter Forty-Seven

Geradin

Biyeskalya frowned at Geradin. "This be not a trick by the weakling to impress me?"

"*The Heir* is not trying to trick you," said Geradin. He hated the idea that this barbarian who constantly insulted Mek was key to keeping him alive. "King Aumekor did not want to ask you himself because he thought your personal distaste for him might cause you to reject this mission."

She walked to a window and stared out at the mountains. "It truly be time to fulfill the prophecy?"

"Yes. And we need you." Geradin might not like it, but he could put up with anything when it came to Mek's safety.

"Then I be ready to serve," said the princess. "What say my father?"

"Before talking to your father about this mission, King Aumekor wanted to gain your consent."

"My father want to come, of course." Biyeskalya sighed. "It be hard to convince him his place be here. How large be the army we are taking?"

Geradin winced. "It's not really much of an army. Which reminds me, are you any good with a bow?"

With a flash, Biyeskalya unsheathed her sword and held it up. "This be my weapon. I need not a bow."

"That's my usual attitude, but the prophecies say we need an archer, and a guide, and a general." Geradin wrinkled his brow.

"You've commanded troops in battle. Is it possible your father would give you the rank of general? And could you guide us through the mountains?"

She stared at him for a few beats. "How large be the force we be taking?"

After rubbing the back of his neck, Geradin said, "There's you, me, another High Protector, Omnimancer Selima, Omnimancer Allonna, a soldier named Holoran, and…an archer, a guide, and a general."

Biyeskalya squinted for a moment. "Nine? Only nine?"

"Fewer if we can manage it. If you could be the guide or the general—or both—then we could get it down to eight or seven."

"Why so few?"

Mek had suspected this question would come, and had ordered Geradin to tell Princess Biyeskalya the truth. "According to prophecy, only four people will make it to the temple to confront the Dark Priestess," said Geradin. "King Aumekor doesn't want to lose any more people than necessary."

"So he need me to keep him alive, but odds be even that I die?" She grinned, to Geradin's relief. "So be it. I face greater odds and be yet alive."

◆ ◆ ◆

King Paskolyik shook his head. "It be bad plan. Who think up such foolishness?"

Before Geradin could defend the plan, Mek said, "I understand if you don't want your daughter involved, but this plan is our one chance to strike at the Dark Priestess while her city is relatively undefended. And a small group stands a better chance—"

"Pah! Be not my daughter that concerns me. Small group be good. Unexpected. But be bad plan. Be not possible take horses through mountain passes here—"

Geradin said, "We could steal some on the other side."

Waving a hand dismissively at Geradin, Paskolyik continued, "—and there still be enemy troops in area. You look and speak like foreigners. You will be spotted and captured long before reaching Dark Priestess."

"We are not all that easy to capture," said Selima, but Geradin could sense some doubt in her voice.

Mek rose to his feet. "These are risks we must take. I'm the last Heir of the Line, and no one will stop me from fulfilling my destiny."

"Aumekorek-Lerid!" Paskolyik's voice filled Mek's chamber. "I think not you be a fool. This be my territory. Sit down and listen to wise counsel before you lead your people—our peoples—to disaster."

The disrespect to Mek made Geradin angry, but it was not his place to correct Paskolyik, especially not in the barbarian king's own castle.

After a few beats of silence, Mek sat down. As if Paskolyik had addressed him politely, he said, "What advice do you have for me, my friend?"

"Good. Now you be thinking. It be foolish to go through the passes and—" Paskolyik shot a glance at Geradin "—steal horses from enemies to ride through enemy territory. Be smarter to take different route and avoid enemy for most of journey."

"What other route?" asked Mek.

"Go north along the edge of the Burn, until you be just across the mountains from the City of the Dark God. Cross the mountains and you be there. Total journey be faster and little chance of enemy armies in the way."

"Traveling in the Burn is too dangerous," said Selima.

Paskolyik rocked his head from side to side. "If you have a good guide, be not as risky as other plan. Not so bad the wind, this time of year."

Geradin had read about the *veteer*, a violent wind that swept across the vast glassy scar of the Burn. Other perils supposedly waited in the Burn for any foolish enough to enter—but since the scorched area was still mostly lifeless even after five hundred years, Geradin wasn't sure how much faith to put in tales of giant man-eating creatures. Even dragons needed a steady supply of food.

"Selima?" said Mek, raising an eyebrow.

"It...may be the better choice," said Selima.

"What do you think, Geradin?" asked Mek.

Geradin shook his head and sighed. "I was so looking forward to becoming a horse thief."

"And who would be our good guide?" Mek asked Paskolyik. "Not you, by any chance?" Geradin had told Mek about Biyeskalya's prediction that her father would come along.

"Such great honor it be, battle alongside the Heir," said Paskolyik. "But there be better guide. You meet him: Serilyon. He travel the Burn and sneak into the City of the Dark One many times, and still he live."

"That would seem to make him qualified," said Mek. "Is he a general? How is he with a bow?"

"He be good enough with bow as a hunter." Paskolyik hesitated. "You be making such a small group. Is very noble, yes, but not so smart. I give you best guide. I should give you best general and best archer, too."

"No." Mek's voice was firm. "I already know I am going to lose at least one of the people I most care about. A larger group only means I have more to lose."

Geradin counted silently. Selima. Allonna. Biyeskalya. And himself. Only three of them could make it all the way to the Temple of the Dark God with Mek. And even that wasn't certain—it could easily be Holoran, Serilyon, and Otunvol, who had been chosen as the second High Protector to accompany Mek.

King Paskolyik nodded slowly. "*General* Serilyon be pleased by his promotion."

◆ ◆ ◆

Geradin awoke to a soft but insistent knock on the door of his bedroom. Was it time to leave already? A glance at the fire barely burning in the hearth told him it less than a quarter of the night had passed since he had gone to sleep. He got up and walked to the door. When he opened it partway, he was surprised to see Nikufed.

"Lord Geradin, I am sorry to disturb you." The manservant's voice trembled slightly.

"Is there something wrong with the king?" Geradin's stomach knotted.

"No, milord. If I might speak with you? Privately?"

"Of course. Come in." Geradin pulled the door open and allowed Nikufed into the room. "Please, sit down," he said, indicating a chair. Geradin walked over and sat on the edge of his bed.

"Thank you."

Geradin waited for Nikufed to speak, but Mek's servant sat silently, looking at the floor. After a while, Geradin decided he would have to give him some encouragement. "Is there something you need to tell me?"

Nikufed looked up, his eyes wet. "He's not going to take me with him, is he? I'm not part of his prophecy, so there's no place for me. Who will look after him?"

"I'll be there to watch over him. And Otunvol, Selima, Allo—"

"Not that way, milord. Who will change and wash his soiled linens? You? Will Omnimancer Selima be cutting his food into bites for him? He needs me to take care of him."

Geradin had not thought about the dozens of tedious or unpleasant chores involved in caring for Mek. But he felt Mek was making the right choice in keeping the size of the party as low as possible. "We will find a way to split your duties among us. He's trying to save your life, Nikufed."

"My life is to serve him."

Geradin sighed. "As is mine. But you can best serve him by going back to Aud Sapeer and being there safe, so you can serve him once he's defeated the Dark Priestess."

"Do you truly believe that, milord? He talks as if he's not coming back."

"What do you mean?"

"Little comments, like how he always wanted to leave the Keep and now he wishes he could see it just once more."

"Listen to me, Nikufed." Geradin stared firmly into the servant's eyes. "I have sworn to protect him, and I will. Even if it costs me my own life, I promise you will see the King return to Aud Sapeer."

After a few moments, Nikufed nodded. "Thank you, milord. I apologize for disturbing your sleep."

"Go with the Light, Nikufed."

◆ ◆ ◆

In the gray light of dawn, Geradin rode beside Mek as they exited the gates of Aldamun. For now, they were surrounded by the full company of Protectors of the Line. To the people of the city, it would appear as if the Heir of the Line was riding to join the armies fighting in Bargas. Only King Paskolyik and the omnimancers who had bid them farewell on the steps of the palace knew any different.

"Wait!" cried a voice from behind them. "Stop! Selima, wait!"

Geradin turned to see Omnimancer Tobalich running down the cobblestone street from the direction of the palace.

"We should see what he wants," said Selima. "It could be important."

So far, only about half the Protectors were outside the city gates. "When our force isn't split, we can stop," said Geradin. He didn't believe for a moment that Tobalich was part of any plot against Mek, but it was best to adhere to good tactics.

Tobalich continued yelling for them to stop until he caught up to Selima. His face was flushed red and his breathing was heavy. "Didn't you hear me calling for you to stop?"

"Why did we need to stop?" asked Selima. "You caught up to

us as it is."

"Well, yes, but—"

"Come to say your goodbyes, have you? I was surprised not to see you on the steps of the palace. I gather you overslept?" Selima's tone was playful.

"It is my fault we didn't stop, Omnimancer Tobalich," said Geradin. "To stop right away would have kept our force divided."

"I see." Tobalich began to dab at the sweat on his forehead with a patterned silk scarf he was carrying, then stopped and stared at it. "I'm sorry. This is what I was bringing you. And this." He separated a necklace from the scarf, and handed both items to Selima.

"More artifacts to augment my power?" she said. "I cannot thank you enough."

"No, they're for King Aumekor and Lord Geradin. I didn't think of them until I awoke this morning. They were created originally for a king who suspected his wife was having an affair. He gave the necklace to his wife as a gift so he could find out."

Mek laughed. "I don't need any magical artifacts to tell me whether Geradin is having an affair."

Geradin felt his face grow hot, and he dared not look at Allonna.

"Of course not, Your Majesty," said Tobalich. "It is you who will wear the necklace. And when you go into battle, Lord Geradin will wear the scarf, tied like a blindfold to cover his eyes and ears."

With a frown, Geradin said, "It will be difficult enough to fight by controlling the king's armor without being blindfolded."

Tobalich grinned. "Not if you can see through King Aumekor's eyes and hear through his ears."

Chapter Forty-Eight

Allonna

As she rode alongside the supply wagon, Allonna could see a blackened patch of ground near the horizon. "Is that the Burn?" she asked Serilyon.

"Your eyes be sharp, milady," he said. "But that be just the remains of an ordinary wildfire." He glanced at her and smiled. "Most people be not so anxious as you to get to the Burn."

"I'm not anxious. It's only that I've heard about it in tales, and I want to see it for myself." Allonna felt slightly embarrassed.

"You see it soon enough. Tomorrow evening. And the day after that. And for twenty days more, you see nothing but the Burn." Serilyon leaned away from Allonna in his saddle and spat on the ground. "Tales. I know many tales of the Burn. Be true, too, not like the storytellers'."

"I'd love to hear your tales," said Allonna.

"Oh, my tales be not fit for milady's ears," he said.

Allonna tried to keep a straight face. "In that case you had better not tell me."

Serilyon grunted. "Well, there be one that be not so bad."

"I'll listen with only one ear, then, in case it's not fit for both."

After clearing his throat, Serilyon began. "This be ten years ago, in the summer. I ride back from spying upon the Shadowed City. You know of the *veteer*? The wind?"

"Yes."

"The *veteer* be strong in the summer, rare in the winter. Most times, it come up from south. The wind scour clean the Burn, polish it like glass. When you see the dust cloud of the *veteer* on the horizon, be but moments to anchor." He reached down into a saddlebag and pulled out a steel spike as long as his forearm. "Hammer this deep into crack in the ground. Tie ropes to self and horse, and cover up till it be passed. If *veteer* arrive too soon, be very bad."

Allonna nodded.

"That summer, *veteer* pass through recently along my path. I know because there be no dust on ground. I still be careful and look for dust cloud to south, east and north. West always be safe, because it be the edge of the Burn.

"But this *veteer* come from the north, over clean ground. There be no dust cloud, so there be no warning. It blow me off my horse and break my leg." Serilyon patted his left leg. "It blow my horse to the ground. I keep tight hold of the reins, and pull myself to my horse. I climb over its body to shield myself from the wind. The straps of the saddlebag be broken—the spikes be gone."

"What did you do?"

"There be nothing to do. The *veteer* blow for a day and a half, and I feel the ground slide under me, the cracks scrape my body. But I be lucky."

"Lucky?"

"When it be over, my horse be dead. The side facing the *veteer* be skinned completely by the wind."

With a small shudder, Allonna wondered what sort of tales he did not think fit for her ears.

◆ ◆ ◆

Allonna cast a ward around herself and was surprised by how effortless it felt. After glancing down at the rings and bracelets Selima had loaned her for this exercise, she decided to make this the strongest ward she had ever made. She poured power into it until the glow was so bright she squinted. The light of the nearby campfire dimmed to insignificance.

Satisfied that she was protected, Allonna focused her attention on undoing the wards Selima had erected. By blocking her own magic from her perception, she could see the wisps of wards around Selima. Each ward flashed in Allonna's vision for a moment before fading out of existence. It hardly took any effort—because Allonna was wearing Selima's enhancing artifacts, the wards had even less power than they normally did.

Another of Selima's wards went down, followed by another. But the overall glow of wards around Selima barely seemed to have diminished. How many were there? With practice, Allonna had progressed to the point that she could undo two spells per heartbeat. By now she must have undone thirty or more. She concentrated harder, trying to speed the process. She began counting each ward as it fell, starting from thirty.

When she'd taken down a hundred wards, the glow around Selima seemed dimmer than it had been originally, but perhaps that was just an illusion. Had Selima truly taken the time to cast hundreds of wards around herself before beginning this exercise?

Somewhere before two hundred, Allonna lost count. Was it a hundred and seventy or only a hundred and sixty? She gave up keeping track, but renewed her determination to get past Selima's wards.

A tap on her shoulder made her flinch. She tried to keep her attention on undoing the wards while turning her head.

Geradin stood next to her. "Selima wins. I'm sorry."

"How did you...?" Allonna tried to find the bright glow of her ward, but it was gone. Her most powerful ward ever had been defeated, and she had not even noticed. She looked down at the rings and bracelets Selima had given her, then stared at Selima. "You held back your most powerful artifacts."

"No," said Selima. "You were facing me in my natural

strength."

Whipping her head around to Geradin, Allonna said, "You did something. Selima gave you an artifact."

He held up his empty hands. "All I did was walk over and tap you on the shoulder after that ward went down. It was amazing—I've never seen one so bright."

"If it was so amazing, why is it gone? Nobody here could undo it." An image of a figure cloaked in shadow sprang into her thoughts. "The Dark Priestess," she whispered.

"Wrong again," said Selima. "I was the one who brought down your ward. Geradin is right, though—your ward was amazing. The lesson I intended to teach almost flew back to scratch me. Another fifty beats or so and you would have gotten through my wards. You have reason enough to be confident in your power, but overconfidence can be fatal."

"What did I do wrong?"

Selima shook her head. "When you think you know, come to me and we'll discuss it. Bringing down your ward took much of my power, and I need to sit down and eat something." She walked over to the campfire, where Otunvol was stirring a pot.

After letting out an exasperated sigh, Allonna said, "How does she expect me to learn if she won't tell me anything?"

"That's just her way of teaching," said Geradin. "If you work something out for yourself, you'll remember it longer than if someone just gives you the answer."

"Do you have to take her side?" Frustration welled up inside her. What good was all her power if she didn't know how to use it? For a thousand years the Dark Priestess had been perfecting her skills, but Allonna only had about twenty more days left.

With a frown, Geradin said, "I wasn't taking sides. I was just explaining—"

"And it's foolish, because half a season from now we could all be dead, so it doesn't matter if I worked something out for myself, because I'm not likely to need to remember it for very long, am I?"

Geradin opened his mouth as if to protest, then shut it. He

looked at her for a moment before speaking. "You're right. I'm sorry, Lonna."

"Selima's the one who should be sorry for not teaching me right."

"No, I mean I'm sorry to have pulled you into all this. If we hadn't met, you'd be safe back in Glicken. I've known since I was a child that I must sacrifice my life to save Aumekor, if needed. My father died protecting the Heir, so I feel like I was born to that purpose. But you...Everything has happened too fast. I can understand why you're frightened to be facing—"

Allonna held up a palm. "You think I'm frightened?"

"You were just saying how we could all be dead soon." Geradin's voice was uncertain.

Raising her eyebrows, Allonna said, "And your idea of how to comfort me is to say you're sorry we ever met?"

"I didn't mean it like that."

The confused look on Geradin's face made Allonna pause. He was trying to help her, so why was she lashing back at him? "I'm sorry, Ger. Perhaps I am frightened, a bit, but what I mostly am is angry that I can't do anything right. The one part of magic that I thought I had learned was wards, but even my most powerful ward..." She shook her ringed fingers at him. "Even with all of these, Selima broke through unaided, which means I'm useless against the Dark Priestess, so I don't know why those stupid prophecies included me in this party."

Geradin reached out and took her hand. "You can undo spells better than anyone. If all you do is *undo* what protects the Dark Priestess, that leaves Selima free to attack with mancy. And don't forget that only you could enchant the armor that will allow me to control Aumekor when the time comes to attack with the sword. None of this would be possible without you. And the prophets knew it."

His praise made her cheeks hot, and she hoped the firelight was too dim for Geradin to notice. "But I know Selima expects more of me. If all she wants is for me to undo spells, why is she trying to train me in offensive magic?"

"You be a fool." Princess Biyeskalya's voice came from off to the right.

For a moment, Allonna wished she could light Biyeskalya's hair on fire. She felt Geradin's hand tighten around hers.

"I am most curious, Your Highness." Geradin's voice had the exaggerated politeness Allonna had heard him use with Lord Regent Kindul. "Is it custom among the Aldamundians to insert themselves into private conversations, or is that discourtesy reserved for those of royal blood?"

The princess strode firmly toward them and stopped a half pace away. "Only a fool rather hear courtesy than truth. Be you a fool, too, Lord Geradin?"

"And only a fool would rather hide truth in discourtesy than speak it plainly." Geradin shifted to a parody of an Aldamundian accent. "Be you a fool, too, Princess Biyeskalya?"

Biyeskalya's jaw clenched and her hand moved to the hilt of her sword.

Trying to ease the confrontation, Allonna tugged at Geradin's hand and said, "Your Highness, why am I a fool? What truth do I not see?"

"You be like that soldier, strong." Biyeskalya pointed to the large form of Holoran seated next to the fire. "But he be not skilled in combat. If he train each day until we reach our destination, still he be not skilled. I be more skilled in combat. So be Lord Geradin and High Protector Otunvol and General Serilyon."

"I know that," said Allonna. "You don't need to tell me I'm unskilled."

"Yet that soldier—Holoran?—It be important that he train each day, improve his skills. For if I be dead, and Geradin be dead, and Otunvol be dead, and Serilyon be dead, he be left to fight to protect the Heir."

Allonna repressed a shudder. She knew she might die, but she had not really thought through the possible combinations of four people who might be left to confront the Dark Priestess. It might be just be her, Selima, Holoran and Aumekor. She felt a sharp pang at the thought of losing Geradin, then understood the point Biyeskalya was making. "Selima intends to confront the Priestess, but trains me in case she dies."

Biyeskalya nodded. "Perhaps you be not a great fool."

◆ ◆ ◆

The tall grasses hid any trace of the road they had been following, but Serilyon seemed to know his way. Allonna slowed her horse and let Selima catch up.

"I will tell you my mistakes," said Allonna. "And then I will tell you yours."

Selima raised her eyebrows. "Very well."

"I was overconfident because I believed you could not undo my ward. But you didn't even try to undo it—you attacked it and eventually broke through."

"Correct."

"I did not layer my ward, so once you broke through, I was defenseless."

"Correct."

"I was so focused on your wards that I did not see what was happening to mine."

"Correct." Selima nodded. "From a practical standpoint, that last mistake was your worst—if you had noticed a problem with your ward, it would have made up for the other mistakes. You could have reinforced it, and I would have lost."

After a moment's thought, Allonna said, "But the root of each of my mistakes was overconfidence."

"A good insight. Someone with your power needs to guard well against overconfidence."

"I hope you will not think it overconfident of me to point out your mistake."

"I did win our little duel." Selima smiled. "But if you noticed a flaw in my technique, I shall be glad to learn better."

"Your mistake…" Allonna took a deep breath. "Your mistake is that you continue to teach me too slowly. Your mistake is that making sure I'll remember a lesson twenty years hence is useless if I die in twenty days. Your mistake is wasting time letting me work things out for myself instead of telling me what I need to do. That's your mistake."

When Selima did not respond immediately, Allonna began to wonder if she had spoken too harshly. She was about to apologize when Selima let out a long sigh.

"Correct," said Selima.

Chapter Forty-Nine

Geradin

The morning sun was high enough that Geradin could look along their path to the east without shielding his eyes from the glare. Serilyon was supposed to be riding point, but Geradin could see the Aldamundian had dismounted and stood atop a ridge two hundred paces ahead. It was too early to be stopping to rest.

"Possible trouble," Geradin said.

"Should we wait here?" asked Mek.

"Serilyon should have ridden back…" Geradin saw Serilyon wave them forward. "I guess there's no danger. But be on guard."

"I'll go find out what it is," said Holoran. He clambered off the back of the supply wagon and began a lumbering jog toward Serilyon.

Geradin almost called Holoran back, but decided it was best to let him feel useful.

After reaching Serilyon, Holoran spoke with him a moment, looked out over the ridge and then down at whatever lay on the other side. He began a slow jog back to the group, who were now less than a hundred paces from the ridge.

"We have to take apart the wagon," said Holoran as he rejoined them. "It's too steep down the other side."

Geradin wrinkled his face. Unloading the wagon, dismantling it, lowering everything to the bottom, rebuilding the wagon, and loading it again would take half the day. He looked along the ridge line that extended north and south. "There's no easier path down?"

"If there were," said Mek, "I'm sure he would have taken us there."

Resisting the urge to spur Gristle into a trot so he could see the problem himself, Geradin stayed alongside Mek as they approached the ridgeline. A sudden brilliance from beyond the ridge half-blinded him, and he brought up a hand to shield his eyes. His other hand instinctively moved for his sword until he realized it was just the sun reflecting off…"A lake?"

"It seems Serilyon has been having a little fun at our expense," said Mek. "We have reached the Burn sooner than he said."

As Geradin's eyes adjusted, he could see Mek was right. Below the ridge, the shiny dark surface stretched to the eastern horizon. At first he thought it was flat, but then he realized it was higher in the middle and curved down slightly to both sides. His eyes flicked back to the horizon and he tried to imagine how much further the Burn must extend to cover half the world. How many cities had been destroyed, with even their stones melted away into the ground? "How could he do it?"

"Most scholars believe the Dark God did not burn the world directly," said Selima. "Instead, he caused the sun to reach out and burn away part of the world."

"No, I meant…" Geradin shook his head. "I just cannot understand why he would do it. I know he was evil, but this…. I thought he wanted to conquer the world so all would worship him, not destroy it."

"I think he was just angry," said Mek. "Why else would he waste so much of his power? He must have acted without thinking things through."

"Assigning human motivations to gods has a long tradition, but it is ultimately futile." Selima sighed. "The Dark God did what he did for reasons that I hope will never become clear."

Geradin furrowed his brow. "You don't even want to know what truly happened?"

"Only the Dark God knows what he was thinking," said Selima. "Would you care for him to return and explain himself?"

"That's a curiosity I would rather leave unsatisfied," said Geradin.

"But the Burning must have depleted his power," said Mek. "Otherwise, why isn't he still around?"

"People have argued this for five hundred years. We are not going to resolve it here on this ridge," said Selima. She looked pointedly at the supply wagon.

Geradin dismounted and beckoned Holoran. "Let's get this wagon apart."

◆ ◆ ◆

Running his fingers over the smooth ground, Geradin said, "At least it's hard enough that we won't leave any tracks."

Serilyon snorted. "Who be fool enough to follow us in the Burn? If the enemy know we come, they will meet us on their ground. They be hoping the Burn kill us first."

Geradin replaced his gauntlet and stood. "Then we'll just have to make certain they are disappointed." He mounted and glanced around at the others. "Everyone ready?"

"Having seen the Burn, be you still certain we need take the direct course?" Serilyon asked.

Geradin looked over at Mek. The safer alternative was to skirt the edge of the Burn so they could take cover in the case of a *veteer*, but during previous discussion Mek had decided they could not afford the extra time. "Are three days worth the risk?"

"Each day of delay carries its own risks. The sooner we reach the City of the Dark God, the sooner this will all be over," said Mek.

"So be it." Serilyon flicked the reins of his horse and started toward the north. The rest of the party followed.

Geradin pulled his horse alongside Mek's. He kept his voice low so the others would not overhear. "Is there a deadline I don't know about?"

"What?"

"By the time we get to the City of the Dark God, half a season will have passed since leaving Aldamun. What difference will three days make, unless there is a certain day on which you are supposed to confront the Dark Priestess?"

"No, there's no deadline," said Mek. "I just want to kill her and be done."

"I see." It was just as Geradin had feared; Mek was allowing his impatience to take precedence over his judgment.

"You think I'm making a mistake?"

"Perhaps. Which route do you think *she* would want you to take?"

"This one."

Geradin let out an exasperated breath. "Why are you playing right into her hands?"

"Because it doesn't matter what she wants. I'm destined to confront her. That's why everything has come together the way it has: you meeting Allonna and Holoran, my betrothal to Princess Kalya, even Tobalich finding that amulet and scarf. The prophets saw all of it, and why would they bother to prophesy about my battle against the Dark Priestess unless it was going to happen? They would have seen that I would choose to travel in a small party, and take this route across the Burn."

"But—"

"I've thought this through, Ger. I have faith that the prophets knew what they were doing, and I'm acting on what they said."

The logic didn't quite seem right. "Have you discussed this with Selima?"

"Yes."

"And what did she say?"

Mek sighed. "She did concede eventually that it was not utterly impossible that I could be right."

After taking a moment to sort through Mek's sentence, Geradin said, "That doesn't mean she thinks you are right."

"No, it doesn't. But somehow, what I'm doing feels right. I think I was meant to fulfill my destiny this way."

Geradin thought for a moment. What would it accomplish to insist on taking the safer route, if that mean hurting Mek's confidence? Better to take this route and use extra caution. "I hope the prophets foresaw an easy journey across the Burn, with no *veteer* to blow us off our horses."

◆ ◆ ◆

Around midmorning on the fifth day, Geradin noticed he could no longer see the hills to the west. The Burn surrounded them, looking the same in every direction. Without Serilyon to guide them, it would be easy to head off course.

"We stop here," said Serilyon. "We rest here until midafternoon."

"Why the delay?" asked Mek.

"During midday, direction of the sun be too unreliable. Better to rest now. We will make up time by journeying after sunset using the Nightglow."

"The direction of the sun?" said Selima.

"When there be no landmarks, it be the only guide. But when it be high in the sky, it may lead you in circles."

Selima raised an eyebrow. "A compass won't work in the Burn?"

"What be a compass?" Serilyon frowned.

"Perhaps you call it something else. A compass is a steel needle that always points to the south."

Serilyon's eyes went wide. "Do you have one of these magic needles?"

After closing her eyes for a long moment, Selima said, "They are not magic. Ostilyan sailors use them for navigation. You mean to tell me you brought us into the middle of the Burn with no way to tell which direction we are going?"

"The sun and the Nightglow be good enough in the past." Serilyon's voice was defensive.

"So much lost knowledge," said Selima, shaking her head. "Cities and people and land were not the only things destroyed in the Burn." She turned back to Serilyon. "It is not your fault. We will do as you say."

◆ ◆ ◆

From his perch atop the supply wagon, Geradin swept his eyes across the horizon. The noon heat made the ground seem to shimmer, but that was the only movement he could see. Most of the party were in their tents, trying to get some sleep before continuing the journey.

"I know I can't keep up," said Holoran, who was brushing one of the wagon horses.

"What?" said Geradin.

"If the party is in danger, you must leave me behind. I wanted you to know that I understand. The wagon team cannot keep pace with your mounts in a chase."

"Don't talk like that. The prophecies say we need you."

Holoran shrugged. "Perhaps I'm needed to slow down what's chasing you."

"We need the supplies, too." Geradin slapped the wagon. "Do you think we can cross the Burn without the food and water?"

"It may be when we're almost out of the Burn. Or after. All I'm saying is, I don't expect to make it all the way to the Dark Priestess, and I don't want you or anyone else risking their lives to save mine. Just leave me behind."

Geradin wanted to object, but he knew Holoran was right. "I know I can count on you to do your duty, Holoran."

"Thank you, Lord Geradin."

Before he could tell Holoran to stop calling him Lord Geradin, a strange ripple in the air to the south caught his eye.

Shielding his eyes from the sun, he tried to make out the shape. Was it really flying, or was that merely an illusion caused by the heat? "Holoran, go wake Serilyon."

"At once, milord."

There was no doubt that the shape was coming from directly behind the wagon. Such a coincidence was unlikely. They were being followed, despite Serilyon's doubts about the enemy being foolish enough to do so. Geradin squinted, trying to get the image to come into focus. For a moment it seemed to resolve into a band of riderless horses, but the image wavered again before he could be sure of anything.

"What be the problem, milord?" said Serilyon.

"Do you see something to the south?"

After a moment he replied, "Yes, milord."

"Can you make out what it is?"

"No, but in the Burn, best to assume the unknown be trouble."

Chapter Fifty

Aumekor

Aumekor signaled his armor to lift him into his saddle. "Wild horses?"

"That's what they looked like," said Geradin. "For a moment."

"The air of the Burn plays tricks on the eye." Serilyon mounted his horse. "Be not likely wild horses follow us."

"Can we outrun whatever it is?" asked Aumekor.

"Yes," said Geradin.

"Not for long," said Serilyon.

"It doesn't have to be for long." Geradin unsheathed his sword, which glowed blue. "Whatever it is will never get close enough to put you in danger." He spurred his horse into a gallop toward the oncoming shimmer.

"Wait, Geradin!" Aumekor didn't like the idea of Geradin riding off alone, but Geradin did not stop. "Allonna, did you ward him?"

"Yes."

"Go after him, Selima," said Aumekor. "Allonna can protect me, but if Geradin needs magical help…"

Selima looked toward Geradin, then back to Aumekor. "My place is—"

"Go. Now."

She spurred her horse to gallop after Geradin.

"Shall we ride, Your Majesty?" asked Otunvol.

"Where?"

"Away. Put more distance between us and whatever it be."

It was obviously what Geradin had intended. Aumekor frowned. "No. I say if we cannot outrun it, then we might as well fight from a prepared position, without tiring ourselves by fleeing. What do you think, Serilyon?"

Serilyon nodded slowly. "Tactically sound."

"Shall I start raising wards, Your Majesty?" asked Allonna.

"Yes. But be careful you do not drain too much of your energy."

Allonna muttered something that sounded like "I never do." A scintillating blue glow surrounded him.

"Why not surround everyone?" he asked. "Our whole camp?"

"I will. I'm just providing additional layers to protect you."

Aumekor looked to see Geradin's progress toward the shimmer, and realized the glow of Allonna's ward made it hard to see out. "Could you make this invisible here, so I can see Geradin and Selima?"

She did not say anything, but the air cleared in front of him.

Already the figures of Geradin and Selima were wavering in the air, and they were not even halfway to meeting whatever was coming. "I wish I could see..." It was a pity Geradin wasn't wearing the amulet Tobalich had supplied.

For a moment, the distant blur seemed to magnify, and Aumekor was sure he saw an armored man on horseback charging forward. That eliminated the wild horses theory. But what enemy would approach from the south?

"Princess Kalya, could your father have changed his mind and sent reinforcements after us?"

"He agree to your plan. He not change his mind unless circumstances alter."

Aumekor considered the possibilities. If the secrecy of their mission had been compromised so it could not succeed, sending troops to retrieve their party would make sense. Or perhaps Omnimancer Tobalich had discovered another artifact that could be useful. "If your father sent someone after us, I hope he included a face Geradin will recognize."

As Geradin and Selima approached whoever was coming, it became impossible to distinguish them in the shimmering air. What was happening? Was it a greeting of friends or a desperate battle?

"I think they've stopped," said Serilyon.

After a pause that seemed to last longer than a Regency Council meeting, the shimmer began moving toward them again. Gods of Light, Aumekor prayed silently, let it not be the enemy.

"I see them," said Kalya. "Lord Geradin and Lady Selima lead the way back on their horses."

Relief washed over Aumekor. They were alive. And as they came closer, he began to make out the details around them. It looked like they were bringing back ten or more riderless horses.

"It really was wild horses?" he said. Then he saw an armored body draped over one of the horses. "One man, ten horses?"

"Thirteen," said Serilyon. "And his armor be not Aldamundian."

Wishing he had eyes as sharp as Serilyon's, Aumekor tried to figure out why an enemy would send one man with thirteen horses, then realized he had read about such a tactic. "Speed. He switched horses frequently so no one horse had to carry his weight for long."

"Perhaps an assassin sent to stop you?" said Allonna.

"Or a messenger," said Aumekor. He winced. "I hope Geradin didn't kill him if he was on our side."

"For an assassin, he be most incompetent to let us see him come from afar," said Kalya. "If I be the one sent to kill you, you not see me until my knife be in your heart."

"Then I'm glad you're here as my protector, not my killer." Aumekor smiled. It was probably a good thing Geradin was still too far off to hear what she had said.

❖ ❖ ❖

"So once we were in hailing distance I told him to halt," said Geradin, "and he replied, 'No one will prevent me from reaching the Heir of the—'" Geradin stopped and grinned.

"The Heir of the—?" Aumekor frowned. "Geradin! You killed him before he even finished speaking? How could you act so rashly? He might have been a messenger from King Paskolyik."

"I didn't kill him," said Geradin. "I didn't even hurt him. If anyone acted rashly, it was Selima: she put him to sleep between one word and the next. He almost fell off his horse, so I rearranged him a bit. Tied him to his saddle."

"Still, you shouldn't charge off like that," said Aumekor. "We had time to make a plan."

"I thought Lord Geradin acted nobly," said Kalya. "Riding against unknown odds to protect his king be an act of courage. In my culture, we value such."

Furrowing his brow, Geradin bowed down on one knee. "I am sorry, Your Majesty. My actions were too hasty."

"No," said Aumekor. He needed to show he respected Kalya's opinion. "The princess is correct. Your zeal to defend me is to be commended, not condemned."

Geradin rose to his feet.

"Can I take a look at our...guest?" asked Aumekor.

"Selima was going to check him over for any magical items or weapons before she wakes him." Geradin pointed outside the camp to the spot where Selima had remained with the horses and the unconscious man. "Until then, it's best that you —"

A shout came from the direction Geradin was pointing. "Where is my armor? Release me at once, woman, or I will—"

After a few beats of silence, Geradin said, "I think she put him back to sleep."

"His accent be from the south," said Kalya. "He be not of my father's men."

"Not from Aud Sapeer, either." Aumekor paused. "Bosperanian, I think."

Geradin took a sharp breath. "Veratur the Betrayer, come to finish what he failed to do."

Aumekor felt a momentary panic, but then logic reasserted itself. "Selima and Veratur would recognize each other."

Selima came from behind the horses, carrying a bow and a sheathed sword. "His armor is of exceptional quality, strengthened by mancy. This is his sword." She drew it from the scabbard. The blade was clear crystal.

"Like the one Kindul gave me for my birthday," said Aumekor.

Nodding, Selima said, "And look at his bow." It was unlike any bow Aumekor had ever seen. Rather than metal or wood, it seemed to be made of a ruby-colored resin. "It's light as an autumn leaf, and it's enchanted in a way I've never seen."

"Can I see?" said Allonna. Selima handed her the bow.

"He's not Veratur, is he?" asked Geradin.

Selima raised her eyebrows. "If he were, I would have killed him already."

"With such weapons and armor," said Aumekor, "to say nothing of his attitude, he must be a noble. Wake him up again and bring him here. No—bring him here, then wake him up."

"I'll get him," said Holoran. He walked around the horses and returned carrying the unconscious stranger over one of his broad shoulders. Gently, he laid the man on the ground before Aumekor, just outside the shimmer of Allonna's ward.

The man looked about twenty years of age. The varicolored padded silks he wore were filthy with mingled sweat and dirt. He stirred, opened his eyes and began shaking his head as if to clear it of spiderwebs.

"I am King Aumekor att'Ordil of Aud Sapeer, the Heir of the Line of Orcan," said Aumekor. "Who are you and why do you follow us?"

The man tried to sit up, but with his hands tied behind his back he could not find the leverage. "Your Majesty! I am

Darilom att'Pivalom, Third Prince of Bosperan, and Protector of the Line of Orcan."

In a flash of blue light, the point of Geradin's sword was a thumbwidth from the man's neck. "Liar. You are no Protector of the Line."

"Careful, Geradin," said Aumekor. What was one of King Pivalom's sons doing here in the Burn? Then Aumekor felt everything become clear. "Did your father send you, Prince Darilom?"

"No, I volunteered. I have come to swear myself into your service, as you promised my father. Have no doubt I am qualified to serve as a Protector. I am the most skilled swordsman and best archer in all the Free Kingdoms. As long as I draw breath, I will let no harm come to you."

Aumekor glanced at Geradin, who burst into laughter.

"Fine boasts," said Geradin, "coming from someone tied up like a Midsummer ribbon."

"Cut me free, give me my sword and armor, and we'll see who has a right to boast."

Before Geradin could escalate the argument, Aumekor said, "I promised King Pivalom that he could send young men to serve as Protectors of the Line. I did not expect him to send one of his sons, but I will accept your oath if you wish to swear it. But first, tell me how you found us. Our mission and our path were supposed to be closely-held secrets."

"Thank you, Your Majesty. Of course, Your Majesty." Darilom struggled again to sit up, but failed. "When my father returned home from Cirkepam and told me of Your Majesty's kindness, I volunteered immediately to serve as your Protector. Knowing that you were journeying to Aldamun, I set sail at once for Bargas. Once there, I purchased twenty horses and rode for Aldamun. Along the way, I encountered your army, and I demanded an audience with you, but for two days I was denied."

Darilom paused to spit some dirt out of his mouth. "On the third day, I was admitted to see someone who was supposed to be you. He did not seem to recall any promise made to my father, until I told him the details. He was so different from the self-assured and commanding person that my father had described that I concluded he was an imposter."

"But how did that lead you to us?" asked Aumekor.

"I proceeded to Aldamun, as I thought the real Heir might have remained there in case of an attack at the Barrier Wall. I was granted an audience with King Paskolyik, who insisted that I was mistaken, and that any uncertainty I had perceived in the Heir must be due only to the pressures of war. So I took my leave of him to return and beg the Heir's forgiveness for my doubting him. But as I was about to leave the city, an old beggar blocked my way. I threw him a bag of coins to move, but he said he must prophesy for me."

The beggar? Aumekor was startled. "And what did he say?"

"He told me I would find my destiny by going into the Burn. Since I knew it was my destiny to serve as your Protector, I rode as fast as I could for the Burn. I assumed you would be going to confront the Dark Priestess, so I traveled north until I encountered your servants."

Kalya snorted. "You rode into the Burn on nothing more than the sayings of that madman? You be fortunate we be here, else the destiny you find be your death."

Darilom shrugged. "If he was but a madman, how did he know where you'd be?"

Aumekor's thoughts swirled, trying to fit the old beggar's prophecies to what had happened since. If the man was a real prophet, that meant Kalya would have Aumekor's child. And that meant his infertility was not permanent. So why, then, did all the other prophecies point to Aumekor being the one who had to confront the Dark Priestess?

Pushing aside the confusion, Aumekor said, "Untie him. Selima, get the oath disk." He believed Darilom, but it was best not to take chances. "Prince Darilom, if being a Protector of the Line is the destiny you desire, you shall have it."

Chapter Fifty-One

Geradin

The sun had long ago set, but the diffuse light of the Nightglow reflected off the surface of the Burn, giving them sufficient light to travel. Geradin rode alongside Mek, with Selima and Allonna close by. Behind them came the supply wagon, with Holoran at the reins. Serilyon was out somewhere ahead, scouting their path, while Princess Biyeskalya and Otunvol were split off to each side. At the rear, Darilom with his thirteen horses had been assigned to prevent anyone else from sneaking up on the party from behind.

"So you're letting him stay," said Geradin.

"I'm letting him stay," said Mek.

"So much for keeping the company as small as possible."

Mek sighed. "He's a great archer. So he fits the prophecies. And prophecy brought him here. It looks like the Gods of Light are forcing me to their path."

"A great archer." Geradin snorted. "We only have his word for that. He also claimed to be the most skilled swordsman in the Free Kingdoms."

Chuckling, Mek said, "Is that what's been bothering you? I'll believe that he may be good, but when Swordmaster Ytanor and my High Protectors all agree that they have never seen anyone to match your skill with the sword, I do not doubt them. And that means I do not doubt you."

Was that really what had been bothering him? Geradin

frowned. Sometimes it seemed as if Mek knew him better than he knew himself. "Even if he were better than me with the sword, we still have a problem: supplies. We could cut into our safety margin to cover him, but we have neither food nor water for thirteen more horses."

"What do you suggest, then? Kill the horses?" Disgust filled Mek's voice.

"I don't like the idea, but it's not as if he values them: he started with twenty. But killing them is only one option. We could just set them free—"

"Which in the Burn is the same as killing them, only slower."

"—or we could send them back."

"Send them back?' asked Mek. "With whom?"

"With someone we don't need now that Darilom is here," said Geradin.

"Serilyon wasn't just the Archer. He's also the Guide and the General."

"Not Serilyon. Otunvol. Now that you've sworn Darilom as a Protector, there are three of us. If you're right about taking only the very minimum number, only two are needed."

"Let me think," said Mek.

They rode on in silence for a while. Geradin looked at the distorted reflection of the Nightglow that seemed to flow beneath them. They could almost be floating in the center of the sky.

"Yes, we can match the prophecies with only two Protectors." Mek's voice had a tinge of sadness. "And I'm glad to be able to spare someone's life. Tomorrow morning, you will take the extra horses and turn back."

It took a beat for Geradin to understand what Mek had said. "Me? You can't send me away!"

"You said it yourself: Only two Protectors are needed."

"But I'm not just one of the Protectors. I'm the swordsman."

"Darilom can be the swordsman as well as the archer."

"You haven't even seen him use his sword." Geradin could not believe they were having this conversation. "Besides, it's my armor that controls yours. I'm the...what was that word? The puppeteer?"

"Yepeto."

"Yes. You still need me for the prophecies."

"Darilom can take that role, too." Mek sighed. "Ger, I'm trying to make sure you stay alive."

"I don't want you to save my life. I want you to keep me here to save yours."

"My mind's made up."

"No." Geradin's voice was firm. "You are risking the entire mission if you don't have the best swordsman controlling your armor when you confront the Dark Priestess. I'm sure everyone else will agree."

Mek didn't answer immediately. After a few moments, he said, "You are right. The best swordsman must be the one to accompany me."

"I'm glad you see reason."

"Tomorrow morning, you will duel Darilom to prove which of you is better."

◆ ◆ ◆

Geradin swung Biyeskalya's wooden practice sword through several positions. The balance was different from what he was used to, but it was better than Serilyon's. Geradin was used to practicing with his real sword because a practice sword could not imitate the effects of the sword's enchantment, but that would not do for sparring. As amusing as it would be to slice right through that crystal sword and teach the newest Protector a lesson, it would not be a fair duel.

He tried to ignore the argument going on a few paces away, but his concentration failed. Swordmaster Ytanor would not have been happy.

"This is madness," Selima said to Mek. "You have carried your obsession with not losing people too far. You can't send Geradin away—you need him."

"If the prophets knew Geradin would accompany me, then he will win this duel." Mek's voice was calm. "If not, then I can ensure he survives by sending him back. It's not madness; it's perfectly logical."

The argument made sense to Geradin, even though he didn't like the conclusion. He would just have to win the duel.

"A madman can proceed with perfect logic from a false premise." Selima wrung her hands. "You can't rely on prophecies to save you from making mistakes. I care for Geradin as much as you do, but having him with us increases our chance of success, and that's what matters."

"Have you so little confidence in Geradin's abilities that you think he will lose?" said Mek.

"Don't change the subject." Selima's voice was sharp.

Mek raised a palm to silence Selima before she could say more. "I've made my decision. The duel will proceed."

◆ ◆ ◆

Two seasons of using an irresistible sword had taken their toll. Geradin almost lost the match in the opening moments because he did not properly anticipate the jarring collision of his blade with Darilom's. Only a swift retreat to the edge of the square marked by supply boxes saved him from Darilom's initial attack. A palmwidth closer, and Darilom would have struck a blow to the body to win the match.

The battle became a purely defensive one on Geradin's part. The inside of his right forearm still felt like it was vibrating and his grip felt weak. And though Geradin hated to admit it to himself, Darilom was the best swordsman he had ever faced. Every attack Geradin parried was followed so closely by another that he could not take the initiative.

Concentrate, he scolded himself. There is nothing but the fight.

He cleared his mind of all distractions. He ignored the tingling in his arm. He forced his fear of being sent away into the hidden shadows of his mind. There would be time to deal with everything else later.

There is nothing but the fight.

He was still on the defensive, but he no longer felt like he was only a thumbwidth from losing. Stroke and counterstroke, he stopped each attack as it came, and he began to anticipate the next. The duel was now one of endurance—if Darilom tired first, Geradin would be able to take the initiative. Whoever made the first mistake would lose.

Wait for the opening.

Darilom's attack was a sliver of a moment slow, but Geradin did not try to take advantage of that. It could have been a trick to draw Geradin into a premature attack—that was just the sort of tactic he himself would have tried had their positions been reversed.

Wait for it.

"Is that a baby dragon?" said Allonna, her voice full of wonder.

There is nothing but the fight.

Darilom's sword hesitated, and Geradin swung swiftly to force it aside, then curved his blade back toward Darilom's torso. The tip of his blade hit Darilom's breastplate with a satisfying thwack. He had won.

"Foul treachery," shouted Darilom, and Geradin was barely able to parry the renewed attack.

"Kill it." Serilyon's voice held the tone of command. "Quickly, before it runs."

"Stop, Darilom," said Geradin. "I've won."

"They're in the way," said Selima.

Darilom continued to attack. "Only because you had your wench distract me."

"Stop now," said Mek. "Ger, *look*."

Geradin lowered his sword. Darilom's wooden blade slammed his chest, but Geradin ignored it as he looked where Mek was pointing.

Ten paces outside their camp stood a black-scaled creature.

Only half the height of a man, it stood on its two hind legs, its swanlike neck balanced by a long, thick tail. A mouth full of sharp teeth seemed to take up most of its head. Its dark eyes were unblinking as it bobbed its head.

Before Geradin could react, the creature turned and sprinted away on its rear legs.

"There be no stopping it now. We must flee," said Serilyon. "Everyone mount up."

Geradin frowned. "Why?" The small dragon, if that's what the creature was, had already covered fifty paces with long strides.

"What about these supplies?" said Holoran, pointing to the boxes and barrels he had unloaded from the wagon.

"No time," said Serilyon. "It bring more soon."

A bow twanged beside him, and Geradin caught sight of an arrow floating out toward the creature. Despite the hundred-pace range, the arrow hit its mark and with a squawk the creature tumbled to a heap on the ground and lay still. Geradin could not help being impressed.

"Well shot, Protector Darilom." said Mek. "Did you see that, Selima? Despite my attempts to prevent it, the prophecies have given me an archer."

"The prophecies do not..." Selima shook her head. "Believe what you will. Then the prophecies have shown you your swordsman, too, as Geradin won the duel."

"He did not!" Darilom pointed at Allonna. "I was winning until she distracted me."

Before Geradin could object by pointing out that a good swordsman must resist being distracted, Serilyon said, "Your Majesty, we still need to move. Where there be one *kolof* awake, a thousand sleep nearby."

Geradin hoped Serilyon was exaggerating. The *kolof* had been easy enough to kill, but in sufficient numbers they would be dangerous.

"We need those supplies," said Mek. "We will leave when the wagon is loaded."

❖ ❖ ❖

Riding beside Mek, Geradin asked, "You weren't truly going to send me off with the horses if I had lost, were you?"

"I realize now that would have been a mistake," said Mek.

"Good." Geradin had been hoping Darilom's complaints wouldn't persuade Mek to order a rematch.

"After all, we may need those extra horses."

Geradin stared at Mek.

After an exaggerated sigh, Mek said, "You're losing your sense of humor, Ger."

"Perhaps that's because I don't enjoy fighting duels for no good reason."

Mek chuckled. "Oh, that is funny. You were looking for an excuse to duel Darilom from the moment he claimed to be the best swordsman. I gave you that excuse."

"Why didn't you say that to begin with? Why make me think you would send me away if I lost?" Remembering how close he had come to losing made Geradin uncomfortable.

"Because I meant what I said at the time. But the *kolof* made me see I was wrong."

"How?"

"Sending you away could not guarantee that you would live—a horde of *kolofs* might have killed you as you journeyed back. All it would do is guarantee that you would be angry with me, and if I died while you were not there to protect me, you would never forgive me. Or yourself. And I don't— What's happening?"

Twenty paces ahead, Serilyon was signaling for the party to halt, and motioning for Biyeskalya and Otunvol to gather in. When everyone was close, Serilyon spoke quietly. "There be a crack in the Burn ahead. See?" He pointed toward a point about fifty paces ahead.

Geradin could not see any difference in the surface.

"The surface beyond the crack be almost a manheight lower.

You not see from here, but there be a swarm of *kolofs* asleep in its shelter. Hundreds, perhaps thousands. I never see so many. We need circle around to the east. If they attack…"

"If they attack, we'll just put a ward around our party and stay safely inside until they lose interest," said Selima.

"Only thing make *kolof* lose interest be more food. If they wake, they eat until there be no more food. Then they start to eat each other. After they eat some, they lay eggs and go to sleep until more food come." Serilyon shook his head. "Take too long. If they wake, we need—"

From the north came a high-pitched cry that reminded Geradin of an eagle.

"South," said Serilyon. "Ride swiftly."

Chapter Fifty-Two

Allonna

Allonna desperately wished she could do what Selima was doing: throwing fist-sized balls of red light at the little beasts following them. On hitting one, the ball would explode—blasting apart the kolof it hit, and killing or wounding its neighbors. Even better, in a horrible way, was the fact that other kolofs nearby would immediately stop and begin devouring the dead and wounded.

But it wasn't enough. Selima had killed perhaps thirty, and still there were hundreds flowing over the glassy plain behind them. Some of the faster *kolofs* had gotten within twenty paces before Selima's mancy or Darilom's archery had brought them down.

Ahead of her she could see Geradin still arguing with Aumekor, who refused to abandon Holoran and the wagon. Otunvol and Biyeskalya rode close to the king.

"It's no use," shouted Selima over the noise of the horses. "How many arrows do you have left, Darilom?"

"Not enough, milady." He leaned over to the first of his string of horses and began to unlatch a quiver attached to its saddle.

"Save them. We need to kill in far greater numbers."

"If we could just kill enough that the rest would stop to eat them," said Allonna.

"How?" asked Selima.

Embarrassed that she had she had nothing to contribute, Allonna merely shook her head.

Darilom took the rope attached to the first horse and reached out to Allonna. "Take this, and hold tight."

She grabbed the rope. "Why?"

He didn't answer, but slowed his horse until he rode alongside the last of his spare horses. He drew his sword and cut the rope connecting it to the others. Then, with a swift sweep of the sword, he slit its throat. It collapsed to the ground and was rapidly left behind.

After a moment of shock, Allonna understood Darilom's plan. As the first of the *kolofs* reached the dead horse, they pounced on it and began tearing its flesh with their mouths. Thirty or forty of them swarmed around it to feed, but the rest kept coming.

Methodically working his way forward, Darilom killed another ten horses, until the one Allonna was leading was the only one of his spares left. Each dead horse distracted tens of *kolofs*, and the horde following the party had been reduced to perhaps a quarter of its original size. Since the fastest *kolofs* were the ones who got to the bodies first, the remaining ones were gradually falling farther behind.

"Give me the rope," said Darilom, and she handed it over. He smoothly transferred from one horse to the other, then killed the one he had been riding. He did not look back as its corpse fell; instead, he drew a cloth from a saddlebag and began to wipe the blood from his sword.

Allonna watched over her shoulder as the *kolofs* surrounded the final horse. It was not enough—perhaps as many as a hundred were still coming.

A red ball of light shot away from Selima and killed one of the nearer *kolofs*. Allonna turned to watch Selima, trying to understand the flows of power used to create the magical weapon.

◆ ◆ ◆

The *kolofs* were almost upon them again, and Allonna could tell from her horse's labored breathing that the short time they'd spent at the slower pace had not been enough for it to recover. She urged it forward and it responded by increasing its pace. Selima's horse did not match strides, and started to fall behind.

"Some of us need stop to fight," shouted Serilyon, "so the rest can continue."

Allonna's heart stuttered when she saw Geradin begin to slow his horse. Even with his enchanted sword, he could not survive against so many. Pulling on the reins of her horse, Allonna slowed. She did not have offensive magic to use, but she would do her best to defend Geradin with wards.

Beside her, a *kolof* suddenly leapt up toward Selima. Its dagger-like teeth tore open one of Selima's bags, and Allonna glimpsed books and pieces of metal scattering on the dark ground. Selima killed the *kolof* with a ball of light, but others raced along only paces behind.

The mobile wards Allonna had carefully maintained around each member of the party were useless against the *kolofs*, she realized. The wards stopped fast-moving objects such as arrows, but even the fastest *kolof* was far slower than that. But strengthening the mobile wards would only slow the party more as the wards dragged through the air.

After a moment of astonishment at her foolishness, Allonna let the power flow through her and out to the nearest *kolof*. She built a mobile ward around it, then added power till the ward glowed. The *kolof* slowed to half its speed while Allonna turned her attention to the next *kolof*, then the next. Out of the corner of her eye, she could see that Geradin had stopped slowing and was now riding alongside her.

"Yes," said Selima. "But use *stationary* wards."

Allonna began casting a stationary ward around a *kolof*, but it slipped past the boundary before she could finish. She needed to cast a bigger ward, and if she was going to do that, why settle for one *kolof* at a time? She reached out with her power and created a ward twenty-five paces across, encircling ten of the creatures. They ran headlong into the side of the ward and bounced back, falling to the ground.

The *kolofs* not caught inside swerved around it. Allonna caught several more in a second ward, then a third. After the tenth there were no more *kolofs* within her range. The horde was being left behind.

Serilyon signaled the party to slow to a walk.

"Well done, Allonna," said King Aumekor. "Well done."

She felt blood rushing to her cheeks. "I should have thought of it much earlier."

"Do not blame yourself," Selima said. "I could have thought of it, too, though using wards like that is something I could not have done. I keep forgetting how much power you have available."

"I think you're marvelous," said Geradin. "That's the second time I owe you my life."

"Everyone stop," commanded Serilyon. He dismounted and began fiddling with his saddlebag.

"Is it safe here?" asked Aumekor.

"No." Serilyon pulled out the steel anchoring spike he had shown Allonna before they entered the Burn. "We have little time. A *veteer* be coming from the south."

❖ ❖ ❖

"The next time my king order me travel the Burn..." Serilyon took a swig from his flask, then pointed a finger at Allonna. "The next time, I insist on having an omnimancer with me."

Allonna smiled at the compliment and nestled more snugly against Geradin's shoulder. Outside the bright blue glow of the ward she had cast around their camp, the scouring dust of the *veteer* streamed by harmlessly.

❖ ❖ ❖

As Allonna was finishing her breakfast the next morning, Serilyon emerged from the supply wagon and marched over to King Aumekor.

"We need change course, Your Majesty," he said. "Any more problems, we risk running out of water before we finish crossing the Burn."

Aumekor pressed his lips together for a moment. "What do you recommend?"

"Head west, to the edge of the Burn. There be streams there from the melting snows of the mountains."

"Very well." Aumekor rose to his feet. "Following this path has accomplished its purpose."

Serilyon frowned. "Your Majesty?"

"If we had not proceeded directly north, then Darilom would not have found us." Aumekor smiled. "You see, the prophecies have a way of working things out."

Despite the confidence in Aumekor's voice, Allonna felt something was wrong with his logic. If King Aumekor had decided to follow the edge of the Burn from the beginning, then wouldn't a true prophet have seen that, and told Darilom to also follow the edge of the Burn? She decided it did not really matter—Darilom had found them, which meant the prophecies were being fulfilled.

◆ ◆ ◆

In Allonna's estimation, traveling along the edge of the Burn was much better than traveling across it. The trees growing on the sides of the mountains provided wood for fires, which allowed roasted meals when Serilyon or Darilom shot game. The mountain streams meant there was water to spare for washing—and fish. Best of all, in the twelve days since they reached the edge, the greatest danger she had faced was being bitten on the hand by a horsefly.

Allonna was filling the teapot from a stream when a child's

cheery voice said, "Can you be my friend?"

Dropping the teapot in the shallow water, Allonna sprang to her feet and looked around for the speaker.

Across the stream, on a rock about five paces away, sat a girl in a brown homespun dress. The girl's large eyes were fixed on Allonna. "Can you be my friend?" she repeated.

"I could be," said Allonna. What was a child, probably no more than four years old, doing here on the edge of the Burn? "What's your name?"

The girl smiled. "Hope. What's your name?"

"That's a pretty name, Hope. My name is Allonna." Allonna paused. "Are your mama and papa around?"

Hope stuck her arm out and pointed partway up the mountainside. "Mama is at our house. I don't have a papa."

"Does your mama know you're down here?"

Shaking her head, Hope said, "You can be my friend. Do you want to play? I have a doll in my house. Mama buyed it in the city for me. It's a pretty doll."

"A pretty doll for a pretty girl," said Allonna. Despite a few smudges of dirt on her face, Hope was the prettiest little girl Allonna could remember meeting.

Geradin's voice came from behind her. "Are you all right? Who are you talking—" His sword swished as he released it from its scabbard.

Hope squeaked and scooted back higher on her rock.

"She's just a little girl, Ger!" said Allonna.

"What's she doing here?" Geradin said in a forced whisper.

"Hope lives nearby. Isn't that right, Hope?"

Hope nodded slowly, her eyes fastened on Geradin.

"Put that thing away," said Allonna, and after a moment she heard Geradin sheathe the sword.

"We can't have her telling anyone she saw us," said Geradin.

Allonna had not considered the security aspect. Geradin wouldn't kill a little girl just to keep her from talking, would he? "Hope, can you keep a secret?"

"Yes."

"I'm your friend, right?"

Hope nodded.

"There are bad people who want to hurt me, so you must not tell anyone that my friends and I were here. It has to be a secret. Do you promise to keep the secret?"

Hope nodded, her face solemn.

"We need more assurance than that," said Geradin. "Can you bring her back to camp?"

Allonna hesitated. "What are you going to do to her?"

"I don't want to harm her. I just want her to make her promise on the oath disk."

She should have thought of the oath disk herself. Allonna beckoned to Hope. "Come here, Hope. I want you meet my friends."

Hope jumped down from her rock. "Will they be my friends, too?"

"I'm sure of it."

◆ ◆ ◆

Selima shook her head. "The oath disk is gone."

"What?" said Geradin and Allonna simultaneously.

"I lost it when that *kolof* tore one of my bags." Selima's voice was matter-of-fact. "After the *veteer*, Serilyon told me it was pointless to try retracing our path to look for the things that fell out."

What else had been lost? Allonna wondered, but decided that subject could wait. She looked down at Hope, who was holding her hand. "What do we do about Hope, then?"

"What do we do about me?" said Hope.

Selima squatted so her eyes were level with Hope's. "Do you live alone with your mama?"

"Yes."

"Who else lives nearby?"

"Nobody," said Hope. "It's all lonely here. But now Allonna can be my friend."

"We all can be friends, but we need to be secret friends," said Selima. "You mustn't say anything about us to anyone."

"I'm good at being quiet," said Hope. "When mama says, 'Be quiet,' she doesn't hear a peep."

"What a good girl you are, Hope," said Selima. "But you must not even tell your mama."

Allonna hated the way they were taking advantage of the girl's loneliness, but what choice was there?

"Is it a surprise?"

Selima smiled. "Yes, it's a surprise."

"A happy surprise." Hope giggled. She looked up at Allonna. "Can I see the beautiful princess?"

"What?" Allonna was sure she hadn't said anything about a princess.

"Mama said my friend would come with a beautiful princess, and a king."

Chapter Fifty-Three

Geradin

Geradin watched Holoran carrying the little girl on his shoulders just outside their camp. She was laughing and telling him to go faster, oblivious to the debate her presence was causing.

"It be a few years since I come through this area." Serilyon waved a hand at the mountainside. "It be possible the girl and her mother arrive in that time."

Darilom shook his head. "It's highly suspicious, Your Majesty. Why would a lone woman bring her child to live in such a place?"

"A woman who seems to know about us," said Selima. "Unless it is a coincidence that she told the girl a beautiful princess and a king would bring her a friend."

"That could work to our advantage," said Geradin. "If we send the girl home, the mother may think her daughter imagined us." He knew Allonna had taken a liking to the girl, and he wanted to find a way to resolve the situation without upsetting her.

"Of course it is not a coincidence," said Mek. "The prophecies have led us here. If the mother knows about Princess Kalya and me, then she may have other information of use to us. Perhaps she is even a prophetess herself. Think what an advantage that would be."

Frowning, Selima said, "We don't know this woman's

motives. Just as anyone else, a prophet could ally with the Dark Priestess."

"She did tell Hope I would be her friend, if she was talking about us," said Allonna. "That's a good sign, I think."

Shaking his head again, Darilom said, "Unless she's using her daughter to draw us into a trap. I must ensure your safety, Your Majesty."

Geradin gritted his teeth. He'd tried to make friends with Darilom after the battle with the *kolofs*, but the Bosperanian prince had merely taken as his due Geradin's praise for his archery, his horsemanship, and his quick thinking in sacrificing his extra horses to delay the *kolofs*. And then Darilom had demanded that Mek put him in charge of security on the grounds that Geradin had done nothing to protect the Heir of the Line. Mek had refused, of course, but that didn't make Darilom any less annoying.

Out of the corner of his eye, Geradin spotted movement near the treeline. He turned his head and saw Biyeskalya approaching, holding a woman by the hair, with a knife at the woman's throat. "It looks like Biyeskalya found the mother."

Mek sighed. "It might have been better to meet her under friendlier circumstances."

Geradin studied the woman's face as Biyeskalya brought her closer. He had expected her to be frightened, but her face was almost expressionless, as if she were resigned to whatever fate might befall her. And then he realized that, even held awkwardly at knifepoint, she had the most beautiful face he had ever seen. Her skin was flawless, her lips were exactly the right shape, her eyebrows had just the right curve—every feature of her face was perfect and the effect of the whole made Geradin forget to breathe for a moment.

Suspicion flared in Geradin's mind. Such beauty could not be natural; it must be the result of a spell, intended to distract any male she encountered. Unfortunately for her, Biyeskalya was the one she had encountered.

Biyeskalya forced the woman down to her knees several

paces outside the faint glimmer in the air that indicated the ward around the camp. "Tell us why you be lying in wait for us."

Mek said, "Prin— There is no reason for such rough treatment."

The woman brow wrinkled perfectly. "You're not raiders?" Suddenly her eyes opened wide, and her teeth flashed in a dazzling smile. "Has the time come already? You're the ones the prophet talked about. Which of you is the Heir of the Line?"

Before Mek could reveal himself, Geradin said, "I am." If this woman was planning an attack, she would get the wrong man. He saw Mek's mouth open, then shut. "What did the prophet say about us?" Geradin asked.

"It is a pleasure to meet you, Your Majesty. The prophet told me that a group of people would eventually come, seeking to kill the High Priestess of Zerul. Among them would be the Heir of the Line and a beautiful princess. And they would have with them someone who would be a friend to my daughter." She looked around, finally spotting Hope being carried by Holoran. "I was looking for her when your guard found me."

Geradin frowned. "Why would a prophet tell you such things?"

"Because I am supposed to guide you into the Palace of Zerul, Your Majesty."

"We already have a guide," said Mek.

"Does your guide know the path through the caves and tunnels emerging in the vaults of the palace?"

Geradin looked at Serilyon, as did everyone else. Serilyon shook his head.

"I didn't think so," said the woman. "The prophet said that was the only path to victory."

"Victory for whom?" asked Mek.

The woman raised a perfectly arched eyebrow, in much the way Selima did when asked a foolish question. "The prophet obviously knew you would pass here. If his goal was to stop you, don't you think you would have encountered the Knights of Zerul, instead of just a mother and child?"

◆ ◆ ◆

"I do not detect any enchantment on either her or her daughter," said Selima.

"You're certain?" asked Geradin. He looked over to where the woman was talking to her daughter. Could she truly be that beautiful?

"Anyone able to hide an enchantment from my search would be powerful enough not to need to hide it."

Geradin blinked and took a moment to follow Selima's logic.

"Despite my best efforts," said Mek, "it appears we will be adding one more to our party."

"I don't like it," said Geradin. "If only we still had the oath disk!"

"You're right, we can't trust her completely," said Mek. "But getting past the guards and into the palace in order to confront the Dark Priestess has always been the weakest part of our plan. I think the Gods have provided us with a solution."

"I hope you're right," said Geradin. "But until we know for sure, I think we should continue the charade that I am the Heir of the Line."

"No," said Mek. "You will apologize to her for deceiving her and explain that you were only trying to protect the true Heir." Turning to Darilom, he said, "Prince Darilom, do you think you can play a convincing king?"

Darilom bowed slightly. "Of course, Your Majesty."

"Geradin, bring her over here and introduce her to the *real* King Aumekor."

Geradin refrained from letting his annoyance show on his face. He walked over to the woman, who looked up from wiping dirt off Hope's face.

"Pardon me, ah…" He realized he had not asked her name during the earlier conversation.

"I am called Ezpetti, Your Majesty," she said.

Geradin grimaced. "About that 'Your Majesty' business—the truth is I am not the Heir of the Line. My name is Geradin, and I'm merely a Protector of the Line."

She flashed her smile at him. "I see. How lucky for you I'm not an assassin."

"Indeed. Please come with me."

She took her daughter's hand, and he escorted them both before Darilom.

"Your Majesty, allow me to present Lady Ezpetti," said Geradin. She was dressed as a commoner and had not given herself a title of nobility nor appended a husband's name, but for etiquette's sake it was safer to promote her to Lady than demote her to Miss. "Lady Ezpetti, this is King Aumekor."

"Lady Ezpetti," said Darilom in an excellent imitation of an Aud Sapeer accent, "we have decided to accept your offer to act as our guide."

Ezpetti shook her head. "I am but a commoner, Your Majesty. But I am happy to guide you."

With a sly smile, Darilom said, "There seems little common about you, Lady Ezpetti. I am happy to be guided by you."

Geradin coughed. No doubt Darilom would stand around flirting with Ezpetti until nightfall if he could. "Perhaps it would be best if we prepared to continue our journey?"

"Yes, Protector Geradin," said Darilom. "Proceed with the preparations."

"I must return to my home to pack a few things for my daughter and myself," said Ezpetti.

"Your daughter?" said Geradin and Mek simultaneously.

"She must come with us." Ezpetti raised an eyebrow. "You don't expect me to leave her all alone here in the wilderness, do you?"

Geradin hadn't even given a thought to what the child would do while the mother was with them. "But it's too dangerous," said Geradin. "Most of us will probably not survive."

"There is always danger," said Ezpetti. "And the prophet said she must come with us."

Before Geradin could protest further, Selima said, "Then she will."

◆ ◆ ◆

The company continued along the edge of the Burn. Hope insisted on riding with Allonna, and Geradin tried to convince himself that the child's weight was small enough that it wouldn't slow down Allonna's horse in fleeing whatever dangers they might encounter. Ezpetti owned no horse, so she rode next to Holoran on the wagon seat.

Geradin pulled his horse alongside Selima. "Why did you let the girl come? I don't remember anything about a young girl in the prophecies."

"Do you know what the City of the Dark God used to be called?" asked Selima.

Frowning, Geradin said, "Well, it's the City of...the Dark God's name." He was uncomfortable saying the name—and the fact that Ezpetti willing spoke the name was another reason to be suspicious of her. Even her name had a Z in it, something which was avoided in the Free Kingdoms.

"Before the Dark God took it and made it his own, it was the original city of the Gods. It was the first city in all the world. For that reason, it was often called the Old City."

"What does that—"

"'An old child,'" said Selima. "We thought Allonna could fit the prophecy because she has not achieved her majority even though she is of age. But 'old child' could mean a child from the Old City, just as 'Aud Sapeer child' would be a child from the City of Aud Sapeer."

Geradin nodded. "So when Ezpetti said the prophet said Hope had to come along, you realized how she fit the prophecy, and that is why you agreed."

With a smile, Selima said, "No. I just realized arguing was futile, as the mother would certainly not abandon the daughter. But perhaps I have learned from Aumekor—

when something happens on this journey, one might as well attribute it to prophecy."

Gristle's ears twitched, and Geradin felt his horse pull to the left. Ahead, between Darilom and Otunvol, he saw Mek's horse shy away from the Burn. Looking out into the Burn, he could not see anything but the bare surface. What were the horses sensing? He flashed out his sword. The blade glowed a pale yellow.

"Protect the Heir," he yelled. Then he heard a low-pitched groan that seemed to come from all around them. He felt Gristle begin to tremble beneath him. "What is it?" he asked Selima.

She was frowning, her head cocked to one side. "I'm not sure. It's like—"

Geradin felt himself bucked into the air. A resounding crack seemed to knock the breath from his chest. He thought for a moment Gristle had thrown him but then he landed painfully, still seated in his saddle, and still holding his sword. Gristle almost fell but recovered his footing.

Otunvol's horse was not so fortunate and fell on its left side, with Otunvol's leg caught underneath. Mek's horse, still recovering from whatever had caused the ground to jump beneath them, stumbled. Darilom whipped a hand out and grabbed Mek's shoulder, steadying him while his horse found its footing.

The blade's glow shifted to a calm blue. Relieved that Mek was safe, Geradin turned his attention to Otunvol, who was pinned under his horse as it struggled, trying to right itself. "Otunvol, are you all right?"

"I've had better days," said Otunvol. His voice was strained.

The horse stopped struggling and lay still, though its side still moved with breath.

"I've made it sleep," said Selima. "Get it off him."

It took a few moments to organize, but with Holoran and Geradin partly lifting the horse, Darilom was able to drag Otunvol from underneath. Selima and Allonna immediately rushed to Otunvol's side and began removing the armor from his leg.

Serilyon returned from where he had been scouting ahead. "Be everyone safe?" asked Serilyon.

Geradin could see Biyeskalya coming back at a gallop from her scouting. "Everyone's alive, at least. Otunvol's hurt; don't know how bad." He took a deep breath to calm himself. "What was that?"

"Earthquake," said Serilyon.

"Aud Sapeer has earthquakes," said Geradin, "and I've never heard a sound like that."

"Look at the Burn," said Mek. His voice was filled with amazement.

Geradin turned to look at the Burn.

The smooth surface had fractured; a jagged line stretched out to the east as far as Geradin's eye could distinguish. The southern side of the fracture was six or seven palmwidths higher than the northern side.

"Just what the world needed," said Geradin. "Another place for *kolofs* to hide."

Chapter Fifty-Four

Aumekor

With one mighty stroke of his sword, Aumekor slew the dragon. Its head rolled, leaving red streaks in the yellow-green grass of the meadow as its body collapsed. Aumekor turned to Kalya, who was dressed in a glittering silver gown. "Are you hurt, my love?"

"No, I be always safe with you to protect me," she said. She rushed to him and he took her in his unarmored embrace. After a lingering kiss, she sighed. "The time draws nigh, beloved."

He reached out and stroked her hair with his fingers. "What time?"

"I be the Princess of Death," she said. She broke away from him and walked over to the dragon's head.

"I embrace you for who you are." He felt a strange calm, even though this had never happened before. Aumekor felt something tug at his shoulder, but he ignored it. In the distance, a voice seemed to be calling his name.

Kalya asked, "Would you like this as a betrothal gift?" The dragon's head was gone, as was the meadow. They were alone in a marketplace, and she was fingering a bejeweled dagger from a weaponsmith's display.

"I will treasure anything given by your hand," he said.

The tugging became more insistent, and he awoke to find Geradin shaking him.

"Mek, wake up."

"I'm awake now," said Aumekor. He blinked a few times, his eyes adjusting to the daylight filtering through the cloth of the tent. "What is it?"

"It's morning, that's what it is. That must have been quite the dream—you didn't want to leave it."

"No, it was..." Aumekor paused. He had dreamed many times of saving Kalya's life, but this one had been different—more *real*, somehow. "Never mind. How is Otunvol?"

"His leg healed well during the night, thanks to Allonna and Selima, so he should be able to ride. The crushed leg of his armor needs a smithy, though. Allonna tried, but..." Geradin shrugged.

"Any other problems?"

Geradin rolled his eyes. "His Majesty the King is being most annoying today." He began removing Aumekor's soiled linens to replace them with clean ones.

It took a moment for Aumekor to realize Geradin was referring to Darilom. "You don't actually have to obey his orders. You're his superior."

"In more ways than one." Geradin snorted. "I don't know why you picked him to play the part. It was my idea."

"I'd rather he be killed in my place than you." Aumekor sighed. "I shouldn't feel that way—I shouldn't play favorites. But it's the truth."

"I suppose I should thank you, then," said Geradin. "But there's no reason I should be alone in my misery: this morning's training will be supervised by His Majesty."

"And here I am lying abed while His Majesty awaits. What a slothful Protector I turned out to be." The banter as he was being dressed reminded Aumekor of Nikufed. With the way the company seemed to be gathering people, he might as well have let Nikufed come.

◆ ◆ ◆

Since he had no control over his movements during the training exercise, Aumekor did not even bother to pay attention to the instructions being given by Darilom. Instead, he let his mind wander back to the dream. Would he ever really feel Kalya's lips against his? And what did the new ending to his usual dream mean? He should talk to Selima about it, though she would probably tell him the dream meant nothing or that his fears about confronting the Dark Priestess were revealing themselves.

He did have fears, he admitted to himself. According to Ezpetti, by taking her path through the caves and tunnels they could arrive in the City of the Dark God in three days, rather than the five it would take crossing the mountains. Somehow, the prospect of confronting the Dark Priestess two days sooner than he had expected made him feel unprepared. Even though he personally could make no difference in the fight to come, he felt like he should be doing something.

Fifty paces beyond the edge of camp to the north, Kalya rode out of the trees. She urged her horse into a fast trot, but instead of coming toward them, she headed northeast, angling into the Burn.

"Trouble. Get to your horse," said Geradin.

After signaling his armor to take control back from Geradin's armor, Aumekor walked over to Windy and mounted. Geradin and Darilom were moving through the camp, quietly telling everyone to prepare to evacuate.

A large shape crashed out of the trees where Kalya had emerged, and stopped. Standing on its huge hind legs, the wingless dragon rose almost three times as tall as a man. Its large head seemed to consist mostly of powerful jaws with long, sharp teeth. The clawed forelegs it held up near its chest seemed strangely small. Its body leaned forward, but was balanced by a long and thick tail.

The dragon sniffed the air for a moment, and then burst into a lumbering run after Kalya, who urged her horse into a gallop.

"Smart. Her horse can outrun it," said Geradin as he helped Allonna onto her horse. "She's teasing it away, but we need to be gone before it gives up and comes back."

Aumekor frowned. "What about the tents and—"

Kalya's horse stumbled. Its lead foreleg bent awkwardly, as if caught in a hole. The horse fell forward, pitching Kalya over its head. She broke her fall with her right shoulder and rolled clear of the horse.

"Kalya!" Aumekor signaled his armor to kick, and Windy charged forward into a gallop.

"Wait, Mek," Geradin called out, but Aumekor kept going. Windy was the fastest horse, which meant he had the best chance of getting to Kalya before the dragon did.

Kalya struggled to her feet. Her right arm—her sword arm—dangled loosely. She looked at her horse, which was thrashing in pain on the ground, then turned and began to run farther into the Burn.

He was gaining on the dragon, but he wasn't sure if he was gaining enough to reach Kalya first. Then the dragon slowed as it approached the fallen horse. It roared, and Aumekor felt his body vibrate from the power of that sound. Windy's gallop faltered, and she shied to the right. Aumekor pulled hard to the left to get his panicked horse back under control. He passed alongside one of the dragon's tremendous hind legs and urged Windy to go faster. Kalya's running had taken her twenty paces further away, so if the dragon stopped to eat the horse they would be safe.

The dragon turned its massive head, and one black eye fixed on Aumekor. Turning to its right, the dragon moved to block Aumekor's path. Daggerlike teeth glinted in the morning sun and its mouth opened wide enough to swallow Aumekor whole.

Aumekor was still pulling Windy to the left and realized he could not turn to the right fast enough. Instead, he leaned forward and pulled even harder to the left. He passed under the dragon's neck as its jaws snapped on air.

One of the dragon's forelimbs, which had seemed puny compared to its whole body, reached out and caught Aumekor's torso in its claw. Only the fact that his enchanted gauntlets were gripping the reins far tighter than his muscles could on their own prevented him from being torn out of the saddle. The jerk on the reins pulled Windy's head back, but she fought it and continued forward.

As the dragon's claw tore away armor and flesh from the left side of his body, Aumekor could not help screaming in pain. Then all resistance was gone and he was free. He pulled Windy back to the right and headed after Kalya. Her silver armor gleamed ahead of him. As he caught up to her he tried to shout her name but could hardly manage a whisper. Perhaps hearing Windy's hoofbeats, Kalya turned, and Aumekor pulled hard to slow the horse. Behind him, the dragon's pounding steps drew closer. He held out his arm to Kalya.

She swung herself behind him onto the horse and yelled, "Go!"

Windy needed no encouragement, and Aumekor let the horse run. The dragon let out long roar, but the sound grew fainter with every moment. Aumekor smiled through the pain —he had rescued her.

"You be wounded," said Kalya. She clamped her left arm tight around him. "Circle back to camp."

"We have to lead—" Aumekor coughed and tasted blood in his mouth.

"Others deal with dragon. You need a healer. Circle back to camp." Her last sentence carried the tone of command, and Aumekor responded by turning Windy gradually to the right.

Geradin, Selima, Allonna and Darilom rode out to meet them. Kalya shouted something to them, but the world seemed to be swirling around and Aumekor couldn't concentrate on her words. His heart seemed to be racing in his chest. Hands lowered him to the ground, and he felt his armor being removed.

The pain faded as Selima leaned over him, muttering. After

a moment, Allonna joined her.

"The dragon?" he whispered.

"Allonna's contained it," said Geradin. "We can deal with it later."

"Kalya—her arm?"

"She'll be fine. You saved her. Just rest and let Selima and Allonna heal you."

Time seemed to wander. Aumekor found it difficult to think straight. He felt like he was suffocating, and he began gasping for air.

Kalya's face appeared over his. "Listen to me. You must listen."

"I'm listening, Kalya," he said. His words seemed distant.

She shook her head. "You no longer call me Kalya, Aumekorek-Lennos."

With an effort, he tried to recall what that meant in Aldamundian nicknaming. He should know, but his mind seemed sleepy. "I'm sorry."

"I make you a promise, Aumekorek-Lennos, and I not break it. I consent to be your wife. But you need promise me, now."

"What?"

"You need live. Promise me you live, my beloved." A tear ran down the side of her nose and dripped onto his cheek.

Beloved. That's what the -lennos suffix meant. His mind seemed to clear. "Biyeskalyana-Lenni," he said, remembering the feminine version of the suffix, "I'm glad I saved you."

"You be strong of will—do not accept death." Her voice was insistent. "You need live to marry me."

He coughed and tasted blood again. "Selima?"

"I'm here, Mek." Her voice wavered.

"I'm dying, aren't I?"

"We're trying to stop the bleeding, but there is so much damage..."

Allonna was crying softly.

What was that prophecy? "'The princess with the magic of death is needed for the Heir to live,'" he whispered.

"My magic cannot heal," said Biyeskalya. "I fear I have only brought you death."

The edges of his vision began to fade, as if he were looking at Biyeskalya through a tunnel, but everything seemed to become clear in his mind. "You are the Princess of Death, and I embrace you for who you are." His voice was barely a whisper. "And I accept what is given by your hand."

Biyeskalya's eyes went wide, and then she leaned forward and kissed him. "Farewell, my beloved."

He felt her dagger slide into his heart, and then the world faded to black.

Chapter Fifty-Five

Geradin

Geradin reached forward and yanked Biyeskalya away from Mek, throwing her to the ground. "You're supposed to save him, not kill him!"

He had hoped Mek's love for the princess would strengthen his will to live. She had played the part of the grieving lover well, until the moment she stabbed Mek. Even if she thought it was a mercy killing, they had to keep Mek alive.

"Let me be if you want him to live," Biyeskalya said. Her right arm hanging limply, she crawled back to Mek's body and took hold of the hilt of the dagger protruding from his chest. She began chanting in a strange language.

Selima gasped. "You cannot do this."

Biyeskalya paused. "Can *your* magic make him live?" When Selima did not respond, Biyeskalya returned to chanting.

Geradin walked over to Selima and squatted down. "Can she do that?" he asked quietly. "Make him live? Gods of Light, let it be possible."

Shaking her head, Selima said, "I do not know. And the Gods of Light have nothing to do with this. I would not allow such desecration if there were any other hope."

"I tried, Ger," said Allonna, "but there was so much tearing and so many places bleeding and I couldn't fix them all because some of them were so tiny and yet they kept bleeding and bleeding and I couldn't get them all to stop."

He knelt before her and took her in his arms, and her body shook as she sobbed on his shoulder. "You did all you could. It's not your fault the dragon attacked him." *That fault is mine. I should have known he would try to rescue Biyeskalya. I should have stopped him somehow.*

Allonna stopped crying suddenly. "The dragon," she said. Her voice was filled with hate. She stood and walked toward the spot where the dragon was caught inside her ward.

Was the dragon freeing itself? Geradin rose quickly to his feet. "Lonna?"

The dragon saw Allonna coming and lunged toward her, then roared in frustration at being stopped short by the ward. Allonna halted a pace away from the ward. The dragon towered before her, more than three times her height.

"What are you doing?" asked Geradin as he rushed to her side.

She stretched out her hands and the ward's blue light flared brighter. The color began to shift into violet and became brighter still. The edges of the ward blurred, and then the brightness faded, leaving only a barely perceptible violet shimmer. The dragon charged again, but to Geradin's relief the ward still held.

Suddenly the inner cylindrical layer of the ward began to collapse in on itself. What had been twenty paces shrank to fifteen, then to ten. The dragon reared up as the ward pushed it back toward the center. From behind, the ward curved the end of the dragon's tail inward. The dragon thrashed in a circle as the inner ward closed to seven paces in diameter. Then the dragon could no longer move on its own as it was forced to stand straight up.

It roared in panic as bones cracked. The roar choked off as blood erupted from the giant jaws. The circle of the ward continued to narrow, and for a few moments more the cracking of bone was the only sound. The circle constricted until it was no more than a palmwidth in diameter even as it stretched up into the sky, a narrow column of gore. Then the inner ward disappeared, and what was left of the dragon splashed down to form a pulpy pool within the outer wards.

Stunned by Allonna's display of power, Geradin didn't know what to say. After a few moments he reached out and put his arm around her, then gently turned and led her back to where the others were gathered around Mek.

Biyeskalya's incomprehensible chanting continued. Mek still lay unmoving with a dagger in his chest—whatever Biyeskalya was doing had not changed that. Geradin wondered if he had somehow disrupted the necromancy by pulling Biyeskalya away after she had stabbed Mek. Unwilling to look at Mek's face, Geradin looked at the others surrounding him.

Selima's eyes were closed and tears lined her cheeks. Darilom kept licking his lips nervously. Serilyon's face had a determined lack of expression. The chords in Otunvol's neck were taut, and his lips pressed tightly together. Holoran stood with eyes closed and head bowed, his mouth moving silently as if in prayers.

And a pleasantly calm man Geradin had never seen before stood next to Mek's head.

Instinctively Geradin drew his sword and pointed it at the man, who was dressed in a varicolored silk robe.

"Who are you?" Geradin asked, and then he noticed his sword was not glowing. For a moment he wondered what was wrong, and then he realized the enchantment was gone. There was no Heir of the Line to be protected. A lump rose in his throat. "Who are you?" he repeated, his voice now hoarse.

The man smiled sadly. "Put your sword away, Geradin att'Balunor. I am Kairith, Demigod of Death." He looked down at Biyeskalya. "You may stop chanting now, my dear. We have matters to discuss, and all that ritual claptrap is rather grating on the ear."

Kalya's eyes opened wide and she abruptly went silent.

Geradin lowered his sword. He had never expected to meet a demigod. This balding middle-aged man did not look like the skeletal horror artists portrayed, but somehow he could not doubt Kairith was who he claimed to be.

"I don't usually collect a person's spirit myself, you understand," said Kairith. "Most of the time I don't even bother with royalty. But it's not every day that someone willingly allows a necromancer to kill him. Willing sacrifices are generally a powerful thing, and when it's royalty...Let's just say I'm interested in how this all turns out." He shrugged. "Of course, barring intervention by one of the Four Gods, I already know how this all turns out, but I find it interesting nonetheless."

"Can you restore Mek—King Aumekor—to life?" asked Geradin.

"Ah, ah, ah!" Kairith waggled a finger at Geradin. "Protocol must be observed. You did not kill him, and you most certainly did not say the proper chants over the body. Believe me, boy, you do *not* want me to deviate from protocol."

Biyeskalya said, "Bring back—"

Holding up a hand to silence her, Kairith said, "Patience, dear girl. He's not getting any more dead right now. Assuming that I had the power to restore him to life, which is a good assumption, by the way, are you certain that's what you want?"

Biyeskalya drew in a breath to begin speaking, but Kairith's hand flashed out to cover her mouth.

"I shouldn't have asked the question. Just be quiet and listen." He removed his hand from her mouth. "Now, Omnimancer Selima, you are a wise woman. What do you think would happen if I restored this body to life, minus the effects of the mortal wound the princess here inflicted on him?"

"He would die very quickly from his other wounds," said Selima.

"Precisely. Restoring him to life would be like undoing a spell. I could do it, as it's part of my domain, but it's pointless because there is nothing gained. And before one of you asks, let me make clear that healing the rest of his wounds is not part of my domain. I'm the Demigod of *Death*. I'm meant to escort the dead to Velia, and the rules of necromancy imposed on me by Zerul are actually an interference with my original purpose. So there's no use asking me to give your friend back to you—it is not going to happen."

"Then it's all for nothing." Geradin's shoulders sagged. He had sworn to protect Mek, and he had failed.

"Did I say that?" Kairith shook his head. "Why would I bother coming here myself if that were true? No, I am bound to do what a necromancer asks, as long as it is within my domain and the sacrifice is of sufficient value. But it's a foolish necromancer who does not think carefully before she asks me to do anything."

"I be not a fool," said Biyeskalya. "I not ask you to restore him to life. I ask you to bring back his soul to re-anim—"

So quickly that Geradin did not see him move, Kairith clamped his hand over her mouth again. Biyeskalya pulled back, but did not finish speaking. Instead, she just glared at Kairith.

"Omnimancer Selima," said Kairith, "have you ever tried to do a spell without sufficient power to make it work?"

"Yes. The spell fails."

"Quite right." Kairith nodded. "And you waste that power to no effect. Necromancy is similar, and many a spell fails because the necromancer thought her sacrifice worth more than it was. Take, for example, someone who kills her own father in order to gain power. Killing a parent multiplies the worth of the sacrifice. However, if her father was an old man with but a few seasons left to live, sacrificing him is not worth much."

"Oh," said Biyeskalya.

Geradin felt frustrated by Kairith's roundabout method of making a point. "Just tell her what she should ask for and be done with it."

"I've told you already, dear boy, protocol must be observed. It's a lesson you should remember—I don't want to have to tell you a third time."

"Or you'll do what? Kill me?" Geradin stepped forward and stood face to face with Kairith.

"Geradin!" Selima pulled at Geradin's arm. "Forgive his impertinence, Kairith. He's distraught over the loss of his friend."

Geradin pulled his arm free of Selima. "I should have died before letting Mek come to harm, yet here I stand without even a scratch. You want a life sacrificed to bring Mek back? Take mine. Better than that—his body is damaged, so put him in mine."

Kairith waved a hand dismissively. "A noble gesture, but your time is not up yet. You will meet me twice more before you die." The demigod gave him a crooked smile. "But that is the future. Let me make this clear: my business here today concerns only Aumekor, the sacrifice, and Biyeskalya, the necromancer."

Biyeskalya took a deep breath, then let it out. "Understand, I be only asking a question, not requesting anything."

Beaming, Kairith said, "Ask away, my princess."

"Could I give up my body to Aumekor?"

"Oh, the storytellers would love that one. The Tragedy of Aumekor and Biyeskalya. He gives up his life to save you, then you give up your life to save him," said Kairith. "But the answer is no."

Annoyed at Kairith's flippancy, Geradin said, "Where I come from, *protocol* does not call for making light of a man's death in front of his friends."

"You are correct, Lord Geradin," said Kairith with no trace of sarcasm. "I apologize. Please let me know if I make any more protocol errors."

"You make this most difficult, Kairith," said Biyeskalya. "If not re-animation, be half-life an option?"

Kairith pointed a finger at her. "I knew you'd think of it eventually. I can give you two days."

"It be my second choice, until Geradin offer his body. But two days be not enough."

Shrugging, Kairith said, "Two days is the limit. You'll have to do the best you can in that time. Ask, and it will be done."

"I ask."

"It is done. I will return to collect his spirit in two days." Kairith looked at the rest of the group. "Safe journey." And he was gone as if he had never been there.

Mek sat up, then rose to his feet.

"Mek!" shouted Geradin. "Thank the Gods of Light. And Kairith, too. And Biyeskalya..." His voice faded as he saw no reaction on Mek's face. The dull lifeless eyes that stared out did not see him.

"Necromancers call it half-life," said Biyeskalya. "His spirit give movement to the body under my control, but that be all. He be no longer the Aumekor we know."

Looking at the standing corpse of his friend, Geradin realized it was not wearing the enchanted armor. Allonna and Selima had removed it while trying to save Mek's life.

"Then you are the puppet-master of the prophecy," said Geradin. "You are the one who must control his sword when he confronts the Dark Priestess."

Biyeskalya nodded. "And we must confront her within two days, or all be lost."

Chapter Fifty-Six

Allonna

The morning sunlight glinted off the Burn to the east. Allonna stretched her tired muscles and wished she had time to sleep. She walked from horse to horse, letting her healing magic soothe the pain and tiredness in the animals. A day and a night of hard riding, pausing only briefly to rest the horses, had everybody on the brink of exhaustion—everybody except King Aumekor. He just ran silently alongside the horses. According to Princess Biyeskalya, in the half-life state a body could run and not be weary, needing neither food nor water, as long as the spirit animated the corpse.

Tears welled up in her eyes as she looked at Aumekor standing lifelessly before her. If only she had been smarter. A mobile ward was only good against magical attacks and rapid weapons such as arrows, but she hadn't thought to put something stronger around Aumekor when he rode off toward a dragon. She'd already been on horseback, so why hadn't she galloped in pursuit, like Geradin had? She could have put a stationary ward around the dragon before Aumekor got too close. Aumekor's death was her fault.

"Why are you crying?" asked Hope.

Allonna looked down through her tears to see the little girl looking up at her. "Because one of my friends is gone."

Hope reached out to take Allonna's hand. "I'm not gone."

"Yes, I'm glad." Allonna stooped down and hugged her. "I'm

talking about another friend. He was a good man."

"Is he coming back?"

Shaking her head, Allonna said, "No, I don't think he's coming back."

Hope looked away for a moment then looked back at Allonna. "Holoran said he would give me a shoulder ride. He's very tall. But I can stay with you."

"No, I'll be fine. Go have fun."

Hope ran off to Holoran, who swooped her up to sit on his shoulder.

Biyeskalya came over to check on her horse, which had been Aumekor's. She looked at Allonna. "You be doing good work, keeping these horses going. We make good time."

"Will we make it there in time?"

"If Ezpetti be truthful." Biyeskalya nodded. "We reach the cave entrance before sundown. If we travel the cave during the night and arrive in the palace before morning, we have time to confront the Dark Priestess before Kairith returns."

"I've been thinking about that," said Allonna. "If we don't get there in time, then we can just do what we planned before. Geradin can control the armor even if Aumekor is dead inside it."

"No," said Selima's voice from behind her, and Allonna turned to face her. "'The Heir must live to confront the Dark Priestess, else all will be lost.' It's a prophecy of Tisuri, the prophecy which led to the formation of the Protectors of the Line. I just hope this half-life is enough to fulfill that prophecy."

"It be enough," said Biyeskalya. "Else why the prophecies about me?"

"I've had enough of prophecies," said Allonna. "Aumekor trusted in the prophecies, and look what happened. If the prophecies come from the Gods of Light, why didn't they give us something useful, like 'The Heir of the Line must not rescue princesses from dragons'? What purpose did his death serve?" She found herself crying again.

"I think I know," said Geradin. He walked over from the campfire, still holding a mug of tea. "I've been searching for reasons all night. Perhaps it's just desperate thinking on my part, but I see one way in which Mek's death can help defeat the Dark Priestess. When he died, the enchantment on my sword stopped working."

"Without the enchantment, your sword be an ordinary weapon," said Biyeskalya. "What advantage be that?"

"Because we now have one of deadliest weapons in the world," said Geradin, and he calmly took a sip of tea.

Allonna knew there were prophecies about the return of powerful magical weapons from the Age of Light, but didn't know any of them were tied to Aumekor's death.

"A weapon?" asked Selima. "Aumekor's father's sword is the only weapon that can kill the Dark Priestess, and we have that already."

"All the enchanted swords of the Protectors stopped glowing yesterday," said Geradin. "No doubt my fellow Protectors in Bargas have been cutting down the enemy by the hundreds using their swords—until the enchantment stopped working."

"So the other Protectors know Aumekor is dead," said Allonna. "But even if they have some special weapon to use if the enchantment stops, it does us no good. Why didn't they give it to us?"

"Geradin, don't be so..." Selima frowned, then said, "Lack of sleep has dimmed my mind. It's likely the enemy knows the swords stopped glowing. And since the Dark Priestess has artifacts that allow her to talk to her generals in the field, that means she knows Aumekor is dead."

Geradin nodded. "Since only the Heir of the Line can kill her, she thinks she's safe. Oh, she may wonder if a new Heir of the Line might be born sometime in the next three seasons—after all, Aumekor was born after his father died—but a baby can't harm her."

"But what's the deadly weapon?" asked Allonna.

Geradin gave her a tired grin. "Surprise."

❖ ❖ ❖

"Allonna?" said Ezpetti. "Can you hear me?"

The sound brought Allonna out of her daze. "Forgive me. I think I was asleep while walking. Is that possible?" In order to spare the horses without losing too much time, Serilyon had suggested walking the horses instead of riding them during the midday heat.

"I could walk your horse for you while you ride in the wagon."

"No, I'm fine." Allonna shook her head to clear it.

"I want to thank you for being so kind to my daughter. I know a young lady your age doesn't need a small child as a friend, so I appreciate your treating her as one."

Smiling, Allonna said, "She's a sweet girl. I wonder that she doesn't have many friends."

"Living isolated as we do, there was no one for her to befriend until you arrived."

"Of course." Allonna should have realized that; the lack of sleep must be affecting her more than she'd thought.

"And it's especially nice of you, considering you don't trust me," said Ezpetti.

Allonna frowned. "What?"

Ezpetti shrugged. "I've overheard enough to know that the one who died was the real Heir. I'm not offended, because you had no cause to trust me. I'm only saying that makes your kindness to Hope…That's strange."

"Strange?" Allonna looked at Ezpetti, who was frowning and staring ahead. Allonna followed Ezpetti's gaze. At first, the terrain ahead seemed what Allonna had expected: the sparsely forested mountains to the left of the Burn's edge, and the Burn itself stretching off to the right. But the horizon was higher and closer than it should be. Then her eyes focused properly and she realized she was looking at the edge of an escarpment rising before them. It extended up into the mountains and out into the Burn.

"That wasn't there before," said Ezpetti.

◆ ◆ ◆

The escarpment wasn't even as tall as two men, but Allonna still found herself awed and a little frightened. The earthquake that had shaken the party two days ago had obviously been much more powerful here.

She watched as Darilom and Otunvol helped Geradin clamber up to stand on Holoran's shoulders. Stretching out his arms, Geradin grabbed the edge of the glassy rock and began to pull himself up. Holoran's well-muscled arms helped push Geradin up, and in a moment he scrambled to his feet atop the escarpment.

"The ground is level from here on," said Geradin, "but I don't see how we can get the horses up."

"Then it is simple. We leave the horses behind," said Darilom.

"Ezpetti, how much further do we have to go?" asked Serilyon.

Ezpetti furrowed her brow. "On foot, it will be dark well before we arrive at the cave mouth. We would have left the horses there, so the journey is no different from that point. Whether we can arrive before midmorning, I do not know."

The prospect of another sleepless night, traveling on foot this time, made Allonna feel suddenly wearier than she already had been.

Looking around at the rest of the company, Ezpetti said, "Trained soldiers may make better time, but not all of us have such endurance. Allonna hasn't slept, and she's been using her magic to keep the horses from collapsing. She's about to collapse herself, now."

"I can do it," said Allonna.

"We may be able to find a place with a slope gentle enough for the horses," said Serilyon. "If we send scouts in both directions—"

"No, we waste too much time if we don't find a passage." Geradin's voice became firm. "Biyeskalya, I'll need you to bring Aumekor. Ezpetti, you'll guide us. Selima, bring whatever artifacts you need and leave everything else in the wagon. Otunvol, Darilom—you and I will assist them, even carry them if needed. The rest of you, take the horses and go with Serilyon. If you find a way through soon enough, you can catch up with us and we'll use the horses the rest of the way."

No one spoke for several moments.

"I don't think there's a better plan," said Selima. "I'll get what I need."

Biyeskalya walked Aumekor over to Holoran. Otunvol and Darilom boosted his body as they had Geradin.

"I should go with you," said Allonna. "You'll need wards." Suddenly she remembered the beggar's prophecy about her friends leaving her behind.

"You will ride in the wagon and get some sleep," said Geradin. "We need you fresh when you catch up with us."

Allonna's vision blurred with tears. He didn't expect them to catch up. He was doing the same thing Aumekor had—taking as few people as possible in order to save the lives of the rest.

After helping the last of his reduced party up, Geradin looked down at Allonna, Holoran, Serilyon and Hope. "What are you waiting for? Find a way to bring us our horses." He turned and disappeared from view.

"You heard him," said Serilyon. "I think our best chance be up the mountainside; I do not like the look of it in the Burn."

Geradin hadn't even said goodbye.

◆ ◆ ◆

Allonna awoke in darkness. For a moment she did not know where she was, then she recognized the creak of the supply wagon's wheels. Faint light made it through the fabric covering the wagon. She started to sit up, then realized Hope was cuddled up beside her. Careful not to disturb the sleeping girl, Allonna managed to get out the back of the wagon. She found herself standing on the smooth surface of the Burn. Above her the Nightglow filled the sky.

Nighttime. She had only meant to take a short nap, just to dull the edge of her weariness. Allonna ran around to the front of the wagon and saw Serilyon leading the horses. They had not caught up to Geradin and the others.

"Feeling better?" asked Holoran, who was on the seat of the wagon.

"Why did you let me sleep so long?"

"Why not? We didn't run into any trouble. And we found a way over."

Allonna rubbed her eyes, trying to get fully awake. "But why haven't we caught up to them?"

"It took too long. Geradin and the rest should be deep in the cave by now."

Gods of Light protect them, she prayed silently. "How will we find them?"

"Serilyon's following trail markers they—"

"Silence," said Serilyon in a loud whisper. He halted the horses he was leading, and Holoran brought the wagon to a stop. "There be a light ahead on the mountainside."

Allonna spotted the bright yellow glow. The light was steady, not flickering as firelight would be. Reaching out with her mind, Allonna could sense the magic of it, and it felt familiar. "It's a light spell. I think it's Selima's. She probably left it there so we could see the cave entrance."

"Stay here," said Serilyon.

"But—"

"Even if you be certain it is Selima's, we do not know what awaits there." Serilyon ran off into the darkness.

Time seemed to crawl as she waited for Serilyon to return.

"Holoran! Allonna! Come quickly." The hoarse shout came from up the hill, and Allonna's heart began pounding hard in her chest. The voice was Geradin's.

She ran up the side of the mountain toward the light. Was Geradin injured so badly he could not go with the others into the cave? A tree root caused her to stumble to her hands and knees, but she got up and continued to run.

As she got close to the light, the scene became clear. Geradin stood next to the cave mouth, which was surrounded by scattered piles of rocks. Someone inside the cave handed him a rock, and he pitched it aside. The pattern repeated itself a few more times before he saw her.

"Allonna, come help. Is Holoran coming?" Geradin's armor was covered in dust.

"He's coming. What's happened?"

"The earthquake collapsed the mouth of the cave." He heaved another rock aside. "We can't get in."

Chapter Fifty-Seven

Geradin

Geradin's hands refused to clench properly, but he could still balance rocks on his forearms to pass them to Serilyon, who passed them to Allonna, who threw them outside. The work seemed to be going faster now, as Holoran was able to carry larger rocks outside by himself.

As Geradin turned back to receive another rock from Darilom, Selima caught his arm. "The sun is up," she said.

"Then we'd better work faster."

"No, Geradin. This plan has failed. Getting to the palace in time is impossible." Selima raised her voice and said, "Everyone stop working."

Rocks clattered to the ground. Various groans of relief sounded in the cave.

"You don't know that, Selima. Perhaps we have until nightfall of the second day. We've got to keep going."

"In which case, you can afford a few moments to rest." Selima pulled Geradin outside and he squinted at the brightness. "Even Darilom and Otunvol have taken shifts."

"Mek hasn't," said Geradin.

"Sit down."

Geradin sat.

"Aumekor's magically sustained. You aren't."

"Then Biyeskalya should kill me and give me half-life. I'd be more use that way."

Selima shook her head. "Don't give up, Geradin."

"Don't give up? Don't give up? I'm not the one who's giving up here." Geradin tried to stand up, but his arms didn't push him up enough and he sank back down.

"I'm not giving up either. I just think the time has come to consider alternatives, and having everyone in our party dying of exhaustion isn't one of them. We don't even know that the path through the cave is open, even after we clear the entrance."

Closing his eyes felt good. Geradin let out a long breath. "What alternatives?"

"Who knows but what the Dark Priestess has gone into the Burn for some purpose, and she'll pass by here shortly? Such coincidences have happened already on our journey. Or Biyeskalya might convince Kairith to extend Aumekor's half-life. Perhaps you could convince him; I think he respects you."

"Respects me?" Geradin opened his eyes. "He scolded me like a child."

"True," said Selima. "I've done the same. But he also accepted your rebuke with grace."

Holoran approached and stooped over him. "You can be quite persuasive, milord. Remember Midsummer Day?"

Geradin was about to say he didn't see how attacking the Demigod of Death with a wooden sword would be persuasive, when he remembered that the attack during Mek's speech hadn't been the only event of that day. "We've come a long way since the Tests of Majority, haven't we?"

Holoran smiled. "The work may be harder here, milord, but it smells better than the sewers."

Geradin found he couldn't keep his eyes open. "If I'm so persuasive, why do you still call me 'milord'?"

"Won't happen again, milord."

◆ ◆ ◆

Someone was shaking his right shoulder. Geradin opened

his eyes and saw Allonna.

"We must move away from the entrance," she said. "Something's coming."

Geradin scrambled to his feet as he tried to estimate how long he had been sleeping. The sun was only partway up in the east, so it hadn't been long. "What is it? A dragon?" He drew his sword and was startled again by its failure to glow.

"We don't know," said Allonna. "There's a rumbling sound inside the cave."

Was the Dark Priestess coming to confront them? Why would she do that, when all she had to do was wait until Kairith took Mek's spirit?

Hunks of rock spewed out of the cave. Some bounced off a ward Allonna had instantly created around Geradin and herself, but most of them went flying down the mountainside to crash to the ground below. Looking through the ward, Geradin could see that the others were safely out of the way.

"What sort of creature does that to rock?" he said.

The torrent of rocks faded to a trickle, then stopped. He and Allonna ran to the side of the entrance, so whatever came out wouldn't see them at first. Perhaps they could surprise it.

Kairith emerged from the cave. He dusted off the front of his robe. "That was an interesting journey," he said. "I don't usually go under mountains, but it was the shortest route to get here from Zerul's palace. Most of that trail is fine, but there were a few tricky spots, like the end there."

Kairith's back was turned toward Geradin, who was still holding his sword. Could the Demigod of Death still collect Mek's spirit if he—

"Yes, Lord Geradin, I could. Put the sword away." Kairith turned to look directly at Geradin.

Sheathing his sword, Geradin stepped forward. "So you're in league with the Dark Priestess."

Kairith raised an eyebrow. "Demigods do not ally with anyone. It's a rule, and we have not the free will to disobey. However, someone—I can't say who or where, naturally—

made a sacrifice and demanded to know whether a certain person had died. I offered to check personally. Fortunately, that request didn't keep me from making my appointment with you today."

Geradin frowned. Why was Kairith telling them this?

"Please," said Biyeskalya. Mek's body stood next to her. "We need more time."

"You have used all the time allowed," said Kairith. "I have no discretion here: it is time for Aumekor's spirit to be taken to Velia. Any further attempts on your part to keep him here are futile."

"What about attempts on my part?" said Geradin.

"Futile," said Kairith. He reached his hand toward Mek's body, and the body crumpled to the ground. "He wants you to know he's sorry for having failed you, and the fault was his alone. Do not blame yourselves."

"You can talk to him?" asked Geradin. "Can you let us talk to him?"

"He's heard every word you've said. But hearing the voice of the dead is a privilege reserved only to those about to die. I'm sorry." Kairith looked around at all of them. "It has been my pleasure. Now, I have a report to give elsewhere."

"Wait," said Geradin. "Giving Aumekor half-life forced us to rush all the way here, and now it's all for nothing? Why did you bother? You might as well have taken his spirit the first time you came."

Kairith shrugged. "Must everything happen for a reason? Perhaps eventually you'll see the truth of the situation." Kairith vanished for a moment, then reappeared. "Goodbye, Lord Geradin. We shall meet once more before you die." He vanished again.

"What do we do now?" said Allonna.

Geradin had no answer.

◆ ◆ ◆

It was still daylight, though the sun was already behind the mountain to the west. Geradin stared into the cookfire, occasionally bringing his cup of tea to his lips. He had always known he might be killed protecting Mek. He had never given much thought to what would happen if he remained alive after Mek died. Without the Heir of the Line to stop her, the armies of the Dark Priestess would sweep the world. What was there left to do but to charge against her and die?

He threw his tea into the fire. It sizzled a moment, but the flames hardly flickered. Whatever he chose to do, it mattered not to the world at large.

Looking up from the fire, he saw Allonna staring at him. He loved her, and she loved him. Why should they waste their lives fighting without hope? They could find an isolated spot, build a home and have children. They could lead a happy enough life.

Perhaps that was what Kairith meant by the truth of the situation.

"Lord Geradin?" said Ezpetti.

"Yes?"

"I am sorry I brought you this way. I truly believed what the prophet said. He had never guided me wrong before."

Geradin sighed. "I believe you. But sometimes prophecies don't mean what we think. I suppose even a prophet could be wrong in interpreting his own prophecy."

"I should have known something was wrong, but I thought it was my mistake. If I'd said something, perhaps things would have been different. I'm sorry." Ezpetti turned to leave.

Selima rose from where she had been sitting on one of the rocks Kairith had ejected from the mouth of the cave. "What did you think was wrong?"

"When I met all of you, I recognized you as the party of the Heir of the Line. The prophet had shown you to me in a vision," said Ezpetti. "But I thought Geradin was the Heir."

"That's my fault," said Geradin. "I claimed to be the Heir in case you planned something against Aumekor."

Ezpetti shook her head. "No, I believed you because I already thought you were, from the vision. When I found out you weren't I was confused. I should have mentioned that what the prophet showed me was unreliable."

"I don't know if that would have made any difference. Perhaps the prophet saw that I would claim—"

Selima gasped and dropped her plate. "Light take me, I am the stupidest woman alive."

In his entire life, Geradin had never heard Selima swear. "What's the matter?"

"Everyone wake up," shouted Selima. "Everybody come here now."

"What is it?" asked Geradin.

"Wait until everyone is here." Selima strode back and forth, wringing her hands during the several moments before everybody gathered around the fire.

"You all have heard the story of how Geradin's father, Balunor, cut the baby Aumekor from his mother's womb. Most of you know that the poison that killed his mother left Aumekor paralyzed." Selima paused. "But that was a lie. Aumekor's paralysis was caused because the umbilical cord was wrapped around his neck as his mother gave birth."

"But..." Geradin was stunned by the revelation. Why had Selima lied about Mek's paralysis?

Selima held up her palm to silence him. "There were two babies born that terrible day. One was healthy, one was not. But I didn't know that at the time. All I knew was that the Heir of the Line was vulnerable, and the Dark Priestess would do all in her power to kill him. Whoever sat on the throne of Aud Sapeer was in danger. So I switched the babies."

For a moment, Geradin almost believed her, but then he spotted the flaw in her story. "It can't be true," said Geradin. "The swords glowed when Mek was in danger, not me. They stopped when he died."

"It's the truth. To switch the babies, I used an ancient

artifact of great power to cast a spell of confusion, so the whole world would think the wrong baby was the Heir of the Line. Even the enchantment of the swords would have been affected." Selima shook her head. "But when I completed the spell, I thought it had failed. No one seemed to have been fooled, because everyone agreed with me about which baby was the Heir. It was a stupid, stupid error on my part—I had not exempted myself from the effects of the spell. It was not until Ezpetti mentioned what she saw in the vision that I realized the spell had actually worked."

Geradin's thoughts whirled. Was Selima telling the truth? Was he really the Heir of the Line?

"'You wish to be remembered for seeking the truth,'" Biyeskalya quoted, "'but shall be remembered best for the lies you have told.' The madman was right."

Darilom kneeled before Geradin. "Forgive me, Your Majesty. I should not have treated you as I have."

Geradin stared at Selima. "You're not just making this up?"

"If I still had the oath disk, I would swear on it, Your Majesty." Selima bowed before him.

"I need time to think," he said. Everyone else seemed convinced. So why did he still have doubts?

Chapter Fifty-Eight

Allonna

Unable to get back to sleep, Allonna finally got up and exited the tent, taking a blanket with her. To the east, the pale light of the coming dawn was beginning to overtake the Nightglow. She pulled her blanket tighter against the chill air.

"Back home there would be snow all around," said Geradin.

Allonna turned to see him placing wood on the remains of last night's fire. "You're up early."

"I got some sleep."

"Want me to make some tea?"

"I can do it," said Geradin.

"Mine tastes better."

"You win."

Allonna fetched some water from the barrel in the wagon and put the teapot to heat on a stone by the growing fire, then sat next to Geradin. He put his arm around her, and they sat in silence for a while.

"Do you believe Selima?" asked Geradin.

Allonna's memory flashed to her first time in Selima's study. Selima had said she would do almost anything to defeat the Dark Priestess. But Allonna couldn't see how lying about Geradin being the true Heir of the Line would help. "I believe her."

"I couldn't even keep Mek alive."

"You think that means you'll fail against the Dark Priestess?" She shook her head. "Geradin, if the Gods of Light themselves were to choose someone to fulfill the prophecies, I can't think of anyone better than you."

Geradin sighed. "What would you say if I asked you to come away with me? Leave all the prophecies behind, and just find an isolated spot to build a little house and raise a family?"

She searched his face for signs he was joking. Running away seemed so unlike him. Then she realized he must have come to the opposite decision, and was just engaging in a final bit of fantasy before doing his duty. She smiled coyly and said, "If there was a proposal of marriage in there somewhere, I'd say yes."

"And what would you say if I asked you to risk your life to defeat the Dark Priestess, and if we somehow both survive, to return with me to Aud Sapeer and be my queen?"

"If there was a proposal of marriage in there somewhere, I'd say yes."

He gave her a small smile. "Then I guess I can base my decision on other factors." He gave her a brief kiss, then stood up. "I need to make a few preparations. Call me when the tea is ready." He strode off to the wagon.

Biyeskalya's voice came softly from behind Allonna. "You love each other."

Allonna turned to look at the princess. "It's rude to listen in on private conversations."

"Then do not hold private conversations by the only fire in the camp." Biyeskalya walked over and sat down a pace from Allonna. "It be time for us to have a private conversation, here or elsewhere; it matters not to me."

"Nor to me," said Allonna. She would not be intimidated. She raised a ward against eavesdropping around them. "No one can hear us now." Selima could probably bypass it, but that didn't matter to Allonna.

"He not make you his queen, so you need release all hope of it."

"Why? Because I was born a commoner? Geradin does not mind. And you forget I am an omnimancer, which gives me the status of a noble."

Biyeskalya shook her head. "I be trying to help you preserve dignity." She leaned forward. "I understand that you love each other, and I stand not in the way if you be lovers discreetly. But I be his queen. It be already arranged."

"You? He hates you," said Allonna. Then astonishment gave way to realization. If Geradin was the real king of Aud Sapeer, then he, not Aumekor, had been betrothed to Biyeskalya. "You can't hold him to that arrangement."

Shrugging, Biyeskalya said, "He ben't the first king to hate his queen, nor the last. But I bear his heir, the prophet say."

"You said that prophet was a madman, and now you believe his prophecy when it suits you?"

Biyeskalya began counting off with her fingers. "He say Aumekor has no future. That be true. He say Selima tell lies, and that be true. He tell Darilom where to find us, and that be true. He say your friends leave you behind, and two days ago they do. If you truly love Geradin, you need be happy if my prophecy be true."

As the princess spoke, Allonna felt her heart sink within her. Blinking back her tears, she said, "Why should I be happy that you steal my love from me?"

"Because I only bear his child if he survive the coming battle."

A tear rolled down Allonna's cheek. Geradin would live, but she would lose him. "I will be happy for him, then." She stood. "Forgive me if I do not care to hear more of your gloating."

Biyeskalya stood, too. "Gloating? You think I be gloating? I be forced to marry a man I love not, who love not me, and you think I gloat? I offer to look aside if you be my husband's lover, and you think I gloat?"

To Allonna's surprise, there were tears in Biyeskalya's eyes. "Then why go through with the marriage? Release him from the betrothal, after he kills the Dark Priestess."

The princess wiped at her eyes with a gauntleted hand, then shook her head. "I learn the lesson too late, but I learn. Resisting prophecy bring nothing but grief. Aumekorek be alive today if I resist not the prophecy. My stubbornness kill the man I love."

Allonna could not believe what she was hearing. "Your false tears will not gain my sympathy. Geradin had you pretend—"

"Do you think I travel so long with Aumekorek and not learn the kind of man he truly be?" She wiped her eyes again. "He be wise, and kind, and strong, and he love me. I grow to love him."

"Then why didn't you tell him?" Despite what she had said, Allonna felt a sudden sympathy for the princess.

"I swear he must save me before I consent to marry. In my pride, I do not go back on what I say, but I plan to tell him he win me by saving my kingdom after he kill the Dark Priestess." She sniffled. "But my pride kill him first. Let not your pride endanger Geradin."

"I will not," said Allonna. "But do not distract him with this. It can wait until after he defeats the Dark Priestess."

Biyeskalya nodded.

◆ ◆ ◆

The men built a cairn for Aumekor from the stones that had blocked the entrance to the cave. On top of the mound rested Aumekor's sword and scabbard. As they all stood in a circle around Aumekor's final resting place, Allonna did not bother to stop her tears. Selima held her close and cried with her.

"I wish we could take him back to Aud Sapeer," said Geradin, "but after we enter the cave, it's possible none of us will return." He looked around at each of them. "The prophecies say only four of us will reach the palace of the Dark Priestess, and the rest will be lost along the way. In all our journey so far, we have lost only one, which means the greatest danger lies ahead. I don't know whose skills I'll need, but if any of you wish to remain behind, you could guard the horses against raiders."

No one said anything.

Geradin looked at Ezpetti. "I do not like the idea of taking a child—"

"There is a grating that must be opened from inside, Your Majesty, and she is the only one small enough to fit through. Besides, she has traveled these caves before and survived."

"Then it is settled. I thank you all for your faith in me." Geradin unbuckled his sword belt and removed his scabbard. "Darilom att'Pivalom, you have proven your courage in battle. You have earned the right to carry this sword as a Protector of the Line. I only wish its enchantment still worked."

Darilom bowed low and moved to take the sword and scabbard.

"Wait," Allonna said. "The only reason the enchantment failed is the sword thinks there is no Heir of the Line. Just undo the confusion spell, Selima!" As she spoke, she wondered why Selima hadn't thought of it.

"No, Selima," said Geradin. "Don't. We have a surprise for the Dark Priestess I'd rather not spoil."

"Oh," said Allonna. She felt her face heat. "I forgot."

Darilom took the sword from Geradin and stepped back.

Geradin stepped forward and lifted the sword and scabbard from Aumekor's grave. "Only with the sword of...my father can the Dark Priestess be killed." He drew the sword and held it up over his head. The finely crafted steel blade seemed to glow in the morning sunlight. "I plan to use it for that very purpose."

◆ ◆ ◆

Ezpetti held out the stick, and Allonna cast a light spell and attached the ball of light to the end. Ezpetti lifted it up. "Thank you. This is much better than a torch."

"You're welcome." Allonna did the same for Serilyon, Biyeskalya, and Holoran. Geradin and the two Protectors would rely on the lights of others, keeping their hands free in case they encountered an enemy. Allonna did not need a stick for her own light: she merely had it float above her head. Selima, of course, created her own light spell.

"I want one," said Hope. "Please, Allonna?"

Allonna found a small stick and attached a tiny ball of light at the end. Hope took it and began waving it around and giggling.

"Are we ready?" asked Geradin.

"One moment," said Allonna. She strengthened the layers of wards around the wagon and horses. No raider would get through to steal them, but the wards would fade within two days. If no one returned before then, the horses would go free. "Done."

Geradin nodded to Ezpetti, and she led the party into the cave. Although the cave passage was narrow, they had not gone fifteen paces before the cave roof arched up to three times the height of a man.

"I used to have to stoop to get through here." Ezpetti's voice echoed. "The earthquake must have collapsed the ceiling."

"We're lucky Kairith came by this route," Allonna said. "We'd still be pulling rocks out, otherwise."

"What I find interesting," said Selima, "is that he came by any route at all."

◆ ◆ ◆

Allonna had lost count of the number of branching passages they had gone through. There seemed to be no order to it: sometimes they took one to the left, sometimes to the right, sometimes one of several in the middle. Some passages were high enough that Holoran could walk through without fear of hitting his head; one almost required slithering on one's belly. Holoran had nearly gotten stuck in that one.

"It would be easy to get lost in here," she said to Ezpetti as they reached another four-way fork. "How do you find the way?"

"I have been through here often enough that it is familiar,

but I should have explained in case we get separated. Hope, show Allonna how we go through the caves."

Hope went to the beginning of one of the passages and pointed her light at a spot a few palmwidths off the cave floor on the right side. There were two crossed lines crudely carved in the stone wall. "X is for no, arrow is for outside," said Hope. She went to another passage and shone her light on an arrow carved in stone, pointing out from the passage. Hope went to the passage they had just come from, and there was an arrow pointing the way they had come.

"Who put those markings there?" asked Allonna.

"The first person to make it all the way through and return," said Ezpetti. "During the days of Zerul, slaves would sometimes flee into these caves rather than face his wrath, and it was always assumed they got lost and died. Then one day a slave returned with the news that there was an exit. The secret was passed down from generation to generation, but shared only with those in the most dire need of escape."

"Why did you need to escape?" asked Allonna.

Ezpetti did not reply for a moment. "It is best forgotten."

Chapter Fifty-Nine

Geradin

The unfamiliar sword felt wrong at Geradin's hip. And if it felt wrong there, it would feel more wrong in his hands during a fight. He should have taken the time to practice with it before entering the cave. He was making mistakes, and he couldn't afford to. For a moment he wondered whether it would cause the others to lose confidence in his leadership if he stopped to practice.

"Ezpetti," he said, "is there someplace fairly wide along the way?"

"There's a large cavern just before we cross into the mine tunnels."

"Unless there's a problem, we'll stop there for a bit."

"It's a good place to rest," she said. "There's fresh water."

The cave passage was wide enough at this point that Selima could come up next to him. She spoke quietly so only he could hear. "What's wrong?"

"Nothing. I just need some time to get the feel of this sword."

Selima nodded. "You're doing well. Aumekor would be proud of you."

"I miss him." The doubts Geradin had been quelling rose in his mind. "Selima, are you certain you're right about the confusion spell? Mek loved being king; he loved the politics and intrigue. He was born to them, I was not."

"I am certain." Her voice was determined. "Now that

Aumekor is dead, the confusion is clearing from my mind. We must confront the Dark Priestess before she realizes that the Heir of the Line of Orcan still lives," said Selima. "I know it may feel wrong for you to think of yourself as the true King of Aud Sapeer, but you must understand you are not betraying Aumekor by claiming the title. It was never his to begin with. Do not doubt yourself—the Dark Priestess will prey on your doubts."

"What if I don't want to be king?" As he said it, Geradin realized it sounded childish.

"That doesn't change who you are. Sometimes we must do things we don't want to."

◆ ◆ ◆

The cavern was more spacious than Geradin had expected. The whole practice yard from back home would have fit inside it with room to spare. Through the middle of the cavern ran a narrow, swift-flowing stream that ended in a pool at the bottom of the cave.

"Best to take water from the stream," said Ezpetti. "The pond water does not taste good."

Geradin turned to Darilom. "You and I both have new swords. What do you say we spar a bit to get the feel of them?"

"Of course, Your Majesty." Darilom drew the sword Geradin had given him and tilted the blade back and forth as if looking for flaws in its workmanship. "Though in my country a man does not truly claim a sword as his own until he has bathed it in the blood of an enemy."

"You may keep to your tradition," Geradin said. "But in my country we have another tradition I hope you will follow."

"What is that?"

Geradin drew his sword and held it in the ready position. "Don't get the king's blood on your sword."

The routine of sparring helped Geradin to relax. He pushed away all thoughts of kingship and prophecy, and focused on the movement of the swords. This new blade was three thumbwidths longer, which gave him a little more reach, but it was heavier, which made it slightly more difficult to suddenly change direction. And the balance was different, so he had to work to find the most effective parrying range.

Soon the movement felt more natural, and the sword flowed easily to wherever Geradin wanted it. He still missed the ability to cut through anything that his old sword had when the enchantment still worked, but this sword would serve very well as a replacement.

◆ ◆ ◆

"Once we enter the mine tunnels," said Ezpetti, "do not cast any spells unless you must. I do not know exactly where the tunnels cross under the walls of the Palace of Zerul, but after that the Dark Priestess is sure to detect any spells."

"Understood," said Selima.

"How likely are we to encounter other people down here?" asked Geradin.

"This part of the mine was abandoned long ago," said Ezpetti.

Geradin looked around the cavern. Other than the passage through which they had entered, he did not see a way out. "Where is the entrance to the mines?"

Ezpetti pointed into the pond. "There."

He should have realized that the water flowing into the pond had to exit somewhere. "How deep down?" he asked, unable to see anything in the water.

"Not very deep. The passage is actually quite large, and it only takes a few moments to get to the pond on the other side. But there's a grating across it that is bolted on the other side. So we'll have to send Hope through to unbolt it."

Frowning, Geradin said, "How do people get through if they don't have a child small enough to go through the grating?"

"Someone from the slaves' quarters tries to come every few

days to see if anyone is waiting, but it is best not to rely on that." Ezpetti turned to Hope and said, "It's time to go through the water and open the bolt."

Hope scrunched her nose. "The water is icky."

"Yes, but I'm sure Auntie Rala will have a treat for you when we see her."

Looking at the small light on the stick she was carrying, Hope held it out to Allonna. "Can you hold this for me?"

"Of course." Allonna took it. "I'll give it back to you after."

Hope waded into the water, took a deep breath, and dived under.

"Auntie Rala?" asked Selima.

"She's not really Hope's aunt," said Ezpetti. "She's one of the head cooks in the palace—and one of the slaves knowing the secret of these tunnels."

Geradin watched the water, waiting for Hope to reappear. Was it supposed to take this long? He glanced at Ezpetti, who was also watching the water, but she did not seem concerned yet.

A head bobbed up. "All done," said Hope.

"Good girl," said Ezpetti. "Thank you."

"Allow me to go first, Your Majesty," said Darilom, "to ensure it is safe on the other side."

Geradin nodded, and Darilom waded quickly into the pond and then dived under.

"He's quite the eager young Protector," said Otunvol. "Reminds me of another—can't quite recall the name, though."

"Me?" said Geradin. "I was never that annoying."

Otunvol grinned and bowed low. "Whatever Your Majesty says, Your Majesty."

Darilom's head reappeared above the surface. "I've opened the grate, Your Majesty. The other side is clear."

◆ ◆ ◆

The mine tunnels were hewn from stone. Brushing his

fingers over the hard surface, Geradin was reminded of the Inner Keep. With a start, he realized that the Keep belonged to him now, along with various lands throughout the Kingdom of Aud Sapeer. "I'd give it all up to have Mek back," he said to himself.

"What was that?" asked Selima.

"Nothing," he said. "Just reminded me of—"

"Stop," Selima said. "There is mancy ahead."

Everyone stopped walking.

"There, where the tunnel forks," said Selima. "It's delicate. Can you see it, Allonna?"

"Yes. Do you know what kind of spell it is?"

"I think it's the remains of a very powerful spell." Selima took a few paces forward until she was a pace from the fork. "It feels ancient."

"How can you tell?" asked Allonna. She moved up next to Selima.

"Come back here," said Geradin. He felt like something bad was about to happen, though he could not identify why. "It might be dangerous."

"The spell is spent," said Selima. "This is like an echo of the original mancy. It must have been—"

"I meant," said Geradin, "there may be danger ahead." He turned to Ezpetti. "Which fork is the correct one?"

"The left, although the right one joins up again after wandering a bit," she said.

"Biyeskalya, Serilyon, scout ahead."

Allonna and Selima stepped aback, while the two Aldamundians moved forward. Serilyon took the tunnel on the right, while Biyeskalya went to the left.

Did the Dark Priestess somehow know they were coming? "Is there anything different about the tunnels this time?" he asked Ezpetti.

"Not that I can—"

"Quiet," said Otunvol. He moved up close to Geradin and whispered, "I think I heard something behind us."

"Go," said Geradin. Perhaps the feeling of something wrong was because he had heard something behind them without realizing it.

Otunvol borrowed Ezpetti's light and began to walk, sword drawn, back into the tunnel behind them. Darilom drew his sword and stood at the ready.

Geradin thought over the tactical situation. The mine tunnels were narrow enough that two men standing side by side could probably hold back a far larger force for some time, especially two men as skilled as Darilom and Otunvol. Should there be someone waiting to attack from behind, that would give the rest of the party a chance to escape—if rushing to confront the Dark Priestess could be considered an escape.

"Darilom, go with him," said Geradin.

Darilom nodded and ran a few paces to catch up with Otunvol. The two of them proceeded slowly down the passageway. They were near one of the openings to a narrow side passage about twenty paces away when Otunvol suddenly reached out and grabbed someone out of the passage.

It was a woman. Otunvol brought his sword up by the woman's throat and said something Geradin couldn't hear.

"Auntie Rala!" Hope held out her arms and dashed down the tunnel toward the woman and the two Protectors.

"Hope! Come back," said Ezpetti as she ran after her daughter.

Relief swept over Geradin. It was only the cook. She had probably been on her way to check if anyone was in the caves, and then had hidden when she heard them coming.

The ground moved with a tremor so slight Geradin wasn't even sure he had felt it. "Did you—"

The next tremor almost made him lose his footing. Then something hit hard on his helmet and he fell to his hands and knees. Rocks fell around him, some as big as his head. His vision blurred, but he recognized Allonna lying on the ground. He crawled to protect her, shielding her head with his body. There was blood on her face. Selima lay next to her, and he stretched out an arm to protect her head, too.

"Help," he said. His mouth tasted of blood; he must have bitten his tongue. Rocks continued to bang off his armor for a few more moments, then they stopped. He looked down at Allonna. He couldn't tell if she was breathing.

Holoran's voice came from behind him. "Get...them...out."

Geradin turned to look. Holoran's light had fallen to the ground, but it was enough that Geradin could see the strained look on the big man's face. The ceiling of the tunnel had begun to collapse, and a massive slab of stone had come down, stopping only a few palmwidths from crushing Geradin, Allonna and Selima. Holoran squatted beneath the slab, his arms holding it up.

"I...can't...much...longer," said Holoran through gritted teeth.

Geradin crawled forward, dragging Allonna toward the fork in the tunnel. Except there wasn't a fork any more: the entrance to the right passageway had collapsed. He pulled her toward the left.

Biyeskalya ran down the left passage toward him. "What happened?"

"Get Selima," said Geradin.

She ran past him and dragged Selima out from under the slab.

Geradin tried to stand but the ground seemed too unsteady under his feet. "Find something to hold up the slab," he said to Biyeskalya. "Hold on, Holoran."

"There be nothing big enough," said Biyeskalya.

"Find something." Geradin checked Allonna's pulse. She was alive. He moved to Selima, who was alive as well. "Wake up, Selima!" She would have a spell to hold the slab so Holoran could get out. "Wake up!" He shook her shoulders.

Biyeskalya pulled him back. "You'll hurt her."

"She has to wake up," said Geradin.

"Geradin," said Holoran, "I...am...done. Thank...you. Tell...Telani..."

The slab fell forward. The sides of the tunnel collapsed inward. Then there was silence.

Propping himself up himself up against the wall, Geradin tried to clear his mind. Holoran was dead. The others had been behind Holoran, except for Serilyon in the collapsed tunnel to the right.

He looked down at the unconscious forms of Allonna and Selima. Biyeskalya was wrapping a bandage onto Allonna's head.

There were only four of them left.

Chapter Sixty

Allonna

The throbbing in Allonna's head was the first thing she noticed. She was lying on a hard surface; she tried to think what it could be. She groaned and raised a hand to the side of her head and found a cloth tied on.

"Allonna," said a woman's voice. "Can you hear me?"

She knew that voice, but it took a moment to recognize who it belonged to. "You can't have him," said Allonna.

"Listen to me, Allonna," said Biyeskalya. "Be you able to open your eyes?"

Allonna thought for a moment. She should be able to do that. Her eyelids opened and she saw two Biyeskalyas peering at her. That couldn't be right. "I'm dreaming. I'm tired."

"No, you need wake up. Geradin, come help keep her awake."

"Lonna," he said. There were two of him, too. "You've hurt your head. We need you to stay awake."

"I'm awake." Allonna notice blood on Geradin's face. "What happened?"

"The tunnel collapsed. You don't remember?"

She began to shake her head, but it hurt to move. "No."

"Can you use magic?"

Allonna frowned. "I'm an omnimancer."

"I mean, are you awake enough that you can try to heal Selima?"

"Selima's hurt?" After she said it, she realized it was a stupid question. Why would he want her to heal Selima if Selima wasn't hurt? Why wasn't Selima healing *her* if Selima wasn't hurt? "I can try." She tried to sit up, but her arms felt wobbly. "Help me up. Let me see her."

Geradin lifted her gently so she was sitting up, supported by his arm and shoulder. Her double vision faded. Selima lay on the ground. Biyeskalya dabbed a cloth on Selima's face, wiping away still-wet blood.

"Be you certain it be wise?" asked Biyeskalya. "What if the Dark Priestess detect the magic?"

"It's a risk," said Geradin, "but we need Selima."

Struggling to focus her mind, Allonna reached out with her power to sense what was wrong with Selima. She felt the magic flow through her, but she couldn't sense anything. She concentrated harder, trying to see the flows of power, but she couldn't. Her throat tightened. "I can't see magic. I can't see it. I can't heal her. What's wrong with me?"

"Calm down, Lonna," said Geradin. "You're still confused. It will pass. We can try again later."

Selima stirred and moaned.

"Selima," said Biyeskalya, "be you able to hear me?"

"What happened?" asked Selima.

"The tunnel collapse. Your head be injured," said Biyeskalya.

Raising a palm to her forehead, Selima asked, "Is Geradin all right?"

"I'm fine," said Geradin.

Selima's eyes snapped open. "No, you're not. You have a head injury. Lie down at once."

"I was dizzy for a bit, but I had a helmet on. From now on, I'm making all my omnimancers wear helmets."

"Lie down," Selima said as she sat up.

"You've got a head injury, too," said Geradin.

"I'm healing mine," she said. She looked at Allonna. "Why didn't you heal him?"

Allonna's eyes filled with tears. "I can't see magic."

"It happens sometimes. It should pass soon," said Selima.

"Lie down, Geradin. You, too, Allonna."

Relieved that her blindness to mancy wasn't permanent, Allonna lay down next to Geradin. Suddenly she said, "Where are the others?"

"Holoran saved us," said Geradin. "But he's dead. The others were farther back, so they're either trapped or dead."

"Hush," said Selima. She put her hand to Geradin's forehead.

A distant bell began to toll.

"I hope that's a time signal," said Biyeskalya.

"It's not," said Selima. "Geradin, you can sit up now." She clapped her hand to Allonna's head. "We have little time."

The pain washed away from Allonna and her mind began to clear.

Selima removed her hand. "That's the best I can do for now. You'll need to rest later."

Allonna reached out with her magic, but sensed nothing. "I still can't see magic."

"You'll have to wait for that to fix itself." said Selima. "If we're lucky, the Dark Priestess only knows that someone used unrecognized magic within the borders of the palace. But she may know where we are, and worse, she may know it was me. We must move from here."

Geradin stood, then stooped down to help Allonna up. "Then let's move."

◆ ◆ ◆

Geradin grunted in frustration. "Another dead end."

"We must have missed a tunnel," said Selima. "They can't all be dead ends."

"It must have collapsed," said Geradin. "It may be behind one of those piles of rubble we passed."

"Quiet," said Biyeskalya. "I hear something."

They all stood still. Allonna listened carefully. Distant, muffled voices seemed to be carrying on several conversations. She also noticed the smell of roasting meat and baking bread.

"Do you smell that?"

"The kitchen," said Geradin. "It must be nearby."

Selima raised her floating light toward the ceiling. A rectangular wooden hatch, about two paces by one pace in size, was fastened into the stone. At one of the short ends, a metal hook gleamed.

Geradin turned to Biyeskalya. "If I lift you, can you grab it?"

She nodded.

Allonna spotted a long wooden pole lying against the tunnel wall. It also had a hook at one end. "Or we could just use this." She reached down, picked it up, and handed it to Geradin.

"This must be what the slaves use." Geradin lifted it up and used it to pull the hatch open. A ladder slid down partway. Geradin unfolded it the rest of the way and it rested solidly on the ground.

Biyeskalya went first, followed by Selima and Allonna. Geradin came last. Allonna watched as he used a rope attached to the bottom of the ladder to pull it up behind them, closing the hatch.

"I be at the top," said Biyeskalya quietly. "There be a hatch here."

The voices conversing above them drifted into silence.

"They're asleep," said Selima. "Go."

Biyeskalya pushed open the hatch. She got out, turned and helped Selima and then Allonna to climb out into a cramped storage room, hardly tall enough to crawl in. Allonna noticed light coming from around a door, so she pushed it open and crawled out into the kitchen. The hatch had opened up inside a cupboard.

The kitchen looked not much different from the kitchens back at the Keep in Aud Sapeer, except for the ten or more women lying asleep on the floor.

Selima emerged from the cupboard, followed by Biyeskalya and Geradin.

"We haven't much time until someone comes," Selima said. "Allonna, can you see mancy yet? The walls of this place drip with it."

Allonna focused her mind, but she saw nothing. "No."

"Then we have no choice. Wear these." Selima removed three rings, a bracelet and a necklace. "They will boost the amount of power you can use safely so you can match me."

Taking them and putting them on, Allonna said, "Don't you need them?"

"Remember when the Tester came to your village, and tried to draw power out of you?"

Allonna's mind whirled back to the Testing she had failed because she had held too tightly to her power. "Yes."

"What I am about to do will be like that, but you must let your power flow to me. Let me take as much as I want, until it starts to hurt. You must not let yourself flare out or the connection will be severed."

Allonna nodded.

"There is also the chance that I will be unable to release your power to you after the battle is done, and you will never have power to work mancy again. That is why this spell is used only in dire need."

Being blind to magic was bad enough. To know she might lose all her power forever was frightening, but it was the only way she could help protect Geradin. "I understand," said Allonna. "It must be done."

"If the Dark Priestess realized we were doing this, you would be a target. So you cannot come with us."

"What? You can't leave me behind again," said Allonna.

"We can't leave her here," said Geradin. "She'll be discovered."

"Go back into the mine," said Biyeskalya. "Once the battle begins up here, it be safe enough down there."

"Please don't leave me," said Allonna.

Geradin stepped to her and kissed her. "I want you safe. Please, stay behind so I can fight without fearing for your safety."

She clung to him for a moment, then said, "I will stay." She blinked back the tears.

"Take this as well, Allonna," said Selima, handing her a patterned silk scarf. "I wasn't sure why I brought it along after Aumekor died, but Tobalich put so much effort into running it down to us I felt it must have some use. I will wear the necklace, so you may follow the course of the battle."

◆ ◆ ◆

Allonna sat on a step of the ladder and wiped her tears before tying the scarf over her eyes and ears. For a moment, she saw nothing but her light shining through the cloth. Her vision faded to black, and as it returned, she saw Biyeskalya running ahead of her down a hallway, sword at the ready.

She felt magical power flow out of her, and Selima's right hand appeared in her vision, throwing a red ball of light past Biyeskalya into the wooden door ahead. The door shattered, revealing some surprised servants.

"Ignore them," said Selima, and the servants began falling to the ground.

Continuing forward, Biyeskalya leapt over the falling bodies.

Where was Geradin? Allonna decided he must be behind Selima. Biyeskalya was risking her life to protect Geradin by making certain she encountered any danger first. Did she truly believe that the prophecy she would bear Geradin's child protected her from being killed?

The door ahead opened, and a soldier stepped through. A shining blue ward appeared across the doorway behind him as he tried to draw his sword. Biyeskalya bore down on him and took off his head before he had a chance to shout.

"Turn right," said Selima.

The surge of power when Selima cast the ward reminded Allonna of the link between them. She forced herself to relax and let the power flow. If she could keep Geradin safe she would be happy, even if she lost the use of her powers when it was done.

Everything suddenly made sense. If she lost her powers, she would no longer be an omnimancer. If that happened, she would not have the status of a noble. And while a king might marry a mere noble instead of a princess, Geradin would not be allowed to marry a commoner. The prophet had foreseen it all.

Allonna's eyes filled with tears, yet her vision remained perfectly clear.

"Stop," said Selima.

Biyeskalya stopped.

"Through this wall here," said Selima. "Stay back." A surge of power left Allonna as a ball of yellow flame shot from Selima's hand and tore open a hole in the wall. Off to the right, Allonna could barely see Geradin standing there. She turned her head to look at him, but she couldn't—Selima was still looking through the hole into the large room beyond. Biyeskalya charged through the hole, and Selima followed.

Tens of Soulless were in the room. Allonna recognized scorpiks, ursiks and serpiks among others. They charged toward Biyeskalya, who shouted something incomprehensible.

Selima's hands swept forward, and the blue shining surface of a ward appeared between Biyeskalya and the Soulless. Then the color shifted up into violet and then disappeared except for a blurred glow.

"Thank you for teaching me this one, Allonna," said Selima. The ward began to shrink, and the Soulless began tearing at each other in panic as they were crushed against each other.

"You're welcome," said Allonna, before remembering Selima couldn't hear her.

Biyeskalya ran around the remains of the Soulless, while Selima sent a blast of yellow fire at the doors ahead. The doors shattered and fell away.

"Wait," said Selima, but Biyeskalya charged into the hole—and bounced back into the room, landing on the floor.

"It's warded," said Selima. She stretched out her hand toward the door. From the repeated surges of power pulled from her, Allonna knew Selima was undoing layers of wards.

A man in armor stood in the room beyond the hole, looking out. "I told your Highness that she would not give up," he said. He grinned. "Nice to see you again, Selima."

When Selima spoke, her voice was filled with hate. "Veratur."

Chapter Sixty-One

Geradin

Geradin suppressed the anger that sprang up when Selima identified the man who had killed his father. It did not matter who the man in the black armor was, all that mattered was that he stood in the way of killing the Dark Priestess. Anger would only distract Geradin from the fight, once Selima brought down the wards blocking the doorway.

Interrupting her muttering, Selima said, "For sixteen years I've hoped to find you. It is time you were paid for your treachery."

Veratur smiled. "Oh, I've already been paid quite handsomely, thank you. But aren't you going to introduce me to your companions?" Veratur furrowed his brow. "The young lady cannot be a Protector of the Line, not unless Wyran's changed a lot since I knew him. She led the way in here, so my guess is she's the Guide." He turned his eyes to Geradin. "Now *he* looks like a Protector. In truth, he looks enough like Balunor that I'd wager this is his son. But aren't there supposed to be four of you? Who could be missing?"

Putting an end to the traitor's chatter would be a welcome relief, Geradin decided. He mentally pushed aside the question of whether Veratur should recognize him as Balunor's son if he was really King Ordil's. Doubts were for after the fight.

"Be ready for my signal," said Selima. "I'll have the wards down soon."

Shaking his head, Veratur said, "You didn't come all this way and forget to bring the Heir of the Line? How careless of you!"

Veratur's remarks were obviously meant to be a distraction. But a distraction from what? Geradin whirled to look behind them. Twenty Soulless had entered the hall, but they were prevented from approaching by a ward Selima must have cast earlier. More Soulless came in through the doors at the far end.

"Why, the only thing more careless would be..." Veratur paused as if searching for an idea. "...letting the Heir of the Line *die*."

"Now," said Selima.

Geradin turned back toward Veratur. Biyeskalya was already charging forward, and Veratur drew his sword to meet hers.

"He's personally warded against magic," said Selima. "Kill him while I concentrate on the Dark Priestess."

Moving toward Veratur and Biyeskalya, Geradin said, "He can't fight us on two fronts."

Biyeskalya nodded and, after parrying Veratur's blow, she dove through the door and scrambled to her feet. Rather than turn his back on either of them, Veratur retreated to the side, clearing the doorway for Geradin and Selima.

At the far end of the large room were rows of Soulless, perhaps two hundred of the creatures in all. They blocked the way to a wide stairway leading up to a platform, where a woman in a crimson dress stood in front of an ornate, gold-encrusted throne. She was too distant for Geradin to get a good look at her face, but she wore a black crown—a band with large spikes rising from it.

Geradin turned his attention to the immediate threat. He and Biyeskalya advanced toward Veratur, who continued backing toward the wall to the right of the entrance.

"That's Ordil's sword," said Veratur, staring at the sword Geradin held. "But you aren't Ordil's son." Veratur turned and ran toward the mass of Soulless at the end of the room.

Geradin and Biyeskalya gave chase. She had been closer to begin with, but Geradin was catching up when Selima yelled,

"Stop!"

He tried to stop, but his momentum carried him forward and he felt the shock as he slammed into a ward just as the stone floor exploded beneath Biyeskalya. He began to fall backwards as Biyeskalya was thrown into the air. Shards of stone flared as they smashed against the ward that now protected Geradin.

After crashing to the ground, Geradin scrambled to his feet. Biyeskalya lay facedown, ten paces away from the jagged hole in the floor. Her legs were askew, like those of a toy doll cast carelessly aside, and Geradin realized they were broken, either from the blast itself or from the impact as she fell. She did not move.

Veratur had lured them into a trap, and only Selima's ward and the fact that he had been two paces behind Biyeskalya had saved Geradin. But now Veratur himself was entrapped: no longer running, he pressed against the ward that stopped him despite the pain it must be causing. "Let me in, Your Highness!"

"Kill him and I will," said the Dark Priestess. Her voice was a harsh whisper, yet Geradin could hear it as if her mouth were next to his ear—both ears.

A series of explosions erupted from the floor ahead and to both sides of Geradin. He flinched, but the stationary ward protecting him did its job.

Debris pelted Veratur from behind and he yelped, but seemed otherwise unharmed.

"I've cleared the area around you," said Selima. "Are you ready?"

"Yes," said Geradin.

With a puff of imploding air, the ward separating him from Veratur went down. Veratur turned to face him, sword up in the ready position. The sword looked familiar, and Geradin realized it was one of the High Protectors' swords.

"Like my sword?" asked Veratur. "Every day, we give it to a prisoner to hold. It always glowed in their hands. I'm sure you would have recognized that glow, *Protector*."

Geradin and Veratur circled each other.

"And then three days ago when we tested it, there was no glow. We tried several prisoners. No glow. I saw it happen once before—on the day you were born, in fact—and I knew what it meant even before Her Highness received confirmation."

Geradin feinted, and Veratur reacted with surprising speed. The traitor was not as fast as Darilom, though, and while it might take some effort, Geradin was certain he could win.

"I don't know what you're trying to prove, *Protector*," said Veratur. "You failed to keep the Heir alive. Coming here only ensures your death."

Clearing his mind, Geradin focused on the fight. He attacked with a rapid thrust which was easily parried, then followed with a continuous barrage of attacks that kept Veratur on the defensive. Veratur slowly backed toward the corner formed by the left wall and the Dark Priestess's ward.

"Even if you kill me, it does not erase your failure," Veratur said between huffs of breath.

There is nothing but the fight.

One of Veratur's parries came slightly late, and Geradin dipped his sword just enough to avoid it. He had a clear path. The tip of Geradin's sword found the joint between breastplate and right pauldron, and he pushed forward with all his strength, driving it into the shoulder of Veratur's sword arm.

Veratur grunted in pain. "Stop. I yield." He lowered his sword, then dropped it to clatter on the stone floor. With his left hand he removed his helmet.

Geradin hesitated, his sword still impaling Veratur's shoulder, pinning him to the wall. Now that he could see the man's face more clearly, he noticed a family resemblance to Darilom. No wonder Darilom had been so eager to prove himself as a Protector—he wanted to remove the stain of Veratur from his family's honor.

"Finish him," said Selima. "The traitor has been condemned to death."

"I can help you," whispered Veratur. "I know her defenses. I once swore an oath to defend the Heir of the Line. I betrayed that oath, but let me redeem it now, I beg you."

Again the voice of the Dark Priestess sounded like it came from right next to Geradin's ears. "Shut your mouth, traitor."

"Talk," said Geradin, "and don't lie to me."

"I'm the only Knight of the Dark God left here," said Veratur. "The rest are fighting in Bargas."

"Tell me something useful," said Geradin.

"She can summon them back in an instant," Veratur said. "Did you know that?"

If it was true, getting to the Dark Priestess would be even more difficult than Geradin had imagined. Unwilling to show that he hadn't known, Geradin said, "What else have you got?"

"The armor of the Knights of the Dark God has a flaw you can exploit. Take a look at this helmet." Veratur lightly tossed his helmet and Geradin caught it with his left hand. "See the joint at the top?"

Geradin's eyes flickered to the helmet. Veratur's gauntleted right hand smacked the middle of the blade of Geradin's sword. Because the tip was still between Veratur's pauldron and breastplate, the leverage gave Veratur's blow sufficient force to tear the hilt from Geradin's grip. The sword came free and fell to the floor. Veratur had drawn a dagger with his left hand, and as soon as the sword was clear he leapt forward. Geradin backed away, barely avoiding a knife-thrust aimed at the bottom edge of his breastplate. Veratur reversed course and grabbed his own sword from the floor, moving quickly enough to interpose himself between Geradin and his sword.

"You're as gullible as your father," said Veratur.

Geradin backed away, and found himself stopped by a ward that seemed to flicker in and out of existence behind him in less than a heartbeat. "Selima?"

"I'm taking down her wards as fast as she can put them up," said Selima, her voice filled with frustration. "But I can't get a spell in to help you."

Veratur laughed. "I guess it's just between us two, then. I

wonder who's the better swordsman: me, with a sword, or you, without?" He approached Geradin cautiously.

When Veratur was close enough to strike, Geradin jumped forward, parrying Veratur's blow with his left forearm and grabbing Veratur's wrist with his right hand. Veratur tried to twist free, but Geradin grabbed the blade close to the hilt using his left gauntlet, and began prying the sword free.

At the moment the sword came loose, Geradin felt a sharp pain in his abdomen, and looked down to see a dagger jutting out from beneath his breastplate. He let go of Veratur's wrist and grabbed the hilt of the sword. Letting go of the blade with his left hand, he swung the sword backhand and sliced through Veratur's neck, severing his head from his body.

Veratur's body fell to its knees and then toppled to the ground.

Geradin looked at the dagger protruding from his waist. Best to leave it in, partially sealing the wound, until Selima would have a chance to heal him.

Selima cried out in pain.

"Selima?" said Geradin.

"I'm fine," she said. She spoke rapidly, and her voice was strangely high-pitched. "But you must get to the Dark Priestess as soon as possible. I'm bringing down the wards between you faster than she can replace them."

"Right," he said. He trotted toward the Dark Priestess, hearing the pops of wards going down before him.

"You can't be doing that," whispered the voice of the Dark Priestess. "You can't have that much power."

Selima's laugh seemed almost girlish. "Who's going to stop me?"

Chapter Sixty-Two

Allonna

Through Selima's eyes, Allonna saw Veratur stab Geradin before Geradin killed him.

"Heal him," said Allonna, wishing again that Selima could hear her. "Heal him!"

The view wobbled and Allonna heard Selima gasp. After a moment, the steady stream of power being drawn from Allonna began to increase. Selima must have activated a short-term artifact to increase the power she could use.

"Selima?" said Geradin.

Selima's voice sounded strange as she replied. It was high pitched, and she spoke more quickly than normal. Allonna remembered hearing tales of mancers in the Age of Light who could speed people up so they could run faster than a horse. If Selima had found an artifact to do that, it would explain why her voice was fast and why she was now drawing more power.

Geradin moved toward the mass of Soulless blocking the path to the Dark Priestess.

"Wait," said Allonna. "You have to heal him first, Selima." Had Selima not noticed the dagger because she was activating the speed artifact?

"You can't be doing that." The voice of the Dark Priestess caused the hairs to rise on Allonna's neck. "You can't have that much power."

The power Selima was drawing kept increasing. Allonna felt

it flow from her and realized this was more power than she had ever used before. Her previous peak had come when she crushed the dragon that killed Aumekor. Yet because of the artifacts Selima had given her the power flow felt like less than a quarter of that.

Selima laughed. "Who's going to stop me?"

"You have a reservoir," said the Dark Priestess. She motioned, and doors opened in the walls on both sides of the room. "The reservoir must be within the palace. Find and kill the fourth human. In fact, kill any humans you find, just to be sure."

The Soulless flooded out of the doors, leaving the way clear between Geradin and the Dark Priestess.

Allonna felt her heart pounding within her. The Soulless were looking for her.

"Stay where you are, Allonna," said Selima quietly. "It will take them a while to find you, and we will have won or lost by then."

The Dark Priestess walked to a small table next to the throne. She reached into a bowl on the table and pulled out a handful of whitish, curved objects more than a palmwidth long, and thick as two fingers. She cast the objects on the steps before her, and as each one hit, a man in black armor suddenly appeared. They were in various poses, as if summoned out of the middle of a battle—which, after a moment's reflection, Allonna decided must be the case. Some of them lost their balance and fell to the ground. One of them appeared already lying on the ground, his head separated from his body by half a pace.

"So Veratur told the truth about that," said Geradin.

"Why did you do that, Your Highness?" asked one of the knights. "The Protectors of the Line were leading a final charge against us. Victory was within our—"

"Fool," said the Dark Priestess, "I'm under attack." She reached for another handful of the objects.

Selima had been following behind Geradin, and was close

enough that Allonna could now see the objects were large dragon's teeth. The Dark Priestess cast them on the steps, summoning more of the Knights of the Dark God. And Geradin kept advancing, as if he cared not that he was outnumbered ten to one and growing worse. If he had been wielding his enchanted sword, she would have thought he had a chance, but without it he could not hope to defeat so many.

Then she realized he had the wrong sword. The sword of his father had been left behind after Veratur had knocked it away, and Geradin was holding Veratur's sword. And that sword was one of the enchanted ones.

"Undo the confusion spell, Selima," Allonna almost shouted. With the confusion spell gone, the sword should realize the Heir of the Line lived and glow again. Surprise was gone; there was no need to keep the secret any more. "Undo it. If only you could hear me."

Selima's draw on Allonna's power doubled almost instantly, and Allonna sucked in a breath at the shock of it.

"Pull back, Geradin," said Selima.

He stopped, then slowly walked backward.

The Dark Priestess cast a third handful of dragon's teeth onto the steps, then returned to her place in front of the throne. As one of the knights shouted orders, they formed into a semicircle and began to advance toward Geradin.

A violet light appeared between the two knights in the middle of the formation, and suddenly the formation was split in two. The knights were swept aside, half to the right, half to the left, where most of them were pinned to the walls. A few were forced out of the open doors.

"That will hold them until I can undo the wards that prevent me from killing them now," said Selima. "You may proceed, Geradin."

He began moving forward again.

"You realize this is all for nothing," said the Dark Priestess. "It matters not how much power you wield, you cannot get around the prophecies."

"Then why do you resist," asked Selima, "if we cannot do you harm?"

"Spare me your childish questions. Obviously the prophets foresaw my resistance," said the Dark Priestess, "and that I did not come to harm because of it. Only the Heir of the Line of Orcan can kill me, and the Heir of the Line is dead."

Selima's high-pitched laugh seemed out of place. "How can you be certain?"

"Because I have a prophet in my dungeon." The Dark Priestess grinned. "And he's bound under magic oath to only speak the truth. Five days ago, he prophesied that the last of Orcan's line would die before reaching me. Then the accursed swords of the Protectors stopped glowing, and yesterday Kairith, the Demigod of Death, confirmed to me personally that the last of Orcan's line was dead, and his spirit was in Velia."

Geradin stopped for a moment, then continued forward.

"Give up, Selima. Turn back, and I'll withdraw my armies for now. I swear not to invade again until after you have died a natural death. It is prophesied I will rule all the world, but I can be patient, now. Stop and you can live out your life in peace with those you love."

"If I pose no threat to you," said Selima, "why make such an offer?"

The Dark Priestess sighed and fingered a black amulet hanging from her neck. "Because I'd rather not use the amulet Zerul gave me. I can only use it once without him recharging it, and I'm not certain when he'll be back."

"Spare me your childish bluffs," said Selima. "My plan has worked perfectly. The true Heir of the Line is approaching to kill you now."

The Dark Priestess burst into laughter. She looked at Geradin. "Did she hand you a sword and tell you that you were the true King of Aud Sapeer, Heir of the Line of Orcan? Let me guess: she said she switched you for another child, and you believed her? It's a children's fable—the prince and the common child swapped for each other—and it goes back two thousand years at least. Veratur knew the moment he saw you that you were not King Ordil's child."

"Selima cast a confusion spell," said Geradin. "It's why no one noticed."

"A confusion spell?" The Dark Priestess raised an eyebrow and looked at Selima. "That's a nice touch. But even with a reservoir as powerful as the one you have now, it's doubtful you could fool the prophets, and impossible that you could confuse a demigod." She looked back at Geradin. "I'm afraid Selima's been lying to you, child. You are not the Heir of the Line, and your only hope of living through this is to turn back. I'll even place you on the throne in Aud Sapeer if that's what you want, since the seat is vacant now."

Allonna gasped. She didn't want to believe the Dark Priestess, but the logic was hard to deny.

"If you knew me at all, you'd know I don't even want the stupid throne," said Geradin. "But even if I did, I have no reason to trust you over Selima."

"I warned you she'd prey on your doubts," said Selima.

"It's simple enough," said the Dark Priestess. "If Selima did actually perform such an incredibly powerful spell, she can undo it with but a thought. There's nothing to be gained by the confusion any longer, so she can prove she's telling the truth by undoing it. What do you say, Selima?"

"I did not cast the spell on my own; I triggered an artifact made by the Gods of Light," said Selima. "That is why it could affect even a demigod. But I cannot undo it without the artifact, which is back in my study in the Keep."

"That's rather convenient," said the Dark Priestess. "I know if *I* were going out to face an opponent as formidable as, well, me, I would take such a powerful artifact along with me." She removed the amulet from her neck. "Unfortunately, I suppose I'll have to use this. But it seems such a waste, because no matter what lies you tell, you cannot win. Do you know what the prophet prophesied this morning? 'The Princess of

Necromancy will not be killed unless she chooses to give up her life.' And, unfortunately for you, I don't feel like dying today—or ever. It's a true prophecy, and it does not depend on whether there's confusion over switched babies or not."

The Princess of Necromancy? Biyeskalya? Selima must have had the same thought, because her head turned slightly to look out of the corner of her eye at the spot where Biyeskalya had fallen. She wasn't there. Selima's head turned back to face the Dark Priestess. Whatever Biyeskalya was doing, Selima obviously did not want to draw attention to it.

The Dark Priestess held the amulet out. A ball of darkness began to grow, floating in the air before her. "Behold the power of Zerul," she said. "His darkness cannot be resisted."

Chapter Sixty-Three

Geradin

By the time the black globe had expanded to three palmwidths in diameter, Geradin could feel a wind pulling toward it. The globe did not appear to have a surface—it looked like a deep hole with no visible bottom. As the globe continued to expand the wind became stronger, but the Dark Priestess seemed unaffected by it. The fabric of her dress did not even flutter.

Geradin decided it was foolish to stand still, making himself an easy target. He began to move to his right, but found it blocked by a flickering ward. He moved to the left. Another ward blocked him. "Selima? I can't dodge it."

"I'm bringing down the ward as soon as she puts it up, but it's still there for long enough that we can't get out." Selima's voice came from directly behind him, and he turned to find her only a pace away. "I'm sorry, Geradin. I thought we had a chance."

Her apology confirmed Geradin's suspicion that she had been lying. "I understand," he said. She had tried to bluff their way into fulfilling the prophecy. And they had come close.

Behind Selima, to his right, Geradin's eyes were drawn to movement. Biyeskalya had dragged herself to the wall and was now sitting herself up against it. Seeing the way her legs were bent, Geradin winced in sympathy for the pain she must be in. Biyeskalya reached out and picked up the sword that was lying on the ground next to the wall.

Geradin suddenly realized he was carrying the wrong sword. Because Veratur's sword was identical to the enchanted sword Geradin was used to carrying, it had felt natural in his hand. He somehow needed to get out of these wards and over to Biyeskalya to get the right sword, to maintain Selima's bluff.

Biyeskalya looked at him and nodded her head. Then she lifted the sword and closed her eyes.

He turned back to face the Dark Priestess. The ball of darkness had grown to a pace in diameter and was still expanding. Pressing his left shoulder against the ward separating him from Biyeskalya, he steeled himself against the repeated jolts.

Biyeskalya began chanting incomprehensibly, her voice loud enough to carry over the rushing sound of the wind. The rhythm of the ward faltered for a moment, but Geradin still found himself trapped.

"So you know the language of death, girl?" said the Dark Priestess. "The words do little unless you know how to use them."

Now that Biyeskalya had the Dark Priestess's attention, Geradin turned so he could run to her the moment the ward came down.

Biyeskalya opened her eyes. "I be not a mere girl. I be Biyeskalya beh'Denori, Princess of Aldamun, and I be the Princess of Necromancy. And within my womb I carry the next Heir of the Line of Orcan. I offer his life to death, that I may have power. With the sword of his father I offer his life to death, that I may have power. And I offer my life to death, that I may have power." She took the sword and plunged it into her abdomen.

The ward disappeared, and Geradin got two paces before it reappeared.

"That's quite an offer," said Kairith, who now stood next to Biyeskalya as if he had been there all along. "A mother offering the life of her own child is very powerful necromancy.

Especially when that child is royal."

Geradin's thoughts whirled. How could Biyeskalya be pregnant with Mek's child? She had avoided him until his death, and there had been no chance after that.

"And the offer of one's own life is also powerful," said Kairith. "Despite that, I've only seen it done three times. I suppose most necromancers consider their own lives too valuable."

"No, this cannot be," said the Dark Priestess. "You told me the last of the Line of Orcan was dead."

"I told you the last child born of the Line of Orcan was dead, and that no more would be born. I'm not responsible for how you interpreted that, Your Highness." Kairith turned to Biyeskalya. "What would you do with all that power?"

"No!" The Dark Priestess's scream was almost deafening in Geradin's ears.

The ward came down, and Geradin sprinted toward Biyeskalya.

A roaring wind approached him from behind. The black globe shot past him. Kairith stepped aside and the darkness engulfed Biyeskalya, gouging a hole in the wall and floor. It continued to travel, leaving a tunnel in its wake.

"She didn't have time to tell me her orders," said Kairith. "All that power, wasted. Such a pity."

Biyeskalya was gone, and the sword with her.

"I killed her and her unborn child," said the Dark Priestess. "I claim the power of their deaths, Kairith."

"Killing two of royal blood is powerful necromancy indeed, Your Highness. But apparently the girl wasn't pregnant at all. I'm afraid you only have the power from one death, not two."

Biyeskalya had lied, Geradin realized, and in doing so had fulfilled the prophecy. The old beggar had not actually said she would carry the Heir of the Line's child, only that he had seen her in a vision telling people that she did.

"Geradin," said Selima, "the globe took down the rest of the wards protecting her."

Without hesitation, Geradin turned and charged toward the Dark Priestess. He was halfway up the steps to the platform when she said, "Kill him, Kairith. Kill him!"

Suddenly the demigod was standing between Geradin and the Dark Priestess, and Geradin found himself frozen in place.

"I told you when we first met that we would meet twice more before your death," said Kairith. His smile was kind. "I believe this is twice more."

Knowing he was about to die, Geradin felt anger rise within him. "So much for 'Demigods do not ally with anyone.' You've allied yourself with her. After all your speeches about the importance of protocol, you do her bidding without it," said Geradin. "I didn't hear her chanting over Biyeskalya's body."

"You are correct, of course," said Kairith. He turned to the Dark Priestess. "I know that over the centuries, you and I have developed a certain amount of informality in our relationship. But I'm afraid that if the other party insists, I must adhere to protocol." He shrugged. "Sometimes it's awkward, lacking free will. But unless you can chant over the body of the princess, you cannot claim the power of her death. And seeing that there is no body, I suppose I must refuse your request to kill him." Kairith stepped aside.

Geradin felt the force that had held him disappear. He continued up the steps until he stood before the Dark Priestess. She did not retreat. He swung with all his might to chop off her head, and the blade bounced off a ward.

"I'm trying," said Selima. "It's just the one ward."

The Dark Priestess smiled. "You have the wrong sword. Even if you somehow are of the Line of Orcan, and Kairith is confused as much as the rest of us, the prophecies are clear that only with your father's sword can you kill me."

Geradin held his sword up against the ward, feeling the rhythm as it flicked up and down. It was too fast for him to swing through it. He needed a distraction.

"I can maintain this for quite a while," said the Dark Priestess. "But your time is limited. Even now, my Soulless are approaching the reservoir. And when they kill whoever it is, Selima will die."

Geradin pushed away the thought of Allonna in danger. There was nothing but the fight. He drew back his sword and struck at a moment when the ward would be down. The blade got a palmwidth closer to the Dark Priestess before the ward reappeared and forced it back. A painful jolt shot up Geradin's arm. He needed to strike faster.

"After Selima's dead, I will have to kill you," said the Dark Priestess, "unless you stop believing the story Selima has made up. You are trying to fulfill a destiny that does not belong to you. But I can be merciful—I will let you return home if you just give up this foolishness."

Geradin swung again, but made no further progress. He need to distract her somehow, get her timing off so he could complete a strike against her.

And then what the Dark Priestess had said about Selima's story and fulfilling a destiny made everything clear as rainwater.

"When Mek and I were children," Geradin said, "Selima told us stories at bedtime. One of my favorites was the story of the sword in the anvil. Have you heard that one?"

As he spoke, he continued to swing his sword, getting a feel for the exact timing of her wards.

"It's about a king who died without leaving an heir," he continued. "Rather than have the nobles fight among themselves to see who could claim the throne, the Gods of Light placed a sword in an anvil, and declared that whoever pulled it out would be heir to the kingdom. There's a lot more to the story, but we've covered the important part."

The Dark Priestess frowned.

"You are right, Your Highness. I am not of the Line of Orcan." Geradin pulled back his sword. "But I will be the *Heir* of the Line."

The Dark Priestess's eyes widened as Geradin swung. His sword encountered no ward, and the blade sliced cleanly

through her neck.
    As it emerged on the other side, the blade glowed yellow.

Chapter Sixty-Four

Allonna

Allonna watched through Selima's eyes as the Dark Priestess's head rolled on the floor and came to a stop by Kairith's foot. She jumped to her feet and almost fell because her vision did not rise with her. "I knew he could do it! I knew it."

Then she saw that Geradin's blade glowed yellow. He was still in danger. And, even though the Dark Priestess was dead, Allonna suddenly realized the amount of power Selima was drawing continued to climb.

Geradin turned to Selima and said, "We have to save Allonna from the Soulless."

"She is in no danger now," said Kairith. "Without the will of the Dark Priestess to drive them, the Soulless are but empty husks. That's why they are called the Soulless."

Relief that she was not in danger mixed with Allonna's anxiety over Geradin.

"Good. I need to rest a bit," said Geradin, and he stepped over the headless corpse of the Dark Priestess and sat on the ornate gold throne. He looked at his sword, which still glowed yellow. "The sword of my father. Veratur?" He shook his head.

"You're bleeding, Your Majesty," said Kairith. "You do realize you have a dagger in you?"

How could she have forgotten about the dagger? How could Selima not have noticed the dagger? "Heal him," Allonna said, even knowing Selima could not hear her.

"The wound is mortal, I know," said Geradin. "But I thank you, Lord Kairith, for not taking me until after I killed her."

"No!" said Allonna. It couldn't be mortal. Why didn't Selima heal him?

Kairith raised his eyebrows. "King Geradin att'*Balunor*, the universe just went through a pile of trouble to seat you on the throne of Aud Sapeer, and now you want to die without producing an heir of your own?"

"I don't want to die," said Geradin. "But last time you said we would meet once more before I died, and we've met."

"And you haven't died yet, have you? Then it is fulfilled." Kairith shook his head. "Farewell, Your Majesty. We shall not meet again until *after* you've died." He was gone as if he had never been there.

Allonna felt like she was falling backwards, then realized it was Selima who was falling, ending up looking at the gold-mosaic ceiling. At that moment, Allonna's ability to sense magic outside herself returned, and for the first time she understood what Selima meant by gathering and storing power. It had always seemed to Allonna that magical power was just there surrounding her whenever she needed it, but now she saw the edges of her stored power, and those edges were shrinking rapidly. Selima was now drawing more power than she had at any time during the fight with the Dark Priestess.

"Must stop," muttered Selima. "Must stop must stop must stop…"

"Selima, what's wrong?" said Geradin. His face appeared before her.

"…must stop must stop must stop…"

Selima had said that she might not be able to release Allonna's power after the battle. Was that the problem?

"…must stop must stop must stop…"

Concentrating on the flow of power connecting her to Selima, Allonna tried to shut it off. The flow reduced to half its strength.

"No!" screamed Selima.

Allonna stopped resisting, and the power flow began to strengthen again. What was she supposed to do?

"Stop it, Allonna," said Selima, sounding like herself for a moment. "Stop it before it's too late. Stop it stop it stop it stop it…"

As Allonna clamped down on the power flow, Selima screamed again, but this time Allonna continued until the connection was severed completely.

"It's gone." Selima began to sob.

"Allonna, if you can hear me, I think you should come here if you can," said Geradin. "Otherwise, get out of the palace and we'll find you later."

She knew that last part was a lie—without her to heal his wound, it would be mortal. No matter what the old beggar had prophesied, Allonna knew she would not leave Geradin and Selima behind. She took the scarf off her head, and after a moment of disorientation, her own sight showed her the mine tunnel beneath the kitchen.

She turned toward the ladder to start climbing and then stopped as she looked up. Her heart seemed to jump in her chest. A leonak, with claws extended and open jaws, was crouched at the top of the ladder as if about to spring.

Instinctively, Allonna raised a shining ward in front of her. The leonak did not react. After a moment, Allonna lowered the ward. As Kairith had said, the Soulless was no more than an empty husk. She shuddered at how close it had come, then she started up the ladder. She tried not to look at the creature as she climbed past.

◆ ◆ ◆

It took her longer than she had hoped to trace the route the others had taken to the throne room, and the torn bodies of slaves and human soldiers she found along the way caused her to vomit at one point. The statue-like Soulless, some of them frozen in the act of mauling a victim, did not ease her mind.

As she stepped through the hole in the wall of the antechamber, she saw four knights in black armor surrounding the open doorway to the throne room. "Get out of my way," she said.

They turned to face her. "Who are you?" one asked.

"I'm the most powerful omnimancer in the world, now that your mistress is dead." Allonna kept her voice matter-of-fact. There was no need to mention that her power was almost depleted, and she wanted to save as much as possible for healing Geradin. "Unlike her, I am merciful to those who do not oppose me."

"Why should we believe you?" asked one.

"Fool," said another. "If she's lying, it won't do any harm to let her pass. And if she's not, I want no part of her."

They parted, and Allonna approached the doorway. A ward blocked anyone from entering. Allonna reached out with her power to undo it—and it did not come down. She tried again using a higher flare, and still it remained.

"Geradin!"

He looked up from where he was seated by Selima, holding her hand. "Allonna. Come quick. Selima's in great pain."

"Tell her to undo this ward."

Geradin spoke with Selima for a moment. "She says she can't."

That made no sense. A mancer could always undo her own spell. Then Allonna realized what had happened: Selima no longer had any control over magic.

She had flared herself out.

Focusing her power on one small area of the ward, Allonna began to break it down. She hoped it wouldn't take too much of her power. It was unnerving to have to think about that; something she had never needed to worry about before. The edges of her power seemed to close in on her.

With a pop of air, the ward collapsed. Allonna ran through

the doorway, erecting a minimal ward behind her, and knelt down beside Geradin and Selima.

"Can you cure her?" he asked.

"Her condition isn't getting any worse," she said. It couldn't. "It's you I need to heal." She reached out with her mind and sensed the wound. "It was smart leaving the dagger in, but I need you to pull it out when I tell you."

◆ ◆ ◆

Allonna used almost the last of her power to ease Selima's pain.

Selima sighed. "Thank you."

"Why did you do it?" asked Allonna.

"I had two advantages over the Dark Priestess," said Selima. "The first was having access to your power, but to use as much of it as possible, I had to give you all my artifacts that increased power flow, except the single-use ones."

"All of them?" Allonna blinked. "Then you knew even before the battle that you would have to flare yourself out."

"And that was my second advantage." Selima closed her eyes.

"How?"

"The Dark Priestess could not match me without flaring herself out. She wasn't willing to lose her power. I was." Selima drifted off to sleep.

◆ ◆ ◆

"Are you ready?" asked Geradin. The blade of his sword glowed blue, despite the fact they were still in the throne room of the Dark Priestess. Selima's wards held most of the Knights of the Dark God against the walls, and Allonna's ward kept out the four who had let her pass.

The pool of her power was growing. Even though Allonna knew she must be gathering power at a faster rate than most mancers, it still seemed very slow. She still hadn't recovered enough to cast the wards necessary to seal all the knights behind them while they made their escape—Geradin could not carry Selima and fight off the knights at the same time. "No. How do they stand it?" she said.

"How does who stand what?" said Geradin.

"Other mancers. Waiting so long to gather power." Allonna shook her head.

Geradin's sword changed to yellow, and there were crashes of metal on stone as several of the knights fell to the floor.

"Can you?" asked Geradin.

Allonna cast a ward, sealing the freed knights again. She looked to the other side of the room, where ten knights were still trapped behind Selima's original ward. "When the one on the other side of the room fails, I won't be able to."

"There are only ten of them," said Geradin loudly. "Not much trouble."

"We will kill you," said one of the knights. "You can't win against all of us."

"Oh, I can't?" said Geradin. "You were all here when the Demigod of Death himself said the universe had gone to a lot of trouble to put me on the throne of Aud Sapeer. You think to waste all that effort?" He swished his now-blue sword through the air. "This sword will cut through your swords, your armor, your flesh and bone, without even noticing. Perhaps, just perhaps, some of you might survive long enough to kill me. But why?"

"You killed the High Priestess of Zerul," said the knight.

"Exactly. Which means that your deceased mistress's empire has no ruler. And who has a better right to claim power than the Knights of the Dark God? One of you could be emperor —but only if you survive what is probably a futile attempt to kill me. My advice is that you just let us go."

The blade turned yellow, and the knights came free.

One of them shouted, "Attack!" and charged toward Geradin. But no one joined him.

"No ward," Geradin said to Allonna.

The knight swung his sword. Geradin cut through the blade and continued smoothly to take off the knight's arm.

"Back off or I'll take your head," said Geradin. "I am merciful when I can be, but deadly when I must be."

The knight backed away, clutching the stump of his arm.

"I trust I've made my point?" said Geradin.

"Take your women and go," said one of the knights. "You have our word you will not be harmed."

"A piece of advice," said Geradin as he lifted Selima up. "Your best option is to form some sort of council, rather than fight among yourselves."

Allonna followed Geradin out one of the side doors into a hallway. None of the knights followed.

"I don't think they'll take it," said Geradin.

◆ ◆ ◆

The journey back to Aud Sapeer was slow and long. Allonna made sure Geradin never even got a chance to use his sword.

Chapter Sixty-Five

Geradin

The western gate of Aud Sapeer was in sight when Geradin said, "Let's stop here for a bit." He reined in his horse, one of three they had purchased after crossing the Barrier Mountains into Bargas on foot.

"What's wrong?" said Selima. Even though she was well enough to ride, her voice had not recovered the firm tone Geradin was used to.

"Nothing," said Geradin. "That is, I don't know if I'm ready for this. It's not every day I ride into a city and say, 'Hello, remember me? I let your old king die, but I'm your new king now, so obey me.'" He grimaced. "Kindul will not be happy to see me."

"Forget Kindul. Unlike Aumekor, you have your majority, so he's not your regent," said Selima. "The people will welcome you as a hero. You've already heard the tellers, wrong as they are on the details, praising the Heir of the Line, savior of the Free Kingdoms."

From the varying and garbled reports they had heard, Geradin had pieced together what had happened in the final battle in Bargas. The armies of the Dark Priestess had been contained after their initial success in capturing half of Bargas, but their numbers were increasing daily. When the enchantment of the Protector's swords had failed, despair had spread though the armies of the Free Kingdoms, and soldiers had begun deserting. Some of the monarchs had advocated surrendering because the situation was hopeless.

Either because they refused to admit defeat or because they were despondent over their failure to protect the Heir of the Line—opinion differed on that point—the Protectors of the Line, plus the armies of Aldamun, Bargas and Aud Sapeer, had gathered to charge into the heart of the enemy. They had done so, and as the battle was joined, the Knights of the Dark God began disappearing from the field. Confusion among the troops of the Dark Priestess turned to terror when the enchantment returned to the swords of the Protectors. At the same time, the Soulless stopped fighting and allowed themselves to be slaughtered.

Seeing what was happening, the rest of the armies of the Free Kingdoms had taken heart and joined the battle. Because the tunnel through which the armies of the Dark Priestess had invaded was too small to allow a large retreat, the defeat had turned into a massacre until they surrendered.

The prevailing theory among the storytellers as to what had happened was that the Heir of the Line had died, and then somehow come back to life in order to kill the Dark Priestess and save the Free Kingdoms. Geradin didn't tell them how much he wished they had that part right.

After taking a deep breath, Geradin said, "I suppose there's no point in putting it off. Let's go."

◆ ◆ ◆

They dismounted in order to pass through the gate.

As they approached, the nearest guard said, "What is your business in—" He stiffened. "Lord Geradin! I mean, Your Majesty!"

Geradin stepped closer to the guard. "What did you call me?"

"I'm sorry, Your Majesty. I was startled, is all. I didn't mean to cause offence."

"I'm not offended. I'm just wondering how you knew...to call me that."

"Everyone knows, Your Majesty. Lord Kindul and High Priest Kogyrinem announced days ago that you were our new king. We've been waiting for you to arrive."

Kindul? Geradin was speechless for a moment, until he realized that High Priest Kogyrinem must have discovered something in the prophecies that showed Geradin was the Heir of the Line. "What's your name, soldier?"

"Nadel, Your Majesty."

Geradin put a hand on the guard's shoulder. "Nadel, I'd appreciate it if you wouldn't spread the news that I've returned."

Nadel nodded. "Of course, Your Majesty, but I doubt I'll be the only one to recognize you."

Geradin winced. "True enough. But I'd rather they not be organized about it."

Frowning, Nadel nodded. "Yes, Your Majesty. I'm under orders to notify the Keep when you arrive, but I'll obey your orders instead."

Not wanting to put Nadel in an awkward position, Geradin said, "No, that's fine. Go ahead and notify the Keep."

"At once, Your Majesty." Nadel consulted a moment with his fellow guards, who turned and stared at Geradin, and then he began running down the street.

"You see," said Selima, "I told you there would be no problem."

◆ ◆ ◆

Geradin had long before decided what his first stop would be on reaching Aud Sapeer, and so they traveled to a small home in a respectable but not wealthy part of the city. As they made their way, Geradin noticed the yellow and blue ribbons decorating the streets. "Is it Midsummer again so soon?" he asked.

"Midsummer Day," said Selima.

"We should have waited until tomorrow," he said.

"Why?" asked Allonna.

"I don't have a speech prepared."

The three of them walked up to the door of the house. Geradin knocked, and after a few moments Telani answered the door.

"Lord Geradin!" she said. "I mean, Your Majesty." She bowed.

"May we come in?" asked Geradin. He had gone through this conversation in his mind countless times, and he still didn't know the right way to tell Telani that Holoran had died saving their lives.

"Of course." She stepped back.

Geradin, Selima and Allonna walked into the small, but homey, room.

"Holoran should be back shortly," said Telani. "My father wanted to speak to him—I think to offer him a job. I don't know if he'll take it though. You know how stubborn he can be."

Geradin stared at her. "Holoran's alive?"

"Allonna!" A little girl ran across the room to hug Allonna's legs.

"Hope?" said Allonna. She burst into tears and reached down to pick her up. "How is this possible?"

Ezpetti came in from another room, her hands covered in flour. "What's—Oh, you've arrived, finally."

"We thought you were dead," said Geradin. "The tunnel collapsed." He shook his head. "I saw Holoran crushed."

"No, you didn't," said Holoran from the doorway. "It's good to see you again, Geradin."

"I think," said Selima, "it would be best if someone explained what happened."

"Sit down, and I will," said Holoran. When Geradin, Selima and Allonna were seated, he said, "I held that giant slab of rock up as long as I could, and then the strength of my arms gave out. I dropped it and it fell. But there were some large rocks that had fallen behind me, and while the front of the slab fell to the ground, the back of the slab was held up enough that I wasn't crushed. Instead, I was trapped."

"I'm sorry, Holoran," said Geradin. "We should have tried to dig you out. But I thought you were dead."

"You can't blame yourself, Geradin," said Selima. "You had a head wound, and the Dark Priestess knew we were there."

"You couldn't have dug me out," said Holoran. "The slab was too big at that point. Believe me, I tried."

"So what happened?" asked Allonna.

"I suppose it's Ezpetti's turn," said Holoran.

Ezpetti had cleaned her hands, and was standing in the archway to the kitchen. "Hope, Otunvol, Darilom, Rala and I were fortunate that the ceiling was stronger at the intersection of the tunnels. But we soon found we were trapped—the ceiling had collapsed in all three directions. We tried digging ourselves out, but some of the rocks were so large that it became clear it was impossible. Eventually we gave up. But then there was a rumbling sound nearby."

"Another earthquake?" said Geradin.

Ezpetti shook her head. "We don't know what it was, but it carved a circular tunnel through the rock, leaving nothing behind."

"I know what it was," said Geradin. "I'll explain after you finish." He grinned—to think that the most powerful weapon of the Dark Priestess had freed his friends.

"That new tunnel intersected with the side passage. Since it sloped upward, we decided to follow it. After a short distance it intersected with another tunnel, and we heard someone moaning in pain. It was Serilyon."

"Serilyon survived?" said Geradin.

"Yes," said Ezpetti. "We dug him out. The rocks weren't too big there. So we all continued up the tunnel, but it ended at a point where its own ceiling had collapsed. So we backtracked to see if there was another way. And then Otunvol and Darilom's swords started to glow."

Geradin nodded. "And since they could cut through rock..."

"Yes. We went back to the original tunnel, and cut through

rock to see if there was anyone still trapped."

"And that's when they found me," said Holoran. "We went back through the tunnels the way we came, out to the Burn. We waited there for two days in case you came back that way, then we took the horses and wagon, and returned along the edge of the Burn. Serilyon went back to Aldamun, and we came here. We got back fifteen days ago."

"Amazing," said Geradin.

Seated beside him, Allonna held Hope on her lap and cried.

"Now it's your turn," said Holoran. "Tell us what happened."

◆ ◆ ◆

"So Biyeskalya saved all of us," said Holoran, after Geradin finished.

Geradin nodded. "And it was Aumekor who saved her, so she could be there to save the rest of us. It was his goal to make sure as few people as possible died, and he succeeded: only two. They are the true heroes in this."

"And now the two of them are together in the World of the Dead," said Ezpetti.

Shaking his head, Holoran said, "She only said she loved him as he was dying because Lor— King Geradin asked her to."

"That's not true," said Allonna. "She grew to love him before he died. She told me. She was upset because she thought she would have to…"

"To what?" said Ezpetti.

"…to marry Geradin," said Allonna. "Because of the prophecy."

Geradin smiled. "When Allonna told me that, I guess I should have been offended that a woman would be upset at the thought of marrying me, but I made an exception in this case." He looked at Allonna, and she smiled back at him.

"There's one thing I don't understand," said Telani. "The prophecy said the Heir of the Line would use his father's sword, but you…" She paused. "I shouldn't have said anything."

"No," said Geradin. "I wondered about that, too. Fortunately, I've been assured that I look very much like Balunor, and not at all like Veratur. The only explanation is that Veratur and my father must have switched swords during their battle."

There was a knock at the door. Telani got up and answered it.

"Is His Majesty here?" said Lord Kindul.

Telani looked at Geradin, and he nodded.

"Yes, milord. Please come in."

Kindul strode into the room, spotted Geradin, and immediately bowed to one knee. "Your Majesty, I would swear my fealty to you. I know you dislike me and will not want me for your Chamberlain, but I will serve you in whatever capacity you require."

Geradin sighed. He had thought this over during the journey home, and he knew what he needed to do. "Lord Kindul, you are correct. I dislike you for the way you treated Aumekor. But he believed you were the best man to serve as Lord Chamberlain, and I trust his judgment. Do not make me regret it."

"Thank you, Your Majesty," said Kindul as he rose to his feet. "If I may ask, will you now take your true name?"

Geradin blinked. "What do you mean, 'my true name'?"

"Otunvol explained how Selima switched you and Aumekor as babies," said Kindul.

"That was a lie," Selima said. "I made it all up after Aumekor died."

Kindul's eyes went wide. "You bluffed your way into fulfilling the prophecies?"

"I tried," said Selima. "I reasoned that it was possible the prophets might have been fooled by the lie, and that is why they thought the Heir of the Line of Orcan was the one who could kill the Dark Priestess."

"And it worked. Amazing." Kindul ran a hand through his hair. "But that means Geradin isn't the king.

"Wrong," said Selima. "My plan failed. It was Geradin who

figured out the true meaning of the prophecy."

"Aumekor was the last of the line of Orcan," said Geradin, "and he died without having any children. I realized that meant his heir would have to be chosen somehow. Why not chosen by the prophecy?"

Kindul nodded slowly. "Whoever killed the Dark Priestess would become the Heir."

"Exactly," said Geradin.

Kindul looked around the room. "I understand that you need to spend time with those who journeyed with you. But as soon as possible, we have much to discuss. There are important matters of state that have been waiting for your arrival. Treaties and laws to be signed. And there is the question of the marriage—"

"What marriage?" said Geradin, standing up.

"The arrangement regarding Biyeskalya," said Kindul.

"She's dead," said Geradin.

"Ah," said Kindul. "Have you informed King Paskolyik?"

Geradin shook his head. "I've been postponing that. But she saved my life, so we will definitely honor Aldamun's request for assistance against raiders."

"Of course, Your Majesty." Kindul nodded. "There are a number of other suitable brides. I could—"

"No," said Geradin. "You need not arrange another marriage for me. I will be marrying my Royal Omnimancer."

Kindul's eyebrows rose. "You're marrying Selima?"

◆ ◆ ◆

Returning on Midsummer Day had to be a sign, so there was one final thing Geradin knew he must do before returning to the Keep.

"Who comes before the altar of Attol?" asked High Priest Kogyrinem as he took the death-day offering box from Geradin.

"It is I, Geradin att'Balunor."

"Who comes before the altar of Beska?"

"It is I, Geradin beh'Elesi."

"Who comes before the altar of Clanni?"

"It is I, Geradin, a Follower of the Light."

"For whom is this offering made to the Gods of Light?"

"For my mother who is dead, Elesi beh'Ehanna." Geradin paused, then added, "And for my father who is dead, Balunor att'Torinil."

He watched as the offering smoke turned white and rose up to join the sky.

Epilogue

Selima

"And so the king married the blacksmith's daughter, and they lived very happily together," said Selima. "And that's the end of the story of the Sword in the Anvil."

"Tell us another story, Grandma Selima," said Prince Aumekor. He was Geradin and Allonna's eldest child, now five years old.

Three-year-old Princess Kalya sat on Geradin's lap. She clapped her hands. "'Nother story."

"No," said Allonna. In her arms was the newest arrival, the Princess Selima, barely a season old. "It's time to say goodnight to Grandma Selima and go to bed."

"Goodnight, Grandma Selima," Aumekor and Kalya said in dutiful unison.

"Goodnight, my dears," said Selima. "I'll tell you another story tomorrow."

The children went out the door of Selima's bedchamber.

"You look tired," said Allonna. "Is the pain getting bad? I can —"

"I'm fine. Henna's taking good care of me." Selima smiled. The pain never went away entirely, but Henna was a competent enough healer that she could ease it.

"It's strange," said Geradin. "I don't recall there being a blacksmith's daughter in that story when you told it to Mek and me as children."

Smiling, Selima said, "Anvils don't just sprout like weeds. There must have been a blacksmith. And there's no reason he couldn't have a daughter."

"No reason indeed," said Geradin. He rose from his chair, walked over and gave her a kiss on the forehead. "Goodnight, Selima." He put his arm around Allonna and they walked out.

"Do you want the candles out?" asked Henna.

"Yes, please," said Selima.

Henna extinguished the candles and went to the door. "Ring if you need me."

The bell rope hung right next to the bed. "I will. Thank you."

Henna went out and shut the door.

Selima let her thoughts drift, and as they often did, they returned to the battle against the Dark Priestess. Tears welled up in her eyes as she tried to remember what it felt like to have so much magical power flowing through her. She knew the joy of it had been beyond anything she had ever felt, and yet she could not recall what it actually felt like.

Even if she could not have that indescribable joy again, it would be wonderful just to use mancy again, just a little. She focused her mind and tried to sense the power that had once been in her.

There was nothing but emptiness.

Selima cried herself to sleep.

❖ ❖ ❖

"Selima."

She awoke. The room was still dark. "Who's there?" she whispered, unsure if she had heard a voice or not.

"It's me, Aumekor." The voice was familiar, even though she hadn't heard it in years.

She must be dreaming. "You're dead."

"Yes," said Aumekor.

"You have fulfilled your duty," said another voice, an even

older memory.

"Balunor?"

"We've come to take you with us," said a third voice—her husband, Pel.

"Kairith was kind enough to let us come," said Balunor.

Aumekor laughed. "It took a little persuasion. He doesn't usually allow more than one friend or relative to go collect someone."

"Balunor and I want to thank you for raising Geradin so well," said Elesi.

"And you did a fine job with our son, too," said King Ordil.

"Yes," said Queen Anutia. "We're so proud of him."

"I did my best," said Selima, still not sure whether she was dreaming. "Who else is here?"

"I couldn't miss the chance to see my favorite apprentice after all these years," said Jiltunok. "You did me proud, my girl."

There was silence for a bit.

"Go on, say something," said Aumekor, although Selima didn't think he was addressing her.

"I know I be not someone you liked," said Biyeskalya, "but where Aumekor goes, I go."

"She's the one who browbeat Kairith into letting us all come," said Aumekor.

Selima smiled. "I thank you for everything, Biyeskalya."

Suddenly, she realized that for the first time in seven years, the pain was gone. She was filled with light and joy. "Yes," she said. "I remember now: that's what it felt like."

"Come," said Pel. "It's time to go."

Made in the USA
Columbia, SC
03 December 2022

8e86bebb-8639-466c-a822-e0ac12972296R01